I0823726

THE MALCONTENTS

ALSO BY

SACHA NASPINI

Nives
The Bishop's Villa

Sacha Naspini

THE MALCONTENTS

Translated from the Italian
by Clarissa Botsford

Europa Editions
27 Union Square West, Suite 302
New York NY 10003
www.europaeditions.com
info@europaeditions.com

First Publication 2026 by Europa Editions

Translation by Clarissa Botsford
Original title: *Le Case del malcontento*

Library of Congress Cataloging in Publication Data is available
ISBN 978-1-60945-937-6

Naspini, Sacha
The Malcontents

Cover illustration by Emanuele Ragnisco

Prepress by Grafica Punto Print – Rome

Printed in Canada

C O N T E N T S

"Out beyond ideas of wrongdoing
and rightdoing, There is a field.
I'll meet you there."
—Commonly attributed to Jalāl ad-Dīn Rūmī

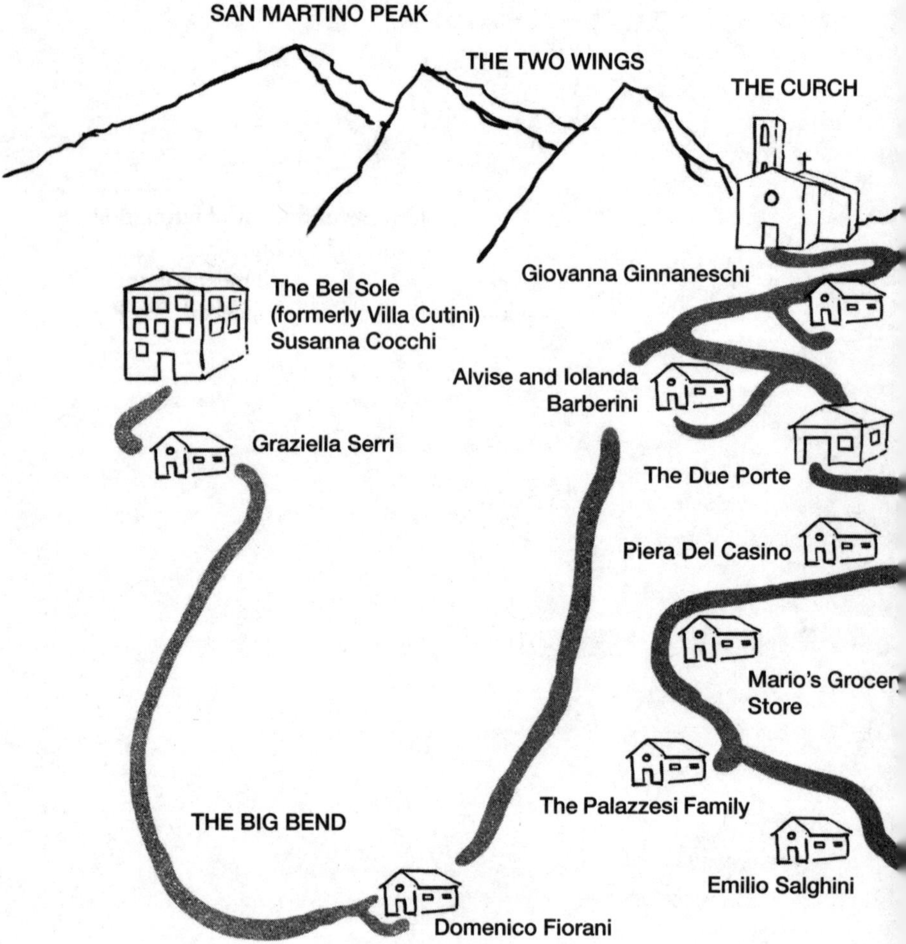

SAN MARTINO PEAK
THE TWO WINGS
THE CURCH
The Bel Sole
(formerly Villa Cutini)
Susanna Cocchi
Giovanna Ginnaneschi
Alvise and Iolanda
Barberini
Graziella Serri
The Due Porte
Piera Del Casino
Mario's Grocery
Store
The Palazzesi Family
THE BIG BEND
Emilio Salghini
Domenico Fiorani

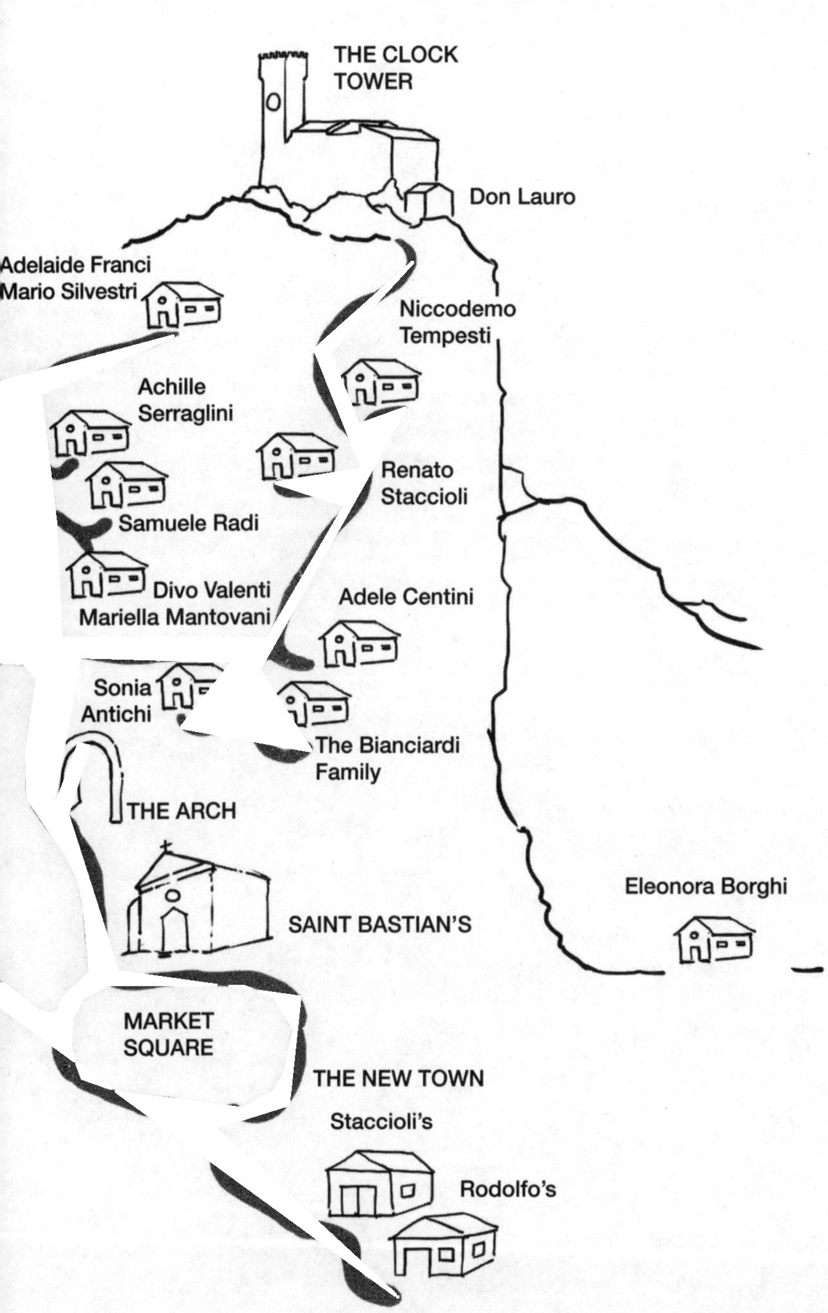
THE CLOCK TOWER
Don Lauro
Adelaide Franci
Mario Silvestri
Niccodemo Tempesti
Achille Serraglini
Renato Staccioli
Samuele Radi
Divo Valenti
Mariella Mantovani
Adele Centini
Sonia Antichi
The Bianciardi Family
THE ARCH
SAINT BASTIAN'S
Eleonora Borghi
MARKET SQUARE
THE NEW TOWN
Staccioli's
Rodolfo's

THE MALCONTENTS

Divo Valenti,
the Retired Miner

They say they saw a flash of silver tear by at breakneck speed on the big road that comes into town after the junction for the grocery store. Filippo, the youngest Nencioni boy, happened to be right there where, if you don't slow down, the hairpin bend will send you smack into the olive grove of that guy from the Marches, the one who never opens his mouth, who's lived here a hundred years but wouldn't let on that he knew you even if you were skinning him alive. Everybody knows Filippo is a bit dim, but he was just minding his own business walking on the edge of the road when suddenly this flash of lightning with the devil in its tail comes by. If he hadn't been young and steady on his feet, we'd be scraping young flesh off the ridge. Like with the Toninelli couple back in '74. It was thirty years ago but people still talk about it. They were on their way back from their seaside honeymoon. He had taken his young bride to a place with beautiful white beaches near Cecina. I'm talking about that big sexy Ferrari girl, Silvia, the milliner. She was something! Even now, there are men my age who still think about her and tear their hair out . . . Anyway, you can bet the little lovebirds were fooling around because they didn't find a single skid mark on the asphalt. They simply shot straight down the hill. The Lancia Fulvia caught fire and left not so much as a trace of the newlyweds. Once a month, old Toninelli takes a bunch of flowers and leaves it on the spot where his son went to hell in a hand cart. Talk about tragedies . . . the man from the Marches has seen plenty of birds land on his olive trees.

Filippo this morning might not have lived to tell the tale. "One second later and I'd have been thrown to the nettles," he was saying this afternoon, down in the new town at Rodolfo's bar where the bougie types go, the ones who talk fancy. Not like here at Maso's, where people act normal. I was only there because I had forgotten that Staccioli, the tobacconist, has a habit of taking Wednesdays off. Mariella says I'm fit to be locked up when I'm without my cancer sticks. She should know. Once, I asked her to get me a carton and she forgot. But she sure remembers the lashing I gave her when I got home from my shift. Every lick of my belt, to this day. At dinnertime she was leaning forward and sitting on one butt cheek. That went on for a week.

This is all to say that the word going around is true: the sleazebag of Via dell'Incrociata is back. How he has the nerve, I don't know. Not to mention the marching band that's probably trailing after him, when people at Le Case don't like any fuss. And yet, there he is, throwing open the windows of a house honored for being once the home of Esedra, may her soul rest in peace. When we were kids, we used to play together. During the war, because of her curly blond hair, the Germans took her for one of their own. She would get all the chocolate bars, but she was good-hearted and would always come and break a square or two off for us kids in the lower part of town. Christ only knows why fate dealt her a grandson like the one who nearly reduced the youngest of the Nencionis to pulp today. Esedra must have realized what she would have to deal with ages ago, when she took her whole kit and caboodle and escaped to safety, six feet under. Leaving the rest of us with that piece of work.

Filippo Nencioni,
the Loafer

They say I'm the village idiot, but the truth is I fuck everyone over and then some. It's easy to call someone an idiot. Maybe one day they'll realize that there's a lot to be gained from acting like one. Like when I pop up at Mrs. Nardini's window. She's a seamstress and women sometimes go and try their dresses on, stripping to their bras. When they see a shadow at the window, all hell breaks loose. Then they see it's me and Mrs. Nardini says, "Don't worry ladies, it's Filippo, one of the Nencioni boys. He's not the sharpest knife in the drawer. It's no worse than having a little lapdog look at you." She even waves at me as she draws the curtains. But in the meantime, there's a naked belly imprinted in my brain and, when I get home, I can look at it under the covers as much as I want. And that's just one example I can think of.

Because I look a bit soft in the head, Babbo has me on permanent vacation from work, unlike my brothers who have to break their backs at the sawmill. At the end of the day, my feet sit under the same table as theirs and I eat more than they do since they're so tired they nod off, slopping their soup like retards. "For God's sake keep away from the blades!" Babbo shouts when he sees me at the mill. "If you don't lose an arm of your own, you're bound to slice two of someone else's off and we'll be paying the debt forever!" And he sends me off with a kick in the ass to loaf around.

The mill is full of my brothers, who wake up in the morning spitting sawdust. There are also some foreigners working there who can hardly speak Italian. They have big heads and low brows. They grunt like pigs instead of talking but they seem to understand one another anyway. There's one in particular who acts like the boss. He's scary. Instead of yelling at his workers, he just shoots them a look and they spring into action like bullets. That doesn't happen when Babbo opens his mouth, though he's the one paying their wages. There's another thing: the quiet foreigner looks like a sculpture. And he never lowers his gaze, not even with my brother Edoardo, who likes playing the boss himself. Once, he ordered him to do this and that, but the man didn't move. There were five minutes to go before the end of his break, and he wanted to enjoy every second of it. Edoardo puffed his chest out: "Go! Move!" The guy just stood there. He was chewing on a cheese rind and staring at the ground. Edoardo started muttering to himself, saying these filthy bastards laze around on their breaks and don't give a shit about being a team. The five minutes passed, and the man got up, tightened his belt, and started busying himself with this and that. The others followed him like kittens. It was like he was saying to my brother, "Your job is to pay my wages." When the shift ends, it's the handsome foreigner who calls his men over to the pickup. He lets two of them sit in the cabin with him and tosses the others into the back like animals. And off they drive, the tires spinning in the gravel.

I couldn't care less. I'm the one that's soft in the head so I go for walks every morning while the others put dinner on the table. I stand in front of windows and I look inside. Especially on a day like today when, even though it's early October, the sun is warming the nip in the air. I walk all the way to the last house, the one after the big bend in the road, near the ruined buttresses of the church. And I knock at Graziella's door.

She's always full of laughs, bless her, even with a hundred years to her name. She usually warms up a little milk in a pan for me and sits me down in the kitchen like a real grandson.

She says the same thing every time, "Filippo, my dear boy, if only I were half a century younger . . . " She takes what she wants anyway. The only problem is it makes me sick when she opens her mouth to take out her dentures because without them, she looks like an old woman. She unbuttons my flies. Then she bends down and says, "Come on, let me get this for you." She takes it out for me, pinching the hood. "Look how sleepy this little goldfinch is!" she says. "The sun has been up for a while . . . Now I'm going to eat you all up. *Yum*!"

When the weather is nice, as I was saying, I sometimes go for a walk as far as the last house, where Graziella lives. She makes me feel good. She gives me a bit of milk. Then she takes out her dentures and sucks my pecker. In the meantime, I think about one of those nice white bellies I may have spied through the window at Mrs. Nardini's house. Graziella swallows as I thump my heels on the ground with pleasure. She takes forever to pull herself back up. She has this terrible habit of saying, "It's all vitamins!" And then she sends me away, my head still spinning and my pounding heart making my breath as shallow as the goldfinch's she was talking about.

This is what happened today, in fact. I was drunk first thing in the morning. I was on my way back to Le Case, weak in the knees, feeling sick at the memory of plugging my pacifier into the mouth of a woman who had been at school with Nonna Santa. Sometimes I see them together at Mario's store and I feel like throwing up when Graziella says to Nonna, "Just look what a fine young man he is growing up to be!" Then she asks me how old I am and we play out the whole farce when she could easily have my cum encrusted around her mouth or on her sweater from the morning session.

I felt drunk though I'd never actually been intoxicated. Babbo always says I shouldn't drink wine as it might go to my brain and give me convulsions. I'm just imagining I'm drunk as I walk back down from the last house, the one after the big bend in the road. I tell myself: "This must be what it feels like to be drunk but without that nice feeling in my balls . . . Or is that one of the effects?"

I'm walking along, basking in these thoughts, when suddenly I hear a buzzing sound. I hear it and next thing I know a ghost seems intent on driving me right off the road into Fiorani's fields, which are already planted with crosses. I'm clinging for life to the guardrail, and the motorbike is already a mile down the road. And I tell myself, "Filippo, a Saint was watching over you."

I don't usually scare easily but today it took at least ten minutes for my pulse to go back to normal. Meanwhile, all I could think of were Babbo's words when my brothers go out on Saturday evening, dressed to the nines for a night out on the town. Babbo always says to them, "Go easy on the shots, lads. It takes a second to fly off the road like the Toninellis. And then the whole sawmill will be on my shoulders with no one to help."

Since this morning, the same words apply to Yours Truly, even though I've never been drunk and they never give me the keys to the truck. Since this morning, I've been saying to myself, "Dear Filippo, they call you the village idiot but don't turn into one for real. When you go and see Graziella to have your pickle pecked, wait five minutes before heading off down the road punch-drunk from all that fresh pleasure. Some loony may come along like this morning and drive you off the road into the fields of the man from the Marches, where there's an olive tree for every person who died taking the bend either too fast or without thinking. And now they're bleating like lambs in the cauldron of Hell."

GRAZIELLA SERRI,
the Fortune Teller

Mariella, my dear, it's not me saying it. It's the tarot cards. Don't be shocked if you see a picture of a coffin. No one is on their way to the graveyard. That's clear . . . This one is a nice card. It means, "News is on the way." But it's next to The Cat and the message the two cards are sending together is, "Watch out for people who are over friendly. They'll smile like they love you and the next minute they'll turn around and poison you."

This place is full of envious people. I know from experience. Ever since poor Martino was called to our Lord, I've been getting a Pasha's pension and all the benefits that go with it. For the other ladies here, that goes down like boiling oil. They've usually got some narcoleptic husband at home watching the weather forecast and not even bothering to say good evening to them . . . Now that I can finally enjoy doing what I want, on Tuesdays I sit at my table with my candles and my plate and shake off all those vipers and their evil eye. When I go into town, I pin a little red satin bow into my bra. You should do the same. When someone says, "Mariella, you're looking well today!" I stick a hand in my pocket and make a horn sign to send the curse right back to them.

But the most important card of all is the one you chose last, the one you placed at the center of the star: The Hooded Man. All of your troubles flock to this card, like crows to carrion. There's something weighing on you. For someone like me with a practiced eye, you're an open book.

Even the walls know it by now. That degenerate has started opening the windows of Via dell'Incrociata, the ones our saintly Esedra used to look out of. You didn't pull this monstrous card out of the pack with your own little hands by chance. It's like living across the street from a villain. That man attracts nastiness, and the nastiness is seeping into your house, which is right there. They say that the devil had to hole up in his house down in the city for days with the shutters closed because people were out on the street waiting for him to come out so they could give him the treatment God intended. Thinking about it makes you want to knock your head against the wall: the case is still open. Well, who did it then? It's always the same story. All the poor folk who fought in the war had to work like crazy with their heads down a mine for forty years to get a moment's rest. Like my poor Martino, God bless his soul. I even get a pension for his silicosis. If someone like him so much as forgot to pay a bill, they would come with a foreclosure order on the house he had bought through terrible sacrifices, the kind that chip your soul to the bone. Just switch on the TV and you'll hear some terrible stories. And then a piece of society's garbage like him comes along and makes a mess like that and what do they do? Allow the case to go cold and let him off as if nothing ever happened. Then people complain when someone gets it into their head to walk into an office with a rifle and shoot their way to the counter just to have a word with the person in charge.

This is all to say, stay away from your balcony. It's the tarot cards saying it. Keep your windows closed on that side of the house even if you need to air the rooms. The breeze would let in the revulsion that trails after that man, worse than the slime of a snail. And tell your dear husband to keep himself in check. I know what Divo is capable of. He's not going to sit back and let anyone step on his bunions. But he would walk down a dead-end road that was seething with snakes and let them slither all over everyone in town. So, let's leave the psycho in Via dell'Incrociata to stew in his own broth. He's breathing our air and that's already worse than a curse . . . This is what the cards are saying. And now, Mariella dear, it's me telling you.

Mario Silvestri,
the Grocer

She has those perfect little hands that look like they've been drawn with a fine-nibbed pen. She slices the salami as if she were turning the pages of a novel. And then there's that oval face that's like a girl's past the first flush one minute, and like a woman's on the verge of discovering the joys of sex the next . . . It may well be that providing the shrews in the old town with groceries has made me as old as the cracks in the wall but the twittering of her voice is all I need to get my blood up.

Early in the morning when I see her standing in front of the roller shutter, I come back to life. "Good morning," she says, and my hairs stand on end with excitement. I suddenly turn into the person I was fifty years ago, when I would go up the alley with the porticoes and see Adelaide waving at me from the first-floor window on Via delle Scalette, her blond curls tied up in a high ponytail. There was always a lock that fell over her face, and I would have killed to touch it. I would get to the store, my hands sweaty and my heart thumping. Babbo would say, "Go and put the Ponenti Family through the wringer. They're hammering in so many nails there'll soon be a laying a railway. They think they're so clever, but we need to eat and shit like the next person." I would take my bike, happy as a clam, and go off to ply the family for the arrears they owed us. The Ponentis would make a song and dance about a bedridden grandfather and little Giacomino whose bronchitis had become chronic. Poor Donatella would come to the door like a mouse sticking her nose out of the burrow for the first time, all toothless and smelly. I would go straight to the point: "Babbo says that if you don't pay up, he'll stop the bread delivery." And she would start blubbering. But that's not what I saw. What I saw was the golden curl bouncing on Adelaide's forehead as the "Ciao Mario" she had thrown out of the window like a rose petal rang in my ears.

It's weird to think how life steamrolls you. Babbo always used to say, "Some walk, others stroll," when he was pushing me to work harder. Now I wonder what for? For half a century I've been walking down the porticoed alley, especially when it's raining, and nothing unexpected has ever happened to me. You could say I've worn a groove in the flagstones of Le Case by taking the same path for so long. I'm the same miserable wretch I've always been, while Giacomino Ponenti was on the news the day before yesterday, boasting yet again about all the factories he has opened in the province. So much for his bronchitis.

Adelaide no longer waves at me from her window. Quite the opposite. She's slowly rotting in the same bed I bought when I finally carried her over the threshold in her wedding dress. Her hair comes away in clumps when I brush it and every day before going down to the store I promise, "Tomorrow, I'll kill you with a pillow, my love." She seems to hear my thoughts, and her watery eyes look like they're imploring me to do it. But lately, as she watches me prepare to leave the house, she's been saying: "Why are you putting pomade in your hair?"

Eleonora, on the other hand, has the beauty of youth. Thinking about it, I realize it's the first thing I'd like to strip off her, even more than her clothes. She walks barefoot over the booby traps of life, and I find myself in the staff toilet, breathing heavily. I look at myself in the rusted-up mirror that has seen me through so many seasons and say softly, "Mario, quit these obsessions right now." Then I throw handfuls of water over my face. I go back into the store and see her behind the counter, already donning her apron. I could run out there and then and shoot myself in the head. Because it's like seeing Adelaide back in her golden days. I would never stop looking at those pretty little hands wrapping the usual wedge of cheese for Giovanna Ginanneschi, who is well on her way to dying a spinster. When she has ordered what she needs, Giovanna says goodbye to everyone, "See you later!" She says it in a way that for once makes me think tomorrow may bring something good. Even though an unbearable sadness immediately invades my heart. "Are you crying for Adelaide while thanking the cancer that has come to eat up her bones?" I ask myself. "If she hadn't gotten sick, you wouldn't have needed a twenty-year-old girl to come and give you a hand with the stingy townsfolk who are always asking for a discount." This is what I think about when at 1:00 P.M. sharp I wipe my wife's ass, a wife who has kept me company all my life. I pull up her diapers and think about Eleonora who has stayed on the afternoon pause at the store, so she doesn't have to go back and forth on the bus. In the meantime, I feed Adelaide, who dribbles everything and starts crying for nothing. "We don't even have a child," she sometimes hisses. "What are we doing here torturing ourselves?"

Eleonora likes listening to stories about the town. She has told me that there are only old people in the Montemassi valley where she comes from. "Unlike Le Case, which is bursting with youth!" I quipped the first time she said it. And with that way she has of tucking a lock of hair behind her ear, she says: "Where I come from, they're all old sourpusses. They don't even say good day to one another. And yet they went through school and the war together."

That's why I tell her about some of the characters that populate these parts. For example, the Isastia widow, who has always acted high and mighty as if the Colonel were still alive and hadn't lost all their land and properties with his gambling. Legend has it that when he lost the last house he said, "I had a great time tonight," and then vanished into thin air. His body was never found. Since then, his widow has lived in a dump where the town jail used to be and yet she still goes around wearing diamond earrings and a gold brooch pinned to her breast. As soon as she comes into the store, she starts picking out the worst looking fruit. Then she has it weighed and pays half-price. Because we give nothing away for free.

There may be no kids in Le Case but there are enough crazies to last a lifetime. Another example is Esedra's grandson, who came back to town from one day to the next with that thuggish scowl on his face. He's had the brilliant idea of leaving the city and finding a safe harbor out of touch with the world in the Maremma mountains, where there hasn't been a rosette on a door announcing a birth for more than thirty years. Maso once said, "A town with no kids is already dead." And he was right.

If I close my eyes, I see a Sunday any Sunday, twenty years ago when the weather was fine up in La Vena or San Martino. Esedra and Adelaide used to like sitting on those boulders shaped like thrones. The kid would toddle around manically near the drop. His mother had already gone off to live in France. Nobody ever knew who the father was, but Esedra always held her head high anyway. The kid had been dumped on her. Adelaide pulled the leaves off the chestnut trees and made headdresses out of them like in the westerns and the kid would tear around in them. "Samuele, if you go on like this, you'll fall headfirst on the ground!" his grandmother would yell. But he wouldn't take a blind bit of notice. There were times when, however loud we yelled, he would just stand there staring into space, completely absorbed, as if a ghost were whispering to him. We were shocked and maybe we should have realized there was something strange going on in that little head of his . . . but then he'd get straight back to his tricks. Thinking about what happened later makes my hairs stand on end. A miscarriage of society like him being flashed all over the papers and the TV news. And then holing himself up here in Le Case like a criminal.

My eyes are well trained, and I could see that when Eleonora saw the lad walk into the store this morning, her heart skipped a beat. She was giving Mrs. Serraglini her change—and there's another one with a story like something out of a thousand and one nights, with a brigand father and the family home bought with blood money from half the region. There was even the priest, Don Lauro, in line at the cash register. The store door slams open, and we all stand there gaping like fish. Eleonora more than anyone. To the extent that she drops some coins, which roll under the counter.

"That's the effect of seeing someone young," I said to myself. And yet, I had clocked him right there and then, remembering his face from the TV news. Whatever happened, my bonny valley lass's face shut down, and it was all she could do to look at the ground. Guessing how things were about to go, I rushed to the deli counter just in time to take the freak's order. She hung back in a corner the whole while. Until he walked out, hardly saying goodbye.

"Do you know who that guy is?" I asked as I went over to her. Eleonora smiled and said she needed the bathroom.

The worst part of my day is when I see her run down to the end of the road at six in the evening to meet that foreigner. He looks as if he's about to pounce and never comes anywhere near the store. He stands there looking surly, wearing work boots, and smoking. Eleonora says, "See you tomorrow" and runs towards him like a trained monkey. He doesn't even greet her. He waits until she is by his side and then turns into Via di Mezzo where he throws his cigarette butt away. While I walk in the opposite direction, up towards home. With my spirit chafing under my shoes at the thought of Adelaide lying in her shit, her eyes wide open with the disease.

I don't want to walk along the porticoed alley any longer, even when it's raining.

Adele Centini,
the Isastia Widow

What I love when I stretch out naked on this little divan is the silence at the beginning. Calamaio comes into Room 112 at the Bel Sole Hotel and finds me here, ready for him. First, he goes to the window and opens the curtains. Then, he lets in a little cold air to make my skin pull nice and tight. He moves the desk he uses to draw on. He takes the sketchbook out of his bag. Lines his pencils and charcoal up on the surface. He sits down without even taking his jacket off. And we take few moments, just looking at one another. Him on the armchair, a few steps away, me on the red velvet bedspread that has been used so often it has molded into my shape. This moment of silence is the very best thing. Usually, he is the first to break it by clearing his throat. Then he leans over cautiously, as if he were choosing his weapon for a duel. He always ends up selecting the stub of charcoal left over from the last time. And he starts drawing.

The second silence is like a lake that disappears into the horizon, where I get lost and which he navigates with the kind of fervor that furrows his whole face. He lashes at the page with nervous scratches that make me think of clawing mice. It's the only sound, mingled with little grunts that sound like grumbles. He even manages to sweat, despite the draught which reaches me full blast. Meanwhile, I plummet into the minutes, with only my trinkets on. In Room 112 at the Bel Sole, the chasm of the past opens up, and I sink into it with my whole being.

Every time I go back, I realize that one September day in 1954 is to blame for everything. I was thirteen, and I bit the inside of my cheeks until I could taste iron for days not to show I was crying. It was a way to banish thoughts about the suffering of the flesh and bury the suffering of the spirit, which had made me practically fast for the three days before leaving. Mamma was angry with me because not eating made me pale and gave me blue bags under my eyes. "I take the food out of my mouth so that you can go to the Isastias looking like a doll!" she snapped, banging the table. Then she rushed to her room, grabbed her powder puff, and came back to dab my nose and add a little foundation around my mouth. "If you wake up looking pale when you're at the Isastias, you need to put it on like this," she murmured as she finished the job. Then she led me to the mirror to make sure I had understood. "Now go and wash your face and when you come back, show me how to do it on your own."

I was unusually pretty, and my mother saw this as compensation for everything else. Including the death of my father, who never made it back from the war in Greece. I only knew him from two photos. Babbo was handsome. Every time I glanced at the picture, I felt an electric shock in my belly: I understood where my good looks came from, but it was my destiny to see it as a curse.

Mamma, on the other hand, was scrawny and ugly with a permanent scowl on her face. I couldn't understand how the attractive young man in the photo could have been betrothed to this woman who walked crooked and, for good measure, had a giant hairy birth mark like a boar's back right in the middle of her forehead. And big hands, almost like a man's. Putting nail polish on them would have been like painting a donkey's shoes.

On me, even a potato sack looked good. But I had that madwoman on my case all the time, trying to tuck a lock of my hair away, straightening my collar, yelling at me for the way I walked. Or else, I would catch her in some reflection spying on me. It made shivers go down my spine, because her gaze wasn't that of a mother towards her daughter. With her beady eyes it felt like she was saying, "Holy Mother of God, I can make some real money with that." Then she would throw herself into her work at the sewing machine. She would pedal away as if she were possessed.

Her husband's failure to return had left its mark. I would ask if I could help with the mountains of washing, especially when the deliveries were due and Mamma was going to have to stay up all night to finish. "Run straight to bed," she would yell, her voice getting more nasal the louder she shouted. "You need at least ten hours' sleep, all the magazines say. If I happen to see you've missed even half an hour of your beauty sleep, I'll have you soaking for a whole day."

We would do it every Sunday before Mass. At dawn, Mamma would go and fill two buckets of Mt. Amiata mineral water from the pump in the square, even in the darkest winter. Even in a hailstorm. As soon as I opened my eyes in the morning, I saw the giant washtub next to the bed. And her, as strong as a man, lifting the buckets with both hands and pouring.

When I was little, I would scream and yell. Jumping into icy water first thing in the morning took my breath away, a thousand nails piercing my flesh. Actually, they felt like bites. Gnawing down to the bone. She would say, "The more you struggle, the longer it will take." So, I would stop wailing and sink to my death in the washtub, my breath trapped inside me, unable to let out a scream. "Look at your beautiful porcelain skin," she would murmur, as if she were washing bone china. She wouldn't give me time to take a breath before plunging my head underwater again, making my brain explode.

One minute in, one minute out, with her saying: "Nine more goes." The water in my lungs burned, and the coughing rasped for two days. One minute in, one minute out. As the minute came to an end, her hand would already be on my breastbone, ready to push me under again.

I would watch my mother from underwater. She used to count out loud and her voice, mingling with the booming of my heart, sounded as if it were coming from the floor as she held me down with the weight of a boulder. After the first ten rounds, resignation set in. I came back up without even opening my mouth to gasp for air. Until we got to the last dips when I turned into someone else. I emerged without even taking a breath. Mamma threw a towel on my head. "What a fuss," she would say. "But look at you. You were beautiful before but now you look straight out of a portrait. The cold keeps your skin firm." Then she started pinching my cheeks to bring the color back into them. I stepped out of the washtub like a reborn Venus.

She made me sit in a chair. Then she would start the brushstrokes as I sat there naked and shivering. She would say, "Now we're going for a walk downtown to show all the little peasants in this shithole who is the fairest of them all."

When word went around that the bigwigs in Le Case were looking for a new housemaid, Mamma hiked the St. Barbara Way to ask for the grace of God. She left early on Saturday morning, with a packed lunch in a bag. "This is what I've been preparing you for," she said, before setting out. "Now stay inside and don't open to anybody, even if Jesus Christ himself knocks."

The pilgrimage took the Montemmassi road, past Meleta, Prata, and Gabellino. She got back Monday evening; the kiss she had given the icon preserved in Niccioleta still impressed on her lips. From Sticciano it was a forty-kilometer hike, one way. The first thing she said when she got back was, "Halfway there, I saw a wolf. That's a good omen." Then she went to bed without eating.

The next morning, I had to wake her. Even though the alarm had been trilling for more than half an hour, there was no sign of life from her room. When I touched her, she opened her eyes. She looked as if she had been lying there mulling things over, like she did in the summer during siesta. "I overslept," she said, her voice completely normal, not slurred with sleep. She pulled herself up into a sitting position. "I overslept," she said again, but this time her voice started croaking. Then she looked at me. First my body, checking what clothes I had put on. Then my face, for my makeup. "I haven't managed to teach you a thing!" she grumbled. At this point she looked at her watch. "The bus will be coming by in twenty minutes," I muttered. She sat there gawping for a minute, her pupils filled with uncertainty. It was as if she had so many things to say and do in her mind at the same time that she froze, bewildered by her disorientation. Then she went ballistic.

The bus was full of mothers and squeaky-clean daughters. "Who knows how many more will be coming down the hills," she whispered, clambering up the steps. She went to say hello to Loretta, sitting next to her taciturn daughter Rachele, who kept her eyes firmly on the ground. "And who is this little flower?" Mamma said, pinching my old schoolfriend on the cheek. Rachele was plump, with a piggy nose and teeth so widely spaced you could stick a finger between them. Her mother had squeezed her into a rented dress. She looked like a badly coated sugared almond and she knew it.

We went and sat in the back. Mamma dug her elbow into my side and whispered in my ear, "Look at them. All these girls together are worth less than one of your fingernails."

That was the day I saw the Isastia property for the first time. The villa rises almost like a castle in front of the old town, at the foot of the road that leads up to the clock tower. When we got to the piazza in front of St. Bastian's, there was such a big crowd in the square that it scared me.

There were all the girls from the Maremma region with their mothers in tow. Mamma eavesdropped on some of the conversations and found out they had come from as far afield as

Follonica and Orbetello. There was a garland of boys around the piazza, sitting on the walls, pressing forward and shoving one another to get a better view. They were all there, making eyes and jokes and laughing amongst themselves. One or two of the girls responded to their teasing and received a slap from their fathers, while their mothers yelled that their hair was now a mess. "Palmiro," one woman yelled over to her husband. "We're here to show Caterina off. So let them look!"

Mamma went off to get a number from a little man who had been positioned at the entrance. She showed me the ticket with my name on it written by hand. "We're going to be here half the night," she complained.

The longer we were there, the more families arrived, each with a daughter or two in tow. One girl was a cripple. People huddled together and started making friends. But if I so much as hinted at a greeting, Mamma swooped down like a hawk, hissing, "Keep your eyes on the ground." Then she looked up at one of the high windows. "They're spying on us from up there and maybe they're already taking notes about which of these idiot girls is being over-chummy. The selection has been going on for a while already."

I was called in mid-afternoon. When my name was shouted out, the hubbub stopped abruptly. There were whispers as the crowd parted to let us through. I walked up to the servant who was blocking the door with his body. The man started blinking wildly as if he'd been stung by a horse fly. He took my numbered ticket without even looking at it. Then he stepped aside, leaving the passage open. Mamma tried to slip in beside me, but they stopped her. "Family members wait here," he said crossly. He pointed me to a corner with a giant empty pot. All of a sudden, I was standing in front of a big woman in an apron, snorting like a bull. "This way," she said, striding diagonally across the hall.

It felt like walking in a dream. I saw the plasterwork on the ceilings, more ornate than the cornices decorating the town church. And then there were the paintings, candelabras, mirrors covering whole walls . . . I felt my heart beating faster as I climbed the stairs following the big woman, who was huffing and puffing. I was breathing wealthy people's air. It smelled of wet wood and a hint of mimosa. As I climbed up, I passed a long-haired cat wandering around calmly as if it owned the whole place. Then we walked down a corridor with lots of rooms leading off it, on a carpet that went from the beginning to the end. We stopped in front of a door with a chink of light coming from the other side. There was a chair in front, and the woman flopped down onto it, flapping her apron in front of her face. "If I survive until this evening, it will be a miracle," she muttered to herself without looking at me. Until there they were. Steps. Whispers. And sunlight pouring over me all of a sudden. I almost bumped into a pale-faced girl who was trembling all over. She looked like she'd survived a massacre. The big lady, with a last-gasp effort, pulled herself back into a standing position. "We're off again," she sighed. She gave me a once-over, looking almost disgusted. "I'll take this one down and pick up another one. If you finish early, wait for me here. And don't touch anything."

I watched the two figures walk into the distance and then disappear behind a statue of a peacock. The corridor smelled musty. All of a sudden, I heard from inside, "Come in." My legs were wobbling. I must have taken a little longer than usual because a louder voice called out, like the end of an echo, "Come in!"

The room was huge. It could have contained my whole house, including part of the back garden and the tool shed. The walls were papered powder-blue, but they were mostly bare. A painting here and there, yards apart. The two big windows overlooking the piazza looked like brightly lit giants. In the middle, the shape of a man sitting at a massive desk.

"That was a bad start," I heard him say. "In this house we

are not in the habit of having to repeat ourselves. Now do me a favor. Stay exactly where you are." I stood still on a chipped floor title. Looking at my feet.

There followed a silence that nearly drove me to distraction. For a moment I thought I was going to faint. I was so apprehensive, my strength drained away. Whoever the man sitting at the desk was, he didn't say another word. I screwed up my eyes and tried to look up but I was blinded by the glare. Eventually, the shape cleared his throat. "Name. Surname. Date of birth," he said. And I answered. The sound echoing around that immense timbered room didn't sound like my voice. I realized notes were being taken on the other side of the desk. "Do you know how to housekeep?" I actually managed to smile and explained that, yes, housekeeping was my specialty. It was practically all I'd ever done but for sure it was the first time I had ever set foot in a mansion like this. "And what is the situation vis-a-vis your love life?" This question made me die of shame. I muttered that I had never had a boyfriend. But that I had had a few pet cats over the years. The words tumbled out of my mouth freely, "Speaking of which, I saw a lovely creature coming up here." The man in front of me chuckled. "He's called Ettore. He steals food on the sly . . ." I heard the chair shift, which made me go stiff. I tried looking up but all I could see was his silhouette. His steps rang out like a grandfather clock striking. "That's a nice name," I murmured. The next minute, he was in front of me. His breath was harsh and hollow. He smelled of tobacco. "Let me see your teeth," he wheezed. I clasped my hands in front of me so that he wouldn't see they were shaking. I threw my head back and opened my mouth wide. The man shifted his weight a hair's breadth, and I was flooded in light again. I stayed in that position for a whole minute. I could hear a whistling sound coming through his nose. And I felt his gaze as if it were digging down into my guts. Then he heaved a deep sigh and went back to his desk. "Wait outside," he muttered, in a nasty tone. "And please ask Esedra to come in."

I was in the room when the announcement was made. Colonel Isastia had found the housemaid he was looking for. I looked down on the piazza through one of the big windows. I saw mothers consoling their daughters. Others were dragging them away angrily, pushing through the crowd. The most upset were the fathers, who had wasted a day's work on the whim of their wives who had been convinced their child would be chosen but, instead, would have to rush back and peel the potatoes.

The driver took us home in the Colonel's car. Every once in a while, I looked over at Mamma, who was staring at the road in a daze. She looked like an animal on heat. Her hands were in her lap, and she didn't even blink when our tires bounced over the potholes. When we got to our destination, the driver said he would be back to pick us up on Sunday at 8 P.M. so that I could start working on Monday morning.

The discombobulation of the day hit me all at once. I threw myself onto the kitchen chair, the skin on my face stinging as if the blood had only just started to circulate. In the meantime, Mamma was already opening and shutting cupboard doors, pulling all my clothes out and emptying the trunks that would go with me to the Isastia household five days later. It came like a torpedo, breaking the silence that had been slowly restoring me. "By the way, just to be clear," she said, picking up the thread of a conversation that had never existed. "The salary will come in useful. You'll be sending it home, of course. But remember we're aiming much higher. As everyone knows, the dear Colonel has been a widower for five years or more. A beautiful young wife is just what he needs to help him tackle old age, don't you think?"

DON LAURO,
the Priest

I love you, dear Jesus, and you know this well. You are my guide and my solace but I'm sorry to say, I really don't understand the punishment you have inflicted on me.

Today it's been two years. Two years of *tick-tock, tick-tock, tick-tock* . . . Maybe watching me going slowly crazy makes you laugh and I'm glad. The truth is that I haven't slept a wink since the days of Moses. *Tick-tock, tick-tock* . . . It may be funny but anyone else in my place would have thrown themselves out of the window. Except that's not what priests do.

Priests don't walk into a pharmacy and ask for drops strong enough to kill a horse, either. I can just imagine Dr. Salghini: "Don Lauro is telling us to have faith all the time. Then when he gets the blues at night, who does he come to for a prescription? A Hail Mary has never calmed anyone's nerves, but benzodiazepine has." Over my dead body will I admit he's right but if it goes on like this, one of these nights I'm going to have to check out for real. I smoke a hundred cigarettes a night. In the end, in addition to the *tick-tock* trick, you'll be giving me a nice case of emphysema. That way we can break open the champagne, and I'll have free rein to fly to the Kingdom of Heaven to see you.

As if the job you called on me to undertake were an easy one in this godforsaken town . . . I was a willing little priest and I wasn't in the least scared of being dumped here on these hills, where, at the beginning of October, the thick fog gobbles everything up and nothing else ever happens. I held you in my heart and I still cherish you with my whole soul, more than before. Even though you've been having a blast playing the joker recently.

Maybe you're still upset about that stupid lapse I had ten years ago? I apologized every way I knew how. And anyway, Mariella hasn't so much as looked at me for a century. She, too, has forgotten that weakness of my flesh. She's ashamed even to think about it and we've all lived happily ever after. With all respect: if this is the problem, you certainly know how to hold a grudge. How holy you are!

Or maybe you're still annoyed by that time I used the money from the collection box to buy a bottle of liquor? Dear Jesus, it's not as if you allow us humble shepherds to wallow in the lap of luxury, while there are those who walk to Rome in slippers that would cost a normal person a year's salary just to look at in a store window. And anyway, I said sorry back then, too. I put the money back the very next day. I get it. What I did was wrong . . . Well, strike me dead then! What can I say? Fling me onto some distant planet and leave me there. But I'd like to see who would come to this mortuary to listen to widows moaning or miners whining like kids because they think they've wasted their life at work or at the kitchen sink. The holy scriptures teach us that the devil hides behind temptation. I would respond that temptation is no match for boredom.

I do my job, dear Jesus. I do it quite well, I think. Take Clara, Giannessi's young lass, for example. She used to sleepwalk and one night she took it into her head to go down to the main square as naked as your Father had created her, scratching herself all over. It was last year, more or less in this season. My eyes were sunken from insomnia. I said to myself: "Don Lauro, my friend. Go and take a stroll, otherwise this constant *tick-tock* is going to strip you of your sanctity, and you'll end up doing something stupid.

By your design, I bumped into her on the road that runs down to the lower streets that give onto precipice overlooking the Maremma valley. It was a sight that would make any normal person hurl and continue to do so in bucketfuls. There was Clara Giannessi on all fours with all the splendor of a girl who has just turned eighteen. And a few steps away, a stray wolf dog with its ears flattened and its back claws scratching at the gravel, ready to pounce.

You watched from up there: I had to throw a stone at that creature from hell. All the while, reciting the Lord's Prayer. But the beast had no intention of giving up on its pretty prey. He was dripping semen and wouldn't have left even if I'd thrown harpoons at him. You can imagine. The dog had been wandering around Le Case looking for leftovers when he suddenly caught sight of that poor barefooted girl with her crown jewels in full sight . . . In the end, I threw a broken roof tile at his head. He let out a yelp and a growl at the same time. When he turned around to look at me with those dark eyes, I yelled, "Get out of here, you obscene Satan!" To get the message across, I lobbed another tile at his face. Only then did he lope off down the incline coming out of the woods. He was still jerking and thrusting as he ran.

Clara Giannessi was there on her haunches in the nude. Her hair hung down and hid her face. I must admit, she scared me more than if I'd seen the devil in the flesh. But I went up to her and said, "Come, little Clara. I'll take you home." I covered her with the jacket I had been wearing. She gave a jolt, as if waking up from a dream. "Don Lauro, what am I doing here? I'm cold," she murmured almost inaudibly, shaking all over.

Dear Jesus, if you require proof of courage, you've had tons from me. I'm just saying. Well, I may have committed a few little sins but, when necessary, I am willing to brandish your Father's name like a sword. Nothing will stop me. Not the drooling devil himself. But if things go on like this, I'm telling you loud and clear: a few more nights and I'll be keeping little Clara company in that place where she was committed a while back.

I was so happy in the cells you had assigned me at St. Bastian's. Church and home, as they say. I spent almost thirty years there and I never once complained about anything, admit it. And then one fine day you have this brainwave, even though there are plenty of other things you're supposed to be doing. That is, to make the rocks Le Case is built on quake. We all know the ways of the Lord are . . . What's the word? Iscru . . . inscru . . .? Whatever. They can't be understood and that's fine by me. Maybe giving the town a good shake every now and again is your way of saying, "Children, do not fear, you have not been forgotten. The eye of the Lord is keeping vigil, even if you live in this bumfuck of a place." There may even be someone who believes it. Up here, the old men say that the old town was built on the back of a sleeping giant and that earthquakes are simply occasional tremors during his thousand-year sleep. People are used to it. When they feel the first vibrations coming, they say: "He's moving. He hasn't shifted since last June," looking up at the lampshade. The quakes are light, hardly shaking a loose stone from a drainpipe. And that was the case two years ago, at three A.M. Most people didn't even notice. The following morning, there wasn't a crack on any of the ancient walls, which have survived the attrition of century after century . . . The only damage in the whole town was the collapsed ceiling of my house. Saving the corner over my bed, with me sleeping in it.

"A miracle!" people yelled when they saw me standing there unharmed. "A miracle!" Dear Jesus, I'm not so sure anymore. I thought it was, to begin with. "Look how the powers that be are persuading me to move."

I liked the idea of moving the few bits and pieces I own to the clock tower. Looking out of the window, I could see as far as the horizon. I said to myself, "At the end of the game, Jesus wanted me to move to the very top of the town to send a clear message: people, Don Lauro is watching over you, which means Christ is, too." Then the *tick-tock* started getting to me. Not to mention the striking every hour. But that's nothing compared to the mechanism. The springs and the crenellated cogs that make the giant hands inch forward over my head. *Tick-tock tick-tock* . . . The harder I try not to think about it, the louder it reverberates in my head even when I'm a hundred miles away. And when it's not that, it's the complaints of these people who have grown up eating nothing but crusts of bread and boar bristles. The local workmen cordoned off St. Bastian's two years ago, and the fences are still there. Not a penny has come into the town coffers to pay for it to be restored.

And then, Jesus my friend, you have the nerve to complain if for once I stick my fingers into the collection box so that I can guzzle down a bottle of booze until I collapse on the carpet and finally sleep as your Father commands?

It would anyway be better than giving in to Dr. Salghini, who fancies he's a scientist. Casting doubt on your word, apart from anything else. That is how he lives, one outright blasphemy after another, putting to the test the idea of holy forgiveness that you have been shooting up my veins for as long as I remember.

MARIELLA MANTOVANI,
the Housewife

Graziella likes acting like a wealthy diva, but she hasn't bought herself a new set of dentures and when she opens her mouth to talk, they dance a tarantella in her mouth. It's hard to imagine that a thousand years ago she was a beauty. She was short in stature, but she had a giant cunt with a thick, dark bush like you're supposed to have at sixteen, when everything is a discovery and it's a waste to slam the door on new experiences. We used to go down to the chestnut woods with our rag dolls. We would pretend we were having tea parties with princes arriving in coaches. Until dolls were no longer enough for us and we started pulling our skirts up, especially on hot days when we would paddle in the stream. Graziella stuck her finger up me and I stuck my finger up her. We could spend a whole July afternoon like that as the Vena flowed lazily past. And I fell in love with her. I still remember the feeling. I'd say, "Graziellina, let's stay here forever, pissing our pleasure into the creek! What could be better?" Then we kissed, like girls at that age do, our hearts thumping at the idea that a passerby or hunter with his swollen desire in his hand might appear from behind the bushes, like a boar grunting at the idea of a tasty morsel for free.

The chestnut trees are still there. They grow taller and stronger every year and in October, like now, they are laden with spiky pods. Whereas we lost our bloom years ago and have stopped thinking the best is yet to come. But I still try it out every now and again. When it's sunny, I face up to the road and make it to the old wash house. Then once I'm around the big bend I walk up to the very same house it would take me ten minutes through town to get to as a girl. Graziella always peeks through the curtain to check. I may be wrong, but I feel as though her leathery old face lights up whenever she sees me at the door. A moment later, she's at the door opening it wide and exclaiming, "Mariella, my dear! What a surprise!"

There's the same smell of cookies as there used to be a hundred years ago in that house. As soon as I set foot inside, a whirlwind of memories hits me. In the old days, we couldn't wait to steal two minutes alone together to chat about our secrets but now that we have all the time in the world without worrying that someone is going to call us back home, the only thing we talk about is the weather and the pain in our legs. Then we sit at the table, and I ask her to lay out the cards.

She learned the art from her grandmother. When she was young, she was already talking about bird-blood candles and plates of piss outside the door at night to ward off restless spirits. In town people used to say Nonna Velia was a witch, the type that summoned the devil in the mirror at three in the morning. Mamma always said, "Best keep her as a friend. Rumor has it that she ruined Benedetti's crops with one look and now he's running to the mayor begging for a crust of bread to keep him going one more day." We used to go down to the stream and do those things we liked so much. Graziellina told me that Nonna Velia knew she was dying but wanted to pass the Tarot art and explain her notebook on herbal remedies first. I didn't really believe in that stuff, but I was madly in love with my friend and all I wanted was to be with her. I used to say, "We're going to have to marry some loser one of these days. But swear to me we won't stop coming to the Vena creek to make out on the sly." Except that the bumpy ride that is life gradually took us in another direction. Her with that toad-faced Martino, and me with Divo, who may be full of cuss words but at the end of the day has never left me wanting.

Graziella was upset when she saw me dancing one evening with the young Divo. We weren't yet twenty and at home they were already saying it was my last chance if I didn't want to die a spinster. So, I took the first man who came my way. One morning on my front doorstep, I found a necklace with a strange pendant made of two stones tied together with hair. "This is how Graziella is telling me she's still thinking about me," I thought. And forty years went by.

Things like this happen in small towns: you grow up together and then you forget, especially when you have kids. A husband's smile grows more and more distant and the days rain on you like hailstorms from one Christmas to the next. Until two years ago when I happen to see that old friend at Mario's and she says: "Mariella, you're looking good! Why don't you come and visit? We can have some tea. Spend a little time together." Just like that, out of the blue.

Since then, once a month, I walk up past the big bend. Graziella is not what she once was, but she tells my fortune for real. It's not an excuse to reminisce about those afternoons in the good old days when we had perfect feet, not like the lumpy, calloused flat irons we have now. Basically, Graziella pretends nothing ever happened and I'm a little disappointed. I know we can't strip and fall into bed for a whole morning at our age with all these folds of fat. But at least talking about it would be nice. Instead of replaying them in my head on my own as I've been doing all my life. But my friend asks me about Divo, whether he's still angry about being laid off at the mine with a pension that won't get him very far. And whether Floriano, the son we sent away from Le Case as soon as we could, is doing well near Siena. So, I sit there without saying anything in particular, playing the part of the old lady. I'm certainly not going to tell her that I have managed to find other ways to cool my blood without any help from her, she who first introduced me to these pleasures at the age of sixteen. Though sometimes I'm so cross with her I would throw it in her face.

I don't know what happens to me when I see men. It started in '65, when I had been married just over a year. Handsome or not, the first thing I think when I see a man is how he could fuck me down there or up the rear, where it feels like a bottomless pit. It must be an illness or something. Or maybe it's just that when both holes are plugged, that emptiness in my belly, where the absence of real love is howling at the moon, disappears. Or again, it could just be a curse Graziella cast over me when I first started seeing this miner who used to laugh and fool around whenever we met. Not like now, when you have to fire a cannon ball at him to get any response that's not an imprecation.

My poor husband Divo. He's always so angry, and at the end of the day, I understand him. Over the years I've had it off with every man in town who has ever crossed my path, from the teenagers to the old codgers. He's the only one who doesn't get a look in, though we still share a bed. We lie head to toe because he snores like a pig and lashes out at me in his sleep, as if in that other world they have told him all the things I get up to in the orchards. Instead of my face, he's had my heels on the pillow next to his for the past forty years.

Divo's hands have become monstrous from work, his nails like claws. And over time, his neck has disappeared. He was born perfectly formed and then slowly became the shape of a gas boiler, all back and nothing else: a miscarriage in reverse. In the winter, when the sheets are icy, it disgusts me when he stretches his foot over to my side of the bed and I feel his big toe brushing my body. And yet in the early days I couldn't get enough of that thing of his, which he'd give me at all times, even after a double shift in the cages down in the Ribolla mines. I don't think I've seen him naked for a thousand years, but I've been washing his underwear my whole life. I send him out dressed like a gentleman, I do. I really have no idea where he's been getting his kicks in the meantime. I don't think about it. I keep up appearances and act like a good wife and that's enough.

Graziella may have a gift for the cards. Everyone knows she does and far be it from me to say she doesn't, but the fact is, she doesn't see these things. Or she doesn't want to talk about them. The last time I saw her she was complaining about Samuele, who's back in Le Case after causing all kinds of hell elsewhere. "If you say as much as good day to him, it's like greeting the devil," she warned me. "Pretend he doesn't exist and shut your windows." As if that were easy. I've watched Samuele grow up, though he left town just as he was getting old enough to slap my ass a little. Some of those boys back in the day used to knead my cunt into ruff-puff pastry as they thrashed about down there. Like Giannone, who lives down near Meleta and has two kids, one of them just like him. We would meet in the dovecot, which stank to high heaven, and where there was always the chance of coming across snakes. I held my legs up high and screamed, "Giannone, get your breath back for God's sake! With all this pounding you'll bust your gut and that will be the end of you!" But he couldn't. He went on grinding into me, staring into space, until something caught in my throat and I wanted to cry, "If you stop now, I'll kill you." Giannone was built like a jackhammer, a bad one. He was like a mule on heat. When he sent me home, my legs felt like mush. Divo would see me walking in as if I had a bar of soap between my legs. "Are you getting arthritis again? It says on TV that the weather's changing . . ." Even worse was the following day when I'd wake up with my flesh cracked right up to my hair roots.

But I remember Samuele with his wispy beard and dark looks. I used to watch him on the street from my window as I chatted to Esedra on the next-door balcony. He was slim and pale-skinned, with a well-chiseled profile. I got straight to the point, without beating about the bush. "My dear friend, if I were thirty years younger, I would make your nephew sing like a nightingale." Esedra laughed while I was thinking, "I'll wait until he's fourteen and one day I'll take him down to the cellar to see what kind of water you can drink through that straw." But I never got the chance before he went off to high school in Grosseto. He left and that was that. Only to end up a year ago on all the news channels.

I'm past it now. I'm too old for lashings of that kind though I would still like it and I wish I still had that sheet of paper where I used to write down all the names of the men who had been inside me. I used to hide it in the kitchen under the plastic cutlery box in a drawer nobody else used. One day, I wanted to add another trophy to the list, but it was gone. I wore myself out for weeks worrying. The idea that Divo might have picked it up upset me more than I would ever have imagined. The idea that he was thinking about all those young men I'd poured my energy into when I had never given him the time of day . . . I climbed into bed every night watching him closely, but he behaved as usual, with that habitual scowl of his that made him look like a leftover Fascist. After a while I let myself feel a little relief, saying to myself, "I must have thrown the sheet away by mistake." The next day, there I was again getting my fill of cock, only without the hare-brained idea of immortalizing the guy's name on a list that might well end up in the wrong hands.

It's true what they say: when you are old, there are some things you enjoy going back to. But sometimes your memory's not up to it. A diary to help relive certain scenes would be useful, and you end up kicking yourself for not keeping one. It's nice, though, when the memory of a raging bull flashes through my mind all of a sudden, like it did just now. This one was from Montebamboli, and they called him Piston. Well, the name says it all. I started chuckling to myself just remembering us lying under the chestnut trees, my panties in my hands. Divo shifts his gaze from the TV set and says, "Why are you laughing? Are you going gaga?" I glare at him as I serve dinner. For a second my knees wobble but then I give my usual answer, "I don't know, it must be the change in the season."

Adelaide Franci,
the Invalid

O*ra pro nobis, ora pro nobis* . . . Don Lauro, do me a favor: open the window a little, it's boiling in this room, and I already feel like I'm at Hell's door. And anyway, I'm fed up with prayers. What's done is done, I say. You can jaw away as long as you like, calling for the Grace of God but at the end of the day what's it for? To confess that I've committed blasphemy or had impure thoughts in my time? In that case, we may as well never be born. That's how I see it. Coming here now that I'm bedridden and may not even live until Friday is all very well. But if the Lord wants to give me a free pass at heaven's gates, let him at least X-ray the person I am, not the one whining because she's reached the last stop. I know who the real Adelaide Franci is and if He's as good as he claims, He that brought me into this world should know it, too. If He gets upset about a fit of nerves or a few harsh words, it's His problem.

Don Lauro, I may be on my deathbed, but I haven't taken leave of my senses yet, and this is another thing I must thank Him for. If I were senile, at least, everything would look new, and I wouldn't feel as though this room and this bed were a cage of woe. I would smile at my husband and throw my arms around his neck as if I were a young girl. And I would hold back my tears as the poor wretch wipes my ass. But that would be too easy for Him. He prefers me to notice everything, to let me be undressed by the man who saw me in the prime of my youth and now almost retches when he pulls back the covers.

Actually, no. If I may, the punishment is even worse. Seeing that we're in the mood for confessions, I have an ax to grind and I'm going to grind it for once.

I'm talking about that slut. The one who has taken my place now that I've got this illness behind the counter at the store where I've spent my entire life.

You should know, Don Lauro, that Sonia Serraglini comes to visit every once in a while, especially on Wednesdays when she goes down to the cemetery to put fresh flowers on her husband's grave. On her way home, she stops over here laden with shopping. You can't imagine how I feel when I see all those packets and smell the freshly sliced mortadella sausage . . . Sonia likes combing my hair. She always says, "Adele, my dear. You need to style these three wisps you have left." And I let her do it. I'm not ashamed with her. And while she's combing, I ask her things. I ask about Mario, how she thinks he is doing at the store. Sonia is a real chatterbox and she and I are a team. She brings me first-hand news.

For example, I've heard that Eleonora acts like a good girl all day but that every evening one of those monsters that have invaded this country from the plains of Albania picks her up and takes her home. All the young lads get out of Le Case after eighth grade with the devil in their tail. Well, at least until about twenty years ago, when there was still someone in town with the stomach to bring children into the world. Now, with no new workforce in half the province, the Nencionis have had to call those Albanian toads in, otherwise they'd have to close the sawmill. One of these workers is the person we're talking about.

"A sourpuss," Sonia says. One of those guys who kill time down at the Due Porte, at Maso's bar. They would traipse in with their muddy shoes and start the rounds. Since they're all animals, things always end up in a brawl. The ones with more drink in them smash bottles on the floor. Once, the carabinieri were called in to pull them apart and a couple of them were sent back where they came from. Well, Maso is no spring chicken, either. His regulars first leaned on the bar when they were young men and have been drinking Campari since the '30s. The strongest of them clenches his mouth to keep his dentures in. You can imagine the kind of fun might be had in a place like that by those men, who were destined to be delinquents and whose only skills were woodcutting and being thrown into jail.

Well, the little saint that Mario has employed to take my place at the store is having it off with one of these individuals. Sonia Serraglini says he has the low brow of a half-wit, though he's actually quite handsome, if it weren't for the bull neck that pulls his head down between his shoulders. And he wears shoes at least two sizes too big, like orphans at the seminary who only ever wear charity cast-offs. No one even knows where the two of them vanish after sundown . . . The only thing I know for sure is that Eleonora arrives on the bus that gets in at a few minutes past seven, the same one that brings the steel plant night-shift workers back home, and that in the evening she slinks off with that horrible man.

Ora pro nobis . . . So, there is something to pray about after all! The point, Don Lauro, is one only and it crushes my heart at every breath. Mario pomades his hair in the morning. I don't know what his brain is telling him but whatever it is, it upsets me. It really upsets me, and I say to myself, "Is this the way our lovely fairy tale, which began with me waving at him out of the window, comes to an end? With misplaced desire for a young girl who could be his granddaughter from a second marriage? That's when the heat starts rising, replacing the hot flashes of my illness. I dig my heels in, scratching the mattress that can no longer stand me and that I can no longer stand, and say to myself loud and clear, "Mario was mine when I was seventeen, and he's still mine! Even though in old age all we are left with are the crumbs of what we were back in the day."

For your information, Don Lauro, it's not easy. You should hear the idiot whistling. The alarm goes off in the morning, and he leaps up like mercury. He's in such a hurry that the day before yesterday, he forgot to leave the window open even a crack for me, a favor you would do for a dog. All he did was check that the phone was on my bedside table as usual and that the handset was correctly placed. Then he slammed the door shut and rushed off.

He's an open book. In the evening when he comes home, I can read it in his eyes: he'd rather have his head cracked open than shut himself up here with the stench of a wife on her deathbed. He brings me some broth. He pulls a chair up and lays a place-setting on the bed for himself. Every now and again he'll give me a little wine, as long as I don't start with the tears. I can't control them; they're waves that wash away all my feelings in infinite anguish. It usually starts with one silent teardrop in my plate. Then I start wailing and tearing my hair out, or what's left of it. I beg him to take me away from this place, which used to be nice, but which now feels like an endless ordeal. He runs into the kitchen and brings me a glass of water. "Drink it all in one gulp, my love," he says. That's how I swill down the drops Salghini prescribed for my depression. I don't even notice I've fallen asleep. The next minute, the alarm goes off, and the fanfare of the day starts all over again.

I must admit, though: the mere fact that the locust comes all the way up here from the valley of Montemassi gives me a reason to go on. I also curse her: without an Eleonora here making a nuisance of herself, I might already have kicked the bucket and I'd be in the great beyond, in your Father's grace. So, here I am playing this game, which makes my blood boil on one hand, and, on the other, renews it by poisoning it.

All this to say that yesterday Sonia Serraglini stopped here on her way back from the cemetery with her shopping, as she does nearly every Wednesday. "I had him right there," she said. Then she told me about a little scene that had taken place at the store, just as that young lass who has taken my place was handing out her change.

The television is always on in this room. The good thing is that, once you've paid the license fee, you get all these re-runs of programs from the old days which are specially designed for old people. In the afternoon, moreover, you get old films in black and white and that's when I start sniveling, though not in the sad way I described before. No. It's more nostalgia: I remember Sundays at the movies with the same husband who, in his seventies, has decided to play the gigolo with that slut. "If only there were another explosion like the one in '54," I say to myself. In her house.

Yes, I lived through the whole thing. I mean what happened with Esedra's nephew. Speaking of the dregs of society. I read about the arrest and followed the shit storm in the press. I heard the daily grind of gossip in people's living rooms and saw the crowd waiting for him outside the courthouse, eager to tear him to shreds. For a while, I even had the magazines brought home. To kill time, as much as anything else, since time was killing me. And I said to myself, "We're not normal here at Le Case. The one time we end up on the TV news, it's for a psycho who killed a little girl for no reason. After Tempesti, who has lost the plot, this is our only claim to fame."

And anyway, I remembered him as a boy, that Samuele. He always used to come to the store to pick up Esedra's shopping, God bless her. His eyes were deep and restless. There was a spark of madness in him that was the same twenty years later, as I saw in the papers. He never made friends with boys his age. There were so few you could have counted them on the fingers of one hand and at a certain point they vanished just like him, to avoid dying of boredom in a town where at five in the afternoon in winter it feels like midnight.

So, listen up, Don Lauro: yesterday morning, this messed-up townsman of ours turned up at the store. "I saw him and my blood ran cold," Sonia said. Everyone knows that, after getting off with a suspended sentence, he has holed himself up here in the family house. Sonia fanned herself as she tried to get the story out. "That Eleonora. You should have seen her. She looked up and blanched, her eyes were like headlights. A tremor went through her body from head to toe. She was shaking so much she dropped some coins from the cash register. Then Mario came forward, because the idiot looked like she'd lost her tongue . . . Does that sound like a normal reaction to you? I smell a rat."

Don Lauro, I really don't know if they're having an affair. But I do know that my dear friend, Sonia Serraglini, knows what she saw. If she says she saw a storm pass over the slut's pretty face, I believe her. And to answer the question, "Does it sound like a normal reaction?" I'd say, "Not at all!" In fact, I would counter: what is the young lass, whom Mario has employed with the excuse that I'm rotting away in bed, hiding? Where does she vanish to, in the evening, escorted by the Albanian buffalo? And let's not forget Esedra's nephew, who has reappeared out of nowhere after narrowly escaping justice by a miracle. He could have disappeared abroad, for example. But no. Here he is, back up in the mountains like an evil eye that has lost its way. Eleonora from Ribolla sees him and her knees practically buckle with excitement.

If it weren't for the fact that the husband I chose when I could still touch my toes is mixed up in all this, I'd let that beetle from the plains piss in whatever corner she wants. But this affects my home and family, and despite the raging disease, I am still in one piece. As a matter of fact, I'm more with it than ever. Mario wants to parade his balls in public and yet he has a wife that loves him as much as when she first met him, when he used to pass her on the street and shake the shiny curls on his head. I'm certainly not going to let him run headlong into ridicule, considering that in Le Case people talk and it takes a minute to sully the reputation built over a lifetime. I'll say more: the idea of butchering that bitch sometimes gives me a little amusement. That's when I brighten up and happily swallow the blood that oozes from my gums like tar. This morning, for example, I looked at myself in the mirror I keep here and my skin looked nice and smooth, especially around my nose. It must be because I'm getting ready for the bell to toll . . . And yet, I'm right: the idea of sending that crazy cow back to the piss-house she came from gives me strength. What is it? Do you want to fight? Take your seats. Adelaide Franci here has never run away from a fight. Which means that, when the time comes, God Almighty will have to add this rancor to the debits column in my ledger if he really has to play Mr. Punctilious.

Tonino Manenti, aka Maso,
the Barkeeper

In my poor old Babbo's day, people used to come all the way from Florence. Things were different then and Le Case felt like the center of the world. I used to pull myself up on tiptoe, gripping the bar with my little hands. I could only just get my nose over the top. And there was Babbo, as fine and sturdy as the cornerstone of the church. He always had a tea towel draped over his shoulder, which he used to dry the glasses. When he saw me, his face would crack into such a wide grin that I could have looked at it all day and I still treasure the memory. He would come forward and say, "Here's my lovely boy!" Then he would pick me up and fly me over to his side of the bar.

In the Spring we would put chairs out on Via di Mezzo, even though the street is narrow and only gets the sun when it is overhead. But my favorite time of year was Christmas, when we used to huddle inside with snow flurries lashing against the windows. The bar would be full of smoke, tangerine peel decorations strung across the room, and the workmen used to spin out the pleasure of drinking until late in the evening. A pipsqueak like me would sit there watching the soccer on TV or listening to conversations I understood almost nothing of. In the meantime, Babbo would flirt with the women who came on their own, especially the war widows. He had a mustache and a high forehead but it was his jocular manner that really got to the ladies. He would wink at me as he walked towards the curtain that to this day closes off the back of the bar where we keep the plastic crates for the empty bottles. There was always some lady or other. "Tonino," he would say. "You take over for a bit!" I never for a second thought about my mother on her own on the other side of town doing her sewing work. I would puff up my chest like a frog and take up my position behind the counter. I tried not to show it but my heart would be thumping as I poured a measure of liquor for whichever hot-faced young man showed up.

My spirit is sapped as I stand here and suddenly see myself in exactly the same place, except that so many years have gone by it makes me want to scream. In a nutshell: one day, Babbo picked me up and flew me behind the counter. And I have been trapped here ever since.

He was shot in Russia during the war. They sent him home with a limp in his right leg. I would beg him over and over to tell me stories about those faraway places and about the bombs. He was always reluctant to talk about it. At times, he would turn morose and sit there staring at nothing in front of a glass of robust wine. Then he would come to with a jolt and go back to the chess board.

It was a game that I had never heard of. He had learned to play during his days in the field camp, in a tent where they would pile up wounded soldiers like him after every battle. Whenever he talked about the game he would say, "There's a whole life in it." I sat in silence, my eyes glistening. Until one day he went down to Grosseto to buy a set.

It was funny to see how the pastime took root here. The old codgers couldn't do without their cards but even they started to stick their noses into the game after a while. The younger men used to come in at opening time to book their place at the "checkered table" as they used to call it, especially on Sundays. The news soon got around and people started to come from Sassofortino and Montieri, even from Massa, despite the risk of being beaten black and blue for the sin of hailing from those places. Tournaments at the Due Porte bar went on for entire afternoons and picked up again after dinner. The winner would take home the whole pot. It was a tidy sum, like a day's wages, together with the satisfaction of thrashing all the brainboxes in the region. Babbo used to tell me that checkmating your opponent is equivalent to sucking their soul dry. The prize might even be a bag full of gold but it's nothing compared to the loser's expression when their king is forced off the board.

The yearning soon wormed its way under the skin of peasants and miners alike, men who had brought all the shit in the world back from the war. Being a doctor or a lawyer was no protection. A cobbler from another town might turn up any time and give you your marching order in ten moves. The big guys would get angry and try and achieve with their hands what they failed to accomplish with their guile, humiliating themselves even more. At the end of the day, when I helped Babbo sweep up, we would often find a tooth or two in amongst the sawdust scattered over the floor of the bar.

The real surprise was when Niccodemo Tempesti arrived. He was a quiet, solitary young man. He looked pretty talentless to me. His mind had been addled by the war but he had returned with a bunch of other soldiers who had been demobbed without any rhyme or reason weeks after the end of the conflict, making mothers, wives, and daughters mad with joy. Niccodemo was by no means the only one paying the consequences. There were hordes of men who would sit for hours staring into space but eventually they came to their senses, partly because playing dead all day when there was no food on the table was not an option. As time went by he, too, adapted to a normal life with no blasts and no fear of being blown up at every step. And he, too, started to step out of the house. The thing was, not only his body but also his nature had changed. He had brought a little light back into his mother's life. She was a widow who had to get up early every morning to empty the night-soil pots and drain the sewage ditches up in the high part of town. A job that was enough to give you a long face before you even woke up. People say she entertained men during the war, the few that were left doing shift work down the mines or in the factories instead of donning battle helmets, that is.

Niccodemo would stand around observing, like everyone else, the matches as they played out on a board placed on a table right in the middle of the bar. The room was always as silent as a grave. Until spectators started muttering when one of the players made a rash move or stupidly lost their queen. The one who had been caught out would sometimes leap up and send his chair flying. But the best matches were the ones where there was a last-minute comeback, when all of a sudden, a disadvantage was levelled and a final deathblow was dealt to the guy who until a second before had been lying back contentedly in his chair after capturing two rooks but had suddenly woken up being cornered by a pawn with his king in mortal agony. There were some who, rather than just a chair, threw the whole chess board with all its pieces up in the air. And ran out of the bar promising never to set foot there again. Babbo would come up to me. "He'll be smarting all week," he'd say. "He'd rather be shot in the head than lose to Tozzini who can't even count to twenty."

One Sunday, Niccodemo's name went up on the board. People went around saying that his mother had had to suck dead skin off old codgers' cocks up in the old town to pay for his enrolment in the tournament. He didn't respond. He simply waited his turn. And when it came, in five moves he beat a man everyone called the Duke, from up near the Clock Tower, with a daughter back home who had been born with no legs like a fish. Duke asked for a rematch, claiming he hadn't been able to concentrate with all the hubbub coming from the spectators, but it wasn't allowed. "Well, I'll go and get my kicks with you know who!" he said, intimating he had a few pennies left over to spend on a hooker. Niccodemo didn't react to the provocation. In fact, in the space of an afternoon, he wiped out ten more contestants. To vindicate themselves, they too threatened to go straight to the same whore and dirty her face. By around seven that evening, they had stopped watching Tempesti with the usual arrogance reserved for newcomers. Then he won the tournament and walked off with a nice wad of cash. The following Sunday, his name was up on the board again.

There are still some photos of that period. Newspaper cuttings. Because our Niccodemo became a celebrity in no time at all. He was unbeatable. He couldn't have been a day over twenty and, while most people went underground to choke on dust for an hourly wage, he brought home a salary with his tournaments. One Sunday, some big shots arrived from Arezzo. They wore white hats and had pocket-watches chained to their waistcoats. One of them put their name on the board. It was Tancredi. I remember because some of the older folk still talk about him. He was unabashed when his turn came along. He took the silver watch out of his pocket and placed it on the table. Looking the rookie in the eye, he said, "Look, kid. If you win, you can take it home." Niccodemo kicked his ass, though the match lasted five minutes longer than usual. Tancredi didn't take it badly. In fact, he opened his arms and smiled. Then he called him outside for a chat.

It's true that when you are born poor and then make a quick buck, you soon lose your bearings. And that is what happened to our townsman. At the Due Porte bar, miners would curse when they read the papers. They'd be shitting iron pyrite for the rest of their lives while this guy had transformed a pastime into a serious occupation. Well-paid, too. With the added bonus of travel to America, with everything you can find there. So, they took it out on chess, as if to say, "We breathe the same air as him. If that goat has succeeded . . . " People were now calling the goat "Maestro." They said he'd bought an apartment in Florence and had married a theater actress for whom the adjective "beautiful" was woefully inadequate. Licking their wounds, the miners would say: "At least I fucked his mother though I have to say she wasn't that great . . . " Then another article would come out and they'd be sick with envy again.

There is one thing that needs to be said: Niccodemo Tempesti never recognized his debt to the Due Porte bar. At the end of the day, his fame started here with the Sunday tournaments. My poor Babbo had to go all the way to Russia and get shot to come up with the idea for the tournaments. But there was never a word of thanks. He didn't even send a telegram when Babbo died in '54.

He came back when he was sixty with a whisky habit, his property squandered away by his wife, and a nest egg he needed to measure out with a teaspoon if it was going to serve as a pension. Then, he sunk back into the poverty he had been born into. Except that now there were no players to conquer in an afternoon, nor was there a whore of a mother who could make up the difference by lifting her skirt. Everyone knew what he was capable of and no one would sit at the chess board with him. And they were pissed off at him because, while they had been searing their lungs at the blast furnace or in the seams down in the valley, he had been strutting around the world like an emperor. Niccodemo Tempesti had won some important matches in later seasons, but that was before he fell apart completely. Nowadays, he lives off the shopping Don Lauro takes him on Tuesdays on his way back from the food bank.

Divo is the worst of the bunch. He sees him sitting alone and doesn't even say hello. Worse, he says nice and loud, "The mine is hard work. Your spittle may be black but at least it puts bread on the table and a roof over your head. Plus, everyone knows that going underground to earn your wages keeps you awake and stops you from giving in to your brain's whims. Not like some people who have tried to make a living without doing a thing but are now pissing themselves with hunger." Then he looks over at me. "Maso, fetch me a glass of something strong. My hands are itching already. There are two kinds of people I can't stand: communists and slackers, which are actually one and the same thing."

Niccodemo doesn't even hear him. He sits there, like now, with the chessboard in front of him. He's not what he used to be but he still insists on the briar-oak pieces, not the plastic ones I've heard they have down in the new town at Rodolfo's bar. It's easy for him to make ends meet; he sells cigarettes. Which means he takes business from me selling liquor and competes with Staccioli who can stick his tobacconist's license up his ass at this point.

Niccodemo is unbelievable. Every day, whatever the season, he comes in at four. For the last twenty years he has always taken the table on the left, under the TV, slightly hidden by the arch dividing the room. He has the dismayed look old men often have. Together with his whisky, I bring the chess board and I say, "Good evening, Maestro." He rests his walking stick on the wall, picks up the glass, and sniffs it for a while, without drinking a drop. Sometimes, he'll mumble, "It smells of peat." Then he puts it on the other side of the board as if the glass were an opponent. He takes out his pieces, which he keeps inside a leather pouch. He sets out the white pieces first, then the black ones.

He turns the board at every move. In the meantime, the whisky absorbs the cube of ice. There are times when I feel bad for him because he can sit there doing nothing for thirty minutes, like a sleepwalker with his eyes wide open. He looks dead. Then he lifts his hand and moves a knight or a bishop . . . he mutters or chuckles to himself. So, I say to myself, "I may have gotten trapped by the Due Porte bar but this poor guy is hemmed into a square, white or black it doesn't make any difference." At the end of the match, he comes up to the cash register. "It's on the house," I say, nodding at the whisky that's sitting there steeping. "Ah," he says, looking around in a daze. "Who won today?" I ask him, to see whether he recognizes me today or plays along with the joke. He looks daggers at me. "I did," he blurts out eventually, his voice sounding like it's coming from the other end of an iron pipe. "Who else?"

When he leaves, Niccodemo Tempesti forgets to close the door without fail. I come out from behind the counter and use it as an excuse to wipe the table. I drink the whisky. Though I really shouldn't, if I know what's good for me, as it'll mean a fight with Salghini when my bloods tests come back with a line of asterisks.

At the very beginning of time, Babbo told me that there was a whole life in chess. Seeing that old man struggle towards the exit it feels a little bit true. He started inside these four walls and one day inside these four walls a bigger match will come to an end. Sometimes I get upset by the fact that he never sent a telegram. Then I tell myself I'm stupid because Tempesti probably doesn't have anybody to thank. He shows his face at the Due Porte as if it were a vendetta. As if to say: "Look what you've done to me." If my poor Babbo had never been wounded in Russia, that poor meathead might have had a completely different life. And so might I.

The truth is that I'm fond of him and I hate to see him get befuddled with loneliness. I've been wondering for days: what if he bumps into Samuele on the street? He may well have an apoplectic fit. After everything that happened.

Rumor has it that Esedra's grandson has been back for a week or so. We watched him grow up here at Due Porte, that little punk. He was never interested in going out into the fields with a slingshot, nor did he get along with kids of his age who were soccer crazy or hooked on some TV program. He liked chess. Or maybe he saw Tempesti as the dad he never had. As a consequence, Niccodemo found himself a son who hung on his every word in matters of chess. It was his way of explaining life, of ensuring the young man turned out alright, not a mess. Rather like trees that bend with the wind if they have no support, Tempesti would lift a piece and say, "With these pieces we build worlds. But we need to be careful because from one moment to the next, everything can fall back on you like an avalanche." I never understood whether he was teaching or revealing something about himself.

The first shock was when Samuele left town. Tempesti sat ensconced at his usual table, drinking one glass after another beginning in the early afternoon: he could hardly afford it, either financially or in terms of his health. When he was drunk, he would set up his solitary matches and start grumbling to himself. But the real blow came with the story of the girl. He never lifted his ass out of the chair in his usual corner while, right above his head, the TV was butchering that pseudo son he was so fond of. It was upsetting to watch: someone spitting at Samuele on the screen while Niccodemo carried on moving his knights and queen, his face ravaged with anguish. The biggest bastards would start chuckling, elbowing one another, and whispering things like, "Look at him now, the big sinner. First, he ruined himself, then he gave airs to a kid who had the seed of madness already sprouting inside him. What else could we have expected from a man fixated with lining up toy soldiers? And he's still at it."

Maybe it was then that Niccodemo Tempesti's mind finally cracked and he started staring into space. It may have happened anyway but what happened with Samuele pushed him over the edge.

Ultimately, this is what I think: maybe he wouldn't even recognize the boy he brought up in my bar. We could bark his name for a whole afternoon and Tempesti would point his stick, gripping it as if it were the rifle that couldn't kill my dad. Or he would die on the spot, his heart shattered by the shock.

Either way, it'd be a liberation.

Adele Centini -2
The Isastia Widow

Calamaio throws his sketch book down. He gets up and starts pacing the room at the far end, shaking his hands as if he had just scolded them on a wood-burning stove. Then he stiffens. He forces himself to take a deep breath. Goes back to the armchair. Rips the paper he had been scratching on so zealously until a few minutes before, and turns to stare at me, his face as stony and his silence as thick as the beginning of the session. He looks as if he's groping his way through a bank of fog . . . All of a sudden, he comes to with a jolt, reminding me of a fisherman who has finally caught his dinner. The fever has wormed its way back in. And he starts drawing me all over again.

In the five days I still had before leaving, I practiced one thing in particular: my entrances. Mamma would make me go into my room and then call me in suddenly. I would appear in the living room at the right speed, with a smile painted on my face. "You look demented," she would say. "Go back to your room and compose yourself." Sometimes she made me wait for minutes.

Serving at table at four o'clock in the afternoon with pretend guests was another thing. "Never look him in the face," she murmured, imagining the scene. "And careful never to giggle under your breath, even if he does something terrible. Another thing you should keep in mind: always show your left profile. You're beautiful from any angle but from that side you are so divine that angels break out in song. Never look at the colonel full-face. Always turn one brow to the right. It should become a habit."

It was like military training. Mamma taught me to launch winks like kisses, stroke fingers while serving tea. "That old trombone won't believe his luck when he sees a little pixie like you in his service. You have the wherewithal to wake the dead, never mind a retired colonel. But when the time comes—and trust someone like me who had no idea how to live in this world, it will come—don't give in right away. Make him sigh for you. I mean to the point that he's climbing the walls. He needs to wake up with your pretty face printed on his heraldry, so that you can take him to your bed that evening and exploit the raging storm that grabs hold of old men of a certain age. The day you open your lovely fleshy lips for him you must gobble him up whole. Including the Villa and all his other properties in Maremma."

I felt hung out to dry. I was leaving home, a fact that already opened up a sinkhole in my stomach. Then, to make matters worse, I couldn't get the old goat's face, the big nose and thick mustache yellowed with cigar smoke out of my mind. The idea of giving myself to him made we want to drown myself in the tub on the spot. And then came the day of my departure. My trunk was already in the car when my mother said at the door, "This is the life you were destined for, my dear." Then she came closer and leaned over my ear. "Don't forget," she said, in a whisper that made my hairs stand on end. "When he's on top of you, don't be an idiot. Take the seed and lock it inside you with four turns of the key."

To begin with, life at the Isastia Villa was awful. Every evening, I tossed and turned in the narrow bed, my pillow wet with tears. Esedra was mean to me. She would only half-teach me household chores on purpose to keep me on tenterhooks. She would tell me off in front of everyone every ten minutes, opening her goose-beak wide and cackling that I was a rustic half-wit. "The colonel has been duped by a pretty face and now I'm the one paying the price of its ineptitude," she complained every five minutes. And she would send me off to sweep the corners of the attic, which was half-empty but overrun with animals that made my skin crawl. One day, I found a big fat spider in my hands. One of those specimens that grow so fat in their den that they can hardly move. I nearly fainted and my skin went on itching all evening. "What's all the fuss about?" Esedra squawked when I raced downstairs, pallid and shaking. "You should feel right at home with all these creepies and crawlies."

At the end of the first month, I was given a Sunday off. I went home and clung to my mother's skirts, begging her not to make me go back to that place, where even the cat was a sourpuss and would slink through my legs to spite me when I was carrying a tray. She listened as I let off steam. Then she gave me a handkerchief. Her face was as smooth as a statue. "And the colonel?" she asked. "Does he look at you?"

I knew almost nothing about him. I would see him at dinnertime, when I helped bring the dishes in. He spent his days locked up in that giant room where I first saw his shape against the light. Every now and again, he would pull a bell cord and someone would bring him a drop of French liqueur. But Esedra was his personal maid. She dressed me down all the time and I spent most of my time on my knees scrubbing the floor. On Friday mornings, I went out to do the shopping at the market, bringing back every penny of the change.

Mamma sat there for a moment looking at nothing. Then she said, "Well, we need to make something not very nice happen to this prime bitch who is making your life a misery. Enough to make her bed-ridden for a month or two so that we can have our way for a while."

Esedra fell down the stairs towards the end of October. Not the whole flight, mind you. Just the last ramp, six or seven steps in all. It happened after siesta, when things started moving again in the house. I called down to her from below to ask her which floors I was supposed to be polishing. She wailed like a siren, "Do I really have to explain every single thing to you from scratch every time?" It was so loud it bore into my bones. She started waddling down the stairs with that backside of hers pitching back and forth like a ship rolling at sea. When she reached the sewing thread I'd tied three times across the banisters, I almost let out a yell to warn her. But another side of me held my tongue. A second later, Esedra took off. She was flapping her arms like a pheasant and it looked for a moment as if she truly believed she could fly. Only to roll down the stairs like a barrel. Stopping right at my feet, unconscious after the knock.

I rushed to tear the thread away and stuff it into my apron pocket. Then I thought better of it, rolled it up into a ball, and swallowed it. Only then did I call for help.

Things went even better than planned: her hip was shattered. She had also lost two front teeth, as if all the slaps I had been wanting to give her had suddenly rained down on that ugly mug that did nothing but spew nasty words. They took her away in a stretcher. She looked like an upturned buffalo on its last legs. The following day, I was given the task of taking the liqueur up to the colonel.

As soon as the bell rang, I would go upstairs with the oval tray, silver with gold trimmings, which on its own was worth more than a year of my mother's wages. I would knock at the door. To begin with, I stood stock still outside as there was not a breath coming from behind the door. I soon learned that the colonel was hard of hearing so I started knocking louder, as if I were playing at knuckles. "Yes," he would say, his voice croaking from having sat in silence for so long. And I would go in, the light from the big windows dazzling me.

In the early days, I had no idea what he was studying so intently. I limited myself to putting his glass down on the food trolley near his desk, which was piled up with documents held with quartz or fool's-gold paperweights. One day, the colonel said, "Dear Adele. You may well be wondering why I make you come up and down the stairs a hundred times rather than stocking this trolley up with bottles." I shook my head. "No, I haven't asked myself that, Sir. It's my job." I didn't stop smiling, not even for a second. He looked surprised by my simple answer. Then he cleared his throat. "The fact is that I know myself. If I had the bottles close by, you would need four hands to get me to bed. It would be a pitiful scene, don't you think? In short, I do it for myself but for you, too." I lit my face up even more brightly, feeling as though I were wielding an ice-bladed knife. "Nothing in this house could ever suggest even a hint of pity, as you say. Especially not yourself." The colonel blinked a few times. Under his drooping mustache there was a wan smile which he held for a while, suspended, as if he were listening to music coming from another room. Then he gave a shudder. He indicated the papers with a nod of his head. "Do you know what these are?" I took a step closer, leaning over to look. "They look like maps, sir. Do they show your properties?" The colonel stared at me. Then his jaw dropped and he broke out into a hearty laugh. "I wish, dear Adele! I wish I did own the whole of Europe!" He had to take a handkerchief out to wipe his eyes. He caught his breath. Then he placed his finger on one of the maps. "This is Paris, for example."

It turned into our pastime. Some afternoons, he even asked me to draw up a chair and sit next to him. I showed interest and always sat on the side that revealed my best profile. As the colonel spoke, I would watch his mouth as he stumbled over some of his words. Then I would smile even more fiercely and look back up into his eyes, which were so soft and lost in that moment of distress.

He was studying the war that he had lost. That was the task that was keeping him closed upon his study rather than going out and taking walks in the gardens of all the villas he owned down in the valley and even by the sea. He was examining every event that had led Italy to its downfall, and he did it with the excitement of a child, mixed with the zeal of a captain watching from the top of a hill while his whole regiment is being massacred. He didn't want to give in to the evidence and he would fly into a rage. "It's all that deranged dog's fault," he snapped one afternoon. "Mussolini, I mean. Adele, do you know who I'm talking about?" Realizing how ignorant I was made me uncomfortable. "I've been hearing about him for years," I answer shyly. "My mother has been sending him a curse a day, ever since I remember." The colonel was easily enflamed at that point. "Quite right, too! A nation condemned just because a swaggering strawman like him gets some insane idea into his head!" He threw himself onto his maps and pointed out where the various regiments were positioned, giving a blow-by-blow account of the action by month and year. "The same cur, always!" he bayed, girding himself for a drawn-out account. "He was obsessed with that madman the Fuhrer, my ass, and yearned for the same toy: State power. But while they invaded France and Poland as if they were off on a camping-trip, our little state was young and fragile, and it still is for that matter. Even in our dreams we would never have the same firepower as the Germans. And yet, that faggot stamped his feet in Rome. He threw tantrums. In the end, daddy Adolf threw him a bone, 'Be a good boy and go and play the invader in Greece. That should calm you down ten minutes, seeing as up here in the North we are all a little busy.' And this was where the debacle started. Our Mack threw himself into the Adriatic and in a jiffy the campaign was mired. The Germans even had to go back there and fix the pickle, splitting off bits of their army that would have been more useful elsewhere. From then on, dear Adele, there was only decline. Though at least the Greek farce was the beginning of the end for those potato-eaters who only open their mouths to give ass. Admittedly, all things considered, the first breach in the German onslaught was down to that pig Mussolini. At the end of the day, I wonder: should we be grateful for his imbecility? I swear, it's driving me mad."

I liked the way he told me stories about the world. Looking at the maps, I imagined us as two giants watching a show put on by ants. In my mind, the maps stretched out into infinity, to the point that I could conjure up the soldiers' days, their marches, their ambushes, the letters they sent home . . .

When I told him my father never returned from the Greek campaign, the colonel looked as though I'd shot him in the chest. Maybe that was the moment he started looking at me differently.

The sun goes down slowly. In Room 112, the colors are imbued with gold in the evening. It's getting colder. I can't feel my legs any longer. Seeing myself like this is a nightmare. A sea of decaying flesh, whereas I used to turn the heads of men, and women, making them die of desire when I walked by. Calamaio digs in with his pastels. But I've never once seen even a half a drawing. "Signora Adele, you must be patient," he says at the end of every session when I insist a little. Then he gathers all his things and puts them away hastily. And leaves, with that trademark scowl on his face, like a little kid who has just had a fight with his best friend.

I went home for Christmas and Mamma popped a bottle of Prosecco when I told her the colonel had taken a shine to me. I told her about the maps and the half-hours I spent with him in his grand study every now and again. Then she interrupted me, her eyes staring into space. "Adelina darling, this is a delicate moment," she murmured. "Let it be as clear as day that you need to fry the dear colonel in the pan of the paramour, not that of the father or grandfather ranting as his life comes to a close. It's true that a fifty-year-or-so age difference is not peanuts, and he may find it hard to get it up. Over the next few days, I'll teach you how to prod horses asleep on their feet. Spurring them on to jump over the ditch."

I was back at the Isastia Villa for the Epiphany. There was no comparison to the mood I had been in when I first dragged myself away from the crests of Le Case. I leaped up the stairs, carrying my own luggage. I couldn't wait to slip my maid's uniform on and throw myself into the housework. I was prepared to put in the elbow grease, as long as I was surrounded by luxurious marble and velvet drapes. To then start at the ringing of the bell. I was in full swing as I threw open the door of the ground floor sitting room, where the colonel received special guests. A woman was sitting there.

She was reading a book on the sofa near the fireplace. The flames lit up her face and I could see right away that she was beautiful. Not as beautiful as me but she had an air of importance about her that gave her an aura. You could see it at a first glance. She put her book down on her lap. She leaned over to pick up a cup of something hot from the occasional table next to her and took a measured sip. Every move she made looked calculated. She was about to start reading again but she must have felt observed and turned around.

Her icy pupils made my blood run cold. Her face was pulled up tight by a hair bun that was so elaborate it looked like a wooden carving. She was wearing a white blouse and a sassy skirt that reached just under her knee. She didn't smile. She didn't do anything. She looked embalmed. Then she said, "Well? Off with you!" I recoiled at the punch in the stomach. I crossed the sitting room holding my head low and disappeared into the other rooms. As well as being beautiful and sophisticated, I realized the woman was a hyena.

Chiara Maria. The colonel's only daughter. In the kitchen they said she spent most of her time in Florence, at her big-shot husband's side. "He's a Lorena on one side of his family,"

Stella, who had been nice to me from the start, explained. "Let that be enough, more than enough." There was plenty of talk though, so I soon learned that her husband had gone up north to deal with some family business. "On her own in those big rooms in Santa Croce makes the lovely Chiara feel depressed and abandoned," they said, not paying much attention to their tone. "So here she is on an impromptu visit, like a viper slithering between your toes. Watch out. With this daughter breaking his balls the master turns into a dog, too."

There were no more cordials. Colonel Isastia sat in his study as usual but he didn't want his daughter to find out about his four o'clock habit. That was why he was in such a dark mood. Before, he had to eat dinner without the usual newspaper he liked to read. Instead, he and Chiara Maria hardly said a word to one another and when they did, it was only about their properties, as we continued to pile dishes on the table as if there were twenty guests. In the kitchen, Stella said, "The good thing is that when the heiress comes to stay, we can stuff ourselves with the leftovers until we get double chins." One evening, they handed me a plate of orange-glazed duck. My stomach turned at the idea, just looking at it, but minutes later I was licking my lips.

In any case, the colonel's eyes betrayed his longing for me. I noticed and gave him a cautious smile, like a hare flashing in the thick undergrowth. He drank a small glass of wine and gripped his knife and fork as if he were clinging to a rope on the edge of a precipice. The afternoons were long. The bell was silent and I went about my day-to-day chores as I used to do under Esedra's rule. To begin with I thought that, given Esedra's situation, we would go through the Rosary again, calling for a new girl to fill the position, the same old mothers and daughters filling the square, and all the rest. But there was no word on the subject and it was obvious why: I was enough, what with my young legs and the dedication of one attached to their job tooth and nail. I sometimes bumped into the Colonel in the corridors. When he saw me from afar, he'd break his stride as if some spirit were pulling his shoulders back. "Dear Adele, how is your day proceeding?" Feasting his eyes on my fresh face. "For me, knowing you are happy is the most important thing," I answered, even bobbing a little curtsey. Then I would walk past him, sashaying shamelessly. I felt his eyes bore into me from behind until I was out of sight. As soon as I turned a corner I would lean on the wall, my heart hammering.

I went back home at the end of February. My mother had put on several pounds. Clearly, the money I was sending home was being put to good use. I told her about Chiara Maria. "With her around, the air is as wintry inside as it is outside," I murmured. "Some of the servants have been whispering for weeks. If this goes on much longer, their throats are going to be dried up by a curse."

She listened to everything I told her, looking bewildered. At a certain point, she said: "So, here comes this little lady determined to bust our balls." She wanted to know everything about her. Even which books she read in the sitting room and the dainties she dangled on the end of her fork and ingurgitated for dinner. "She's mad on cheese," I told her. "She eats tons of it, mostly with fig jam or honey. Even for breakfast." I also told her about the billionaire husband who, according to everyone in the Villa, couldn't have children. In fact, Chiara Maria had not produced as much as one brat. Many said that was why she was so sour. I then added that we didn't have to put up with it for much longer because the news was that she was about to leave. On Tuesday morning, to be precise. Mamma suddenly stopped stirring the polenta, as if someone had whispered something in her ear. And said, in the tone of someone who can see the glint of a pile of gold, "Does the dear heiress like fresh raviggiolo cheese? We'll give her baskets of it, wrapped in fern leaves and anything else we can find."

Chiara Maria Isastia came off the road on the big bend at

three o'clock that afternoon, witnessed by a drayman on his way home from Civitella. His name was Nello and I would sometimes see him at the market selling chili peppers he picked in the mountains and strung up like good-luck horns. He told the carabinieri everything about the accident: how the car had skidded on a carpet of grit that someone had thrown down on the bend. That smidgen of gravel was enough to send the colonel's daughter and her driver over the edge. In less than a second, they had both ended up shearing the tops of the olive trees.

At the Villa, the comings and goings of important people meant that for the two days before the funeral, we servants couldn't so much as lift our heads for a second. The only time we could breathe was at night, even though my bones were tired through by the time I got to bed. But despite the tiredness tearing at my spirit, I couldn't fall asleep right away for thinking about the four lit candles around the dead body. And there was another worry wearing me down: my mother. I tried to get her out of my head but as soon as I closed my eyes, I saw the car skid. And her lurking in the bushes wrapped in her black dress, lying low after the accident like a hunted animal.

I couldn't be sure. It might have been a bona fide tragedy. And yet, if a saint had laid his eyes on me, he would have seen the doubt I harbored. It spoiled my days. I went as far as asking myself this question, which I would pose against my will: Could my mother have done it?

Not a peep from the Colonel. They said that when he heard the news, he took himself to his bed without saying a word. That he did nothing but look out of the window. "He's lost a war and a daughter," Solino, the kitchen hand who did the heavy work, said. Solino was munching on a slice of bread with prosciutto fat on it. "Do you want to know what's going to happen to the merry-go-round? The colonel is going to die and we'll all have to get off. Eat as much lard as you can, while you can." Then he sliced another bit of fat off the ham and ate it, skin and all.

I went up to the room at mealtimes but there was always someone there. I left the tray on the side table in silence and withdrew. When I came back with dinner, the lunch dishes were exactly as I had left them. When I brought them back down to the kitchen, they soon found their way into some servant's gullet.

The Colonel didn't even go to the funeral. Not participating in a daughter's last rites felt blasphemous, adding to the bestiality of the sudden death that had shocked the whole province. They prepared his uniform dripping with medals but he didn't get out of bed and even refused the mulled wine they wanted to feed him with teaspoons. Stella and I were the only ones from the household to go. We sat in the back, in the last pews which divided the Florentine relations from the normal people from Le Case, who nevertheless flocked to follow the carriage with their heads bowed to show their respect because almost every one of them had a son, cousin, or nephew employed on one of the family properties. I saw Chiara Maria interred next to her mother in the family chapel. Stella touched my elbow as they laid the last stone. She crossed herself and pointed her chin at the gates: it was time to get on our way because it was getting dark. When we got back to the Villa, I felt ten years older. I felt the weight of the old building drowning in its silence on my shoulders. Its creaking was more noticable. The way the house breathed was different, as if a shadow were sitting on my chest. In that place there was a father who had not accompanied his daughter to her grave. My blood ran cold just thinking about it. All of a sudden, I felt as though the floor was tilted, inviting everyone to roll into a hole.

A week went by. Then two. Solino came with me to take up the meals. He would pull the colonel up with his oxen-arms and prop him up with two pillows. I missed one of my vacations with my mother and spring was beginning to make its presence felt. But the Colonel was not coming back to life, even though he had started holding a fork on his own. He needed to be watched at all times as they feared he might prong himself in the neck and then we would all lose our jobs from one day to the next. The rest of the time he needed to be supervized, too, and the task fell to Marcello, who was also his chauffeur. He took it in turns with Stella, especially for the night shifts. "If he survives until the middle of August, it'll be a miracle," Solino would say as we came down the stairs together. Then, one day, I took courage in both hands. I told everyone in the kitchen that I'd had an idea that would keep us all employed. As I was speaking, Santo came in. He spent most of his time outside looking after the plants in the big garden behind the house that overlooked the whole of Maremma. He was the gardener even though he was missing an arm, which he'd lost in the Apennines fighting the Germans. Santo never said a word and always ate alone in a corner. But this time he came forward and said, "We need to try it. Even if it means another war. We must try." Then he went back to his usual spot, near the little gate at the back of the building.

The following day, we took up the Colonel's lunch. Solino pulled him up into a sitting position and I placed the tray carefully on his bed. We watched the colonel eat so slowly that it made you numb. His eyes lost in a place only he knew, where he had locked himself for weeks. Every now and again, I would lean forward and wipe his mouth with a corner of the napkin. When he had finished, he took the coffee bean he liked to keep in his mouth at the end of every meal and was about to lie back down again. But I called out loud and clear. "Colonel. Today something different is going to happen." He didn't even look at me.

I took the dishes and the tablecloth with an embroidered border off the bed. I set the glasses and cutlery aside. I sat on the edge of his bed and unrolled one of his maps in front of him. It was a map of Europe, just the upper part. I pointed at a random spot. "This is where the Krauts passed by when they were invading Switzerland," I said. I moved my finger. "And this is the Hungarian front, where the Italians won hands-down . . . "After a few minutes of chatter like this, eventually Colonel Isastia shifted his gaze and looked at the maps. Solino's eyes were wide with wonder and he barely stopped himself from making a comment. I was equally surprised, but I couldn't stop. "When France declared war on Italy, for us it was like a stab in the back," I continued. "It was April, 1941."

The colonel blurted out something. He was kicking so much that he nearly fell out of bed. "Hogwash!" His voice was as thick as hardened mucus. "It was the Italy of that wretch the Duce stabbing the French in the back! Great show: the cheese-eaters already had the Germans at home. And it was June, 1940. I won't even correct the other nonsense. But for your information: What Italy won hands-down was only a gigantic, immense, filthy dishonor!" That was when he looked at me. He was still bewildered, but his eyes were less glazed over than they had been all this time. It was as if he'd been pulled up over the lip of a well after days and days in the dark. "Adele, you are a good, dear girl," he murmured. "But you need to keep house, forget the maps." Then he was shocked to see Solino in the room. His face went hard. "By the grace of God, can you tell me why the cook's aide is here in my bedroom? Wearing his work clothes, to boot? Has the world gone to wrack and ruin?"

Domenico Fiorani
the Peasant

They call me "the man from the Marches" and then they complain if I walk through the market without looking up once to say good morning. I wish a bomb would fall on all of them. At the top of my death list, I'd put that upchuck of a father I've been landed with. One day, I'll go up to him and say, "Mimmo, lovely day!" And *ta-da*, I'll stick a carving knife into his flabby belly.

Sometimes I dream about it. I wake up all sweaty with my heart hammering. At the same time, though, a sense of joy gallops through me that I never experience in my everyday life. So, I lie there for a minute and say to myself: "By God's grace, the strength has come to me. I'll have to go to jail but at least I won't be spending the rest of my days with a knot in my stomach." Then the dream fades away. I need to go into the kitchen. I grab the big bottle and drink straight out of it, gulping down the wine I need to get back to sleep. When the cock starts crowing, I feel like shooting myself in the mouth and it's always you-know-who's fault: the first person I meet in the morning. Starting my day with a Goddammit.

He didn't even bother to give me a name. I replay the scene all the time. I emerge from the guts of some mother or other, he takes one glance, and, filled with that disgust that is stamped on his face and that I'd chisel off if I could, mumbles "Domenico" to the registrar. His same name. As if to say, "Wash the shit of that wretched woman off him and let me go home. I have olive trees to prune."

Nothing says he's even my father. There isn't a single letter or photo at home. Nothing. This is where I get the feeling that I sprang from a legend. One of those nasty ones. If someone asked me to tell them my story, I'd have three little turds to share: I'm from Pergola, in the Marches; giving birth to me split my mother in two; and the year after that tarbrush I ended up with as a parent brought me to Maremma, where we didn't die of hunger as we may have done elsewhere, and where I've stayed ever since. The end. Anybody who says, "hey, that's some bad luck," would get their teeth smashed in at once. And in any case, nobody ever asks me to tell them my story.

When I was a kid, I used to do it myself at supper time. At a certain point, I'd turn to Babbo and say, "Was Mamma beautiful?" If he was in the mood for a long chat, he'd lift his eyes from his plate and say: "Eat!" But more often, he'd pick up the remote and turn the TV up to hear the weather.

The trouble began as early as I can remember, and doubled when I went to school. I had to get myself up in the morning when he'd been tilling the earth for at least an hour already, walk up alone from the hollow to the town in all seasons. I would eat a piece of cheese on my way. The other kids would see me arrive with mud on my boots and they would make fun of me because my breath stank of feet. On top of all that, Mr. Serafini, may he rot in eternity, would call on me. "Fiorani, to the blackboard!" he would shout, pointing at a nice little math problem waiting for me. I never opened my mouth. I was ashamed of speaking in front of the other kids. Whenever I walked past them, they would blow raspberries at me. After minutes of silence, Mr. Serafini would say, "Well, at least with that chalk dust on your hands you'll be looking cleaner when you get back home." He meant that the white chalk would cover the dirt under my fingernails. Two years ago, when they found the teacher dead as a doornail in his home, I went to Maso's bar and drank myself into oblivion.

It was at school that I started to think about it. The thought still haunts me to this day. What if that horsefly of a father I find myself saddled with bought me at a Friday market like this one in '66, pulling me out from under the stall of a family that was so poor they were barking up the wall? He never had a wife called Mary, though he sometimes said he did just to show off. He needed a slave to make dinner for him, that's all. Someone to lend a hand in October when he had to lay out the nets under the olive trees, prepare the mats in the cellar, get the ladders, and find the rakes for picking the green olives, the ones you can eat, which make good money.

I just don't get that level of ignorance. When I was a child, I would get holes in my socks and ask him to darn them. Walking with my naked heel rubbing against the nails in my boot-heels made me hobble like a crippled chicken. The blister that formed every day made me cry and the contact with the leather made me stink of death. He used to say, "Do it yourself, it'll be better," which is the same answer he gave me whatever I asked. If I needed a pair of pants one size bigger, "Do it yourself, it'll be better." If I asked him to look over my homework, "Do it yourself, it'll be better." And on it went, to this day. Including the fevers that I had to bring down with wet rags, even when I nearly fainted getting out of bed. In the end, I stopped asking.

I suppose I can say this: if that spit of the devil who says he's a relative of mine has done one good thing in his life it is not to have taught me a thing. Now my strong hands can do anything: make a soup just so, and split logs in one fell swoop, though I learned the hard way by amputating my little toe at the age of twelve.

This year the trees were bursting when autumn arrived on St. Matthew's Day. All I needed to do was look over at my neighbors' fields to see merry bands getting ready for the olive harvest as if they were gathering for a party: cousins, grandparents, grandchildren . . . my heart felt like stone. At our place, the harvest always feels like a death knell, and I'm pretty sure the olive oil is affected, because it kicks you in the teeth with acidity. The dirty bastard screams at me to get out of bed and all the hairs on my body stand on end at the sound of his voice. We head off for the olive groves without saying a word. He hammers in the stakes where the land slopes downhill and I lay the nets under the trees. He climbs up the big ladder. I start raking off the olives on the lower branches. He wants me right under his nose. If I go off for a second, he calls out, "I can't see you." I would set fire to the whole grove, with him in it, if only I could. Until a few years ago, I thought he was checking on my work. Then I realized that he couldn't care less how I rake the olives. What he cared about, if anything, was that I didn't move around near the foot of his ladder in case I decided to kick it from under him and crack his head open on a rock. Just to give you an idea of the trust that exists between father and son.

At Le Case they think we are from the same stock. The truth is, every minute of the day, we are desperate to rid ourselves of one another. When we sit down for dinner, the first thing we do is check where the knives are. A glance across the table would have been enough for both of us to lose our appetite if we hadn't been breaking our backs working all day.

I was eight when the Toninellis had their accident. It was after midnight and I was already asleep. I didn't even hear the crash. But I did jump when I heard the door of my room suddenly yanked open, like when the wind opens the doors of the rabbit cages if you don't secure the hooks properly. I rubbed my eyes and saw that animal standing there in his work pants and night sweater. "They've landed in our patch," he said, gesturing for me to follow him outside.

I'd never seen a dead person. Then, on one perfectly ordinary night, I saw two. Babbo shone his torch onto the last olive tree in the bottom row, where the trees cling to the rocks. I saw the car that had flown off the hairpin bend and landed head-first down there. One of the back wheels was still spinning. The tree was split in two. But that was not what got to me. It was the woman's torso on the ground, looking for all the world as if she'd been buried in that olive grove up to her waist. She was standing with her arms splayed open and her head bowed, her hair covering her features. My knees turned to pap when I saw her shoulders shuddering as if she were coughing.

I felt that swine grab my collar from behind and hold me up. "It's the nerves firing," he said. "The other part of the body is still in the car." He shone a cone of light onto the car with its windscreen shattered so I could see the whole gruesome scene. There was a tangle of twisted metal. Inside, the woman's bottom half was dangling, dripping blood onto the concertinaed car bonnet. "If you're going to throw up, do it far from here," he said, walking away. My head buzzing, I found myself sitting on the ground without realizing. There were little white dots shining in the depths of my vision.

It was pitch dark. Aside from the shiny white dots, the only light was the torch that was still illuminating the wreck. Some suitcases had burst out of the Lancia Fulvia after the impact and were now scattered around under the trees. Babbo was running around picking them up and taking them back to the carcass of the car, which reeked of gas. I watched him bend down, looking for new treasure. Every now and again, he put something in his pocket. Then I heard a voice a stone's throw from where I was sitting. I leaped up yelling.

There was a man. His legs were in an unnatural position. But he was moving. He was whimpering like a kitten. His face was clean. Not a drop of blood. Babbo turned his torch towards him and did nothing as the man desperately tried to open his eyes. But they kept fluttering shut again, as if he were fainting a hundred times in a row. "I'm going to call Dr. Salghini," I said, preparing to run even though my body was not responding. I felt Babbo's hand tightening his grip on my shoulder. "Don't you dare, numbskull," he grunted, handing me the torch. "Hold it up for me."

I saw him empty the poor guy's pockets. Then he grabbed the wallet. I thought he was checking for ID to see who he should call. Instead, he pulled some bills out and squirreled them away somewhere. He ripped the gold chain off the man's neck. Then he grabbed the man's limp hand, trying to pull the wedding ring off, but thought better of it. "No," he muttered. "Better leave this on." And he pulled himself back up.

"Silvia . . . " the guy started whining, as if he were calling out from another world. "Silvia . . . " Babbo grabbed him by the arm and started dragging him towards the split olive tree. He dumped him there like a sack of potatoes. I followed him to the woman's torso, which was now immobile. He grabbed her in the same way and heaved her to the site of the crash, dropping her in front of the Lancia Fulvia's bonnet, right under the other half of her body. Babbo turned and looked in my direction. "Go fill a can with paraffin from the tank. And bring a rag while you're at it."

I was eight years old and my head was still buzzing as if a bumblebee had flown in there. I went to the shed and grabbed everything. When I got back, my father was scuttering around collecting bags and clothes. But now the man was speaking, without the deliria of shock. He sounded tired and every word was a spasm. "Who are you?" he groaned. "Where am I?"

Babbo took the can and started pouring paraffin around the woman's torso and along the path where he had dragged her. He did the same for the furrow he had made dragging the man's body. Then he ripped the rag in two. He dipped both pieces in the fuel and got his lighter out. He turned towards me. "Run into town," he said. "Knock on Dr. Salghini's door until he wakes up and tell him that a Lancia Fulvia has flown off the bend."

I stared at him, my eyes wide as saucers. He realized I wasn't moving and thrust his arms up in the air as if he were herding a cow. I started running. Behind me, I could hear the voice of the poor man calling out for Silvia who was split in two. But I was running with the devil at my heels. I ran up the path, out of the hollow, and onto the road. Only then did I stop to catch my breath. At the bottom of the ridge the flames were already raging. And then I heard the explosion.

The carabinieri came. The Toninelli's flight was even in the papers. The funeral was attended by everyone in Le Case but people also showed up from the nearby hill towns and from the ones down in the valley. A frightening torrent of faces. I kept a newspaper clipping. It says there hadn't been such a crowd since the mine shaft collapsed in Ribolla. Except there weren't any government officials at this funeral. The only one not to join the funeral procession was that grouch of a father of mine and I think that's one of the things the town has always held against him, because, let's face it, not mourning such deaths was bestial on his part. I was there. I wanted to show I was different to him. Also, I could take a good look at how city people dress. I got home that evening to heat dinner up on the fire and I found the ugly mug sitting at the table counting money. He was weighing in his hand the gold he had stolen from the newlyweds' bodies and cases before setting fire to them. Winking at the treasure he said, "This is our compensation for them killing a perfectly healthy tree."

Ever since '74, many little favors have been raining down on our olive grove from the hairpin bend, but if it's daytime, you have to be careful because the neighbors, or anyone walking in the woods, might see you. If it's an accident at night, it's another story. There's the crash and then you have to sit and listen carefully for about half an hour, without turning the light on. After a while I hear my father's bed springs and that's when I get out of bed.

It's odd, but there are lots of car crashes on that bend. The town can put up as many road signs as they see fit but there are still some drivers who seem to aim straight for the guardrail, at high speed. Mostly kids who have spent the evening tanking up on wine. Or young couples who can't keep their hands off each other. But a road is a road, whatever anyone does, and it doesn't give a damn. Or, again, they may be out-of-towners who have never navigated these hairpin bends before. Time enough to yell something, and then it's *arrivederci*.

I had to admit that freeloader who was my father was right, though if he died in the next ten minutes, they would have to take me to hospital because I'd be splitting my sides laughing. All those cars raining down onto our olive grove have decimated our trees. Not a single person ever comes to say sorry. They come and collect their dead and that's that, thank you very much. While here there's someone who has never had a day off, who's been spitting blood since he was six. Every five years my father goes down to Grosseto to sell some of the gold. In '87 we got a new tractor, and it's still going like a dream.

Recently, though, the kitty has been running dry. It may be because they've resurfaced the road. It may be because powerful cars nowadays are not what they used to be and they can handle the skid. The harpin bend has stopped spitting out miserable wretches for us to strip search, even though I go out at night every now and again and throw a film of grit on the blacktop to encourage someone to recklessly slam on the brakes. But it's no use.

The last little birdie was two years ago. We only noticed the following morning because the motorbike had gone over the edge without breaking through the guardrail. It was clear nobody had seen it. Which meant we had all the time in the world and left stuff on him so that people wouldn't think ill of us. I was tempted to make him vanish altogether, given that there wasn't a living soul to tell anyone to look for him on our land.

"I might keep the motorbike," I said. "I'll spray-paint it and in a year's time start using it as if it were mine." Babbo narrowed his listless little eyes. "You're prison enough for me," he said, rifling through the dead man's pockets, "and you haven't even found a wife yet."

But I'd love a shiny new motorbike. I imagine it as red, with a roar so loud it would make the old men who wile away their time at Rodolfo's bar swear at me. With a ring-ding like that, I'd make women wet between their legs. And I'd stop going to see Susanna at the Bel Sole Hotel. "Marry me, Domenico." That's what she says. And she holds me close and kisses my neck all over. She makes herself up as if she were a girl but the grooves around her mouth are so deep her lipstick doesn't fill them in, which makes me want to look the other way. On some days, I'll be hammering away at Susanna for half an hour or more and nothing happens. I end up leaving in pieces while she lies there naked on the bed wailing, "You used to find me attractive, even though I'm ten years older than you." In any case, I always pay for my own coffee at the hotel bar.

Of all the women in their fifties like me, I'd like Giovanna the most, even though she's overweight and doesn't take care of herself. Like every Friday, I'm here at the market stall with my fresh produce, overboiling at the idea of seeing her pass by with her beautiful, fleshy lips. Sometimes she leans over the crates and asks how much something is. I look at her chubby fingers, their little nails painted pink. I always feel a blow to the stomach and say to myself, "I'd happily die squeezed like a little mouse between those buttocks." I wanted to shout right in her face, "You still don't get it? Apart from the outsiders, you and I are the only singles in their fifties left in Le Case. We really need to get together." But it's a miracle even if she looks askance at me, asking how much I charge for a pound of courgettes, only to leave by the old town road without passing back here even once. Little does she know that I have a nice little gold necklace for her. I think about nothing but how to surprise her with the gift. It was in the pockets of a stage-manager from Volterra who tumbled down on us Sunday night. The pendant is a red stone carved into the shape of a goldfish.

Yes, Giovanna's giant ass straddling the back of a motorbike would be quite a sight. With me driving like a devil taking those curves down to Perolla head on. I'd open the throttle like a dipshit, knowing exactly when to brake . . .

About ten days ago, my hopes were raised momentarily. I see a bike racing along the road to Siena. There I am hoeing the ground when I hear a rumble in the distance. I take my eyes off the ground and say to myself: "Judging by the speed he's going, he's going to end up here in smithereens any moment now." Hoping to break the spell of two years without any gifts, I had in fact scattered a handful of grit on the bend the night before.

I watch the final hairpin bends with my chin on the handle of the hoe. Meanwhile, I take a look around: not a leaf is stirring in the neighboring fields. The hunters' rifle shots stopped mid-morning. I can see that retard Nencioni, who sometimes likes to take a walk to the top of San Martino, sauntering along the bend. "This is going to be an easy little morsel," I say to myself, even though it's the middle of the day. I'm ready to throw the hoe down and run to the trees where the chump is about to land. But what does he do? He brakes at the last minute. Worse, he revs up as he goes into the hairpin as if to say to me, "Giovanna's ass is mine." Then he disappears.

I would have been happy even if he'd crashed into a chestnut tree a few yards further on. But the Lord never listens to the prayers of a peasant.

In town that's all they talk about, even though Maso gestures to us to change tone when that old goof Tempesti is at the Due Porte bar. That's when Divo hams it up on purpose. "Anyone who comes back to Le Case must have messed up for real. Or never messed with anything at all."

I tend to agree with him. But sometimes I feel like answering him back. "Are you any better? You've spent your whole life breathing in dust and now you're sticking it up your nose. While your wife has planted the horns of a cuckold into you enough times to split your head. At it with the priest, even. And with me, before I had even turned twenty."

Even Jesus would be anxious all the time if he were Divo. His eyes flash in perennial anger and everyone nods and says Yes, thinking back to the sex they had with the woman who would be making his dinner that evening. You can tell who the cuckolds in the town are: they drink a lot and their wives look as though they've walked straight out of the hairdressers even when they're a hundred years old. And they act like Fascist pigs. Then one day they might go down into the cellar and shoot themselves.

"I saw him early this morning," I said at the Due Porte last night. "That Samuele, I mean. He was running, wearing sweats and sneakers. He was coming down from the old road. Then he turned into the alley that runs along the Parisi land and went up towards the rocks."

I die of laughter when Divo gets angry and goes beet red. That's why I needle him. "I'd make that guy run," he muttered. "With a kick in the ass. Past the clock tower and up to the edge of the outlook."

I don't care one bit about the gossip concerning Esedra's grandchild. What I do care about, if anything, is that flashy silver bike he keeps outside his house. I've been watching him come down to the hollow for three days, and for the past three days I've dropped my shovel and followed him. I watch him as he vanishes and then I take the shortcut up the hill along the creek path like I did when I was a kid. Mind you, when I was a child, I climbed up easily but now I need to stop five minutes at the bench by the water-fountain, just inside the old town walls, to catch my breath. From there, all I need to do is dodge the low roads and I'm at the turn for Via dell'Incrociata.

It's a beauty, that bike. You would think it could speak. It calls out to me, "Mimmo, get your ass on my back and let's go be cool." Sometimes I touch one of the knobs. Just for a moment because Mariella may happen to glance out of her window and think I'm nosy. Or suspicious, which is worse. Then I leave, returning the same way I came. Only this time it's downhill, my cock is dangling, and my legs move on their own. All the while I'm thinking to myself, "My friend, with a motorbike like that, you'll make all the Giovannas in the province die to be with you."

The dog of a dad I'm dumped with doesn't want to hear anything about it. On Sunday afternoons, I go back home drunk and try and talk to him. "Maybe I'll go and buy a bike with some of our earnings." To get myself something after half a century of staining the clods of dirt with my sweat. Or to find a wife. "We shouldn't be seen to have money," he answers, and I feel like slashing his throat with my bare nails. As if the antennae of the tax police would be alerted by someone like me, who has worked all his life, just because one day I decided to give myself a reward. "Showing your gain and you show your brain," says the mongrel dad who would rather talk to ants than to me. So, I run out of the house and scream at the trees, tearing up handfuls of the high grass that grows around the ditches.

Because I have been working, going to the market, and stripping bodies clean for an eternity but the time for a reward never comes. And without a silver motorbike, I really don't know how to win myself the prodigious ass of Giovanna, who wanders around the old town with her fleshy, pursed lips. And who looks at the latest batch of cucumbers with more gusto than she looks at me.

Sonia Antichi,
the Serraglini Widow, Housewife

Yes, Achille my love, it's true. I bent over backwards to put a proper meal on the table for you, but you never said a kind word to me. You liked stroking Pepita more than me. You'd pick her up by the collar and put her on your lap as you sat in front of the television. And there was always a stain too many on the floor tiles. You would see a smudge on a window that wasn't even there. Mother Mary is the only one who heard the curses I sent in your direction over the years. Until one day she answered the oaths I had spat out in anger and you slipped on the icy slope on St. Lucy's Day, cracked your head on Barberini's door step, and that was that. Poor Iolanda. The next morning, she opened her front door and found you sprawled there like a beggar. "His eyes were still wide open," she says whenever she talks about it. "But his face looked normal, like someone waiting for their turn at the barber's. Until I saw the blue stain on his temple." They came to give me the news and for a moment I felt I was coming back to life. "Are you sure?" I asked. But confusion and despair soon came crashing down on me. "What am I going to do without Achille?" I asked. "Whose pants am I going to mend?" Because it's true. With you chewing me out all day, by the time I got to bed my stomach was a knot of nerves. But now I'd give an arm and a leg to see you cross the room huffing and puffing with a scowl on your face. Meanwhile, I've already thrown two calendars into the fire.

You used to take me furtively under the cover of night.

Sometimes, I would wait an hour in the dark and my belly would catch fire when I felt your strong hands on me. I would tremble with anticipation, my heart galloping like when I was a little girl waiting for my stocking filled with almonds and tangerines. You never said anything and that is what I liked most about it. I felt your kisses on my mouth and on my forehead. And I lay there completely still, taking you in. Our breath mingled without looking each other in the face. Full of love, I could drive you crazy. Even at sixty, we were as beautiful as the whole world.

I don't know what happened to you. Maybe they put a curse on you at birth. You could hardly bring yourself to say good morning when we woke up. During the day, you would only look at me if you had to, and your affection was reserved for the cat. I used to die of jealousy. I would spy on you in your armchair with pussy purring away on your lap. I would lock myself in the bathroom and look at myself in the mirror as if I were unhinged. "Are you really jealous of a cat?" I would ask myself. There were days when I almost burst out laughing. Then at night in the dark, you would turn back into an angel and light up my whole body.

Now that you're not here, Achille my love, the worst part of the day is when night draws in. I eat on my own with Pepita brushing against my legs, begging. Most of the time, I put my plate on the floor without even touching it. And I come here to this bed, like now, mauled by the dark and the silence crushing my windpipe. I lie on my side of the bed, as always. And I imagine the rustle of the bedcovers and you climbing in unexpectedly. Sometimes I think about it so hard that I can almost feel it happening. I hold my breath, a little abashed by the idea of being petted by a ghost and a little overwhelmed by the wave of love that makes me call out, "Achille, is that you?" But you never answer. I turn the light on and sometimes see that the sheets have been lifted by the cat. She curls up into a ball where you used to put your feet. So, I pick her up and hold her on top of me. And that's how we both stay until the morning.

Angiolino came this morning. I tell him every time, "You should call me first so I can get used to the idea." But he's deaf in that ear. Every now and again, he decides to drop in on me on his way back from his errands. He's always shocked when I open the door and almost drop to my knees, sending my slippers flying all over the place every time I open the door. One of these days I'll bang my head like you and that will be that for me, too.

This is the punishment you reserved for me: a twin brother who looks like an exact replica of you. The way he walks and his voice, too. Angiolino comes into the house talking about the weather and I'm blindsided. I drop everything and my heart hammers against my breastbone so hard I feel pins and needles under my skin. I watch him wandering around the house and I feel like asking him the same question I cry out at night, "Is that you?" Then I bustle about putting the coffee pot on, while he blathers on about all the old books he digs out in peoples' cellars. This is the only difference between you two: Angiolino talks. If he had his druthers, he wouldn't shut up for a minute. After a while he goes back to the subject of when he lived in Switzerland, where everything was great, and he didn't feel like he was wasting his time. "Here in Le Case, people hardly read the newspapers and when they do, it's for the horoscope or soccer results," he says, in your voice. In the meantime, Pepita has already jumped into his arms. While I feel weak at the knees and ready at any minute to blurt out, "Let's go into our room and turn the light off for ten minutes, shall we?" Once I tried switching you over in my mind's eye and the thought of it was enough to send me all over the place. But I don't know whether the idea disgusts me or attracts me, and that is enough to drive me to distraction.

It happened one evening in the days after the funeral. I

didn't know how to get through the night. All of a sudden, I put my coat on and cut across Via di Mezzo, flurries of sleet whipping my face. When Angiolino opened the door wide, for a moment he looked like he'd seen a ghost and I felt the same looking at him. He said, "Sonia, you came all this way in your slippers? In this weather?"

Achille, my love, your twin has one thing going for him: he isn't easily satisfied. Le Case has done its best to turn him into a zombie, with no aim in life, like the rest of us whose feelings have been hardened by the snarling mass of days that never change. But he has resisted. With the books and other junk that he fishes out of cellars. The rednecks in this town will trade their old stuff for a couple of cents and your twin spends all night locked in his study straining his eyes in the lamp light. He loves looking at things from the past. He could go through a whole afternoon in front of a chair with its woven caning caved in, imagining the backsides that had sat there a hundred years before. He reconstructs the lives of people who lived perched on the mountaintops centuries ago. It's a way to escape Le Case at full tilt, and I don't seem capable of doing it. Not even in my imagination like he does.

That evening, he invited me into his home. "Sonia, come and warm up in front of the fire," he said. I answered, "I'd throw myself into the flames." Then I turned to look at him and he shook. I must have looked desperate. "Why are you staring at me like that?" he asked after a while. My response was to jump on him.

Angiolino let me kiss his mouth and face that evening, without saying a word. I went on relentlessly, my hair flying loose from its pins. I wouldn't stop, even after fat tears crash-landed on his face without my noticing and I tasted salt. I wouldn't stop, even when something bit my heart and dragged it somewhere else. Until I ended up sitting on the floor with my skirt pulled up. I was crying so much it terrified me because it felt as though I would never be able to stop. That was the worst part of it: I knew that the tears would stop but that the convulsions would go on forever. And that made me wail even louder.

Whenever I think about it, I feel like sending you to hell for real: not only did you leave me your twin, but he's a fag to boot. Here, in Le Case, there are people who won't even say good morning to Angiolino. Divo spits on the ground when they cross paths. And it's been at least thirty years since your twin set foot in the Due Porte bar, which is always full of hunters, old men, and old-men hunters, who are there ready to provoke him with high-pitched voices and other jokes like the peasants and drunkards they are. In the old days they would count to ten before starting, in case it was you, but now that you've cracked your head open on the Barberini's door step, they have no doubt and start gassing as soon as they see him in the distance.

To tell the truth, there have been days when I've thought about it, too. "Just my luck to have a fag as a brother-in-law!" It would have been nice if he had liked pussy, at least. I might have been able to have a quick pet on the sly thinking of you. But Angiolino is hung up with taking it in his back pockets, even though he's too old for these things and I'm willing to bet he does nothing more with his dick than a five-minute rub with his hands. I can just see him there, peering through the shutter slats and playing peeping tom with that devil who has come back to darken Esedra's door again.

This afternoon he talked about him, that Samuele. "His grandmother and I used to bid good night to one another," he said. "She would knock on the ceiling twice with her broomstick and I would answer with a tap of my heel." Then he looked at me, his eyes wide. "Sonia, imagine how I felt when out of the blue, in the middle of the night, he started moving furniture around. I didn't know he'd come back. I said to myself, 'Listen, poor dead Esedra can't find peace.'"

Rather a hundred ghosts of that saintly woman than Samuele

in the flesh and blood, I say. The spying I do for Adelaide at least keeps my mind busy, otherwise my thoughts go for their usual spin and always come back to the same place: where you came unstuck. I keep my friend's rotten blood running. With the excuse of taking up arms against a twenty-year-old bimbo. Even though the mangy old woman is stuck in bed, she's refusing to give in to the disease and is still alive.

Achille, my love, maybe you've been looking down on me from up there and I expect you were shaking your head when you saw me making that scene with Adelaide. And yet, Esedra's grandson has brought on a storm in the veins of that girl from the valley. What I saw the other day at Mario's store put a flea in my ear. And that's why I've started setting my alarm during the day.

It rings at two, when everyone has finished washing the lunch dishes and are having their siestas. At that hour, Le Case is a ghost town. In the alleys there are nothing but cats. So, I set myself up in the narrow passage that goes from Via dei Frati to the clock tower. From that position, I can see the whole store window. On cloudy days, I can even see inside a little because there is no sun reflecting off the glass.

That Eleonora girl may be a treasure, with her big beaten-doe eyes and all the rest. But she's hatching a plan and that's no longer just a hunch on my part.

For example, the day before yesterday I was lurking there. It was the third day, and I was starting to say to myself, "My friend, you're looking for entertainment but there isn't any here. Go home and have a good cry as usual." Then the grocery door opened. I thought, "There she is. She's going for a little stroll." I waited for her to turn into the portico leading to Via delle Gabbie and I started tailing her. When I was a girl, I was good at finding hiding places. They blamed it on the fact that my grandfather had been a bandit, with a wild air about him, his blood sucked dry by the laws of the day which hit poor people harder, as usual. With a band of kids, we used to meet up at St. Anthony's church up at the rocks on the edge of the precipice. The huge slabs looked like giants. We would climb right up to the twin pinnacle, which from a distance looked like a pair of wings. When the north wind blew the sky clean, we used to say, "Let's go up to the Two Wings to get a view of the sea." If we were lucky, we could see as far as the mountains on the island of Elba. But that's not what I was interested in. All the kids used to shield their eyes from the sun and look towards the Gulf. I looked the other way. Below me, the Maremma valley looked like a boundless green pool. And I would say, "A long time ago, my granddad was king of all this land, as far as the eye can see and further. But I never met him. One day, before I was born, the carabinieri came and shot him in the head."

So, the day before yesterday, I was tailing the little flirt while thinking back to when I still dreamed about having a landlocked pirate as a granddad. I saw myself as I was back then, when I couldn't wait for my tits to grow, to become an adults so I could pick up the conversation that a pistol had cut short. I wanted to take Maremma back, since it was rightfully mine. I would live there in the woods with my merry band of brigands, bandanas tied around our necks. We would rob the rich and give to the poor. To make our point, we would go straight to the bastard carabiniere's nephew's house, drag him out, rip him apart, and scatter the pieces at night around St. Bastian's.

Achille, my love, when I was a girl, I dreamed of adventure but life gave me you. I'm not complaining. It was your cold expression that weaned me of my obsession with taking back half the region by force. Instead of becoming a bandit, I turned into a good little housewife. I shed my bandana for a headscarf. Now that you're no longer here, I need to keep my mind busy. I clean all the rooms in the house thoroughly, twice over. The next morning, I get up and start again.

I didn't notice to begin with, but that Eleonora girl was taking me in a precise direction. Straight to Esedra's house.

She was standing at the corner waiting, with no idea that Yours Truly was on her tail. I said to myself, "Either she's an idiot or she's a spy." I flattened myself against the walled-up door in the alley, the one that still hides the room where local anarchists used to hold their secret meetings. I watched the girl standing in the portico shadows. She looked unsettled. She kept sticking her head out like a frightened animal and then pulling it back in again. She was struggling with something, undecided down to her marrow. She wiggled her legs as if she needed to pee. A little further on, in the square where the school used to be, was the house in question. Seeing it shuttered up always gave me the shivers.

Achille, my love, I don't know what that devil of a girl disguised as a fairy is up to. You should have seen her. At one point, her legs must have given in. She was propping herself up on the stone wall of the alley like a drunk on the way home from the Due Porte bar. And she was talking to herself. Until she let out a deep sigh, as if she were steeling herself to come out of hiding. Except that she didn't. The clock in the tower struck four and she almost jumped out of her skin. She turned on her heels and started scuttling back down the street. I was dying of nerves, almost melting into the walled-up door. I said to myself, "Now she'll see I'm tailing her and what am I supposed to tell her?" She slipped by like a ghost, preoccupied with getting back to the store in time for her afternoon shift with pomaded Mario, whose age and lust for young flesh had turned his brain to mush. She was gone in a flash. There could have been ten of me in that tomb-like doorway and she still wouldn't have seen me. She vanished down the alley.

I must have inherited something of my grandfather, the man who used to eat bread and cheese with that saintly bandit, Tiburzi. My grandmother always said, "Cosimo would simply vanish. You took your eyes off him for a second and, poof! There wasn't even the stench of old goat left behind. The following day, I'd turn around to get a pan and there he was, kissing me all over."

These are the facts. There's a depraved man on the loose in Le Case. He's living in Esedra's house, sullying her memory just by being there. There's also an apprehensive young girl who is spying on him, looking for all the world as if she is dying to see him.

In the meantime, I'm spying on her to keep Adelaide's blood coursing through her body.

To add insult to injury, peeping through the shutters on the first floor of Via dell'Incrociata, there's one more set of eyes that doubtless never misses a thing Samuele does. Because, it must be said, the man may be perverted but he is also good-looking. Angiolino, your twin, I mean. I don't want to imagine what he does with those hands of his when Esedra's grandson gets on his knees to scrub the tiles in the courtyard downstairs.

At the end of the day, I have accepted the abandonment, Achille, my love. Because we spend our lives hunting one another like animals, nerves gnawing at us as the days here in Le Case go by like little explosions of nothingness. The world is on course at a trot while we are stuck here, the only jolt of excitement being when the earth shakes a little.

Thinking about it: once this generation of old people has gone, it'll be my generation's turn to die. Then there will only be empty houses in the old town, which already looks deserted. The thought makes me feel even worse because the idea of dying in a vacuum, chained to a bed like Adelaide without anyone looking out for me, is like a stone in my stomach that won't go down or come back up. We all have it, up in the old town, even though we pretend we don't. We iron out our faces when we say good morning, our smile a rictus in a skull. They may have closed the looney bins, but I would invite a clever doctor or two to come up here and take a stroll: they would find plenty of cases that require meds. Le Case is filled with silence. Behind every door, there are rooms that echo with solitude, the ugly kind that makes you go feral. We're wretches dragging ourselves down to do a bit of shopping. We are all lost, our eyes watery from the drops Salghini prescribes and the drinks Maso hands out. Look at me, Achille, my love: to fill up a sliver of my afternoon, I've started trailing young girls, one in particular who has latched onto a madman and struck up a rapport with a low-browed foreigner.

And then I curse myself and I curse you a little, too, because when I used to climb up to the top of the rocks as young Sonia, my light was still bright. But Le Case snuffs out your soul. Le Case is a black heart planted right in the middle of the big belly of Maremma. It disguises itself with dreams and then sticks them up your ass with a vengeance. You start life fantasticating up at the Two Wings and then you pickle your brain at the Due Porte, clutching a wine bottle.

If only you'd been a little more like my grandfather, who is still screaming inside me, like a calling that was never heeded and died a pitiful death. That Cosimo who vanished and reappeared like a ghost. The same man who once took a young girl under a fig tree and left my poor mother in her belly. Nonna told me, "He came to the house, with his bushy mustache and a pistol in his belt. He looked at my father and said, 'Dear Alceste, your daughter is pregnant on my account. Here's the money . . . and be happy because catching a brigand's load is like winning the lottery.'" Nonna Dalia's eyes shone and she sometimes had to wipe her eyes dry as she told the story. "There was never a day without bread on the table," she said. "Never any trouble. Then a monster of a carabiniere came along and we were thrown headlong into poverty."

But I had you, Achille, my love. As far as adventure was concerned, you were out of breath even after climbing the ten steps to the church in the old town. When you set off for your shift, you looked as though you were facing the death squad. And you never once said, "Look at this delicious dish my lovely little wife has cooked up today!" Not one kind word, not one comment . . . Just never-ending long faces, all the way down to the floor. But at night you became an angel. You stroked my hair with your strong hands. And then the wave of feeling rolled over me, crushing the breath out of me. When you were done and had gone back to your side of the bed, I used to lie there looking into the darkness. My flesh was a light gown, trembling. And I would say to myself, filled with contentment, "Nonno Cosimo may have been the king of the woods, but making love to my Achille makes me bigger than the whole of Maremma."

EMILIO SALGHINI,
the Doctor

The thing about being a doctor in a town like this is that, in the end, you recognize the smell of every single apartment. You could blindfold me and lead me to a random front door and I would be able to say, just like that, "Here we are at Graziella's house." Or, "Someone here loves barley, so this must be the Nardini's place. If, on the other hand, I smelled turpentine and stale onions I would have no doubt, "Greetings to Maestro Calamaio, obsessed with catching a likeness with a paint brush!" I could go on until tomorrow morning describing every stench, herbal infusion, or effluvium of slow-cooking delicacies in grisly detail. That way, when a call comes in like yours, I prepare myself. If I have to get my bag and rush to a deathbed, for example, I open the jar of Vicks VapoRub. I dip my finger into the ointment and rub it into my mustache. At least the menthol and camphor wafting up my nose protects me from the fetid stench of dead skin, boils erupting with pus, or toenails that stink like a corpse. With the added bonus that I'm not put off my food for life.

When I was little, Mamma used to yell at me when she saw me sniffing at the food in my plate before eating. "Stop being so fussy," she would say. Babbo was the same, "When you grow up, you'll find a nice little surprise between a woman's legs that smells like codfish." When I was sixteen and told them I wanted to be a doctor, they glanced at one another. And burst out laughing. She said: "What, you? Even so much as touching a piece of meat with the same fork you used for your pasta disgusts you! Imagine palpating an old man's rectum." But she asked my opinion when she first got ill, a hundred years ago. She would watch me from her bed, her head propped up on the bedstead. One morning, she started, "Emilio, dear, feel my belly, will you? It's making this strange grumbling sound . . . " Three months later, they buried her next to Babbo.

I'm talking to you out loud but I could be talking to the wall. Admittedly, in your family you are a match twice over. Twins: both dwarves, both deaf-mute from birth. It's pretty easy to imagine what went on under the covers around here, back in the day when there were droves of first cousins and little else. And this is the result. Two little monsters who, against all odds, have seen off all their relatives and now live together like husband and wife, continuing the tradition of perverting nature at the community's expense. But you are still creatures of this world. And I swore an oath many years ago.

Your house smells of broth and musty wood. But in the background, there's a smell of cat piss even though there are no mousers around. If it weren't for this, it would be a nice apartment, full of books as it is. They line all the walls, often stacked double. That's what you must fritter away all your disability pensions on. The State has certainly lost out with you two. Life expectancy for little doohickies like you is usually around forty or so. But you're past sixty and still going strong. Maybe we should call a TV program to show the world how people here live longer, thanks to the air we breathe at Le Case. Even the ones who came into the world wrong.

You know, I've come to the conclusion that the quality of silence is different in the homes of the deaf. The silence feels a little put out at not being appreciated. Which makes it shout out even louder, like a spoilt child. You notice it immediately when you come in from outside. If I were blindfolded and walked through your front door, the smells are not what would strike me, though they would give you away immediately. It would be the silence. It's like a hand digging into you.

The only sounds are your mongoloid grunts. Especially yours, dear Giuliano. You never stop whimpering and you don't even notice. It's as if the cat that pisses all through the house is stuck in your throat.

Your sister, on the other hand, is more composed. Look at her, Giuliano. She looks like a plump rag doll whose stuffing has shifted, filling her up here and emptying her there, making her deformed. Of the two of you, Piera has the bigger head. But her petite hands and feet look as though they've been carved out of wood. When I tap her on the back, instead of coughing, she turns around and looks at me with those cat-fish eyes of hers. And like a fish, she gawps and blows bubbles. A wheeze comes out, like the caw of a magpie. And I am in awe, thinking of the design of whoever put us here on Earth: the two of you in the middle of nowhere, banished to Le Case, serving your sentences even though you are innocent. A punishment which is twice as severe for you because you are also mortified in the flesh. My anger rises at the thought and my mind goes to Don Lauro, for whom all the suffering brought about by our useless existence is grist for the mill and then he lives off the proceeds. "It's God's design," he says. It may well be. For me, though, if there were really a white-bearded God in this universe, the sketch he has drawn up here on this hill looks more like the scribbling of someone who was so bored they let the pen roam around the edge of the page and then forgot all about it.

It's alright for Don Lauro to say, "You'll be getting the real prize in the great beyond" and then continue with the usual rigmarole, the last shall be the first, etcetera etcetera. At the end of the service, he passes the collection box around and everyone rummages in their pockets. Because it would be foolhardy to make enemies in heaven after all the heartache down here in the sewer. In my opinion, it should be the other way around.

One day you arrive at the gates, and St. Peter writes you a check right there and then to pay you back. With apologies from the company.

That's why people in Le Case run to the confession box, kneel on the wooden step, and whisper their guilty secrets through the grate. I prefer two deaf dwarves. I drag out the check-up and I talk and talk and talk as the freaks' little beady eyes focus on my mouth and read my lips.

Because saying the words you harbor deep inside out loud is like opening the cages of a hundred baying mongrels. It takes the weight off, momentarily. But the dogs come right back to disembowel you.

So, I tell the deaf-mute dwarves again about Alfredo, my son. One morning forty years ago, he didn't wake up, just kept on dreaming, as he would for the centuries to come, the same dream he was having the night of September 9, '76. It was important for me to be sure that it was a good dream. Such a wonderfully happy dream that it stopped his young heart just before he turned twenty-three. Vilma didn't want anyone to touch him. She sat on a chair by his bed and kept vigil over him. If I came anywhere near, she would jump up like a spring with a nervous titter. Whispering like a spy, she would say, "Tell those people to keep quiet. Can't you see Alfredo needs to rest?" She went on like this for three weeks, even after the funeral. When she went to Mario's to get the groceries, and someone came up to her to offer their condolences, she would rebut their advances almost playfully. "Okay, my husband's face may resemble a fat old toad's but aren't condolences a bit much?" she would joke, before turning her back on them. One morning she took the bus to Grosseto, saying she wanted to take a stroll around the Thursday market. And she vanished. Into thin air. They searched along the banks of the Ombrone but it was no use. So now you know why I have no son, because he was kidnapped by a dream, and how I have a wife who, from one day to the next, was erased from the face of this earth.

And yet, dear Giuliano, I keep going. I took an oath, and almost every evening I recite it from memory. Don Lauro has his litany of prayers, but I only need one, written by Hippocrates. Every morning I open my surgery and one sick person after another strips off on my table. Sometimes I can see they have advanced cancer, and I don't say a thing. Instead, I give them a pat on the back and send them home with a prescription for cough syrup. Or I prescribe a strong pill for their nerves. The family always invites me to the funeral, and they don't seem to mind that much. "He was doing so well," they say. "And then in just under a week he was laid to rest in the grace of God." I don't say a word. In fact, for a week I have this good feeling I carry around with me, which puts a little wind in my sails. I think about the poor wretch or the weary, bored widow I released from their suffering. I go up to Maso's bar and have a drink or two, and gaze out at the world around me. I might see Divo, and I wonder how the swelling in his goiter is doing and whether he has noticed it yet. Or I may meet poor Adele on the street, with her early-onset dementia. I take pleasure in watching her trudging up the hill, thinking that the osteoporosis that she has never done anything about will one day make her bones crumble and she will have a fall. If she's lucky she'll die on the spot like Serraglini two winters ago. Otherwise, she'll have to spend a few months in bed with her hip or femur bone broken. At that point, she'll be close enough to the grave she can dance her way there.

Dear little friend, Piera will meet the same end, and for once I can say it out loud, though talking to you is like singing to an ant. The old doll can hardly breathe because of her heart, which is having its last waltz. If we're lucky, she'll be gone before the end of the month. Who knows? Maybe tomorrow you'll wake up to find her lying next to you as cold as a stone with her mouth gaping open like my boy, the son I once had. Then you'll be heartbroken, and you will follow her. That is, if your poor afflicted sister's death doesn't make you throw in the towel on the spot, in which case, a nice dive headfirst into the muddy waters of the Pecora.

I feel sorry for myself, if anything. Who will I go and tell my stories to? All my acts of charity that nobody knows anything about? Giving and giving and never being thanked wears you down after a while. It would be nice to receive a word of comfort every now and then. But this town is full of philistines, whining from dawn to dusk. And yet, as soon as you get a little pain, you dig into your miserable lives like tics. Let your lives go, I say! Life's a waste of time, so why not close the curtains and be done with it? If it were for me, I would prescribe a digestive concoction for everyone instead of antibiotics, in a last-ditch effort to reign in all this profligacy. Followed by a bullet between the eyes, which would at least make the walls of some of these sitting rooms a bit more interesting.

As I have already said, however, in Le Case the people are thick-skinned, and some of them try to put a spanner in the work I undertake with such affection. As if they were doing it on purpose to thwart me. Take Mrs. Franci, for example. She's about to leave us, it seems, but then she ends up hanging on, all skin and bone, her hair in patches. When I go and see her, she's all set for a chat. I check her blood pressure, and the results confirm she's no better off than an animal on its last legs. Her bedsores are starting to get infected, and that should be enough on its own to free her from her stinking deathbed. In short, everything is prepared for her to take her last breath. So, I say, "Adelaide, I'm very pleased with your progress. You're doing very well." She doesn't listen and plows on with her prattle. You should see how bright her eyes are! The only thing that comforts me is that I can't understand a word of her drivel and I'm thinking to myself, "At least the dementia has set in. This must be the peak before the final fall." I go back two days later and she's stable but her jabbering has got worse and that seems to be enough to keep her blood flowing.

Adelaide is gossiping relentlessly about a certain tryst between a young girl in the valley and that boy Samuele, Esedra's grandson. I find it hard to listen to because, while she may well be insisting on staying alive, I can beat her at that game and insist on checking her condition all over again. In terms of probability, she should have been dead at least a month ago. Meanwhile, hearing her idle talk of young men rampaging around town brings a lump to my throat, worse than if I'd swallowed poison. At this point I ask you all: what is this new generation for? I swear, it's something I think about a lot. All I need are these young things coming along and raising the average age of the town, making my task far more difficult despite all my hard work. Luckily, I got a phone call this morning from Silvestri, which gave me some comfort.

"She's fainted," Mario said. When I got to the store, he was standing there, his face set as if he were on his way to a funeral. The girl was laid out on the counter in the store room. Mario had rolled up her apron as a pillow to raise her head. "She's breathing alright," he mumbled, like a doting parent. "Her eyes flutter open every now and then. I talk to her but she can't see me. Then she drifts off. Is it serious?"

Dear Giuliano, dear Piera, we folks at Le Case don't get much of a chance to touch young flesh, you know. One of the last women left is big Giovanna Ginanneschi. But when you unbutton her blouse, the rolls of flesh are enough to put you off. I tell her she's doing all the right things and recommend eating a slab of lard with three thick slices of bread dipped in oil. You have big bones, I tell her. You need to gain at least fifteen pounds to sustain yourself. Sometimes I see her panting up the long Via di Mezzo, and I'm happy to see she's struggling to walk and that she's holding a hand up to her heart as if it's about to burst. It takes a long time to clog the arteries of a woman her size. But I don't have a train to catch.

Eleonora, on the other hand, is in her first bloom. "I'd know how to make you better," I thought as I bent over her pallid little face. I got my smelling salts out and put them under her nose. Her eyes opened wide and she looked around. She took a while to work out whether she was on this side, in the world of the living, or the other.

It was odd to see that girl in Mario's storeroom, on the counter where they usually pile up supplies. It felt like I was reliving the time when Adelaide fainted and hit her head on the tiles two years ago, the first symptom of her sickness. It makes you wonder whether slicing Bologna sausage for ancient customers causes fainting spells. "Let me go and shut the door," I had said at the time to her concerned husband. And I said the same thing this morning, "Let me go and close the door." Meanwhile I told the girl to stay still so that I could at least measure her blood pressure. When I tried to loosen her collar just a little so that she could breathe, she pulled back, her lower lip trembling. She had the same reaction when I attempted to roll up her sleeve. "I'm fine," she kept on saying and she was probably right. Maybe a little anemic. I could see it in her eyelids, which were pale and lifeless. Iron deficiency. That must be why she fainted in the store. Apart from this, Eleonora, who had taken Adelaide's place there, was a monument to good health. Then I noticed the bruises.

They stood out like peacock tails against her pale skin: dark purple, black, and yellow smudges. I had glimpsed a big one on her throat as I'd loosened her collar before she had buttoned herself up again. There are more on her arm, deep impressions of finger marks. "Someone is abusing this girl," I thought to myself, but said nothing. Instead, I produced one of my patent smiles that were meant to say, "Dear girl, you are the picture of good health!" I tapped her knee to check her responses and asked Mario to bring his apprentice a glass of sugar and water. He didn't ask me for a certificate.

This is all just to say that Adelaide's stories are idle gossip, animated, no doubt, by her sickness and by her envy of this new little pony trotting around the store where she used to work. What is for sure is that Eleonora, with her dark expression, isn't in a good place right now. Someone is roughing her up at home. One day, if I'm lucky, there'll be an "accident" and the threat of the younger generation will be halved.

I could never say these things to anyone, not even in confession to Don Lauro. He doesn't give a fig about the confidentiality of my profession and would call the carabinieri after a split second. Speaking of that little priest, in the last two weeks I've noticed that when I go and see Mario's wife, the sleeping drops I prescribe her are never there. It just so happens that, the day before, our beloved officiant had passed by, so assiduous is he in his duties as deathbed advisor. I may be wrong, but he may well be stocking up on deep sleep . . . so this is why I've decided that the next time I bring round Adelaide's prescription, the concoction is going to be a little different, both to encourage the sick lady to take the leap into her grave and to poison that empty chatterbox who's always tooting his trumpet, counting off people's sins on the tips of his fingers, and then committing a worse one himself by stealing drugs from a woman on her deathbed. I know he does it because he doesn't want to give me any satisfaction. Don Lauro is obsessed with his faith. He would rather be flayed in the town square than come to my office and ask for a prescription for the poison of his choice like everyone else does.

Dear Giuliano, this might be the last time I can talk about my plan to someone who is alive. Or, at least, to someone who looks human. People need to know that I'm not done yet. Here, at Le Case, there's evil that needs to be extirpated and to do so, we need to free all its captive souls, like birds from a cage. This shell of a town must be scooped out and emptied, its windows left dark, its streets filled only with spiders.

Le Case is a monster that grows fatter with every breath we take, and my task is to snuff them out one by one, until the only breath left is my own. When the monster is hungry, the earth from which it came trembles, giving us cold sweats and making our hearts hammer. But its long agony is already upon us. Month by month, the bells toll for the dead in the church at the top of the town. The funeral processions are getting thinner and thinner, considering some of the inhabitants are already six feet under and others are bed-ridden. In the old town, every now and again, the light stops shining through the slats of one more set of shutters. The monster's breath is getting more and more labored . . . the day will come when I can finally deal the town its final death blow by shooting myself in the mouth.

GIOVANNA GINANNESCHI, *the Spinster*

Here, my lovely pooch, one for you and one for me. Gobble it up. You're so lucky you can stuff yourself without gaining an ounce of fat. I'm so jealous I could strangle you. One for you and one for me. There you go . . . every cookie is manna from heaven for your empty belly. Whenever you see me reach into the box for another, you nearly choke on your chain, your mouth foams, your nails rasp at the floor. Your little yelps sound like a child falling down a dark well. I love making you crave my crispy butter, caramel, and hazelnut cookies. Mamma always says, "Don't feed that creature. It'll give her too many calories and she'll be pooping everywhere." She doesn't understand that it's a ploy. If I didn't come down here, I'd finish the whole box in no time, the rolls of flesh on my legs would double, and my hips would grow wider and wider, filling out my clothes until they tear. That's why I give one cookie to you for every one I eat myself. This way I can keep the cravings at bay. And the burgeoning rolls of fat under control.

Mamma used to say something else, though recently she seems to have changed her tune. She used to say it was a matter of bone structure. "You're well-built," she'd say. "You need to stop thinking of it as a disease. Dr. Salghini agrees. Or do you think you know better than a man of science?" Then I look at my naked body in the mirror and see how deformed it is. Sometimes I stop and study myself for a few minutes, to the point where I can almost see beauty there. In the reflection, I see Giovanna heavy with some kind of inexplicable accumulation, and in the end the fat doesn't matter. Giovanna is still there, though her ankles are ruined under the strain of countless quintals.

One for you, one for me, my pooch. The truth is they should have caught it in time, when I was about twenty and I was just beginning to lose my figure. All the signs were there. I was one of the last young people to stay in Le Case but nobody looked at me even then. Mamma would come into the room, where I still sleep, and stroke my back. "My dear girl," she would say. "Don't take it so hard. Would you really like to marry one of these neighborhood derelicts? It would be such a waste!" Nothing has changed since then. Except that I'm over fifty and getting my first hot flashes

You know, I would actually have liked to know what it feels like to let a man in. A man I'd fallen head over heels in love with, as uninhibited as a small boat in a storm . . . I don't even know what it's like to be kissed. I don't know a thing, pooch. And now I've gone past the point of no return. Maybe it happened when they started calling me Big Giovanna and in everyone's minds, I'd become this great big blimp lumbering up Via di Mezzo, hair glued to my forehead with sweat even in midwinter. "Here comes Big Giovanna," they all say, and have been doing for years.

I don't know where this frenzy to stuff myself comes from. There are some nights like this one when I wake up all of a sudden with an insatiable appetite, as if I hadn't eaten a single crust of bread since the beginning of time. And I'm not the type to go to bed without my supper. I'm so hungry I feel like hollering. I'm shaking all over. The pit in my belly is so deep that if I don't fill it, I'll fall right in. I suddenly turn into a dragonfly and flit around the house barefoot, as light as a shadow, having shed my short-of-breath elephant's body. It's dark and I feel like a ballet dancer en pointe when I go and open the fridge or the larder door. I grab some snacks or stubs of salami sausage and go down the stairs with my heart in turmoil. I hole up down here with you, dear little thing, so that I can go halves with you. You hear me coming at three in the morning with some delicious little morsel. You know that if you make a noise, you'll wake Mamma up and she'll hurl herself down here and send me right back to bed. Goodbye snack.

There's nothing to save now. Whatever might have happened if I'd managed to keep my craving under control is now on the scrapheap. And anyway, Dr. Salghini is always pleased with my lab tests. "Giovanna, my dear, it's your constitution," he says every time. "Take it or leave it." And I take it. More and more weight, that is. As for the rest, my blood pressure is perfect and my dizziness is a symptom of the change, which is coming on fast. Three months ago, the doctor gave me a big smile and said, "Giovanna, dear, that's the way life goes. I was your pediatrician once and now here I am telling you the hot flashes mean your monthlies are soon coming to an end. Which means good riddance to the hassle. Are you happy? Be prepared for some weight gain, though. It's normal." I burst out laughing.

But it is after his home visit that my Mamma changed. Maybe she was still hoping to reel in a man for me and suddenly realized I had aged. She saw that my neck was ringed with rashers of quivering lard and my pendulous double chin was hanging perilously low. She halved my portions of pasta. After two slices of bread, the loaf was whisked off the table. When I looked for jam in the larder, it was not on the shelf I'd been stealing it from since I was six. The result was that my night hungers got worse. I woke up with only one thing on my mind: "If I don't demolish that half-salami sausage in the fridge, I'll throw myself off the roof terrace." Two minutes later, I'm with you, dear pooch. At least the stairs burn some calories.

There's some kind of battle being waged. For the last three months or so, even breakfast has been stripped back, despite Dr. Salghini's recommendations: "The bigger the build, the more calcium is needed for the bones." Which is taken from the same songbook as my mother's, though now she's changed her tune, she's too ashamed to utter such things. Her shopping is rationed and she only puts what is needed for the next day in the fridge. From one day to the next, the crisper drawers at the bottom have been filled with vegetables. There's never more than a couple of inches of wine at the bottom of the bottle. When I'm hankering after food at night, munching on three carrots is taking a bite out of a cloud.

The fact is that by starving me, Mamma is also depriving herself, though she doesn't need to at all. I inherited Babbo's build. When he died, we had to hire the Roccostrada's men to carry the coffin from the old town down to the hearse. At the end of the meal, Mamma picks the crumbs up with a moistened finger, sticks it in her mouth, and sucks it dry. She would sell me down the river to get her hands on a slice of pine nut pie to dip into her milk, but, instead, she gets up and starts doing the dishes. I've shrunk almost two sizes in three months. And she often strikes up that particular conversation. She talks to me from the kitchen sink with her back to me while I'm watching TV, my leg jiggling with nerves from eating a meal fit for birds. "That Mimmo looks like such a nice man," she says. "He's a hard worker! He may be a bit quiet but that's not necessarily a bad thing . . . what do you think?"

Do you want to know what I think, my dear little pooch? I think that there's a difference between looking for a husband and scraping the bottom of the barrel. If that country bumpkin had proposed ten years ago, I might have given him the time of day. But the very idea of getting engaged now makes me sink into a well of miserable despair. Not to mention the fact that he does seem to want to get his hands on me, and he could be carrying meningitis in from the fields.

Back when we are at elementary school together, we used to see him climb up from the hollow, with those boots he'd hammered nails into full of mud. He stank like a wet mule and hardly said a word. He had a crush on me in third grade. One morning, he waited outside school to give me a note. I didn't even read it. Actually, I ripped it to pieces and threw the confetti in his face while all the kids laughed.

I've thought about it over the years. If I had to vote for the moment that I brought the evil eye on to myself, I would probably settle on that morning outside the old school gates. Mimmo loped off, having been made fun of and spurned by the big ones. And I was laughing more than anyone else, with that merciless meanness that kids have. Then I shake my head because if there really is a God governing things, and if he's punishing me for that day, then we'd be back to square one. It's not fair to brand someone forever just because they behaved like idiots when they were practically still in diapers. And yet it's always felt like a curse: me turning into more and more of a barrel with every year that passed. Not a single living creature looks at me nowadays. Mimmo is the only one. The same Mimmo who once dared write a note containing the only sweet-nothings I have ever received, which I didn't even bother to read.

On market days, he watches me walk past on the road. His hang-dog expression makes me sick. Mamma knows the peasant has a weakness for me and she exploits it. The bags of vegetables we take home from his stall are always stuffed with extras and he charges us half of what they're worth. As if I cared two hoots about that rabbit food. Give me a rasher of streaky bacon any day.

Then this summer I fainted in the square. Dr. Salghini's verdict had only just come in. I was taking the iron supplements but still felt dizzy, especially in the heat. That morning Le Case was burning like the devil's own belly. All of a sudden, I found myself on all fours, the shopping rolling out of the bags onto the street. When I came to, there was a ring of faces shading me. Among them, my mother's, yelling at me. I didn't understand a thing. All I heard was a whistle in my ear. A whistle with no sound. Like a breath of wind forced through a crack. Or rather, a punctured tire on a bike. And that's what I thought. "There must be a puncture in my brain. Maybe I'll deflate a little."

First, they helped me sit up. Somebody gave me a packet of sugar. Mrs. Barberini fanned me with her hankie. I eventually came back to the land of the living but I felt weaker than I'd ever felt. I couldn't even lift my arm. Suddenly, I felt a tremor come over me and my heart started beating for no reason, making me short of breath. I was drenched in sweat. Cold sweat, that made my clothes stick to my skin, revealing the lard underneath. This was when the horrible scene took place, in front of the whole town.

They tried to pull me back onto my feet, dear Pooch. They heaved and hoed but they couldn't lift my ass from the ground. Worse, I'd fall onto my backside every time they gave up, and they had to prop me up from behind otherwise I would have folded with my legs sticking out and landed on my back again. I'd already started crying. If someone had pulled out a gun, I would have begged them to finish me off right there and then, ten feet from the door of St. Bastian's. Divo said he wanted to call social services because there was no way they could move a deadweight like me. He had taken his shirt off and was there in his undershirt. He was dripping like me and the veins in his neck were as thick as ropes. He was having difficulty catching his breath, with his hands hooked into his belt. At one point, he even smiled to spur me on. But there was pity in his look and it took my breath away. It felt like he was saying, "Poor woman. It would be better for her if this was the end and then that would be that." Sonia closed my eyes and prayed that my life would come to an end there and then. I was praying so fervently that I felt as though I was actually flying. I took off and floated up to the clouds.

When I looked down, I thought I could see the little square

way below me. I was about to say, "The agony is over," but my mother's face was right in front of me, cutting off every possible comment. "My darling," she said, drying the sweat from my brow and the tears from my face. I didn't know what was going on. I felt as wobbly as before but I was standing up and everyone was yelling, "Shall we call Dr. Salghini?" or "Giovanna, come and sit in the shade for fifteen minutes to cool yourself down."

Mimmo was there, my dear little pooch. The same Mimmo I had mortified with a handful of confetti with his words written on them. He was holding me up from behind but I couldn't feel him. Having seen this beached whale in the middle of the piazza, he had rushed headlong to my side, accomplishing the task that three men had not been up to. He walked with me to the church steps, which were in the shade, and he sat me down on the bottom step without saying a word. Nor did I utter a word to him. In fact, being indebted to him of all people made me a little nervous. Mamma had been handed a fan and wouldn't stop waving it in front of my face. She was the one who gushed forth, thanking him a thousand times for what he had done. I looked at my feet. I was slowly recovering my strength. The group of rescuers and onlookers had already begun to disband. Eventually, Mimmo left, too, and all I could give him was half a smile. When he was sufficiently far away, I whispered, "No trouble. He's been lifting bundles of firewood all his life. I was easy." Dear little pooch, there are days when I ask myself whether I shouldn't just give in. It's not easy to find a man who knows how to ride a woman like me. But then I feel sick at the idea of falling asleep in the same bed as that red neck. He made me feel sick when I was eight and I feel exactly the same now. Mamma started it. Practically every evening she bangs on about the same thing. "By the way," she said the other evening, after a miserable little weight-watching meal she had cooked, though her efforts are in vain. "They say Fiorani's new olive oil is ready. Tomorrow let's go down to the hollow and get ourselves a nice big can to see us through the winter, shall we?" I got up and went up to my bedroom without saying a word. I opened the drawer and pulled out my diaries. I like re-reading them every now and again to help me cry a bit.

One for me and one for you . . . Vanish. That's what I feel like doing sometimes. Like that girl from the store who's been missing for a week. They've turned her parents' house and her boyfriend's place inside out but there's still no sign of her. No letter, no note. Swallowed up by nothingness for no reason. Lucky her. One day Mario comes back to the grocery store from his lunch break and Eleonora has gone. Whenever I see her picture in the newspaper, I say to myself, "Dear girl, either you've been really brave, or you've been unlucky." Then I sit back and enjoy all the gossip about the case. I pretend they're talking about me. It may be a game for the deranged, but it feels so good. Because when someone just vanishes like that, people take a good look at themselves and still don't understand. When someone disappears and their body is never found, people start insinuating that there has been a secret plan carried out without anyone's knowledge, not even the husbands, wives, or children. A year or two later, people start talking about martians.

I wrote it in my diary in '76, when I was nearly twenty. I want to disappear, I wrote, filling in the margins with his initials. I may have never savored a kiss, or enjoyed a man's carnal favors but I know what true love is. And it has a name. Someone who broke my heart in two, not once but twice.

It's a story you could recite from memory, dear little pooch. Whenever I come down to spend time with you, we always end up circling around the same subject: Alfredo. But some gaping holes can never be filled and I've never been able to replace the feeling that used to beat in my heart as I ate dinner with my stomach in a knot. Back then, my body was not like the one I lumber around in now. I thought of nothing but him. Nothing else mattered. I was in my prime, with the arrogance that comes of youth. Then it all ended. There's nothing worse than allowing someone to experience the effect of their beauty and then taking it all away so cruelly and so quickly.

Still today, I think of Alfredo walking down these streets in the summer, in the old days when the fair rides used to come to town. He always had a cigarette tucked behind his ear, his hair quite long on both sides and falling over his eyes. Most of all, though, it was his laugh that stopped the blood in my veins. I could hear all the world's answers in that white-toothed guffaw. One evening I made my mind up and sent Valentina Cocchetti over to watch his reaction. She was more brazen than me and lives in France now with two kids studying in Paris, like the ones you see in the films. I spied on them from afar while I was squeezing Sabrina Gori's hands to relieve my tension. She married a dentist and sends me a Christmas card every year from Florence, and I've never sent one back. "I'm going to die," I said, my heart beating like a drum as I glanced over at Valentina surrounded by a group of boys, in the midst of which Alfredo's good looks shone like a flaming torch. "Why isn't she coming back?" I started asking after a while.

"I want to vanish," I wrote back in the summer of '76. August 6, to be precise. The tears are flowing now. I couldn't help seeing my friend's face tossed back in full-throated laughter, and Alfredo taking the cigarette out from behind his ear and offering it to her. That might be the moment that the old Giovanna, who was still beautiful and not yet deformed, actually died.

I was paid with the same coin as when I was ten and refused the advances of a certain snot-nosed Mimmo in front of the school gates. The first few days I bleated my desperation. I woke up crying at all hours of the night and buried my face in my pillow. Mamma brought my lunch into my room as if I were sick. I handed it back an hour later without touching a crumb. By the end of the month, I was as thin as a rake. I spent my days staring at the ceiling in the shadow of the tragedy that was consuming me little by little. I heard my mother say, "My dear girl, you're still in your prime . . . " or, "The sea is wide and full of fish, you'll see . . ." Babbo would simply open my door a little and peek inside. Then he would tiptoe away because he was never good with words. Until something changed. One day, the pain was maybe worse but at least I could breathe. Except that I had turned sour.

It was already the beginning of September. One day they saw me creep out of my den. Pale, with tousled hair and wearing only a T-shirt that went down to my knees. I took a few unsteady steps as if I were a skeleton and sat down at table with my parents. Mamma smiled. "Darling," she said, making me choke on my soup. Babbo poured me half a glass of wine. "About time," he muttered. The television was on low, like in hospitals. I sat there staring at the food on the table. Then, without saying a word, I started eating.

I made up for all the meals I had missed over those weeks of agony. The more I stuffed my face, the more I wanted to stuff my face. Mamma rose to the occasion: cracking eggs, frying cutlets. Babbo cut slabs of bread like there was no tomorrow. Or he would take out jars of artichokes, rounds of cheese, and sides of prosciutto he had been hanging to cure. After a while, their relief at seeing me a little rounder turned into concern. They filled my plate and I hoovered the food up without a moment's hesitation. I wanted more. Is it possible that I had decided to kill myself with food? That I wanted to end up beached on my chair? I was always hungry. I would polish off a whole bar of chocolate and follow it up with half a pear tart. I would eat fig jam by the spoonful until the jar was empty. Still not sated, I would gorge myself on fruit, eating all the peaches and plums in the fruit bowl. It was then that I suddenly went stiff and my eyes popped open as wide as they could. Mamma ran to get a towel, expecting the worst. Babbo jumped up saying, "I'll hold her head." And I let it out.

A burp. A giant belch, a hunter's salvo, so prolonged it shook the glass in the windows. It was big and smelly. As the gas was released, I gripped onto the table as if there had been an earthquake, a bad one. One of those quakes that brings the ceiling down. I was as shocked as they were. They gawped. We were in the eye of a storm. I felt like something was evacuating my belly. It was as if I were ejecting a ghost that had bedded down in my body. For a moment I was scared. There was so much gas coming out, I felt I didn't have any air left to breathe in. I thought I was going to die of a belch and instinctively I planted my feet on the ground and stood up. Until it was over. The silence that followed shrouded us as if the ceiling had really come down on our heads. I took a deep breath. I looked at Mamma, who was glaring at me as if I had just murdered someone, "Is there anything else to eat?" I asked.

Adele Centini -3
The Isastia Widow

Calamaio gives me a look that may pass for a smile and closes his sketchbook. He starts slotting the pastels back into their case. When we get to this point in the proceedings, I always feel like I should be consoling him, but I wouldn't know what for. He sits there, his face so long it's under his feet. He throws me shy little glances as if he were begging not to have to say anything. "How did it go today?" I ask, leaning over cautiously to grab my bath robe. Every joint feels like it's about to come apart. As I move my head, I hear grains of sand grinding at the back of my neck. He attempts a smile but still manages to look as despondent as an effigy. "Well . . .," he says, looking like a teenager who has just tucked his dick away in a hurry after being caught red-handed having a go at it. This makes my hackles rise a little. "Will I ever be able to see one miserable drawing?" Calamaio hangs his head. He leans on the back of the armchair where he has been sweating until five minutes ago. "Well . . .," he says again, this time with a sigh of encouragement which means I know I'll have to hear him through. "Adele, my dear, I can't get it right," he murmurs as if he were pulling his guts out and putting them on the table. "It's there somewhere. I can see it in my head but when I try and catch it with my pastels, it's gone. It's driving me crazy."

I've been waiting patiently for two years but I don't insist. Calamaio picks up his things and turns to look at me before leaving the room, giving me a little bow with his head. "If it is convenient for you, we'll meet again next Tuesday at the same time," he says. I usually don't answer. I just smile. I watch him open the door softly. He closes it behind him just as softly, rotating his body as he goes. I am left on my own in Room 112 of the Bel Sole. The first thing I do is light a cigarette, the only one in the week. Then I go to the window and take in the eyesore, the boundless lake that is the view from this place.

After recovering from the trauma of his daughter's death, the colonel lost his head, in particular for me. The plan Mamma had laid so carefully soon came to fruition. He looked at me with a spark that was so intense that it took my breath away, because it was the spark of a nut-job full of yearning who walks ten feet off the ground. It was amusing to begin with. The colonel realized that there were other ways to spend the little time he had left other than with his maps: with a girl in the full bloom of youth like Yours Truly, for example. Radiant and beautiful enough to light up his old age on the very brink of death.

Everyone in the household was giving me sideways looks but I insisted that nothing had changed and denied that I had my eyes on him. They shook their heads and said they would never dream of thinking anything of the kind. "The point is, you need to get on with your work," Stella said, winking at me. Solino added, "Rather you than some other snake." Santo stopped saying good morning to me, as did Ettore.

The colonel made me get up early so that I could accompany him on his tours of his properties. The tenant farmers were already treating me like a countess, bowing their heads in greeting. When we traveled around, I clocked Marcello's shrewd expression in the rear-view mirror and realized he was gunning for me, too. When we arrived at our destination, he even came around to open the door for me.

And yet, the lord and master never laid a finger on me. He would gawp at my face, for sure, but he never tried anything else. I told Mamma at the end of April. She dropped to her knees and gave thanks to St. Barbara. When she got back up again, she said, "Seed or no seed, we have him on a leash now. All we need now to do is tighten the noose. Inch by inch, even the Molossians were thrown over."

The days I spent with the colonel were long and happy. One morning he said, "Dear Adele, today I'd like to take you somewhere further than your eyes can see. Put that way, it scared me, and I felt something tear inside me when I saw the Ribolla valley stretching out in through the windscreen. I'd never ventured so far from the foothills, where the peak of Mt. Roccastrada was visible from every neighborhood. It was like losing sight of one of one of your parents. And then, all of a sudden, I saw the sea. It opened up in front of us at the end of the road that ran alongside the railway. And there was the Gulf of Follonica. The one I could just make out from the top floor of the Isastia Villa but only on the clearest days. From up there, it was little more than a mirage. A slice of sky that had crashed down to earth, the island of Elba floating on it like a ghost whose outline you could only guess at. I had once drawn the scene on a window with my finger after misting up the glass with my breath. But now everything was before my eyes and I felt as though I was floating in a dream. There was enough water in the sea to drown me.

The colonel owned an elegant building on the esplanade. It was called Villa Marta. "It's my mother's name," he said. We made a surprise visit to the family that was taking care of the property. The custodian went deathly pale when he saw his master at the gate. He didn't open it immediately. He stood there staring, words failing him. "Am I allowed to come into my own house?" The colonel said without even saying good day, in that cantankerous tone he often adopted with servants.

I glimpsed the hall for a second. Then I ran outside, jumped over the parapet, and sunk my feet into sand for the first time in my life. I didn't dare go any further. The horizon was so vast it made me dizzy. I had never felt so insignificant or imperiled. Maybe I was scared the sea would swallow me. Then I felt someone at my side. It was the colonel. He, too, looked at the horizontal line in the distance. The island looked as if it were protecting our eyes from the immensity, keeping us from seeing it all at once. "I want to take you to France," he said after a while. He didn't say anything else and I didn't answer. When I turned around to look, he had vanished.

It was a strange life. I took what came and if there were no specific orders to the contrary in the morning, I would don my work clothes. My tasks in the Isastia Villa did not last long: once I had taken the colonel his breakfast, I received my instructions for the day, which usually included taking my apron off. Nevertheless, in the evening, I would go back and sleep in my scullery maid's cell, my head spinning with the novelty of it all. By day, I was thrown into a kind of paradise. At dusk, I took up my place on earth.

As time went by, the kitchen staff started giving me looks, despite their initial sympathy and the fact that it was thanks to me that the colonel had revived in the first place. However, without me doing the work, they had to divvy up the chores among themselves. I was taking home the same pay as them even though I was out on day trips and they had to work twice as hard. To make matters worse, the colonel had taken it upon himself to give me an education. If we didn't go out, we would spend most of the afternoon in his study sitting at his enormous desk with the quartz and pyrite paperweights. He marched up and down like a soldier talking about history and geography. I liked literature, too, and that's where he reeled me in. After our sessions, he would go down to the main living room. He would choose a book from the giant bookcase that filled the whole back wall of the room. "Here is your homework," he would say, handing me a tome.

Maybe Colonel Isastia was shaping me up to be a wife according to his specifications. He tried to rid me of all the rough trappings of a girl born to poverty and ignorance. When he'd had enough, he sent me to eat with the others. As soon as I appeared at the kitchen door, a tomb-like silence fell. Nobody said a word during the meal and Stella no longer served me the tasty bits. On the contrary, she took the last scoops of the ladle and flicked the food onto my plate with a look of disapproval, like a plasterer dabbing a wall with lime.

When the colonel pulled out the book on etiquette, I knew he was getting serious. Mamma had prepared me well in this respect, especially with regard to my manners. And anyway, no training could compare to my mother's efforts when my beauty first started to show, despite my attempts to thwart her. Colonel Isastia created little situations, citing, for example, a commander he disliked intensely; dead he may be, but the colonel would have liked to dig him up and hang by his feet in a public square. "Just to say that this situation could be real," he said. He would impersonate this commander, changing the way he walked and spoke. He took three steps back and turned into him. Stepping forward again, he said: "Greetings, Signorina," bowing to kiss my hand. There was a whole repertoire of expressions for that one gesture. Once I saw him shudder with disapproval. "Adele, heaven forbid!" he roared. "You stroked the back of my hand with your index finger. Do you know what that means?" I shook my head vehemently. Catching his breath, he said, "It's best you don't know." And he had to drink a sip of cordial to recover himself.

We crossed the French border in late June. This time the tug was even stronger. I felt as though the world was swallowing me up so entirely that I would be spat out as another person. I was ostensibly Adele Centini but there was fresh blood coursing through my body and it gave me heart spasms. Seeing myself strolling down the avenues of Montecarlo was like imagining myself on the moon. I gripped the colonel's arm and was terrified we might get separated if he stepped away for a second, even if it was only to buy tobacco. I sipped champagne and it all tasted the same. The streets echoed with the language of Martians and the food they brought to the table was so unappetizing that it made me miss Stella's scrapings from the bottom of the pot, even though they had been served with a dollop of venom. The evenings were the worst. Once I bade the colonel goodnight, I locked myself in the room of the hotel whose name I couldn't even pronounce. I felt completely alone. I was homesick down to my marrow.

The colonel needed me for a lot of reasons but there was one that stood out in particular: feeling good about himself by showing me how important he was. My never-ending amazement was a dish he never tired of tasting. After his daughter's death, he must have lost a cog or two, though it wasn't apparent from the outside. I caught occasional glimmers of it, especially when he went into a frenzy. His eyes would shine and it would terrify me. I said to myself, "Any minute, he'll lose his mind and I'll be stuck in this place where I wouldn't even know how to ask for a glass of water."

It happened most often at the casino when he was gambling at the card table. The first few times I didn't realize because I was distracted by all the gold and crystal, reflected to infinity in the mirrors. My jaw dropped at the wealthy women's dresses, twinkling with diamonds, their hairstyles, and the long cigarette holders they dragged on. One evening, I saw a woman with a cat on a leash and thought I'd ended up in a madhouse. The waiters couldn't abide my being without a glass in my hand. As soon as I emptied one, they rushed to bring me another. I responded with a smile because that was the one thing I knew how to do.

The colonel, on the other hand, ordered an expensive bottle which usually lasted all evening. He wanted me to sit by his side on a stool in full view of all the players. One evening, he said, "They see this lovely piece of female flesh and they go cross-eyed looking at their cards. They're thinking, 'This old man is enjoying top-quality meat.' They sense some power in me. I win half of the hands. It's called strategy. A bit like in the war: if you look well-armed the enemy is less cocky and goes mad thinking things over. Then, *ta-da*! They make a mistake." After a winning hand, he would rake in the chips, turn to me flushed from the drink, and wink. Another time, when the games were over, he pulled out a promissory note. We were walking back to our rooms. As we walked and I held him upright, he said, "This is a little apartment in Lorraine." He folded the note and put it back in his pocket. A little further on, to disguise my feeling of ignorance, I commented, "I once had a classmate in elementary school with the same name. She was from the Braccagni estate. She was called Lorraine Battaglini. She had a lisp." Colonel Isastia spent the next ten minutes falling apart laughing. He had to lean his back against the wall and put his hands on his knees because the convulsions had turned into a coughing fit that he didn't seem able to recover from.

It was already July by the time I returned and finally, one Sunday, sat opposite my mother at the kitchen table. I was a river of words. I told her about France. I'd even been to visit the galleries. She sat and listened but she wasn't interested in me or any of my stories. She stared at the trinkets and the dress the colonel had had specially made for me in Grosseto. All of a sudden, she said, "Isn't it about time you had a little property with an income made out in your name? Or that villa by the sea that seems to have gotten under your skin. Tell him I need it. Tell him I need the sea air to cure my lungs." I sighed deeply. I pulled a sheet of paper out of my bag. I placed it on the table.

I told her that the colonel had already given me a property on Via delle Scalette, near the Isastia Villa. It was one of the many apartments that had been converted from the jail in the old town. "It was abandoned, so the colonel had it done up for me," I murmured. "Right now, as we speak, somebody is taking the trunk with all my things in it, old and new, to that address."

Mamma's eyes lit up. She gave a quick lick to the corners of her mouth, where the saliva had been accumulating. All she said, though, in a voice that sounded like a snake hissing, was, "It's a start." A moment later, I dropped my elbows on the table, cradled my face in my hands, and burst into tears.

Eventually, she picked up a little ladle and yelled, "Remember this?" But I was still desperate. I didn't want to move into that apartment. I far preferred my little scullery-maid's cell next-door to Stella's. I sometimes used to let Ettore on my bed to keep me company. "I'll kick you in the ass all the way to Castel di Pietra, you'll go flying like Pia did once!" she screamed. "You don't spit on the grace of a saint! Nor on the kind heart of a colonel with no heirs who has decided to tinge your blood blue. What do you want to do? Go up to him and say, 'Thanks a lot but I'll do without'? As if our property portfolio was stuffed full. Shame on you!"

Mamma calmed down only when she saw me go seriously pale. I had been crying so hard my breath had grown shallow, my throat was constricted, and a terrible weight was squeezing my chest. My head was spinning and my mother had moved behind me to hold my chair still. The front of my dress was soaked in tears. "So much drama," she whispered in my ear, stroking my hair. "Come on, breathe calmly and it all will all blow away." She went to get a bottle of vinegar and poured a few drops onto the palm of one hand. She dipped a finger in and rubbed it under my nose to help me get my breath back. "I grew up with bad nerves," she murmured. "Not over whether to accept a house or not, mind you. It was hunger that woke me up at night, ripping my belly open bare-handed. There was little point in calling out for my mother in those days." She saw my color return after a while and went back to her seat in front of me. She touched my hands. Sounding like a real mother for once, she said, "What on earth is going on in that little brain that I gave you? What's with all these feelings?"

Ghosts. Everyone knew in Le Case. In Via delle Scalette you could still hear the prisoners' screams. So many of them had killed themselves, grating their wrists to a pulp on the walls, having gone crazy locked up in those three-foot crypts. And now they were pacing the rooms, dragging their chains, and lifting you off the ground by the hair when you least expected it. Even in broad daylight, people avoided those alleys if they could. Rumor had it that during the war, the Germans had turned them into officers' quarters but only stayed three days. "And it was no mean feat to get those bastard Nazis to flee," I'd heard Stella say, back when she still liked me. Even the cats took the long way round when it came to that street. The construction company that had gutted the building had all those empty conversions on their hands and no one wanted them, even to give away. Just looking at the narrow street gave you the shivers. It was steep and rose out of the base-rock like a maze, with irregular steps. "I'd rather go and sleep in a corner of the graveyard," I moaned. Then I looked at Mamma and said, firmly, "This evening when I go back to the Isastia Villa I'll go and see the colonel and give him back the deeds."

She looked bemused, as if she were about to burst out laughing. She got up and disappeared without saying a word. I heard noises from the other room. After a while, I went to see what she was doing and I saw an open suitcase on her bed. She shot me a glance. "The pathetic little ghost who can pull ownership of an apartment out from under my feet has not been born yet," she said. "I'm coming with you. You'll say to your dear colonel, "My mother needs medical care." He can't object to that. In the meantime, I'll write to Antonelli. He's been writing to me for ten years to get this apartment back so that his daughter can move closer to him." She folded a thick woolen sweater. And looked at me. "Let's start squeezing a little money out of this turnip, shall we?" she said.

That evening, she was waiting for me in the market square.

We walked that short stretch together. Mamma was holding a saucepan wrapped in a dish cloth with our supper in it. Every now and again, she lifted a corner and stuck her nose in, her nostrils inhaling the smell. "Capon this evening!" she exclaimed, and then carried on walking contentedly.

The colonel helped us sell the house I'd grown up in. He sent us a notary and no one asked us a penny in stamp duty. That same morning, we went to the bank and opened an account. As we signed our names, Mamma almost fainted because she couldn't believe we had more savings than we could keep hidden under a floor tile. I was the center of everything, and I behaved with my mother exactly how the colonel behaved with me: I showed her how important I was. I was opening up new horizons for her after a lifetime spent worrying and staying up all night pedaling away at the sewing machine. But having her in the house was not easy. She would wake me up early in the morning, an hour before dawn, and start getting me ready for the day. As I sat in the tub, she would scrub my back so hard she practically flayed me. Then she had to dress me and do my hair and makeup. "Just a touch," she always said, her tongue between her teeth in concentration, as she dabbed my cheeks with blush. She reminded me of an artist putting their signature on a painting. When I had my monthlies, she would frown. "If he decides to take you today, don't say no but keep your petticoat on. You don't want him seeing the vile stuff the first time. There are lots of ways to assuage a man's passions. Why would I have given you such a shapely mouth, if not?" As she said this, she gave me a little smack on the lips.

But it didn't happen, and Mamma was getting a bad liver worrying. "He has this lovely rose in his hands and won't even touch a petal," she complained, her eyes betraying the expression of someone who has seen the world go to seed. Colonel Isastia continued to buy me hats and diamond trinkets, educate me and teach me how to collect rents from his properties.

But he never laid a finger on me. Not even a grandfatherly kiss on the forehead. One morning, he gave me a wad of cash and said, "Call Marcello and have him take you to Grosseto to buy some clothes for the winter." It was already November, and in Le Case the mist was so thick you couldn't see your feet. We stopped on the verge under Meleta, our fog lights on. Marcello was in a rage. He would have preferred a day off rather than having to drive down those hairpin bends to the valley. I tried to get him to chat, reminding him that for me being there was preferable to being on my knees scrubbing the floor. "It's like being inside a cloud," I said as the white film clung to the windows like milk. "Mist like this makes me feel as if I don't even exist," I went on. "You could slit a man's throat and not even God would see you . . . " Marcello threw me a look in the rearview mirror. As I was speaking, I had already opened the top button of my shirt.

Achille Serraglini, *the Dead Man*

The hardest part is getting up in the morning and putting his clothes on. I wish I didn't have to look in the mirror, because every time I do, I get cold feet—my reflection looks as if it's ready to walk off on its own. I'm always expecting it to pull a face, burst out laughing, and say, "Hey, twin brother, you look good in my sweater." So, I shave as fast as I can, choking on my own breath first thing in the morning. Angiolino made a point of shaving every day and smothering himself with that sissy eau de cologne. By the time I leave the house, I'm feeling queasy, which is perfect for bidding the whole neighborhood good day.

Then I have to cross the old town holding my head high rather than staring down at the ground as I was used to doing. I have to send greetings up to the old ladies on their balconies rather than walking straight past with my hands behind my back. People call me over, "Angiolino, there's a treat for you in my cellar!" or "Angiolino, I've just come across a box of bagatelles in my attic . . . do you want to take a minute and have a look?" And there I am, speaking in my pervert brother's dulcet tones. As I shower them with exaggerated smiles, I feel like a calf who has just realized the slaughterer's knife is about to slit its throat.

Almost a thousand days have gone by and I'm still not used to it, not even a bit. Almost a thousand days of play-acting. Every morning I go down to Staccioli's to get the papers. I drink a warm latte at Rodolfo's bar. Then I stride back up as if

I were a busy priest on his rounds while my guts are cramping with enough gas to send a rocket off. Usually at that hour there are already a few characters at the Due Porte bar starting their day with a glass of white wine in their hands. Divo, in particular, who never misses a chance to spew cruel words. Sometimes, he snorts and spits on the sidewalk when I pass by, just to punctuate his words. But I don't bat an eye, even though my soul is crying out to give him a proper thumping. To smash his face in the gutter and yell in my own voice, without the embarrassing falsetto, "My dear town cuckold, look who's back from the dead. These are Achille's hands. Don't you recognize them?" And then smash his face until his teeth cave in.

The truth is, it's not at all easy to take on the guise of Angiolino. The more time passes, the more his clothes weigh on me, as if his pockets were producing cannonballs. I only regain my natural color at the end of the day when I close my door and turn the key twice in the lock, leaving all the deception outside, even though it never really abandons me and yells even louder in the silence. When I see myself in the living room in my dead brother's red dressing gown, I hear a voice half-whispering, "I'm going to do myself in." But then I think about Sonia.

There are no two ways about it: she takes the most effort. There are days when I feel like saying, "Look, it's me," and hugging her tight, like a soldier coming home after two years away at war. But then there would be some explaining to do. The urge subsides and I repeat for the umpteenth time, "Dear Achille, there's no going back now. You'll never get so much as a fingernail of your old life back." I force myself out of the house, ostensibly for a constitutional, although I haven't eaten a thing. I knock at the door of the house I paid for with more than thirty years of hard work in the mines, shoved up the sphincter of Maremma. And when Sonia comes and answers and sees this clown in front of her, she always looks as though she's about to pass out. She grips onto the door handle, her eyes red, and murmurs, "Ah, Angiolino, you're having a little walk I see," as if she were trying to convince herself she wasn't conjuring up a ghost. This breaks my heart all over again, though it is also cold comfort for someone as pathetic as Yours Truly: "She's still mourning me," I think. "She hasn't forgotten me yet."

Sonia never talks about me. Her hand trembles when she hands me a cup of tea. Pepita meows and starts rubbing herself against my calves. Because she knows who I am. So, I pick her up and put her on my lap, even though Angiolino hardly ever did. I put Pepita on my lap and sit at the kitchen table for a quarter of an hour.

The best moments are the silent ones when Sonia leaves me on my own saying she has to go to the bathroom. Although I know she goes there to take deep breaths in front of the mirror . . . Anyway, when I sit there and for a second, it's as if nothing has ever happened. There's me and the cat I adore. There's the smell of the life I once had. Except that my presence is as out of place as a profanity in church. The wife I left behind has lost so much weight and she has a dazed forlorn look. Every time I go and visit her, I feel like I'm pushing her closer to the edge of a kind of madness. Even though I would love to stay, I force myself to leave, inventing some cellar I have to rummage through, like my twin used to do. She nods her head and bites her lip. She walks down the corridor with me, where photos of us when we spent a month every summer at the seaside in Follonica are still hanging. Eventually, she throws me out on the street and slams the door behind me as if she has fainted against it.

It's probably mean of me not to give her a call and warn her but if I did, she would steel herself and the element of surprise would be lost. If she's not expecting me, on the other hand, I turn her world upside down from one moment to the next and that is when I have to get a grip on myself because I'm sorely tempted to doff that stupid hat I have to wear every day and say,

"Dear wife, there's someone else in that urn. I'm alive and well and seeing you makes my heart swell with passion."

I wish my twin had been less of a faggot, at least. Sooner or later I would have gotten in there and plugged the hole my passing left in its wake with the same passion that Sonia enjoyed previously. She would have given in to me out of desperation, like that evening early on when she crossed the old town in slippers in the middle of a storm that would have uprooted century-old poplars. She stopped just in time. If she had kissed me any longer, I would have melted then and there, by the fireplace, and told her the truth. As things stand, I have to play my part to the bitter end, thrusting the hands I would like to raise against the gossips hanging out at the Due Porte bar deeper into my pockets, and acting like a guest in my own house. All the while, I continue to crawl along the Via di Mezzo like a living ghost.

To begin with, it was odd receiving condolences for my own death. People would stop me on the street and say, "Dear Angiolino, sorry for your loss." "I know. There's no one like Achille . . . " I would answer, grief-stricken. But as soon as I turned the corner, I would touch my balls for good measure. Then the votive offerings started.

Ever since Nencioni opened the flood gates and let those Albanian barbarians in, people in Le Case have been spending their bonus money on security grates for their windows. I used to say to Sonia in no uncertain terms, "I didn't pay off the mortgage to live in a prison. If I ever find one of those animals scratching at the window, I'll give them a good talking to, with a stick."

It was past midnight. There was no way I was going to be able to get any sleep. All of a sudden, I heard someone touching Angiolino's door. I was sitting by the fire with the tongs in my hand. I said to myself, "Look at these snakes. They've made a copy of the keys." I went into the hall and stood by the coat rack. I heard them working on the lock slowly, as quiet as pickpockets. As soon as I saw the figure walk past, I stepped out of the shadows yelling as loud as I could: "What's all this, then?" And bludgeoned the guy with the iron tongs right behind the knees.

Rolling on the floor in agony was Maso, not some foreign thief with patches on his ass. I had shattered his bone with such force that his mouth was stretched wide but not a sound came out. He looked at me for a moment and passed out. I stood there staring at him. I said to myself, "What is Maso doing here on the floor, with Angiolino's keys? What can it mean?"

The answer came spontaneously. It wasn't rocket science. Even a kid would have figured in out. Later, as I was driving him down the hill on the Perilla side towards Grosseto, he wailed like a siren. "Bastard!" he moaned, his voice as muffled as a trumpet with a mute in its bell. "You knew it was Wednesday today!" I didn't say a word because between cries of pain Maso was confessing. "It's been ten years, not one day! And this evening you beat the crap out of me! Okay, you lost your brother . . . but why take it out on me?"

In short, I discovered that our dear bar keeper at the Due Porte had been having an affair with that particular relation of mine who is resting eternally in a burial niche with my name on it. They'd meet at midnight for a quickie, usually on the third day of the week. This was the debris of my twin's life that had landed on my lap. "You could at least say sorry!" he went on, snot dripping into his mouth. "What have I done to you? Why did you beat me, and why are you looking at me like you're disgusted?"

It was easy to make up a story for his wife. We told her that once he had thrown all the last drinkers out into the coolness of the street, he had closed the bar as he did every night. And that I had gone out to get a breath of air since sleep had had no intention of knocking at my door that evening. I had been walking along minding my own business when I had heard a moaning sound. When I turned into the passageway where the water fountain was, I found him on the floor in agony.

"That'll teach you to stop acting like a teenager," Clelia yelled at him as she accompanied him to open the roller shutter. "Am I supposed to tolerate a seventy-year-old like you coming home stinking of Vermouth?" He scowled, his leg set straight in the plaster cast, but he didn't close the Due Porte, not even for one afternoon.

And yet, his face melted whenever he saw me walk past. After a week, the drinkers had forgotten the Serraglini family was in mourning and they were back to hawking up loogies on the sidewalk and making comments. Maso gripped tight onto his crutches, sighing like a lover. He looked like a parrot on a perch. He stared at me with that death stare of the betrayed Sicilian. I realized he was still in love with me and that I had cut him off just like that. After all, killing your twin is one thing, taking it up the ass for him is another.

Sometimes I ask myself point-blank, "Achille, are you sorry you caved your brother's head in?" I think for a minute and answer with my gut. "Not in the slightest, my friend. If anything, I'm proud of it."

Physically, and in the way we walked, we were identical. For the rest, we were as different as night and day. For example, I never cared about old stuff and I never wanted a Swiss boyfriend. He would send me a card every Christmas which went straight into the fire without even peeling the foreign stamp off first. When we were kids, I would spend afternoons looking for some nice chard seeds to plant, while he sat at a desk over his books, growing sick of life. Going even further back, the pack of kids I used to hang around with didn't even want to come over to our house for a snack in case they caught whatever disease he had. At school, I always sat on the other side of the classroom to show everyone what was what: my brother was born a pervert, but I was different.

Angiolino got in my way from the very first day he came into this world one minute after me. He made my mother cry and my father angry, but no amount of belting would set him straight. Quite the opposite. As soon as my father got his belt out, Angiolino would speak in a girl's voice to spite him. They wouldn't invite me to parties so as not to have to invite him. If he liked something, I had to say it was for faggots. If he went for white, I chose black, and vice versa. People wonder how I came out so bad-tempered and muscular . . . But later, the world went crazy and he suddenly became the popular one.

That was difficult. He was shooting blanks with a clove-footed mountain creature. A goat with a bank account worthy of the thousand and one nights whom he had met in Siena in a boudoir with crystal chandeliers and wall-to-wall mirrors. They would arrive laden with gifts and all the relatives would fall at their feet. Except me, who wouldn't even shake his hand. Even less that of his red-headed cheese-eater friend with a face like a half moon who was always happy for no reason.

Sonia would say it so often she made me weep: "That big cellar in the Bianciardi house is up for sale at a bargain. It's adjacent to our wall here. All we'd need to do is knock through the kitchen and we'd have a millionaire's basement." I would reply simply, "I'm a miner." For a normal person that should have been enough. And yet she would go on in the same tune, "The old people have been dead a while. All the other Bianciardis have a life elsewhere and don't give two hoots about the apartment here . . . it's gift-wrapped with a bow on it! It would double the value of our property!" As if with an extra hobby room, we wouldn't be just the same as always. I felt like taking her on a tour down the mine shaft to make her understand once and for all how a spade-face like me makes a living. Then, one afternoon out of the blue, Sonia said, "I told

Angiolino." I stared at her without saying a word. She stuck her hand in her apron pocket and pulled out a sheet of paper. "He says it's an investment for the whole family . . . this is the contract with all the permits."

I went straight to that twin brother of mine to tell it to his face. "I won't be indebted to anyone," I said, tossing the crumpled contract on the floor at his feet. He had this way of looking at me, like a second-rate actress about to bleat out her lines. I decided to make myself even clearer, "I don't need to be spoon-fed. I don't need that faggot you've dragged over from abroad to give me an extra room . The obscene spectacle of the two of you mincing down the street in town is more than enough." Angiolino's face changed suddenly and he looked like a peeved squire. To make me even angrier, he said, "The cellar is in your name now. If you don't want it, let it go to ruin." And that's what I did for the next ten years.

Every now and again, Sonia tried to bring the subject up. "It's such a waste having the keys to that room and letting it rot." Worse, she hated the fact that we twin brothers wouldn't speak to each other even at a distance. Not even a phone call on our birthday. I was fine with it. In the meantime, I made Angiolino pay the property tax on the giant cellar. If an injunction were to come in, I would go straight to Via di Mezzo and donate the place to the local council.

When the Swiss boyfriend died in an accident, I went into the kitchen and popped a bottle of champagne. From one day to the next, after a lifetime out in the world, that twin of mine came back to live in Le Case. Sonia was close to him and made sure he didn't suffer too much heartbreak. I saw her go out, carrying a crock pot with a lid on it, and I didn't bother to ask her where she was going. Then, one day, Divo made the mistake of looking at me as he was making a rude quip, thinking I was the other twin. I gave him the whole treatment: twenty days in hospital and two months at home with his leg in traction.

But he made me pay dearly for all those broken ribs and his squashed nose that looked like a tomato. The thrashing he received ended up in the local paper, with Yours Truly named as the responsible party. Then I had to hand over my life savings to that cuckold and the to the lawyers in Ribolla. But there was never enough and eventually Angiolino was called in to empty his pockets. When Sonia told me she'd convinced him to help, I answered by saying, "It was his duty. Divo's drubbing was Angiolino's fault." I still think it was.

There is no doubt, life is full of funny twists. My twin brother disgusted me so much I wanted to climb the walls. He incarnated all the things that were wrong with me, bagged up into one body. Now I've turned into him. I walk like him. I talk like him. I wear his clothes that smell like a girl's. But I still have to be careful, even as the thousandth day approaches. Last month I was coughing so loud the windows shook and, in the end, I had to call Dr. Salghini to come and check out my chest. I didn't want to die twice, the first time in the open and the second time out of sight. Salghini arrived carrying his doctor's bag, his face like a death knell. As soon as he walked in, he stopped in his tracks and started sniffing around, his big fat nose in the air, filling up his lungs with deep breaths. "There's something not quite right here." I was standing there in those dainty little sandals my brother used to wear in the house. "It looks fine to me, Doctor. Let's get on with it. I need a check-up. With all the catarrh I've expectorated we could open a jam factory . . . "

"Expectorated." In order to stay in character with the man who still poisons my days even though he's dead, I've had to study his vocabulary. I wouldn't have dreamed of using words like "querulous" or "puerile" before. When I go to my old house to pay Sonia a visit, I drink my tea with my pinky up in the air and say it's "exquisite."

I must say, though, Angiolino may have made me sick but I can imitate him perfectly. Everyone falls for it, even my wife who slept in the same bed as me for a bucketload of years. I know his face so well, identical to mine but peakier, with a needy expression, especially when he was running out of money after having to pay back Divo's medical expenses. "Achille," he would say to me, "Why don't you sell me the Bianciardi cellar back? I need some breathing space." I always had my answer ready, "I've never asked anything of you, so why don't you follow my example?" His eyes would glow like hot coals. "I've been eating nothing but bread and onions for a week. When you really needed help, I chipped in without batting an eyelid. You're just mean, that's all." And he loped off, holding back his crocodile tears. I shouted after him, over his head as always, "I'm different. Especially from you."

When he came to tell me that he'd found a little treasure, though, his expression was different. There he was, with an old book in his hands that he'd found in a dusty attic somewhere. It was called *The Mysteries of Paris*. I shrugged my shoulders. "What am I supposed to do with that?" His expression tightened. "I'm not interested in the book. It's the sheet of paper inside that interests me." He opened the tome and took some yellowing sheets out from between the leaves. He started reading them out loud.

They were random sweet nothings scribbled down on April 7, '84 regarding me and Mariella Mantovani back in the day when we were making out in the Ponentis' vineyards. Sins of the flesh committed when I was thirty and horny after ten years with a ring on my finger. That woman had the devil in her, I tell you. She threw herself into things as passionately as if she were actually in love, but she never climaxed, even after I'd jiggled around for over an hour and was starting to get bored. "I love you," she would moan, her eyes sparkling. Then she would urge me on. "Achille, go on. Don't take any notice if I scream out in pain. Harder, hammer me harder." The fling lasted a few weeks. On my way back home after my shift, I would go up to the old town the back way, avoiding Via di Mezzo. Mariella would come from the alley, the one near the Pretella gate. We would run out of the old town and tumble onto the grass like teenagers. She kept saying, "I love you," and this scared me because getting on with what we were doing was enough without gift-wrapping it. We weren't exactly planning on starting a family. Then I would go home to Sonia and tell her I'd missed the two o'clock bus. Or that I'd stopped in the square to meet my buddies down at the benches outside St. Bastian's. One day she said, "You've missed the bus after work a lot in the last month, and you normally fly straight back like a homing pigeon. Anyway, I can't imagine you sitting on a bench blabbering. I wish you talked a bit more when you're home, that's all!" That's when I stopped the affair.

And now, there was my twin, with those memories hidden in a book that must have been gathering dust in Le Case for at least two decades, left there by Mariella who knows when. Angiolino stopped reading and looked me straight in the eye. "Are you going to sell me the cellar now? Or would you like me to send these love letters to you know who?" That bastard. After all the kindness Sonia had shown him. There he was using her to blackmail me. I was about to say something when he stopped me, waving the sheets in my face. "I have a copy of these and I'm the only one who knows where. Think carefully before opening your mouth." I lowered my eyes and didn't speak for a whole minute. Then I looked up. "Let's go and see if that damned cellar is in a fit state after all the years we've let it go to wrack and ruin. Then we'll decide on a price."

Sonia, with a rag in her hand, saw me come back in from my walk, but I didn't hang my jacket up. Her jaw dropped when she saw Angiolino. Seeing us together after so long must have given her a shock. She watched me take the key off the hook to the cellar that had never been used. "Shall I put the coffee pot on?" she said. I didn't bother answering.

Trying to turn the key in the rusty lock that had been untouched for so long nearly broke my hand off, but in the end the door creaked open. In the dim light that filtered in from the street, it was the first time I had ever set eyes on the Bianciardis' cellar.

A curse nearly escaped my lips: the cellar was amazing! It was full of abandoned furniture. There was even an old racing bike, exactly like the one our poor Babbo used to have. There was a stone arch dividing the space in two. Angiolino opened one of the drawers in a dresser. I heard the rattling of tools. And then I heard him say, "This place is a gold-mine." I scoffed, "I know what a mine looks like. This place is a palace in comparison." My twin wasn't listening. He was feverishly opening and shutting cupboards, lifting up sheets that shed fat spiders and giant lice. Then he pulled an old vinyl record out of somewhere and wiped it clean with his coat sleeve. "I can't believe it . . . " he started whimpering. "I can't believe it . . . this alone is worth ten of these cellars." He started to turn around to show me his treasure. The blow to his temple knocked him to the ground hard.

I pulled the door to, leaving a chink of light so that I wouldn't bang my own head on some old piece of farm equipment. I put the table leg back where I had found it, in a damp, rotten basket full of filthy junk, and squatted over my brother, feeling for his face in the dark. I covered his nose and mouth with my hands and started counting in my head: "One, two, three . . . "

By the time I got to twenty-four, Angiolino had stopped struggling. He'd been kicking like crazy and reaching out with both hands for something to grab on to. But he had been weakened by the strike to the head. "Thirty-eight, thirty-nine . . . " I held my head right back so I wouldn't get any scratches on my face. I listened as his heels banged against the flagstones, echoing around the cellar. "Forty-eight, forty-nine . . . "

Angiolino died when I got to sixty-four, exactly his age. And then they say it's all coincidence. Just to be sure, I held on for another two minutes at least. Holding my twin brother's head in my lap for the first time in my life made me feel a modicum of tenderness. But then I got to my feet. I had to clean myself up a bit. I locked the door of the cellar and went home. When Sonia saw me hang my jacket on the peg, she murmured, "Don't tell me you've made up your mind." I looked at her and nodded.

That night I took her into my arms for the last time. I buried my head in her hair so that I could breathe in the smell of her. I hugged her tight and kissed her on the forehead and on the mouth. We never talked while we were at it, but this time she whispered, "Why are you trembling?" I answered her with more kisses, on her neck and all over her body.

After making love, Sonia fell into a deep sleep. I waited until the bell up in the tower struck four and then I got up. I dressed in the same clothes I'd been wearing the day before. I stood in front of our bed for a couple of minutes, trying to send my tears back where they came from. I leaned down and gave her a kiss on each eyelid. She hardly moved. I left the house, going past the kitchen where Pepita was dozing on a chair, and stroked her one last time.

Back in the cellar, I started undressing Angiolino. He was already stiff and as I moved him, little bubbles of gas popped out of his mouth. At one point, I thought I was going to have to use the table leg on him again. I dressed him in my own clothes, down to the underpants. And I put on his, drenched in that disgusting effeminate perfume. When I had to put my wedding ring on his finger, I felt sick because it felt like I was marrying him.

Before leaving, I checked out the alley both ways. The half-hour bell rang. I said to myself, "Le Case is dead at five in the evening, so at five in the morning there won't be a soul." I went back inside, heaved Angiolino over my shoulder, and headed out into the thick December fog.

I placed his body in a sitting position, his legs splayed sideways, on the Barberinis' doorstep, at the point where the ice on the slope makes it slippery. Then I walked straight back up the hill again. Jingling in my pocket were the keys to the house I've lived in ever since, like some freak, to borrow a turn of phrase from my inverted twin. At least I can still go out and get the newspapers in the morning.

What made the whole thing believable was the stubble that had continued to grow on my dead brother's chin overnight, giving him that shadow of a beard that I usually sported. I was more worried about our hands, because that was how people could have told us apart. Mine were the hands of a worker, while his were as soft as a maiden's. One of those girls who leaf through books all day and put cream on their hands at night. Yet, one look had been enough to convince the whole town and it was Sonia who sealed it with her wailing. "Ever since he retired, he started going out early in the morning sometimes. I told him he wasn't young anymore. Those slabs of ice that form in December have split more than one head over the years. Achille, my love, Achille . . . " she moaned, "what will I do without you?"

They didn't even do any tests. The man they had found dead on the doorsteps was me. He had my wallet, my ID, my wedding ring on his finger. The deep ridge on my ring finger would have given the game away but it was winter and I covered myself up and wore gloves. Even now, I keep my left hand hidden when I go out in public. The furrow left after years of marriage is hard to conceal.

When they came to give me the news, I answered the door in this frilly dressing gown, the one I still wear when I'm at home. I made a scene and pretended I was going to faint. During the wake, I greeted everyone in silence and kept my eyes on the ground. Ditto at the funeral. I walked on Sonia's arm, my gloved hands deep in my coat pockets. I felt a little dizzy when they plastered the burial crypt closed with the last tile. I had been so involved in the unfolding of events that for a second, I convinced myself I was being interred. I felt like I had disappeared into the tomb and in some ways, I had. People thought my vertigo was a symptom of grief and they walked me home.

Living Angiolino's life led to endless discoveries. To start with, to avoid being caught out, I wolfed down all his books. I tidied up his notes and diaries. I wasted reams of paper practicing my twin's writing and signature. Then something happened and I finally understood that my situation was a double-edged sword: my brother had been an antique dealer and art lover and the more I digested his world the better I liked it. Angiolino had been good at his job. While I had wasted my life toiling down the mine shafts so that I could buy a fridge when I got back up, he had gone around looking for abandoned treasures. Treasures that I have now inherited as if they were a gift. I don't feel a bit guilty, though. The most precious things in the world are worth nothing compared to witnessing Sonia's expression after a betrayal. I'd rather she believed I'm dead than unfaithful. I'd rather she went crazy. I'd rather the idea of my love for her stayed as solid as the foundations of St. Bastian's, forever.

This house is magic: every day some little object turns up. Dried flowers and postcards from faraway places drop out of books. And I continue to add to the accumulation of old stuff, an accidental connoisseur. Then, last month, this funny thing happened: I'm rummaging around in the Ginanneschi cellar, fighting off the cobwebs, and what do I come across? A record. Exactly the same as the one Angiolino had in his hand a moment before bashing his face on the floor. I tell the family I want to show it to the trader that comes up to Le Case every couple of weeks to check out my discoveries. Just as my brother did when he was still in the land of the living. Then I walk down the Via di Mezzo with his last words hammering in my head: "I can't believe it . . . I can't believe it."

It's a 78-rpm disc in a black sleeve with no writing on it. The label on the record must have once been gold but it's now a faded yellow diarrhea color. The date is illegible. It's full of scratches but none of them are deep enough to make the needle jump.

When I died, the ownership of the cellar that once belonged to the Bianciardi family was passed on to Sonia. I was the one to persuade her, "Sell it. You'll be able to set aside some savings, which is never a bad thing." The Ginanneschis were interested, even though they live two streets away. People seem to like piling up all the junk in their lives, without ever throwing anything away. They made an offer on what would have made me a very nice basement if I hadn't been such a blockhead. In order to make space for their own bric-a-brac, they had to get rid of the clutter that was already there. Even the memory of what remains can be paid for with a check. And yet, they saved that record. Who knows why they set it aside and took it down to their underground cellar carved out of the rock. Only for me, of all people, to find it last month.

Laughter. The disc has laughter recorded on it, on both sides. When I first heard it, it gave me a turn. I wondered, "Why would someone record all this mirth? What for?" I listened and listened. Angiolino's gramophone is gilded. There's a hissing background noise but it works like new. Guffaws. Like sea waves. First there's almost nothing, a quiet chuckle, then it rises to a peak: people hooting with laughter, rolling in the aisles. It's real. The kind of cackle you can't command. You would notice if it was a choked titter in the throat. There are also knee slaps, and people stamping their feet as if they desperately needed a piss. Then all goes quiet. Getting ready for a new burst of high spirits all over again.

When Giancarlo came up to Le Case, I showed him the record at the end of a long sequence of knickknacks and pictures by country bumpkin Sunday-painters that had hung over some fireplace or other in the region. He inspected the first bits and pieces without registering any excitement. When he came to the 78-rpm disc, his pupils suddenly shrank to the size of a snake's. "And this little treasure?" he said, attempting to get his hands on it.

Out of everyone, Giancarlo is the one who has put me in the greatest jeopardy. More than Sonia and all those characters I grew up with, working shifts together for a lifetime. The trader from Amiata was all of a sudden having to deal with a different Angiolino. An Angiolino who talked about antique books and vintage craft work in a random manner. One of the first times we met up, he said, "Maybe you're still grieving. Your head is not straight yet. You know better than me that in this job you can be cheated and lose a few months' earnings in no time at all. You need to get some rest." I knew quite a bit about Louis Philippe armchairs, which the attics of Le Case seem to be bursting with, even though they usually need re-upholstering. I had just left my life behind and I still thought that a pink marble washstand with a bowl and pitcher attached was one of those things you would dump in the landfill together with broken washing machines and mattresses that have rotten under diseased backsides.

I told him I'd bought the record from a family, without giving any names. And that for the moment it wasn't on sale. Remembering my twin's last words, I said, "I know it's quite valuable but I don't get why a piece like this is worth anything. I have read about it somewhere but I can't remember where."

Giancarlo asked me if he could listen to it. He watched me as if I were handling the holy grail. When the disc started to turn, he closed his eyes. There were the first mumbles, the throat-clearing I knew by heart at that point. Followed by the first snickers. Until the full-blown chortling burst out. "Marvelous," he said. To him, it was akin to angels singing.

It worked like this. They put people in a theater somewhere.

On stage, they mimed actions and then recorded the audience's guffaws. They sold the discs to poor wretches who spent their lives scraping at the depths of misery, breaking their backs in the dark to bring what passed for dinner to the table. At the end of the day, these poor bastards sat around the fire and wound up the gramophone to hear people who were better off than them, howling with laughter.

Giancarlo looked possessed when he said, "Just think, they're all dead. There are probably fewer than five of these records still in circulation. In the whole world, I mean. I know some collectors with a taste for the macabre who would sell their mothers to get their hands on this reliquary. I can make you a very good offer." He has been wooing me ever since. The last time, he made eyes at me as if he were willing to pull down his pants if I let him take home that recording of rich people eaten by worms over a century ago splitting their sides.

I can't stop listening to it. It makes me shudder but the urge is stronger than my capacity to resist it. Like when you sit and watch a daddy longlegs with legs like pube hairs and see-through bodies hiding behind the furniture: your hairs stand on end with disgust but you still sit and stare at them for hours. As I listen, I move things around, or open a tome I haven't looked at yet sitting by the fire . . . two days ago, I made a new discovery.

There's a loose tile between the bedroom and the sitting room. I've always known it because as I walk past, it makes a tapping noise. The other day, I bent down and looked a bit closer. The ceramic tile came up in my hand.

The first thing I thought of was my father who always said, "The apartments in Le Case have eyes and ears. I'm not just saying it." When I was a kid, I used to fantasize about this all the time. I imagined a town where every room led into another room in an infinite chain. A town like Le Case which ended up being one house, full of stone and brick passageways that led into every single dwelling, including the churches and the tower. At the time, I dreamed of stepping suddenly out of the Ferrari's wardrobe and spending an hour devouring their sex-crazed little flower.

Angiolino didn't deserve it, but he had a father who cared about him anyway. Babbo always said, "You were born twins so I had to work twice as hard." And in order to prepare the ground, he divided the nice house he had inherited from his parents and put the ground floor up for sale. It was the '50s, the roads had been rebuilt after the war, and the Maremma valley was as good as new. Anyone who wanted to start out again and make an honest living found fertile ground here. For example, Mattafirri started baking cookies in the cellar and selling them in the stores. He was so good, and there were so many requests, that he transformed the house into a bakery. And he bought our ground floor, which was nice and spacious, and brought his lovely Esedra with him. Babbo looked us straight in the eye and said, waving the receipt in our face, "With this nest egg, I'll buy an apartment for the first of you to get married." Now Sonia is sitting there in that apartment, wilting in front of my eyes.

I peered down into the gap under the tile. In the middle, there was a cork set in the cement. A stopper. I pulled at it and it came away.

A hole. Between the bedroom and the sitting room there's a hole that goes all the way to the floor below. The bottom of the cork has been painted white, in order to camouflage it against the ceiling downstairs. Who knows when?

Because Babbo was not the type to blow his trumpet for no reason. When I was a kid, I'd take stories of hidden spy holes and secret hiding places to bed and think about them for hours. "They were precautions that were necessary in the old days, when the Germans would burst in unexpectedly with their rifles drawn," my father told us. I thought back to those words as I looked down through the hole. "There were lots of partisans who came to Le Case to get themselves patched up or to get a decent meal after weeks hiding in the woods." It was like in those cartoons where pictures have eyes, or a piece of a wall suddenly opens into a portcullis and reveals a burial crypt. At the time, nobody bothered covering the peep holes up with plaster. My father simply closed off the stairwell and split the building into two parts, handing the downstairs keys over to Esedra's husband. If I'd known it was there when I was a kid, I would have spent my days face down on the floor.

I sit there with my thoughts. Dead people's laughter around me. And I say to myself, "Dear Angiolino, now I learn you're a peeping Tom to boot." A moment later, I'm flat on the floor.

Peeping into Esedra's living room is a stab in the stomach because I was born in that room and I haven't set eyes on it since I was eight years old. I feel suddenly homesick, as if that room were spying on me. "Look, Achille. I'm still here and I remember those days . . . " This is what it feels like it is telling me through all that silence. In the meantime, I squash my face against the dusty edge and when I get up, there is a grimy mark on my cheek.

There I am, stretched out like a madman, going over and over this discovery in my head. All of a sudden, I hear two loud bangs. A second later, I see Chiaretta's son walk right under my nose. I jump up with a jerk, pulling a nerve in my neck as I do so.

We all used to fancy Chiaretta. Not as much as the Ferrari girl but almost. She had a look about her, as if she were on view in a store window. She had pale skin, red lips, and gray eyes. A soulless gray, or rather a gray has stolen your soul. Chiaretta wasn't the kind of mare you could rein in easily under the covers at night. She was born in Le Case like all of us, but she acted as though she'd descended upon us from another world. She hardly ever laughed and, more than anything else, that was what made me fall in love with her. In fact, I resented it when she started going out with that foreign guy, even though I already had Sonia under my thumb. People said he was French, or German . . . Whatever, he stuck a baby in her belly and there she was, pregnant. After giving birth, nobody ever heard from them again, they vanished off the face of the earth . They left the baby for Esedra to look after, a gift for her old age.

I'm watching the kid now through a hole in the floor. He's been the hot topic in Le Case for the past twenty days or so. They say he has done something terribly wrong and has come back here to lick his wounds. I've never been interested in gossip. What I know is this: if Samuele's grandmother had not been mother and father to him, if he had not been her light and life, I'd be looking through this spyhole into the darkness of an empty apartment instead of a room with a kid walking around in it. We all have skeletons in our closet we have to deal with in the middle of the night.

And yet, the first time I heard movement downstairs it was a shock. After the Swiss boyfriend died, Angiolino took full possession of the apartment and he often used to say, "Lucky for me that Esedra is there. She knocks on my door every afternoon and we chat about this and that for half an hour over a cup of tea. Or we sometimes shell some roasted chestnuts together. We knock goodnight to one another: she knocks on the ceiling and I knock on the floor. It's her way of staying close."

When I first heard those steps a few evenings ago, I thought it was my twin's ghost, from when we were young and used to live downstairs, when it was part of the same house I'm living in now. I stayed up all night, my heart in a little ball. I had prepared a speech just in case his head suddenly rose up out of the floor. "Dear brother, are you trying to torture me even after your death? Let me die so that I can come over there and murder you again, I'll send you into the hell of hells. Aren't you happy with the price I'm paying? I'm not even sullying your reputation. Now look at me, Angiolino. Look at me and answer this question: which of us do you think is the real ghost here?"

The tile presents you with a stark choice: either you look or you listen. Two days ago, I nearly twisted my neck trying to get both my ear and my eye lined up with the hole. A bit of one and a bit of the other, according to what is going on. Because there are some things going on down there that are really quite peculiar.

I saw Samuele standing in front of the door. Only from the waist down and back-lit. He was talking to someone who had come over at two o'clock in the afternoon when most of the inhabitants of Le Case were deep into their siesta. I turned my head, making the bones in my neck crunch. My ear flattened over the hole. I heard a girl's voice say, "You won't believe what has happened." Then there were some movements. I swapped my ear for my eye.

The light had change and there was Eleonora, the girl Mario hired to work in the store after Adelaide was taken ill. She was standing there hugging herself as if ice were eating her from inside, and she was shaking. She looked around and muttered something I couldn't make out.

Samuele was standing a few steps away staring at her. He was shaking his head. I stuck my ear back on the hole. "I can't go back," she wailed. "Let me stay here. Nobody saw me coming."

I was so desperate to see the scene that I heard a crack in my neck. My head was ringing so loud that for a second, I thought they would be able to hear it from downstairs. But they had other things on their mind. Eleonora was gesticulating, he was answering in short outbursts. I had been in the same position for so long that I started to get pins and needles. Blood was pumping in my temples as if my heart had been moved to the middle of my skull. I saw the girl go stiff. He came to her side and hugged her tight.

I turned onto my back. It took a while to get my breath back, my blood prickling my skin as it started circulating normally. The recorded guffaws had stopped playing a while ago, the needle had jumped the last groove of the 78-rpm record and was bumping up against the label. I said to myself, "I don't know what's going on. Evidently, Samuele and Eleonora, Mario's assistant, are having an affair."

At my age, and with the awkward role I have to play, I shouldn't be thinking these things, but I would gladly have taken the place of that crooked grandson Esedra had brought up and accepted the girl's effusions. "Let me stay," she had said. "I can't go back." I would have let that Eleonora stay with me in a flash, with her dark eyes and rolling tears. If only to sate the lust that has been lying dormant in my body for so long. I can't even pleasure myself because, if I do, my brain splits into two and I feel as though I'm giving my dead twin a handjob. It makes me want to retch and whatever urge I may have felt shrivels to nothing.

Ultimately, what I'd really like to know has nothing to do with whatever troubles these two young people are going through: did Angiolino use to spy on the house downstairs? If he did, he must have done so when Esedra was still alive, when Samuele had the peach fuzz of a fifteen-year-old. The idea of it makes my skin crawl with disgust because it proves I had been saddled not only with a faggot for a twin brother, but also with a pervert who may have got his kicks by peeping at children . . . What really kills me is that, the way things stand, I am right here doing the same disgusting things he did, including the peeping. I am living under an eternal curse that is punishing me yet again for having taken the life of my own flesh and blood. Suddenly, I see the snapshot of me that emerges at this point in the story: in my body and in my everyday life, I am imitating the gestures and obsessions of that brother whose heart and soul are constantly flitting around the apartment where Sonia lives so that I can't even make love to her under the cover of night anymore.

If he had died at birth, it would have been better for everyone. Sometimes I see Sonia walk up the street carrying her shopping on her way back from the graveyard. I have to hide in the nearest alleyway to get my heartbeat and shaking under control, just like when we were young ourselves. The difference being that, back then, I would rush back home to practice in the mirror inviting her to the midsummer ball, where everything started. Whereas now, I'm stuck here inside these four walls. In the background, there's a record hissing on the turntable. With dead people poking fun at me.

Susanna Cocchi,
the Hotel Proprietor

Sergeant, I assure you that I, the undersigned, believe in the rule of law, not that of the church. If I really must demonstrate my respect, I'd rather bend down and kiss the stripes on someone like Lieutenant Corsi's uniform rather than the hem of a priest's robe.

Don Lauro is a decent person. I don't mean him. Even though he has the approach of a crow dressed in black that caws when it smells tragedy in the air. In these fitful days, you can see him hurrying through the streets as if he had a pan on the fire, while the real work is going on here at the carabiniere station where no time is lost reciting the Lord's Prayer and the officers are trying to give a name to the delinquents who are ruining the tranquility of this town. Because here at Le Case that's how it goes: nothing happens for a thousand years then one fine day, disasters strike all at once, and then some . . . I'm talking about what happened to poor Filippo, the youngest Nencioni kid.

What can I tell you? Even the stones know that he was reputed to be a half-wit, though many people claimed he used it to his advantage. Maybe that was his way of winning the game: living off his family, waited on hand and foot, never having to lift a finger to move half a log at the sawmill. But he was a good kid. He wasn't wild and his smile was so pure his eyes shone. Whenever I was about town, he would always ask me the same thing, "Signora Susanna, is there a lot of business at the Bel Sole? Can I come and see the tourists?" In the Summer he had his favorite spot in the breakfast room, which is the same as the lunch and dinner room. Filippo used to like seeing new people. I used to let him take them their warm milk and cocoa, as long as he didn't bother anyone with his stupid questions. Maybe I shouldn't be saying this but one morning he even saw his own dad come down the stairs with that little woman from Montemassi who has been doing the accounts at the mill forever. It was almost midday. Filippo lifted his head and was about to shout something to get his father's attention. I caught him just in time by yanking him away by one ear. "He's a client too," I told him. He gawped at me with that half-wit stare. Then he shifted his gaze to the door and saw his father close it behind him, giving the secretary's backside a pat as he went out. After that, he went back to eyeing the French visitors.

Sergeant, just to be clear: our job is to provide rooms to whomever asks for them and to keep other people's business to ourselves. What happens in there is a no-man's land. As long as I keep within the letter of the law, needless to say. We even have a back entrance, which is useful for people who don't want to be seen around the Bel Sole at an unusual time of day, especially in the afternoon, because that's when our rooms fill up and the lampshades start to swing. There could be an earthquake and they wouldn't know it.

Oh, if I wanted to, I could write a cuckoldry primer, arranging all the intrepid husbands and playful wives from half the province into alphabetical order. An array of different people who come up to the Bel Sole, locals and out-of-towners. In fact, there's a certain level of activity at the bus stop. Especially when the 4:00 P.M. bus pulls in. But any bestiary of these sexcapades would be without end. Normal people can't even begin to imagine what goes on in a hotel room. An example? A couple married forever arrange an illicit tryst and order a nice bottle of champagne at their bedside. I mean, couldn't they fuck at home without forking out so much? The thrill of waving cash around must help the gentleman raise his flag and moisten the lady's beaver . . . If you told some of these stories, people would say you had gone soft in the head. Some days are chili-pepper hot, with husband downstairs and wife upstairs. Each with a lover. That's when we have to work double shifts because our customers' privacy is paramount, and we want to avoid scenes in the corridors at all costs. Then there are husbands who are queer, wives too, who discover pussy late in life. Daughters with fancy lovers from Civitella while their mothers, dressed to the nines and made up for a party, have it off with visitors from Sammontana. Just to say that blood is thicker than water . . . This is why we need to keep a calendar. A phone call from a certain gentleman with his dick in a twist? I check the list of bookings and say, "Sorry, nothing available." Which means, "Listen, handsome, there's already someone here airing out your family stink ." The man gets the message and moans as if he were in agony. He hates the idea that he's not the only one in the family engaging in subterfuge. He books another day.

This is what it means to manage a little hotel in the province of Maremma, where the two-timers, both men and women, never stop. Then they all go to Mass at eleven on Sunday. It must be the boredom, or creeping old age, that ruins them all. So, they resort to a bit of flabby hanky-panky, and every now and again we have to call an ambulance because some old geezer's heart flits from his balls to his throat from one moment to the next.

Sergeant, this is all to say that we need a hundred eyes open even in low season. You certainly can't blame me if we haven't been taking poor Filippo's words seriously, may his young soul rest in eternal peace. Like everyone else, we only noticed when it all blew up in our face.

Sure, he would talk about it sometimes. He would approach me with the air of a spy and say, "Signora Susanna, I've found a treasure that needs digging up. When I've put it in the bank, I'll reserve a room in the hotel, too. Maybe for a whole year." He was so cute . . . He had decided that he wanted to be considered a client. "It's a shiny treasure," he went on, his face melting into a marshmallow mush. "I dig a little on Sundays, up there in the woods a hundred yards past the Bel Sole. But don't ask me where! I'm not stupid, you know."

The blast two days ago made all the windows in the hotel rattle. I said to myself, "After all the earthquake warnings, Le Case will be swallowed whole by a sinkhole." I peered out, expecting to see the old town sliding down, but nothing had changed. Then I looked over at the woods and saw a column of black smoke.

From what I read in the papers, they found a crater surrounded by tree trunks, split open like the backside of a heifer on heat. And scraps of iron with still-sizzling flesh seared onto them. They recognized poor Filippo from shreds of his clothes, shreds which continued to flutter around all afternoon and ended up being snagged by the branches of the chestnut trees or strewn across the Bel Sole car park. As well as the fine dust I had to sweep up myself. I talked to him as I worked, "Filippo, here you are in dust motes. You should have told me the treasure was an undetonated WWII bomb, sitting there buried since 1943." I was stupid not to have asked for more details and I should be arrested on the spot for not doing so. I've been itching all over for two days. The thought of the dead boy's ashes landing on my skin drives me crazy and I wash my hair one more time.

This is what comes of leaving a retard son to prowl the streets like a stray. In this ageing town, Filippo had no friends and so he connected with anyone who paid him any attention. He once said to me, "Babbo doesn't want me messing around at the sawmill because I'm such a moron I may come a mucker. His way of protecting me is to cut me loose so I can wander around all day. Anyway, I'm not complaining!" And this is what you get.

A closed coffin with nothing inside. Just a photograph, a clump of hair, and a pair of half-burnt shoes. Since the explosion, I can't eat in the evenings because it feels like I'm munching on sand and my stomach clenches. I end up talking to him. I say, "Filippo, my dear boy. Stop flying around the hotel in particles. You're making us all sick with nerves . . . "

I feel a knot in my stomach, Sergeant. One I won't easily forget. It's always unsettling to think of a lad that age up in heaven, however challenged he was. This is where Don Lauro disgusts me because, in the face of a tragedy like this, the church pews fill up again and he chants to his heart's content to the old folk. "Let us pray for his poor innocent soul," he says. And everybody sits there, heads bowed. Two hours earlier, they would have slammed their windows shut if they clapped eyes on Filippo Nencioni in the street. Now that he is dead, owing to practically everyone's neglect, they're queuing up to say, "Poor boy." If they'd only listened to him for ten minutes rather than turning their heads the other way; they all avoided being stopped in the street by his nonsensical babbling. It was only because he had no one to talk to. And then we act shocked that a lad like him kills time up in the woods and eventually comes up with a little surprise. The procession of filthy-minded old folk I saw this morning behind the hearse was so disgusting I wanted to machine gun the lot of them. And if I had, I'd still be here with you, dear Sergeant, confessing and thinking I would spend the rest of my days in jail. But at least my heart would feel lighter for having cleansed the world of such scum. The kind of crud that cannot be bleached white by sitting in a pew at St. Bastian's for ten minutes.

The truth is that in Le Case, things come back to haunt you after sixty years. They originate before you're born and ride out all the storms just so they can detonate in your hand when the moment is right. Le Case is full of traps, the worst of which are the sick, twisted minds of its inhabitants. This is why, Sergeant,

I intend to carry on talking and to touch on another subject I know you are concerned about.

I still remember people snarling and lashing out when old Nencioni gave those Albanian migrants work at the sawmill. It wasn't that long ago. Two years at the most. My fellow townspeople, who make me want to throw up, would elbow each other whenever a boy whose roots were on the other side of the Adriatic walked past. "They're here to steal our jobs," they would grouch. As if this place was brimming with young muscle willing to exert itself in anything remotely tiring. The last young people in this town couldn't wait to get out at least twenty years ago and they never regretted it, abandoning forever their family homes as their parents' bones were polished off by worms. The nastiest were the women perched on their terraces with binoculars. "The riff-raff we didn't kill off during the war is back with a vengeance," the calmest of them would say. It took less than a month for the waters to settle and then suddenly all the rooms at the Bel Sole were taken, especially on Sunday morning. The church bells up in the old town would call the faithful to mass while down here the third-floor rooms were taken by storm. The same ladies, well into their sixties, who used to burble from their balconies were suddenly giving themselves a makeover, flitting in an out of the back entrance like shadows, kicking their cracked heels in the air while a young buck slammed into them, and receiving a return delivery of their own nasty words directly to their nether regions. Young lads who knew at most a couple of Italian words but knew the language of insult by heart and knew how to shove it home to the hilt, commas and all.

I may be venting a little, Sergeant, but events over the last few days have fanned my anger. The inhabitants of this cesspit sit there waiting for an outsider to come by so that they can sling a few insults. It makes them look good in their own eyes because for a moment they feel important, even though life has always denied them this pleasure. I used to pity them a little but all that's left is disgust. Some days I feel like putting the hotel and all its contents up for auction so that I can shoot off with my nest egg to the other side of the world where people don't behave like dogs. Dogs that have spent their whole lives chucking down the same chow, dogs who pat each other on the back to congratulate themselves on Le Case having the best dog-treats ever.

Yes, I'm talking about the young girl from down in the valley who seems to have vanished into thin air. And here we are back to square one with the same doggerel as Filippo. Until a moment before, nobody took a blind bit of notice. If they did, it was just to gossip about how fast she climbed up to the old town. Now they look like a pack of penitents, cradling their faces as they murmur the Rosary. Of course, Don Lauro is laughing through his butt cheeks. More and more heads fill the pews and he can't believe his eyes. So, he puts on a pained look and bangs on about lost sheep and all the rest. Then he passes around the collection box.

Sergeant, I couldn't tell you what kind of girl she was, that Eleonora, who disappeared three days ago. But I do know what people were raving about and I'll leave the rest to your imagination. As usual, the crudest versions came from the mouths of the vipers slithering outside the old town walls and it's easy to understand why: Eleonora was young and they were not. The Albanian she was seeing was the one everyone fancied but I've never seen him near the Bel Sole. So, I'll say it loud and clear. If anyone asked me where to look for that girl, whose only fault was that she was in the flower of her youth, I certainly wouldn't go and turn inside out the apartments of those poor wretches who came over on boats to work for Nencioni and receive a pittance at the end of their shift for the trouble. I would go and search the cellars of those characters who are grinding with envy. The same characters who talk behind your back one day, and crawl on their knees in tears to the gates of the cemetery the next. If only they would burn in hell. Right now, while I'm talking.

And yet, it would take so little. If Le Case teaches you anything, it's that you need to content yourself with very little if you want to be happy. The town does you in when you are still in diapers, stripping you of any prospects you may have imagined for yourself, and at fifteen there you are wearing the same outfit that you grew out of a good while ago. If you lack the will or the means to leave this town built on a rock, you suddenly find yourself looking at the old walls from a new perspective. Once, they were the gates to the world. Now, they are the walls a prison and, rather than make your eyes glitter, they stifle you. Then you start lowering your sights. You say, "There are people who are worse off." And this is the cardinal sin that Don Lauro should be accusing everyone of. Because it turns into an alibi and eventually you start to believe it. You convince yourself that, given the way things are, this little hill town will provide you with the bare necessities for a sad excuse of a life. My mother used to repeat it like the Hail Mary, "Susanna, go and take a look around! Don't get het up about the hotel. Owning a property is an opportunity, not a cross to bear." But I didn't listen to her. If I had a votive card with her face on it, I'd be kissing it all day. Ruining your life for love is stupid enough, but trashing your whole life for a mere gesture of affection, what's more, one never to be reciprocated, is a curse, a curse that has been cast on me. By the time I realized, the train had already left the station and I had grown old standing on the platform. The age when I might have had children was waving goodbye to me with its little hand. It's like poor Filippo's bomb, except that it detonates in your heart all of a sudden, extirpating the whole town and Maremma with it. I wish it would blow up. The wasted days holler inside you forever, never leaving you in peace, not for an instant. Just like the promises that have never been kept of a peasant who has settled here and comes to visit with the excuse of a cup of coffee when he's feeling horny. First, he says, "Susanna, I'll marry you tomorrow." Then, suddenly, "We're too old now. We'll be the laughing stock of the whole town."

So, Sergeant, here is my version of events: the blame for everything lies squarely with this town. Le Case is like a tree. The things that happen to the people who live here are its rotten fruit. Poor Filippo was blown to smithereens because anyone who clings to the rock of St. Bastian's is on a mission to be indifferent and to curse everything and everyone. Even the disappearance of an attractive young girl from the valley is the result of this attitude. The character of the people in this town is like that of a monster, who every now and again lets out a roar, moving the curtains and making the ornaments look as though they have a life of their own. There is a moment of giddiness. To keep us all on edge. To tell us that we all belong to him rather than to ourselves. Anyone who leaves in time is saved. The ones who come back to these vertiginous heights go slightly mad. Or they are monsters seeking silence . . . And then there are all the others. Take the gang of Albanians with no homeland, Sergeant, who ended up here as outcasts. Or other characters such as Lieutenant Corsi, for example, sent from Viterbo to serve in a town where the mist makes it feel like it's perennially autumn. To the extent that you feel like saying, "To deserve a posting in Le Case, our dear lieutenant must have blotted his copy book. For eternity."

Giovanna Ginanneschi - 2
The Spinster

It happened one early morning. I was having breakfast. I heard Babbo coming back in from his walk to the Due Porte, where he goes to read the paper. He would bring me a fresh donut sometimes. As soon as he walked in, I heard him at the end of the corridor say, "Serena, come here a minute." Mamma scurried to the door and I heard the two of them talking softly. After a while, they came and stood outside the kitchen, peering in. I noticed that Babbo hadn't taken off his jacket or beret. Mamma came in looking grim. At one point she had to grab a chair and sit down. She tried to plaster a smile on her face, but it looked like the snarl of a death mask. "Darling . . . " she stammered, not knowing how to go on. She swallowed, took a deep breath, and started again. "Darling, something rather bad has happened . . . "

I stared at her, sucking on the cookie I had soaked in my barley coffee. I continued chewing even after she had finished. She tried again, her whole body shaking, her voice reduced to a whisper, "Honey, did you hear what I said?" I reached out for another cookie. Dipped it. Sent it down. My eyes on the television. It suddenly felt like Mamma was speaking in tongues, a stream of meaningless words coming out of her mouth.

Alfredo had died in the night. His lips were barely parted when they found him, just enough to let the ghost of his soul fly out. Alfredo broke my heart twice. And I turned into a 200 pound lard-ball of love, stuck at the starting line.

I didn't go to the funeral. At least, I don't think I did. I can't remember. Nor can I remember the months that followed. Alfredo went to bed one evening and never woke up, which meant I was never able to get my revenge on him for picking the slightly older, bright-eyed, giggly Cocchetti girl over me. Everyone else got on with their lives. Even her, my best friend. She solved all her problems two years later by getting pregnant. I, on the other hand, had run completely adrift.

Thinking about it now, I couldn't even really say I was grieving. Sleep took over. I was wandering between two worlds, in a no-man's-land: two worlds that only came together if I stayed still and stared into space. Alfredo's death had reached a place deep inside me and an invisible hand had extinguished the last glimmer of hope. I ate, that's for sure. Non-stop. And I went for walks around town. I would take a different route through different alleys every day of the week. When I got back home, Mamma had a pink pill waiting for me next to my morning snack. I took a white one in the evening with my last glass of milk before going to bed.

One for you, one for me . . . When I first met you, my dear pooch, I knew right away you had been abandoned just like me. You were a stray mutt, belonging to nobody, lost-looking, withheld love swelling your teats, deforming your body. You picked me. We half-greeted one another down in the Brigantino alley but we were both shy. Then I said, "Come home with me. I'll make you a hot meal. It may help a bit."

Anyone could see that you were only putting one foot in front of the other because that is what we are told to do: put one foot in front of the other. But there was no finish line on the horizon. Just a vague line where the sky meets the earth in a dark glow, an infinite waste of space. In your eyes I saw my own distress. And yet, you had made an effort: you had curled your hair, painted your nails bright red, put on a nice dress as if you were going out somewhere special when it was just an ordinary weekday afternoon.

Do you remember? We used to talk until dinner, my dear little pooch. We had the house to ourselves, Babbo out on his shift, Mamma on errands, collecting extra orders from the dressmaker Nardini as she does every two days. So maybe it was Tuesday. "I might want to kill myself," you said. "After Alfredo, there's nothing left." There were no tears. You stared down at the table, with a determined expression, like when Babbo got his packed lunch ready for a double shift at the blast furnace in Piombino. I had put the kettle on and the water was boiling, so I jumped up to make tea. Instead of bringing you a second cup, I emptied the boiling kettle over your head.

You shook your body once, that's all. From behind, I could see the long hair stuck to your shoulders. You didn't move a finger. When I moved to the side, I saw that your mouth was wide open, but you were not making a sound. It was a silent scream. You looked at me, just briefly. The skin on your face was purple, your makeup dripping into your mouth. Then you fainted from the pain.

Now you can't even remember your name, little pooch. You've lived in the dark for an eternity, chained up and choked here in this room. Your hair has grown so absurdly long that it'd stretch to twice your height if unraveled. You haven't stood up on your two feet for forty years, your knees are stuck in a position that makes you look like a locust with transparent skin. Your ears shriveled after that scorching shower and now, all these years later, they look like the ends of balloons after they've been tied. Your eyes, too, have gotten worse with age. And you speak in guttural grunts, with no words. When you hear me coming at night, you wheeze like an animal. It's how you celebrate when I bring along an unexpected bite of something special.

That day, long ago, I was standing over you, the dripping kettle still in my hand. I heard Mamma saying, "What's going on? Did you spill something? The mop is over there where it usually is."

I had been so engrossed, I hadn't even heard her come home. I didn't answer. Until she came into the kitchen. "What are you playing at? Statues?" she joked. Then she saw the bag on the chair nearest her. She came closer and when she saw you on the floor all the color in her face drained out. "Honey, what have you done?" she said, her hand over her mouth.

There was no way I was going to let you commit suicide. If I had to go on living, you had to carry on living beside me. Putting on some lipstick and throwing yourself over the precipice behind the church in the old town was too easy a way out. Maybe you didn't understand at the time but it was in your womb that it all started. That's when everything began to go wrong. The day Dr. Salghini was feeling horny and shot his seed into you, creating a baby boy. In one second, the two of you had conceived a new life and destroyed another that was still to come. My own. It was nearly Christmas, and Alfredo had been dead less than three months. I had already gained more than twenty pounds.

You were the only one who knew exactly what I felt. I could read it in your eyes, my dear little pooch and even now, words cannot describe all those shades of blinding darkness. Leaving me on my own to deal with the pain, when you were the one to generate it, would not have been fair. I was suspended between two worlds. I suddenly understood that if I shared the madness of it all with you, I might be able to get back on track, at least in the eyes of most people. The condition was that you had to go on living.

When you tried to get up, I was scared. One eye was half-stuck down from the burn, and your face was blistering. "They'll send me to jail," I said. Mamma shook her head. "Don't be stupid," she answered. With a determination I had hardly ever seen before, she walked around the table, took the kettle out of my hands, and hit you on the head. You fell asleep like a little angel.

I've heard the story of Nonno Dante since I was in diapers but I like telling it to you every now and then when I creep down the stairs to see you. He spent the war hidden in the woods but one day he was shot by the Germans. The bullet went into his leg, just above the knee, smashing the bone into a thousand pieces. He screamed out in pain when they tried to move him but one night, they brought him here to this hidey-hole carved into the rock Le Case is built on. Mamma says the town is full of secret rooms like this one, though most of them were walled up after the Americans came. There are some old people in the town who still threaten people with them. "Watch it! I can open up the secret room if I feel like it" What they are trying to say is that behind the bricks and mortar, they've stockpiled the rifles and revolvers they once used to fight the Fascists.

Mamma says Le Case is full of hidden treasure that has been forgotten. Where wounded partisans were once held, now there are pots of gold that families have set aside over a lifetime. When there are no children, the family line dies out, and there's no one to leave their inheritance to. Entire bloodlines die out, when behind every wall there may be a hidden stash melting into the stone over the centuries.

Behind this wall you lie, my dear little puppy. There are twelve, steep steps to get down here, under a trap door that opens under the kitchen floor. The tiles are the same all over, exactly the same, so when the trap door is closed nobody would ever know it existed. This is where Nonno Dante fought his last battle, before shooting himself in the temple at the age of 24. While he was convalescing, he kept asking whether his brigade had blown up the cabin up at Mt. Alto, the one built by the Germans. "Have they taken down the antenna?" he would ask, while his wound was rotting, weeping serum. One morning a squad of eight gendarmes came and broke our door down. Some collaborator had reported him. Mamma was only six but if anyone asks her, she says she remembers it as if it were yesterday. The Fascists got straight to the point and asked where the hiding place was. Nonna Ambra denied its existence to the very end, weeping and wailing as she was roughed up by the policemen. When she realized that they were going to search the house from top to bottom, she leaned on the table and tapped her heel twice on the floor, the arranged signal. One of the men slapped her across the face so hard she fell to the floor. The gendarmes dragged her and her little daughter away with them.

The Fascists, who were worse dogs than you, my dear little puppy, had no way of knowing that Nonno kept an arsenal down there in case he ever needed it. There were three British hand grenades and fifteen revolver shots. The first policeman to open the trap door and peer down got a bullet right between the eyes. Nonno shouted, "You'll never catch me alive!" and lobbed the first grenade up through the trap door. It rolled under the table and blew the kitchen to smithereens, and with it the infamous traitors who were still in the house.

Nonno Dante's act of resistance was written up in the papers later. Mamma still has the cutting and she goes back and reads it whenever she needs to give herself courage. She reads about her father's exploit, fighting off the Germans for a whole day from the bottom of this cellar with a festering leg. They couldn't go back into the house. My grandfather, who had fought with Garibaldi back in the day, was ready to pull the safety off the grenade as soon as he heard a floorboard creak. Or he would shoot into the air just to show that he was ready for them when they came, with an arsenal at his disposal. "I'll take you all out with me!" he shouted before firing his last shot. At himself. Even though the gendarmes knew he had shot himself, they stayed outside for hours, surrounding the neighborhood, calling for reinforcements. Time went by, but the gendarmes ignored orders to go in and put a stop to the skirmish, and ended up getting arrested themselves. They were happier deserting than storming this house. Hair and brain matter were still dripping down the walls from the last soldiers who had tried to storm the place They waited outside, squadrons filling the alleys around the house, leaving their other positions unguarded. The news spread and reached the ears of the partisans in the woods outside the town. At six that evening, an explosion echoed around the hills. There was black smoke coming from the antenna on Mt. Alto.

All this to say that this pit here has witnessed many a story over the years. Including yours. You still live here, with no teeth, your skull showing through your translucent skin. One day, forty years ago, I boiled your head, my dear puppy. Then Mamma bade you goodnight with a nice knock on the head with a kettle. She shifted the table with her hip and opened the trap door onto this cellar, carved out of the rock back in the eighteen hundreds when Nonno was still a kid.

To begin with, you struggled a lot. We had to wait until Babbo had gone off for his shift. Then we would clamber down and give you a few drops of water and some leftovers. "Well, you were the one who wanted to disappear," I said to you as I prized your gag off, avoiding your bites. You howled like a harpy but there was no point in telling you your caterwauling was buried in the belly of the bedrock. You refused to eat, so I force-fed you and then you puked the whole lot up all over yourself. Mamma came down with a mop and pail, especially after we decided to strip you naked because down in this pit it's hot in summer and cold in winter. You pissed outside the pail on purpose and grew skinnier by the day. "She's decided to let herself go," Mamma said one afternoon as I rubbed your skin dry with a cloth and you just sat there as usual without saying a word. "Pretend you're dead for real," I whispered in your ear. "What do you care? Imagine you've jumped off the Tolomei cliff and this is Hell. Except that there's someone here being nice to you." You stared at me without any reaction. I left the cloth in the pantry and burst the last blisters on your face that were still weeping.

The good thing was that you had already one a little crazy and being buried alive in a dark pit all day sent you off the edge altogether. It was strange: every day when I came down the stairs you were more like a little girl. You started talking again but by the end of the month you hardly remembered that you once had a son. You went on about a certain Emilio with a well-tended little mustache you had fallen for but had never dared speak to. I tried hard, but I couldn't imagine Dr. Salghini as a young man. He disappeared, and you were going on of twenty. You talked about a fling with a dipstick builder from Valpiana with nice hands, though they were calloused from hard work.

Mamma wanted to finish you off and take you out one piece at a time. "What if Babbo finds her?" she would say. I had to explain it to her all over again: without you I would go gray in no time at all. "If she survives, I will," I insisted. Anyway, you had turned into a newborn. You would get excited as soon as you heard me open the trap door. You had regressed so much you couldn't speak any longer, though it wasn't like the beginning. This time, you had simply forgotten your words. "She's just pretending," Mamma would say. But I could see your eyes in the naked light of the bulb. They were the eyes of a devoted little puppy who was thankful for small mercies. Just like now.

It was quite funny when, in the evening, Babbo would sit at table and say things like, "Sometimes there's no end to bad luck. Imagine Dr. Salghini. First his son dies, now his wife has vanished into thin air . . . " They had even trawled the Ombrone looking for her. In the papers there was a picture of her from twenty years ago. She was the talk of the town.

Forty years have gone by and it feels as though I'm reliving the whole thing. The girl who has just disappeared is the same age as I was when I locked you up down here. Even back then I played the same game: I imagined I was you and felt a wave of relief wash over me. We shared the same pain, like twins with the same blood in our veins. You vanished and became evanescent in your grief. So, I vanished too. I used to enjoy listening to the idle chatter in town. "She must have fallen down some ravine," they would say.

Babbo died on January 6, '83, the feast of the Epiphany. Remember? That morning Mamma and I had gone to St. Bastian's for the eleven o'clock mass. When we got back there was a strange silence, because the silence of a death in a house is different to a normal silence. "Gaspare, are you there?" Mamma called out after hanging her coat up. She stood there looking down the corridor. "Gaspare?"

"He must have gone for a walk down to the Due Porte," I said with a shrug. I didn't really think he had. I noticed the TV was on in the kitchen. The volume had been turned down and it was barely audible, so that's not what gave it away. It was the images: the shadows in the room shifted very slightly.

Mamma took a few steps, her face gray. "Gaspare?" she kept calling, her voice little more than a murmur. We reached the kitchen door. I was about to look in when her scream stopped me in my tracks. "Gaspare!"

You were there on the ground, dear little puppy. In the daylight, you looked like a mythological creature, an unbelievably pale skeleton. You were crawling on all fours, like you are now. There were cartoons on the TV, and your eyes were glued to them. You didn't budge when Mamma screamed. Your hair was down to the ground and you were crouched there like a toad, with the gaze of a sleepwalker. Your iron chain, one link loosened, hung down your side. There was a pool of piss under you.

The worst thing was the upturned chair. Babbo was on the other side of the room in a sitting position, his back leaning against the cupboard under the sink. His face scared me to death because his staring eyes looked abnormal. As did his mouth. It looked like his jaw had been dislocated from screaming so hard. His hands were curled up like claws. A puddle was forming under his pants.

Dr. Salghini said his heart had given out. "Of course," he added, "his weight didn't help matters. Even though his latest tests came back perfect . . . he was taking the pressure medication I'd prescribed, wasn't he?"

Only Mamma and I knew the truth and just thinking about it made my blood curl. I imagined Babbo sitting at the kitchen table with a cup of coffee, the paper, and the TV on low to keep him company. His usual daily routine. When suddenly the trap door flies open and a balding, bony creature deformed by burns leaps out at him, bellowing and howling. The shock must have been so great that he jumped out of the chair and his heart stopped. The last thing he was expecting that morning was a monster rising from the belly of the earth to drag him down into the underworld.

"My poor Gaspare!" Mamma despaired, to begin with. "He must have gone through the gates of Hell . . . " Keeping you locked up in Nonno Dante's pit had not been easy for her to digest but after January 6, '83, she developed a taste for it. It's always a struggle and whenever I leave the house on my own, I have to issue stern warnings. And yet, when I go downstairs sometimes and find you in a corner trembling and wheezing with tears, I tempt you with cookies because you're scared to approach me. When you finally look up, I see the bruises in the light of the bare bulb. It drives me crazy with fury. Mamma needs to stop hitting her on the sly. Babbo may have had the heart of a little red robin but he could have eaten less salami! Maybe that way his heart wouldn't have burst when the trap door under the kitchen floor suddenly flew open.

One for you and one for me. This is all to say that I'm very, very fond of you, my dear puppy. In the beginning, I kept you locked up so that I wouldn't be the only one grieving, but over time, you have proved to me that we can survive anything. You were the closest thing I had to Alfredo, who ruined my young life for good. The closest thing to him that I could keep for myself. I keep all the newspaper cuttings in my diary. The first article reports the tragic death of my unconsumed love, who died in the flower of his youth. Then there are all the articles about your disappearance. I go through them every now and again and they make up a family album.

I don't know why, but I've started cutting out the articles about this girl who has just disappeared. I must be feeling nostalgic . . . And yet, when I think about this Eleonora from down in the valley, I feel a rush of excitement in my blood, like I do in the Spring. I pore through the articles for hours as I make up grim stories in my head. Oh, I've always been on the imaginative side . . . at least it keeps me company. And I wonder to myself, "Which house has she been locked up in?" Mamma is always saying, "In this town there's so much to uncover." Which makes me imagine other pits, other walled-in cellars and caves. Maybe, in one of those holes, there's an Eleonora like you, my little puppy. An Eleonora in the early stages of her agony, bearing the burden of having inflicted pain on others and paying the penalty for it, without even knowing why.

The girl's disappearance has made me reevaluate things and an idea has been playing on my mind for a few days now. An idea that started with the gossip in town about Graziella and her tarot cards, which she uses to guess what people should do to save themselves from the evil eye. I would like to find out if she knows any particular secrets. Such as the fact that I've been holding a certain little creature down here all these years. Ultimately, this is the question I keep asking myself, "If she can detect evil in people, what is she waiting for to yell out to the world the exact spot where this new girl is being held against her will? Or has she already been buried for a while?"

When I said this to Mamma this morning, her eyes lit up like head lights. "What is this nonsense?" she exclaimed. "Don't you know that it's all bunkum? Only cretins fall for that stuff. Graziella gets a pension worthy of a princess, she certainly doesn't need to round it up with tips from us." But I was ready for her argument and had prepared a salvo I knew would touch a nerve with her. "I want to hear what the cards say about that Mimmo guy," I said, with a coy expression. "You've talked about him so much that he's gotten into my head. But I want to go alone."

I know what everyone else says about Graziella: that she's a witch. As for the rest, she gets a widow's pension from that Martino I hardly remember because he was all work and no play and hardly ever went into town. I also know he went through the whole of elementary school in the same class as my mother, back in the day when the windows of the old school shook every time Grosseto was being bombed.

In short, there's something rotten in Le Case, what with girls disappearing and retards detonating bombs from half a century ago. The blood of the whole town is stirring and I'm no different. Even Mamma is flushed. She thinks out loud and she's become obsessed with ways to make us filthy rich. She never stops talking about it. When she's not banging on at me about marrying Mimmo, she starts with another crazy idea. "I want to buy a house on Elba," she says when she's on a roll. "So that I can spend my final years looking at the sea." I sit there in silence. As soon as she realizes I'm not keen on the idea, she starts yelling, "You're a prize product of Le Case! You're as hard-headed as everyone else in this shithole. Would it really be so disgusting to be able to strut around in a fur coat like a real lady someday soon?"

She rushed into my room like a whirl wind. I hadn't seen her so animated for years. "Either someone has died or we've won the lottery," I said, not knowing whether to laugh or start yelling. Mamma beckoned me over to the kitchen table and laid out a sheet of paper. "The latter," she muttered. "Even though it is someone else's win."

I couldn't make out much. Rather, what I could make out felt like a bad joke. After a while, I lifted my head. "You've bought a cellar in Via Stretta?" A minute later I had become the whirl wind. "Have you lost your mind?" I shrieked. "You've just sunk almost all our savings into an extra room? I may be menopausing, but those arteries in that pea-brain of yours must have suddenly hardened." She sat there as I let off steam, observing me almost with a challenging look. "Are you done?" she said when I finally slumped into a chair with my heart in my throat and a bug in my tush. Then she told me a story. And I'm going to tell it to you, puppy. If only to convince myself that, because I'm up to my ears in debt, we're not going to be living under the Sticciano railway bridge in a couple of years' time; or that I won't have to marry Domenico Fiorani and end up sleeping on a mattress that stinks of sheep.

There was once a couple whose surname was Bianciardi. Sourpusses both, Mamma said. Born and bred in Le Case. People called him Manolo, even though his real name was Stefano. They called him that because he was good at manual work of all kinds. After the war he didn't sign up for work with any of the mines. He liked getting up in the morning and having a different task every day: this pipe to fix, that ceiling to paint . . . "He could till the land, loosen bolts, and whitewash with the same skill," Mamma said. "He could fix shoes, engines, hinges or spouts." Off the books and at a discount. Everyone in le Case had Manolo's number on hand near the telephone. Then, one fine day, Bianciardi stopped working. "It happened in '67, out of the blue." Mamma remembers it as well as she does her Hail Marys. "Once the mayhem over their win was over."

I was still a young girl when it happened, but I can remember the hoopla. The news was on TV and in all the national papers: in Le Case somebody had guessed the results of all thirteen soccer matches and won the jackpot to the tune of one hundred and thirty-three million. People said good morning and good evening to one another with their eyes peeled, X-raying every detail as they walked past. And the lucky winner was out there somewhere, without telling anyone. It went on for months. After a while, people started complaining that this so and so, whoever it was, could at least have given something to Staccioli, since it had been the tobacconist who had sold the millionaire ticket that Thursday, apparently like every other. But nothing came of it. Not a peep. People kept track of anyone who skipped town for a half-day in case they had gone to the notary to sign under the dotted line. The malcontents in the town grumbled, "Best stay as we are. Money only spells trouble." And their livers would turn green with envy. The one time the goddess of fortune had paid a visit to this mountain town, she had planted a kiss on the forehead of one of its inhabitants who wouldn't even buy you a coffee at Maso's bar. Whoever the scoundrel was, they were continuing to lead a normal life, like Divo, maybe, or Salghini even, who blathered every now and again, "If only it had been me . . .," and then went straight home to drown himself in a pint of strong red wine, attempting to act like his days were one big celebration.

A year later, when Bianciardi suddenly stopped leaving his house at six every morning, the idea that he had won the jackpot caught fire immediately. If you bumped into him in the street, he would tell you that he had back ache or his knees were hurting. "I need some sun, the kind you get at the seaside," he would tell everyone. "To oil my joints a little. All these years of work come back to bite, you know." And he would go on about having arthritic hands that kept him awake at night.

But the townsfolk have long memories. It had become clear as daylight that he had been the lucky winner and he had made up every possible excuse never to pick up his tool kit again. He started living like a recluse in Le Case, and only went out when he couldn't avoid it. Their children had already left town a few years before: one bound for college in Siena, one gainfully employed in Florence. Kids who were only seen in town when they were very young because there were relations to visit. Manolo, it appeared, was receiving a state pension but he had also paid into a private scheme which he always used to boast about. "I'm setting aside a little just so we don't end up suffering in poverty in our old age." He would look at you dolefully with those bovine eyes. "Does it seem fair to you? You work for a century so you can spoil yourself in your old age without worry, and then everything you've set aside flies out the window because you have to spend it all on drugs." Now the blindfolded goddess had given this hard-working citizen a massive retirement fund. In Le Case, there were some people who thought, "What about me? Haven't I broken my back as much or more than he has? In any case, I would have given some of the money to charity at least . . . " And as they moaned, they swilled down brandy shots.

Well, pup, the story I'm telling you follows the same pattern as all the others: there's a gleam of light at the end of the tunnel and then darkness swallows you up and you have to start again, except it gets even harder. People talked about them with such venom that soon bad things started to happen to the Bianciardis. "First the wife died," Mamma tells me, looking sincerely upset. "All of a sudden, her blood was running thinner than water. That was in April. By the end of May, she was ready to go six feet under." In town, people doffed their hats when the funeral procession went by but at the same time they were muttering things like, "If you're not born to it, wealth can wear you out. Manolo can enjoy his millions on his own now, sitting by the fireplace. Or maybe he'll hand it all down to his children, who will run through it in less than a month, being typical products of this place, and end up with holes in their pockets like Tempesti."

And yet, Bianciardi was different. After the shock of his

wife's death, he stayed holed up at home for weeks on end. Until his neighbors smelled something sinisterly similar to decaying human flesh. When the carabinieri broke down the door, they found Manolo sitting in an armchair covered in flies holding the TV remote. They said he must have been there for at least three nights. Since it was summer, the body was already in advanced decomposition.

"All the papers relating to their win must be walled up somewhere at home," Mamma says, when she gets worked up. She starts pacing the house, making her skirt swish and sway. "The Bianciardis used to take partisans in, too, during the war. The Bianciardis had hidden wells dug into the rocks." Then she stops, staring into a void. She looks at me and says, "When I saw the For Sale sign, I thought 'This is Jesus doing us a favor. Knowing the soccer spread win was wasted on these people, he's now handing it over to the first bidder with a bit of backbone. And the Serraglini family, who haven't set foot in the place for years and have left it to go to seed, can go to hell. They've been sitting on the capital keeping it warm for us."

I really hope so, my dear puppy. Because they'll come to foreclose on everything soon, right down to the gums in our mouths, and I'll be rolling down to Fiorani's house in the hollow surrounded by grime. "The children come to town in cars that don't look at all fancy," I hear Mamma whispering when her eyes start glittering again at the idea of the hidden treasure. "And you can see from miles away that they buy their shirts at the market. Which sends a clear message: no money. Maybe they don't even suspect that their parents had collected the manna that had rained down from the heavens. Maybe they wanted to wait before telling them. And then they were so frazzled by the whole palaver that they croaked. Manolo must realize that you can't spend millions when you're in a grave.

After the sale went through, we emptied the cellar of all the filth that had been rotting there. We saved a few ornaments to decorate the house with, even though I didn't like the idea of displaying bric-a-brac belonging to dead people on the sideboard. Anyway, I scrubbed everything with bleach. Other trinkets went into our own cellar, the one that gives out onto the big road. There were some pieces of furniture that were a pity to throw away. We also wanted to call Angiolino, who knows about these things and sometimes discovers something worthy of a museum which he can sell to make ends meet happily. But when he came to look over the pile of junk, the only thing he bought was the record I had set aside, handing over two twenty-euro bills without batting an eye. I even thought to myself, "What if the real treasure is this disc?" Then I thought about my mad mother's profligacy. "We'd better start earning back what we've spent."

Then I wonder why hunger holds me in its grip at night. It's not surprising, with all these thoughts going around my head! Mamma spends whole afternoons knocking on the walls of the cellar we have bought at the risk of being reduced to a diet of bread and water. She knocks softly, her ears flattened against the walls. Then she marks a cross with a pencil wherever she thinks it sounds empty. The big cellar that once belonged to the Bianciardis is now filled with crosses, each of which we'll have to drill with a teaspoon. "We can't exactly use a sledgehammer," she blurts out when I ask her. "Sonia's on the other side and she mustn't notice a thing. Imagine if we suddenly knocked through the bricks and made a hole into her kitchen. There would be a repeat of Babbo's heart attack, exactly the same scene."

I think about the appointment I have made with Graziella to see whether she has understood what makes me tick and maybe even give me some answers. In the meantime, Mimmo Fiorani is watching and waiting for me with his arms wide open like a trap. The precise trap Mamma wants me to be snared by, especially if her expectation of a treasure suspended in the middle of nowhere comes to nothing. Forget the cookies, if that happens, my pup: we'll all be baying like hungry wolves. And if I did go and shack up with that peasant, who would take care of you? Mamma is filled with such hatred that she would sneak downstairs and break a broomstick on your back. That would be her only chance to vent after her umpteenth disappointment. So, I say to myself, if at the back of your head there is still the ghost of a person, pray. Pray furiously, pup. That the treasure so lusted after by that mad woman gushes from some brick or other. Otherwise, you'll see me rolling down to the hollow, a trophy for the man from the Marches. And there won't be any more midnight feasts. Only beatings.

Adele Centini - 4
The Isastia Widow

On the dresser in Room 112 there's a porcelain statuette of a peasant girl. She stands there holding out an empty plate as though she were begging. I take my diamond earrings off and put them on the plate. I unclasp my pearl necklace. Then the fine gold chainmail bracelet. Last but not least, my ring. The whole lot ends up in this girl's plate. I go into the bathroom. I start running a bath, without any foam. My mother always used to say, "Soap turns your flesh to dough." She would be more likely to go into the kitchen and come back with a handful of rock salt. Or she would squeeze three lemons into a glass and pour the juice into my hip bath. "Your skin will come out as firm as an iron bar," she would say.

However, time doesn't stand still and when I drop my bath robe, I feel like my heart skips a beat. The mirror is shockingly brutal. I look away, trying to forget as quickly as possible. The ageing process is a theft, a doubly hateful one for anyone who was once beautiful.

Colonel Isastia didn't take me but his chauffeur started doing so whenever he had the chance. I was not in love with him in the slightest and I told him to his face. "Marcello, if you do me the disservice of falling in love with me, you will never see me again." And then I let him have his way with me, discovering a new facet of my beauty, a ferocious one. A nod from me was enough to make him kneel at my feet. More than with his body, he feasted on me with his hands and with his eyes. When we were done, as we were pulled our clothes straight, he would dip two fingers back inside me. He would wave them in front of my nose and mouth. "The Colonel uses eau de cologne," he used to say. "I get my perfume right here. Your wetness will keep me going me all day, it's much better than holy water."

I didn't tell my mother anything. She would have gone crazy if she had found out I was having an affair with the driver rather than working on Colonel Isastia, who was still at the mercy of my smiles. Except that instead of taking me into his bedroom, he told me all about the Greeks. Even the walls had sensed it by then: it wasn't a wife he was training up but a replacement daughter. He had seen a glimmer in me and devoted almost all his time to my education. Then the day finally came. It was a week before Christmas.

He called me into his study and, like every morning, I arrived in my maid's uniform. "Adele, my dear," he said. I could tell right away that he was nervous. He felt the need to get up from behind his giant desk to talk to me. He walked over to the big window on the left, which shed a dull gray light on the room. He clasped his hands behind his back, standing to attention. "I wonder whether you have heard rumors concerning a brother of mine?" he started. "I have made it very clear that his name should never be uttered in this house. But we all know that servants have loose tongues and that they use them mostly to speak ill of their masters, thus licking the wound of their poverty."

I looked at his shape. "Is that a question?" I asked, my heart thumping. "Anyway, no. Never has any news of any close relative of yours reached my ears this year . . . What is his name?"

He snorted. "Adele, I've just told you that I wouldn't say his name even if I were under torture. I'd rather cut my balls off and feed them to my hunting dogs." He turned imperceptibly towards me. "Speaking of which, Santo says there has been a new litter. Do you know anything about it?" I had to admit that I didn't know anything about that either. "In any case, the fact is that the good Lord has seen fit to punish me with this encumbrance who walks around town with the same blood as me. A miserable wretch. I can just see him in those flea-ridden taverns raising his glass to Chiara Maria's death. And to mine. But may God strike me down with lightning if I ever allow that leech to get his grubby hands on one square inch of the last parcel of land on the edge of Maremma!"

Even a jackass would have understood where the man was heading with this prelude but when he dropped his daughter's name into the conversation, cold, salt water seeped into my marrow. He had never talked about her and, all of a sudden, he had mentioned her in passing as if "Chiara Maria" were ordinary words. I felt the floor shift under my feet as the Colonel twisted his body around to face me. "Does it sound reasonable to you that a father's dalliance with a servant girl should put one tiny particle of my property at risk?" I shook my head so violently it almost came off my shoulders. Colonel Isastia let out a deep breath. He suddenly looked tired. "I could make a donation but that brute would contest the will the following day," he grumbled. "He would go on and on until he managed to get some kind of concession." There was silence. I stood there, my arms hanging by my sides. "They say there is only one way," he continued, as he started walking towards me. His steps echoed around the room. Eventually, he was so close that I could smell the stench of tobacco. It felt like I was being catapulted back to my first day, the one where the piazza was thronging with girls applying for a job here. I batted my eyelids, almost expecting to wake up from a deep sleep and to hear something like, "Thank you, Signorina. We will let you know in due course." Instead, the Colonel grabbed my hand. And murmured these words, "Adele, dear, would you do me the honor of accepting my hand in second marriage?"

That evening, Mamma swooned, laughing and crying all the while. This time, it was me having to fetch the smelling salts and give her little slaps. She opened her eyes, saw who I was, and fainted again. She behaved as though I had brought her news of my own death. I gave her spoonfuls of wine to get her blood running again. Eventually, her eyes opened and she didn't pass out. She stared at me. "If you have a little girl, we're calling her Barbara after the saint. Agreed?"

The news was kept secret until the last minute. The Colonel was afraid that rumors would get around and his wretched brother might get it into his head to hire someone to get me out of the way so that, when his time came, he would be the last man standing. "Look around you," the Colonel would repeat, without ever touching me even though we were engaged. "You need to have eyes in the back of your head. The people you mix with at the moment are the ones who will be bringing you breakfast in bed. Nothing poisons the blood more than someone else's unexpected wealth. They would be willing to lose what little they have just to see you sinking back down into the mud alongside them, or eating scraps left over from dinner with the dogs.

I carried on the same life as before, with tours of the properties in the morning and lessons in the afternoon. When we got into the car, Marcello would keep his eyes on the road without once looking at me in the rearview mirror. Then during the afternoon siesta, I would take off as few clothes as I needed to give him direct access for a quickie. He would have stripped my skin off if he had had his way.

Mamma and I left Via della Scalette a week before the wedding, when the Colonel made his announcement. It all happened so fast: we arrived at the Isastia Villa and all the servants were lined up at the entrance to welcome us, including Stella and Solino. Only Santo was missing. The house servants had been the first to hear the news. The evening before, I had resigned my position as favorite scullery maid and the next morning, I crossed the threshold as the lady of the house. "Her command is my command," the Colonel thundered, his voice resounding throughout the entrance hall. "Her needs are mine. There is nothing to add."

Colonel Isastia gave Mamma rooms on the top floor, near where I used to sleep, but no wall was enough to keep her at bay. She never left my side. The only time she rested was when I closed myself in the Colonel's study, where he now deigned to show me the account books with figures lined up involving six zeros or more. At dinner, my mother sat next to me. She would take my portion from the serving dish. She would taste a forkful and wait for a bit. She would only hand me my plate after she was sure she was still alive.

With her at my heel, it was practically impossible to give Marcello an assignation. In any case, Colonel Isastia was about to make me his wife. Once again, my world was being transformed and I let it happen, without opposing any resistance. One day, I walked into my room and found my mother sitting on the bed. It was awful. The first things she said was, "Shameful hussy!" Then she leaped to her feet and ran towards me, flapping the skirts of her new dress that fit her so badly it was like a snub. You can tart some people up as much as you like but their poor origins stick with them like ringworm.

She closed the door, careful not to make any noise. Then she waved a scrap of paper in front of my nose. "Someone slipped this under the crack for you," she said, without giving me time to read it. She whipped it away, crumpled it up into a ball, and stuck it in her mouth. She swallowed it in one gulp, like a goose. "What is this about? Do you think we have gone through this whole palaver just so that you can have it off with the first miserable stable hand you come across?" She hissed like a viper. "Imagine if the Colonel finds out! He'll throw you back into the gutter. And I'll kill you."

Mamma saw me go pale. I was suddenly sobbing my heart out. She immediately came to the wrong conclusion. "Listen, I don't want to hear you're in love, or any nonsense of that kind!" Her voice was all air and her pupils flashed as if they were about to take flight. "If I hear a single word about this again, I'll throw myself out of the window on the spot. I've survived two wars but this would be the last straw."

I went to the bureau in the corner of the room. I pulled the chair our and slumped into it. She looked at me, paralyzed with fear. I took a deep breath. Then I said, "I couldn't care two hoots about this Marcello." Mamma crossed herself and threw a look of gratitude. "But there is more," I said. "I may as well tell you now since it will come out sooner or later anyway." I lifted my head. "Do you remember three months ago when my courses didn't come?"

She gasped. "What do you mean? They came. I washed your rags for a week and gave them back to you fresh and clean as usual."

I had to lower my head again. "It wasn't my blood. I went into the kitchen on the sly and dipped my rags into the meat they serve for dinner even though the Colonel hardly touches it."

Mamma took a few steps back and ended up back where I had found her.

"I did the same last month, too. And I would have done the same in a few days."

The silence was deep enough to drown in. My mother's gaze was so lost that she looked as though she was in another world that only she had access to. Then she muttered, as if I weren't even there, "This little bastard . . . " She looked as though she was sleepwalking. She mulled over the news as if she were telling a story to a ghost. "You should have told me back then. Now the thing has grown, a knitting needle won't be enough to get rid of it without bringing the rest of your guts out with it . . . All this just to get a bit of flesh on the side, when I've been teaching you good manners all your life."

I didn't say a word. I could feel a few big tears roll down my face and drop into my skirt but I didn't dare take a breath. In the meantime, she was racking her brain to find a solution. Then she got up and went to the window. She opened it wide, letting the icy air in. "Mamma!" I yelled, leaping to my feet. She was standing there like a statue, her face whipped by the wind, her gaze directed outwards. Just as she used to force me to do as a child when she put me out on the balcony at dusk. In the nude. All of a sudden, she turned around like a missile and came back into the room. "It's not the time to be imbeciles," she said, walking towards me with that lopsided gait of hers. I thought I was about to get a slap on the face but, instead, she clasped my face in her hands. "I have a solution right here in my head. Let's get ourselves to the wedding so that we can rest our backsides on all the land. There's so much of it he'll never keep track. On your wedding night you need to be clever and coax the dear Colonel inside. You're not a daughter to him. He'll find a young wife who is eager to kindle the dry old twigs of his old age. You'll see, he'll be encouraged by the drink at the banquet. At the end of the following month, you'll give him the news. He won't be surprised when his son and heir is born premature. It happens all the time. Especially if the mother is a sixteen-year-old who has been hungry most of her life. You don't have the strong womb of a breeder brought up in the lap of luxury, that's for sure.

They let me choose the flowers and the decorations. Meanwhile, cards and gifts arrived from all over Tuscany. "The Colonel wants to go to Paris to recover from the wedding," my mother informed me. The sole idea made my heart leap into my throat. Paris felt like an expression rather than a real place. Where I came from, if someone walked by dressed to the nines, people would say, "Look at them, strutting like they've just come back from Paris." Or, "Speak plain, will you? You're not from Paris." Now, in the spring, I would be setting foot there and it felt like I would have to walk into a dream. Mamma grabbed me by the collar. "Don't dare even think about it! Any shock and the thing could detach, and you'd need forceps to get it out. And then what would you tell the Colonel? A newly conceived creature doesn't come out with the head of a calf. There'll be no Paris for you. In fact, you'll be taking bed rest, without any doctors meddling in your business."

Marcello had no idea. The good thing was that the day the announcement was made he could hardly bring himself to look at me, acting somewhere between offended and fawning. I was depriving him of his merry-go-round rides but at least he wouldn't have to deal with the problem of a third child, born out of wedlock to boot. The note Mamma had swallowed had been his only attempt. Since he had never received an answer or a knowing look, he went back to being a chauffeur and that was that. Luckily, between my mother and the Colonel's brother, he and I were never left to our own devices or sent down to the valley on some errand or other, missions which until not long ago gave us the chance to try out as many positions as we wanted.

The wedding was imminent. One morning, the Colonel called me into the living room to open another round of gifts. Mamma was sitting in a corner on one of those antique chairs that were only supposed to be for decoration. She watched me unwrap the presents as if I were a star of the stage. If I pulled out a hand-painted dish, she would clap slowly. The last gift was a small sky-blue box with a white bow. I looked at the card. It was from Esedra. "Dear woman," the Colonel murmured behind me. "She practically raised Chiara Maria. I owe her more than she knows . . . They say her hip is getting better now, even though the fall left her bones as fragile as glass. She gets an invalidity pension but it's not very much and yet she has sent a gift. I'll have ten bottles of wine sent to her immediately. Come on, Adele. Open up."

I pulled the bow loose and opened the box. It was a tiny little glass horse lying on a blue doll's cushion. The Colonel smiled. "This means more to me than all the silver that has come our way so far." He picked it up and placed it on a shelf in the big glass cabinet beside him. The miniature horse stayed standing, resting on its tail and back hooves. By pure chance, a random ray of sun caught it and refracted a rainbow onto the wall. I was bewitched for a moment by the little light show. But I suddenly felt a kind of itch that distracted me. I looked down and saw a fat black scorpion. It was right there on the back of my hand, its pincers wide open and its raised, hooked tail dripping with poison.

I started screaming like crazy. I wanted to bite my own flesh. I was so hysterical I unbuttoned my shirt and shook my hair out. "Where is it?" I yelled as the colonel looked on in shock, asking what I was making such a scene about. Eventually, I heard a crunch. I looked up and saw Mamma lifting her foot. She'd crushed the scorpion under her shoe, its yellow guts spilled all over the floor. But the stinger was still moving. I stopped hollering at that point but my knees buckled under me. Colonel Isastia caught me from behind just in time. Despite his age, he managed to hold me up.

Solino came to the door, summoned by all the racket. "What's going on?" he called out. He ran to his master's side and helped him stretch me out on the sofa. "We need some smelling salts!" But the servant didn't move. He stared at the ground with his mouth open like a codfish. I could see him out of the corner of my eye as if through mist. Then he came over to me. "Smelling salts are not enough," he said. As he said this, I lifted my head and saw the drops on the floor.

Mamma hurried over. "Good heavens!" she cried. "The Red Baron decides to pay a visit now. Of all times!" I tried getting up so that I could leave the room right away but I suddenly felt a rush of heat in my belly that traveled up to my eyes. A second later, it was as if someone had stuck a pitchfork through me from one side to the other. I started yelling so loud that it felt like it was outside my body, in a voice I had never heard before. Meanwhile, a red stain spread through the lilac skirt I was wearing. The last thing I saw was Stella's face, who had run into the room alongside all the other servants. She lifted my skirts and peered underneath. She dropped it right away. "Call a doctor! she blurted out, looking deathly pale. "Adele is bleeding out in front of our eyes."

Alvise Barberini,
the Retired Factory Worker

That voice of hers hammers through my brain like a long, crooked nail.

"You've looked in the chest, haven't you? Well, look in the broom cupboard then. Anyway, let this be clear: this is the last time! I have things of my own to worry about and they're not trifles, either. Maybe you take me for a spinning top that does nothing but your bidding but you're wrong there. One of these days, I'm getting on the two o'clock bus and that will be that. Alvise, my dear, this wasn't the life you promised me. I pray every day that we could go back in time to that autumn festival in '69, you know? When your twinkling blue eyes made me feel a little giddy. My poor mother always used to say, 'Watch out for the men who come up from the Tatti or Ribolla side: they're either crazy or about to become so.' But I was an idiot and didn't listen to her. I fancied blond men with thin mustaches like the American film stars . . . And, in the meantime, I had batted away all the most popular suitors, like Paride De Lorenzi, for example, who used to make all the girls in Sassofortino drool with lust. Whenever I go down to the valley and see the villa he has built near Meleta, I say to myself, 'Iolanda, this could have been your house.' And all those other admirers I could cite . . . But no! I chose an Alvise like you, who was born a slacker. You may have been good looking, my friend, but if the good Lord sent me back to that infamous day, I swear that I would shoot myself rather than go down to that dance in my best dress . . . What are you waiting for? Have you looked in the pantry?"

*

That evening I hadn't even wanted to go down to the autumn fair. Gilera had persuaded me, obsessed as he was with girls from the hills. "I undressed a married woman from Roccastrada every day for a week." He had been at it so hard that he had a giant welt he attempted to cure by filling his underpants with talc because the blister made it painful even to walk. "Gotta get some pussy in these hillside towns: they have appetites like tigers," he used to claim. "And we're sitting here staring at the signpost outside the town. It looks more like a gravestone than a welcome. It feels like we're already six feet under."

Gilera had always behaved as though he was wasted here. So, that evening we took him for a ride up to the peaks, even though a storm had been brewing all day without ever breaking, lightning flashing on the horizon. We were up there: me, him, and poor Gianni who we used to call the Little Guy from Montieri. We were well into September by that time, but our shirts stuck to our backs in the heat. Looking up at the mountains, we saw fog cloaking the ridge.

Everyone in the area had come to Le Case. By the time we got there, the locals had already been tippling. Gilera stared them down deliberately because he liked fist fights almost as much as he liked girls. When he was spoiling for a fight, he was so hot-blooded that it took two of us to drag him away. Unlike Gianni, who flew away like a bluebottle.

We ordered a flask of wine and sat on the low wall in the piazza to watch the dancing. It felt like we were in another world. We were inside a cloud: a thin veil around us that was invisible from close up but shrouded everything in the distance in mist. The streetlamps and strings of fairy lights seemed to multiply. Gianni kept elbowing us in the ribs and rubbing his face with his hands. "Is it my eyes, or do you see everything double, too?" Gilera looked over at him, all serious, and said, "What? Everything looks normal to me." Gianni paled and started experimenting with his eyesight, screwing up his eyes like old people do.

The band was at the other end of the piazza and it felt like they were playing from a faraway corner of heaven, even though the speakers relayed the sound over to us. The dancing couples twirled in circles, melting into a blur in the gray mist and then coming back into focus, with clean outlines and bright colors. "I'm going to be sick," Gianni said. Gilera took no notice. In fact, he tapped me on the shoulder. "There's a girl giving me the eye," he said, his wine-breath hitting me in the face. I turned around and identified the precise point his diabolical eye was fixed upon. At that very moment, a giant bank of fog hit Le Case and a second later we could see nothing.

" . . . And anyway, this fixation with chess needs to come to an end. Look at you. You've turned into an old windbag. Wouldn't a little walk be better for you? At least you would get out of the house for ten minutes, apart from anything else. All the other old men spend their days propping up the counter at Maso's bar but you're here underfoot. You like showing off your squeaky-clean house, don't you? But God forbid you ever wipe up one particle of dust. Alvise, dear, you won the lottery when I came along, mark my idiot words. Have you looked in the window seat? That Calamaio is already out and about and he'll soon be ringing our bell like the waste of space he is, always coming to make our lives hell at three on the dot. On Sunday, I ask you! My dear Alvise never says, 'Luigino, what about a rain check for today's match? I'm taking this wife of mine out for a ride up to San Martino so she can get some fresh air after breaking her back every day this week, poor thing.' No, something like that wouldn't happen even in a world of dreams. Better to stay in like two zombies, staring at the chess pieces without saying half a word to one another. If only a worthy opponent showed up for you! It wouldn't have to be a champion. But really? An elementary school teacher? A man who has decided to retire to a town with no children, like a recluse, spending all his time in a cellar painting? His pupils' playfulness must have had done him in. That friend of yours is always so gloomy, it's like having a dead man walking beside you. This house could do with a bit of joy, you know! But what am I saying? God forbid! Never! Better to spend your Sundays here, walled up in silence, and me locked up in the kitchen with the TV volume on low for fear of disturbing these brainiacs while they're thinking out their moves. Better to wear yourself out like now, turning every room inside out, looking for that heirloom that came from a market but that Calamaio likes seeing on the mantlepiece because he brought it from Florence with all his love. And now you can't find it. I wish it had at least done him good. Get a move on. Have you looked in the window seat or not?"

A milky sea. The band stopped playing and Gianni was bleating. He was groping around for Gilera but he found it disgusting to be touched by a man and kept shoving him away. We couldn't even see our shoes. Here and there we heard the muffled shattering of glass as bottles and glasses went flying, as if it were happening in the next-door room. Most people were laughing. But there were a few worried voices, especially women looking for their children. "Michele," one yelled. "Michele, stay there. Don't move!" A kid started sniveling. "Someone's just trodden on me!" he cried. More noises were added to the fray.

The lead singer used his microphone to tell everyone to stay calm and have a good time but a second later, there was a crash and from the curses that echoed around the piazza through the speakers we understood that someone had walked into the drum set and upturned the cymbals and snare drum. Gianni started yelling, "I told you we shouldn't come! Are you there?" I heard his voice getting further away as he yelled, as if the fog were erasing him. I realized that Gilera was no longer by my side as I reached out with my hands to check. I knocked the wine flask over and it smashed to the ground. I instinctively took a few steps back. I had no idea what was in front of me or what was behind. Gazing at the swirling gray fog in the glow of the streetlights made me feel seasick. Gianni was still whining but he sounded more like the chirping of a chick that has been locked up in a cage. In the meantime, blindly placing one foot in front of the other, I had made my way into the middle of the crowd, which sucked me into its midst. Outlines of bodies knocked into me, making me turn, like a skittle. All I could see was the glimmer of a face, followed almost immediately by a blind shove. Suddenly, I felt a hand fishing into the back pocket of my pants but when I spun around, there was nobody there. My wallet had gone. Then there came a loud beastly bellow. "Somebody touched my girlfriend!" Everybody started moving and I ended up squeezed in the middle. I heard people fall all around me, and one started yelling, "My arm! My arm!" That was when the crush started for real. Everyone was pushing and shoving their way towards what they thought was the way out of the piazza. It was like a wave. The throng dragged me along and I could do nothing about it. A kid knocked right into me. I tried to grab him by the collar to lift him to safety but all I found in my hands was a fistful of fog. People were calling out to one another and begging for help. The heftiest were able to elbow their way through, leaving a shitstorm behind them as unruly drunks dished out punches. Then I saw a shadow coming straight for me. And I received a head butt that knocked me for six.

" . . . as if that disgusting painting that we have to display in our sitting room were not enough! If only it was a nice sunset or a picture of kids playing around a fountain . . . that would be too much to ask! Naked women lying across a sofa who knows where and who knows when, that's what Calamaio specializes in! He likes breathing in those depraved Parisian airs, that man does. The airs of a bygone era which he copies out of books, making our main room look obscene. The sideboard! Look at the back of the sideboard . . . I'll have a heart attack today and that would be the least of it. Oh, I would gladly go back to kicking you every night, what do you think? You have made me throw my life away in this shit show when I could have been living in a villa on the Meleta cliff. This will cost you dearly, dear husband, and there'll be interest to pay on the sum, thanks to the Sunday torture you force on me once a month. If only you could see the way De Lorenzi still looks at me when he sees me on the big road in the new town. He goes by in his flashy car and sometimes he winks at me, and I can see he is sighing. Just so you know: the lady standing here in front of you still gets a look or two from certain people. I know you see me as a carer for your old age but these skirts here still cause a stir when I'm out and about! Now that Giampiero has flown the nest, there's nothing stopping me leaving this place, changing my destiny to what it should have been back then. But then who would look after you? You can't even wash your own feet when your back plays up for a week on end. And I'm not an animal. I would love to enjoy Paride's wealth but without being tormented by Alvise rooting about the house like a cretin, unable to do so much as fry an egg. So, I look up at the ceiling and I say loud and clear, 'Is there anyone up there that knows how it goes? I'll play the perfect wife to the bitter end, as long as the agony of watching this man sitting there all day in silence comes to an end soon. What's the point of eking out a life stuck in an armchair? If only he would keel over and knock his head on the ground like Serraglini, it would be curtains for him. And this lady standing here in front of you would have a peaceful old age at least, without having to pick up after him and clean today, tomorrow and the next day.' Look at what you make me say. If these words are worse than curses, it's not my fault. It's your long face that has put them in my mouth. Never a compliment, never a nice word . . . All your attention goes to playing chess with Calamaio, who I have to treat as though he was the king's liegeman. What is it then? Maybe you've found out you're a faggot in your old age? Like Angiolino, whose only link to his brother is his name, which he sullies with that disease that has always ravaged his back side. Is that what's going on, Alvise? Have you changed sides? It would be a liberation for me, don't you believe it. And a reason to leave this place, finally, where I am slowly dying, inside more than outside, without so much as a thank you from anyone . . . "

The fog vanished as quickly as it had arrived and turned into a fine haze. The whole thing lasted no more than five minutes. The bank of fog simply melted away, leaving everyone looking around nervously. As the cloud lifted, it unveiled an unprecedented scene. While before there had been a party raging in the piazza, now it looked like the aftermath of a battle.

There were women who had lost their sandals in the chaos and had trodden on glass, wandering around with their feet bleeding. There were kids who had wet themselves, bawling their eyes out. They floated between the supine bodies of those who had broken a bone or two, trying to attract attention. The surly young men were still fighting, their girlfriends yelling at them to stop. The priest, meanwhile, was dragging all the old people away from the bedlam and getting them to sit on the wooden benches. Some people were throwing up because they had been dizzy with drink and disoriented with the fog and now couldn't stand up straight. But most people were where they had tried to get out of the piazza and nobody could understand why, in their collective madness, they had all cast around blindly and ended up stumbling against a wall several yards away from where the street led out of the square. They had plowed their way there like beasts of burden with nowhere to go. They had run the risk of crushing the people in front of them, who they now saw were in bad shape, bruised all over or collapsed in a faint.

I kept on seeing little white stars out of the corner of my eye because of the blow that had sent me flying to the ground in a corner. I heard someone say, "Your nose is bleeding," and that was the first time I saw her.

She was wearing a yellow dress, with one of those low necklines that dip just above the bosom. One of her shoulder straps had been torn off. I could see a vein in her neck pulsing. Her eyes were such a bright green that, in the midst of the gray mist, looking into them felt like peering into a secret garden. I said to her, "Your forehead is bleeding." She reached up with her hand and then looked at her fingers. She had just managed to give me a smile when she collapsed onto me, her eyes rolling backwards into her head.

There were faces to patch and little kids fished out of the melee by their parents but I was wrapped up in a different story. It was as if the fog bank had conspired to land on Le Case in order to make sure I bumped into at the woman I was holding in my arms. I was amazed to find myself stroking her hair, expecting some furious provincial oaf to come along any minute and yank her away with a slap. Instead, Gilera suddenly appeared. "I wasn't wrong," he said, looking dazed, as if he himself couldn't believe what he was about to tell me. "The girl was ogling me. I caught her in my net under the fog." It sounded as though he was trying to convince himself. Then he brought me into focus. "But the craziest thing of all is this: I'm not so sure I screwed the one I meant to. The fact is, I was there in one hole or another, with the husband yelling, 'Mariella! Mariella!' And she was gripping onto my hand with all her strength as if to say, 'Don't say a word and carry on with the drilling' . . . If I tell anyone, they'll think I've gone mad." He had only just noticed the girl I was holding. He pointed at her with his chin as he always used to do, as if he was always a little disgusted by everything. "It looks like you've had someone fall at your feet today, too. But she's a child. She can't be more than sixteen, or seventeen maybe? Listen to me. People like us need to look for nooks and crannies with experience. That's how you learn. That's where you find out how real women behave. I mean the ones that suck you dry. The ones that when you're done, it feels like they've eaten your dick and you forget you even had one for a week."

Gianni joined us, too, with blood dribbling out of his nose. As he walked, he let it drop into his cupped hands and a little pool had already formed. "Do you want to take it home?" Gilera asked him, suddenly manic again. And he thumped him with his elbow making Gianni's hands fly up to his face, splattering the blood everywhere. "You're a moron!" he yelled, his face looking like jam. Gilera had already forgotten about him. His gaze shifted to the piazza where they were still picking up the walking wounded. He took a pack of cigarettes out and lit one for himself. He exhaled the smoke that swirled into the mist and mingled with it. "What an evening, guys! I want to carry on having fun tonight." And he started staring down a burly-looking young man who was standing there looking murderous in the middle of the piazza.

" . . . Bring me those drops Dr. Salghini prescribed me, will you? What was it he said? 'Twenty drops, as needed.' Put thirty in, then, even though when I take them, the taste of ammonia stays for hours and I get heart burn for three days in a row . . . I can feel I'm getting anxious. All because of that crock of shit, Calamaio. If only he had been blown up that time near the portico. If only the Arno had broken its banks again when he was in Florence, like it did in '66, and washed the old teacher with a hobby for filling our house with the filth he buys and paints all the way to Pisa. Aha!

Maybe this has been your game from the start: to drive me crazy and tread me down with your heels into a coffin-sized patch of earth before my time. And then hole yourself up here like two circus dwarves, throw grappa down the hatchet and twiddle those little contraptions on the checkerboard. Alvise, dear, I know what they say in town. I wasn't born yesterday, you know. They say Calamaio acts like little lord Fauntleroy with that forlorn air of his but that as soon as he goes down into that cellar where he spends days at a time, he dons his wizard's hat. A wizard with an unhealthy interest in women's flesh, like a disease. Just look at the paintings he copies from some depraved artist from the last century . . . So, you think I don't know about our hero's strolls to the Bel Sole, do you? Especially on Tuesdays, I hear, when even the poor Isastia widow goes out for a walk on the big road dressed up in her costume jewelry. It takes courage to pick up the crumbs of confidences from a woman who has gone off her head. Your comrade in silence risks a lawsuit, you know. It's criminal to put ideas into someone's head when they are demonstrably incapable of discernment. You can see it from a mile off. If that poor woman had even half a relative to defend her, Calamaio would already have been cautioned. But there is someone on her side, Alvise dear. Just so you know. We may be homespun here in Le Case, nobody denies it, but there's a difference between being a little rough at the edges and behaving worse than animals, believe you me. So, I'll tell it as it is, from the heart: when the teacher's story comes out in the papers, and mark my words, sooner or later it will, I don't want to hear any associations with this house. Don't you dare spoil my old age like you did the best years I had. What an idiot I was to knock you over that day and let you chew me up completely ever since . . . Have you looked in the cabinet under the stairs? First bring me my drops, though. I swear, if I have a heart attack, I'll be coming back to haunt you every night from under the covers. Even if I had to beg Christ in person for the pleasure!"

The first time I ever bumped into Iolanda, my nose almost exploded. But I wasn't the only one to interpret the fog bank as a sign. A week later, I took her a little engagement ring. She accepted it emotionally. She still had a plaster stuck to her forehead, covering the gash she had made crashing into me. You can still see the fine scar today but only when she furrows her brow and in the right light. It looks like a strand of angel hair that vanishes as soon as she changes expression. When I see it, it feels for a second like I'm looking at Iolanda as she was back then, when we used to eat bread and onions, which felt like a gift when we did it looking into one another's eyes. "You're so handsome," she would say all the time out of the blue, on a perfectly normal day. I was always struck dumb by it, like an idiot, because I never expected her to say it. "You don't need to answer," she would murmur, before I ruined everything by saying something ordinary and trite. "You're handsome, and that's that."

I was already employed at the sawmill that old Nencioni had opened, may he rest in peace. On Sundays, I would go down to the Due Porte bar for the chess tournaments and Iolanda walked lightly alongside me. Even though she was pregnant. When my name was called, I would go to the table with my soul on fire under everybody's gaze but especially hers. Before moving, I would whisper in her ear, "If I win, I'll take you to the seaside for two whole days, like rich people do." She would kiss me on the mouth. "Looking at you is like looking at a wider sea than the real one."

I was good. Nine times out of ten, I got to the final match against Tempesti. I would end up with him at the other side of the table looking down, still traumatized by the war since he had actually fought there. Unlike me who had only heard explosions far away. In any case, Niccodemo Tempesti wasn't a player. He was something else. And yet, there was one time when I made him sweat bricks and it was the talk of the town in Le Case for weeks.

We were at the point after the opening move where the battle begins for real, when you can get a measure not only of the brains at work but of much more. One second before, I had been casting my eye over a match that was about to unravel as usual and then, *boom*! There were my pieces. They were floating in a sea of different moves and I could see clearly where each of them would be leading. I felt as if I were God watching all the hustle and bustle from up on a cloud and thinking it was entirely normal, without any mystery. I moved a knight and all the spectators started groaning as if to say, "You're making a mistake." Some even started sneering. They took Tempesti's countermove for granted, ready to clinch the game with a slap the face as he always did: checkmate in a few moves, a rook or two crashing into you like a train from another planet, nailing your king to the spot. But he didn't make a move. He didn't even look at the board. He looked at me. Straight into my eyes, with that grim look of someone who has been robbed of a priceless secret. A hush fell over the room. When the all-time champion finally moved a piece, it felt like a layer of ice had formed over the bar. I countered right away moving my bishop forward. It was all there, glitteringly splendid under my gaze, now a saint's. Tempesti fell into my trap and took a knight. But his hands were shaking and he wasn't entirely convinced. A moment later, he found himself cut off by my queen. The bar exploded with shock.

I tried to catch Iolanda's eye but I couldn't see her as everyone was crowding around the table, excited by the prospect of seeing the champion after his downfall. Him, of all people. I heard a voice saying, "Your turn." It was my opponent's voice and he didn't usually speak. He had made his move. It was the endgame. So, I looked down at my board and my blood ran cold, the ice seeping into me. Because the chess pieces had gone back to being simply chess pieces. I couldn't see paths or trajectories anymore. Suddenly, I was no longer God.

Even though I was ahead, I was steamrolled in a minute. At one point, Tempesti leaned over and tapped the king I was defending, finding fault with it. It fell off the board. Maso brought him the bag with all the bets in it. It weighed more like four days at the seaside than two, with a restaurant meal thrown in every night.

A sometimes think that I lost Iolanda that day. Giampiero had been swelling up her belly for six months. We went home in silence, putting one foot in front of the next as we made our way through the alleys. Arm in arm but without our usual cheerfulness, which usually resisted even when I lost a game. It felt like there was a spirit sitting on our heads. A spirit that looked at me, mostly, and said, "The one time everything is going well for you, you throw it all away." I felt a crack opening up inside. A mixture of shame and wanting to eat my heart out. But there was more. I didn't know what to call it exactly, because for a moment I had had a hot-shot's vision of the game and it had felt like going into another world where everything was crystal clear. A kind of bliss and at the same time, a tragedy.

I've been trying to replicate this feeling for forty years because the only thing I want to do is experience it again. It's an obsession. A church steeple could collapse a yard away and I wouldn't notice.

" . . . Ah! Those drops are a blessing, I tell you. I feel like I'm floating already. Even though they make me want to puke my guts out with that stench. When you take them, it feels like they're digging a hole inside you. But that's not the only reason. My stomach turns at the idea of a certain hotel room where that sicko you bring to the house locks himself in with a woman who is not of sound mind. I don't want to even think about the scenes that play out on that bed. It would be enough to give even the devil a hell's itch. And we invite this charming specimen into our front room, because otherwise the gentleman here in front of me goes into a deep gloom, then who is the saintly soul who has to put up with him? Me, of course. Who else? As long as Giampiero was living here, we played a different tune. At least I had a speck of credit. I used to say to myself, "As soon as this lad is settled, I can pull my oars in." Well, that didn't happen. Now I have two big babies to take care of, and they don't give me a day off even on Sundays. And that's not counting how depressing it is to see the two of you with your heads hanging over the table like two statues. Three hours go by without a word, without a moment of pizzaz. There's just the dull thud of your steps between games when you take the corridor in turn to go and dribble your piss out. Alvise, dear man, does this sound normal to you? At the end of the day, the only reason we get married and grow old together is to have a little companionship, just enough not to feel that life has not done us in completely. This is true for you, too, since I don't think you have laughed out loud once since '72. It's not easy living with you. Always acting like a babe in the woods. Always shrouded in that deep silence that would be a killjoy even for the Virgin Mary, with Joseph and Jesus in tow. To shift one hair on your head, I have to talk for two and by the end of the day, my voice is as hoarse as a crow's. You're not going to succeed in dragging me down into your bottomless pit, my dear. I was born with a backbone and I want to get to the end of my life without bending over for anyone, thank you very much. Who knows what goes through that head of yours? Who knows what cast a curse on one of those cogs, turning you into a ghost of a husband, without even a glimmer of the cheerful Alvise I met so long ago. My poor old mother always said, 'Just look how this fairy story started: with a gash on your head. And that says it all.' And here I am still, eating my heart out."

In the meantime, I've brought up a son. In the meantime, I've filled four hundred and thirty notebooks. On every page there are three or four games with notes. For every game, I note down the date and time and then rows and rows of moves: A3-F8, C1-H6, G3-F5 . . . A life's worth of them fill the shelves in the cellar, divided into years. Sometimes I go down and pick out a random notebook. It's quite shocking to see the drivel I used to write when I was thirteen and knew nothing about the world but wanted to write about it. So, I put the notebook back and feel a shudder of shame. Which, in the end, is the shame of having experienced a flash of genius and then having wasted the rest of my life poring over the details in a vain attempt to recapture it. Thinking about it makes me feel sorry for myself. I look at the rows of books and say to myself, "It feels like I'm so far out at sea that coming back to shore would kill me." A second later, my flame lights up again and I dig down into the mine of my chess moves.

Some days Iolanda asks me point blank, "Can you tell me once and for all what you stare at for a whole hour without lifting a finger? You look possessed. What is it? Is it that you want to follow in Tempesti's footsteps right to the bitter end?" But there are no words to explain it. Or, rather, there would be but they are hidden in the helix of a sequence that if I'm lucky I can see in the distance, like the flash of a shooting star, there for a second and then gone. Leaving me with my stomach in knots.

It was Sunday in the summer of '93. Giampiero had had an appendicitis the week before and we had taken him home from hospital to convalesce. As soon as I set foot outside, anyone I bumped into asked, "How's the lad doing? Did the operation go well?" I reassured everyone with the same words and went on doing so as I walked into the Due Porte, where I was taken by storm. I ordered a glass of wine from Maso, which I rarely do even today. He poured a glass and set it on the counter. "It's on the house."

People were taking up their positions in the other room. I realized as soon as the people I knew started leaving and left off with their words of circumstance. There were clumps of heads huddling in the corner, near the entrance. I turned back to Maso. "What's going on? Has there been another jackpot like in '66?"

He was drying the aperitif glasses, those long ones with Campari printed on them. His lips curled into a smile. "Haven't you heard yet? he said. "We have a very important guest in Le Case today."

Niccodemo Tempesti's career was already waning and not long after that he suddenly moved back here for good, before falling apart altogether and becoming a shadow of his former self. That morning I was shocked to see him sitting at the same table where he had embarked on his career, emptying the pockets of most of the workers in the neighborhood.

He was already getting long in the tooth and had developed a double chin that made him look like an ambassador. He was wearing the kind of suit folk like us only ever see in the movies. And he had a white silk scarf thrown around his neck despite the summer heat. The scarf belied his origins: every other minute he would use a corner to wipe the sweat off his face. He had grown a bushy, almost-Mexican handlebar mustache. To complete the picture, he was sucking on a cigar, spitting out thick clouds of foul-smelling smoke as arrogantly as a carabinieri sergeant. That turned me off him straight away.

I had been following the man's adventures through the years, poring over the articles that came out in the papers. I had even glimpsed him on TV one night at 1 A.M., a repeat of a tournament final against a Chinese player that he had lost. Now he was here and everyone was challenging him to a game, as if they were going on a fair ride. They enjoyed getting thrashed on the spot. The games lasted two minutes at the most. By the time I realized that the eddy of onlookers was pushing me towards the chess master, my heart started thumping.

They had taken the old chess table out for the occasion. The umpteenth challenger came forward with a moronic smile and was knocked out in five or six moves. The shoving from behind continued. I suddenly found myself on the verge of settling my ass on that chair. Like at the dentist's. Next, please. They had already put all the pieces back. I was ready for the challenge, which was not going to be the walk in the park it had been with the others since I knew what the qualities of a genius were. "I'll do my very best," I said to myself confidently. Then I saw a shadow flitting quickly across the room to my right. A second later, the chair was occupied by someone else. Someone who had been more on the case and less hampered by mental blowjobs.

It was Samuele, Esedra's grandson. A thirteen-year-old living in town with no friends whom I would see occasionally walking around the neighborhoods. Tempesti didn't even look up to see who was on the other side of the table. He picked up the white pawn and moved it straight to E4.

I took a sip of my wine. In a matter of seconds, it would be me in that chair. And I was better than these amateurs who were crowding in the corners of the Due Porte.

But the boy was not perturbed. Tempesti was the one who looked dumbfounded, if anything. His moves mirrored those of his opponent for the whole opening—he took no initiative. "He wants to test the boy's instincts," I said to myself. "Making me late for dinner. Iolanda must have already served the first course. I can just imagine her swooping to the door like a siren." But it was a unique opportunity for me to see whether I could maybe recapture that inner eye I had once thought I had many years ago. "To achieve great results, you need to learn from great players," I convinced myself. "Even though my baked pasta may be getting cold."

Everybody was ridiculing him but when Samuele made a skewering move with his bishop, there was silence in the room. Tempesti laughed out loud, which made his belly bounce and pull on his shirt buttons. "Tempesti's making him play the queen's bishop," one person commented. But others muttered, "The lad is putting up a good defense, though." Tempesti sacrificed a knight moving the other. Samuele ignored this and moved his queen, jeopardizing the opponent king's diagonal escape route. Our townsman, who had beaten a champion around the world, grimaced. "Let's not exaggerate, now" he grunted. And he shifted a pawn, just to put his adversary's strong piece in its place. Esedra's grandchild didn't even react to this and, rather than pulling back, made a horizontal move, risking the same knight that was already under the bishop's eye. By doing this, he got himself out of a sticky spot and gained a tiny advantage. Everyone laughed. A good opportunity had been thrown to the dogs in the most stupid way, dictated by arrogance. But a moment later, we were all catching our breath. The white rook had lunged all the way to the other end of the board, breaking through the defenses. And nailing the black king to the corner.

All eyes were on the board. Everyone was trying to understand how it had happened and looking for a way out before the master chess player made his move, which would turn the situation around in no time all. But there was no way out and I had realized that a while ago. The great Niccodemo Tempesti had been insolently checkmated. I kept my eyes on his mustached face rather than on the board. And I saw a part of him, somewhere inside that self-important carapace, die. It was as if a drop of red-hot molten metal had shot through him, traversing his body from head to toe. But he was an experienced player and stifled his dismay, making the whole scene look like a prank. "Anyone in your place would have taken another path," he muttered, looking at the boy with the air of a father. "You were brave. And I must say, you have some talent . . . At this stage of your life your main enemy is your impatience to win quickly."

There was a kind of applause. "Tempesti is a great champion," they all said, breathing a sigh of relief. "He gave Esedra's boy a test run and didn't mind losing to him for once." But I had seen the concern in the man's pupils. And he still looked bewildered, even though he had gotten up to drink a glass of wine with people who used to treat him like a dog and were now fighting over who would be standing next to him. A shadow had come down over his forehead. Every now and again he threw a look over at the corner of the bar as if, instead of the chess table, there were a smoking crater there. "They've taken your toy away," I thought to myself, allowing myself to enjoy a moment of mean pleasure. I was celebrating my enemy's brutal defeat at the hands of a boy. A quiet boy with a disastrous family history, exactly like his. Samuele had come out of nowhere and had stolen his scepter. I knew it. I recognized in Tempesti's expression the same terror that had consumed me when my brief moment of glory had come to an end. But I had only savored that treasure for a moment, and then I had been forced to give it back. Samuele had simply stuck it into his pockets and then walked off. Transforming Tempesti from a champion into someone with the tragic fate of living a normal life.

" . . . There he is! He's just turned onto our street, shuffling like a convict dragging a chain. And still no sign of that crappy heirloom. Of course, you'll be making up excuses, won't you Alvise? You're worse than a sleepwalker. You could least have made a note of where you were hiding it. He's a friend of yours, isn't he? You may as well take the truth and shove it in his face. 'Dear so-and-so, it's nothing personal but that catafalque of yours is an eyesore and every time you leave this house, we hide it to give ourselves a rest from all that filth. You should be glad of the fact that we've housed it this long.' I'm not getting my hopes up. It would take a man with hair on his chest to say something like that, not a big snail with no shell like you, exterminating us with your long face. Three men could take me by force and you wouldn't lift your little finger. But I'm washing my hands of it this time! Calamaio comes to see you and you'll be lucky if I bring in a tray of tea. I don't know whether you've noticed but that man looks at my calves. And he always says, 'Iolanda, dear, you've never looked better,' in that voice that sounds like a piece of velvet drenched in desire. The very thought of it gives me goosebumps but at least I get a compliment thrown in my direction, proving that I'm not thirty years past my sell-by-date for men. You're the only one you can't see it, and that makes my morale take a plunge. A husband should be a husband, a task that I haven't made too hard for you. Imagine if I were the kind of woman who enjoyed being ridden, like Mariella! If I'd been a heifer scratching my fanny against every post! And this is what I get for being a saint: a cod fish with a hobby of filling up notebooks with chess moves, like those kids who get obsessed with collecting soccer cards. And I even have to be nice to the man. 'Welcome Luigino, dear,' I say. He kisses my cheek and I can feel the flames of hell rising from my slippers and licking my legs. His eyes are small, languid, and that ash gray color that make him look like a madman of the first order. But I don't want the embarrassment. I've spent my whole life taking care of the little things and if I've learned anything it's that the devil is in the detail. Lying to me about Calamaio's little gift is like telling me that I don't have an eye for detail when you know perfectly well that taking in the details is the skill for which I always win the gold medal. So, go and look down in the cellar, you deadbeat sleepwalker, you! For once, give this poor earthquake victim a hand, cursed be the day she said good evening to you after her head hit your mouth. Or the man will be here any minute and he won't find that trinket from the market in its usual place. Then he might go and tell Isastia who isn't right in the head and is incapable of holding her tongue and in no time at all, the whole neighborhood will be starting to think that Mrs. Barberini is ungrateful when she receives gifts. And my whole world will fall apart. Needless to say, whatever happens, it's your fault."

It may have been at the beginning of the month. I was having a coffee at the Due Porte when someone said that Samuele had come back to Le Case to hole himself up for a bit.

The shock was the same as it had been in '93. In an instant, the huddle of heads around Tempesti, dressed like a local Al Capone, came back to mind. More importantly, I thought of the years that had followed, when the chess master was forced to come back to these mountains, declining slowly but relentlessly into poverty, which still clings to him today. The boy stuck to his sides every day, like a son. I used to walk into the bar in the afternoon and get an attack of heart burn on the spot. Because I was supposed to be the champion's heir, not that surly kid with peach fuzz. Niccodemo Tempesti should have trained me as an antidote to his decline.

Sometimes I would sit two tables away pretending to watch the soccer results on TV like most people in the bar. In the meantime, I would follow their moves and keep my ear cocked. But they used to whisper, those two, as if they were confabulating about where to bury some treasure. They would stoop over a board with their foreheads almost touching and talk, talk, talk. I wanted to throw a hand grenade into that corner. Then I would go home and try to create a similar chemistry with Giampiero when he came back from college on Saturday. But he already had girls on his mind, and I had to teach him the moves from scratch every time. 'Tempesti has gotten a crush on his own murderer,' I thought to myself. 'He sits there playing the father the kid never had, waiting to grab everything back with a surprise attack.'

But Tempesti never got to that point, When Samuele left Le Case, the great champion fell headlong into a depression, rusting like an old weather-beaten scrap of iron dumped in a field. His pupil had abandoned him, taking the flashes of genius that the chess master had carried in his head for a lifetime with him. Tempesti started to see the game with the same eyes as everyone else and, like many of them, found refuge in drink in order to pick at the scab. I would see him sitting at the chess board on his own with all his pieces lined up in limbo. One day, I took courage in both hands and stopped in front of the table. Without saying anything I bent over and moved a pawn forward. That gesture cost me my soul. Even proposing to Iolanda didn't cost me as much effort.

Niccodemo Tempesti glanced up suddenly and saw me there. But he didn't look me in the eye. If anything, he stared at my mouth, as if he had to give a signal, a sign of some kind. He wasn't interested in anything else about me. I attempted a tight smile. He stiffened a little. He let out a kind of growl and got up, already blind drunk. He didn't say a word. He staggered to the door and left. Leaving me with my opening gambit like a lousy dog scratching at the door.

When Calamaio applies his brain to the chessboard, I sometimes pretend that he is Tempesti, the man who rejected me just like that, years before, and has refused to even greet me ever since. Making it clear that I, Alvise Barberini, was not worthy even of being on the threshold of that secret world that he has anyway drowned in alcohol in the meantime. And so, I slaughter Calamaio when I play against him and dip myself in his blood up to my elbows. There are some matches when I eat his heart out so enthusiastically that he looks up, a little worried. "I'm happy to come and play," he says, "but you don't need to go at it so aggressively. It's bad for your arteries, you know."

At the end of the afternoon when I go to the door with him to say goodbye, I am energized, like after a hundred-meter sprint. One time, he came close and said, softly, "My friend, I enjoy giving you the chance to vent. But we could sometimes go up to San Martino for a stroll, for example, and get some fresh air."

They're not bad. Calamaio has a thing about Toulouse Lautrec, whose paintings he copies all the time. Calamaio feels as though he was born into the wrong century and the wrong place. So, he shuts himself down in his cellar listening to French music from that period on the record player. That is how he disguises the conviction that he has thrown his whole life away teaching kids from Civitella who, after learning their three R's, go on to spend the following seventy or so years on the Maremma peaks doing what animals do without a single ambition: that is, eating, drinking, sleeping, and shitting out more kids. But I, too, have wasted a lifetime and that is why I get angry if my companion of so many battles leans over to teach me a lesson. "You can't talk!" I said to him then. "You spend your whole time down in that cellar of yours." And he made me pay for it by not coming to the house for two whole months. When he came back, I was like a lamb to the slaughter. Once, I was about to give him a victory. But then I changed my mind.

I saw him. Samuele, that is. He's a man now, no longer that earnest boy who had stolen my chess master. His manner is the same, like those people who sneak around on the sly. In fact, in this respect he is worse than before, especially after what happened two years ago when his face was plastered all over the TV news.

I used to run home so as not to miss one second of the crime reports. I would devour every article that came out. They pilloried Esedra's grandson in the public square and I laughed my balls off, without ever showing it. Iolanda's jaw dropped as she watched the programs. "If I think of everything that poor woman did," she would say. She couldn't believe what she heard. "The world has gone to the dogs," she continued, her eyes narrowing in front of the TV. "That scumbag walks free, even though they know why he did it. Playing chess so much must have prodded the monster's brain to come up with some explanation persuasive enough to sway judge and jury. Anyway, what makes my blood run cold is hearing Le Case in connection with crimes of that ilk. That's how the townsfolk are all thrown in together, from where that madman hales. We were better off when nobody knew anything about us. As if we didn't have . . ."

"As if we didn't have our own problems! First and foremost, giving a semblance of humanity to this marriage that is unraveling, dear Alvise. It's like spitting blood. If only I could vanish into thin air! Like that girl they are looking for now through half of Maremma without a trace. Or like Salghini's Vilma who, after finding her son dead in his bed on Christmas night, only lasted as long as Boxing Day. She opened the door and vanished, without even leaving a note. Every now and again I think about Vilma and I imagine her on some desert island, maybe with a new husband and another son, neither of whom have the faintest idea about the tragedies that occur up in these mountains. Maybe she has found some happiness. I send her all my nicest thoughts and then I say to myself, 'You were brave, my friend. You had the courage I lacked, still chained up here in my sunset years, my guts baying in my belly like caged dogs.' Or she ended up in the waters of the Ombrone. But even for that she needed to have her head screwed onto her shoulders, didn't she? As you can see, I'm still here. In any case, don't imagine that certain ideas don't cross my mind every now and then, even just to experience the thrill of possibility. Just because you see the same old Iolanda doesn't mean that the millstones aren't working in this heart of mine. The same millstones that day after day crush the life out of you and make you wonder, 'What if I suddenly didn't exist anymore?' And that's when I start to imagine the scene: Le Case is still Le Case and Giampiero brings flowers to my grave on All Saint's Day. At the Due Porte bar, my name would be on everyone's lips for about ten minutes and then Maso would go back to mixing fizzy drinks as if a fly had been swatted away. There would be fewer vegetables to weigh at the Friday market and Don Lauro would heave a sigh of relief because, when I go to confession, I start talking and can't stop and I use up more than half an hour of his time. Sometimes he tells me to stop, inventing an excuse like he needs to go to the bathroom. Then he tells me to recite a few Hail Marys . . . I suppose he wouldn't actually be relieved but I couldn't say that my death would leave a giant gap in anyone's memories. I don't care about that. Because when I kill time by imagining my death, I like looking at you, my beanpole. To begin with, I feel pure pleasure at the idea of you in this house alone, quieter than ever, but gathering dust balls around you, putting dinner together with string, unable even to take a bag of spinach out of the freezer. More than anything, I imagine you alone with a speech bubble of me trumpeting in your ear, 'Now you'd like to open up that oven of a mouth of yours and exchange a few words like normal people do, wouldn't you? But this dear wife of yours has been fed to the worms and you are condemned to silence for the rest of your days!' The maddest thing is that I spend so much time imagining you stooped over the chessboard in a house that swallows you up in its silence that I end up crying my heart out on my own. Because without this wife of yours you wouldn't even know where to find your own dick, and I can't bear to think about you going out shopping looking like you've just come out of exile. Mario would give you the cheese rinds or worse and would never tell you about the bargains. And you, like an idiot, would hand out ten-euro bills like nobody's business. What happens every time is that I wake up in the night with my hair drenched in sweat from a double dose of anxiety. And I say to myself, 'Alvise has ruined my life but if he dares make even my death a misery, I swear I'll kill him!' Then, since for a second I find myself in the mood, I start handling you the way you really like it. The fact is, you're weak my friend. You wouldn't last an afternoon without your Iolanda following you around the house like an attendant. You wouldn't even have the courage to hang yourself from the beam in the kitchen, as Vilma may have done thirty years ago in the middle of the woods, only to be eaten up by the animals, since they never even found a toenail. So, I'm saying it now and forever hold your peace: if with Calamaio you are planning to give me a heart attack out of sheer exhaustion, let it be clear that between the two of us, you, dear husband, must go first. I'm used to my problems now and I can deal with them. And anyway, I wouldn't lack the courage to throw myself off the precipice if it had to give in to a situation with no possible solution . . . There's the bell! Have you looked under the bed? That would be the best place to hide that piece of trash from the market. Like a potty, it would be perfect for emptying your bladder into in the middle of the night."

I keep an eye on that Samuele. Every day he walks past my road carrying heavy bags loaded with shopping. It must be the good mountain air giving him an appetite. Or maybe it's all those interviews with the gossip magazines that have earned him a tidy income that he can throw about however he wants. And who cares about that poor girl Clara whom they found dashed on the rocks in Corsica? He spends his days shut up in the house. I used to avoid him and choose a place at another table but now I prolong my early morning walk and go up Via dell'Incrociata from the portico near the old school. His shutters are always closed, even at midday. Samuele must live practically in the dark. The thick fog is already there in the morning and sometimes it sits there until lunch time. It suits him, like a tailor-made outfit, because he doesn't want to see anyone's face. The only person he talks to is Mario at the grocery store. Poor thing, they haven't given him a break since his assistant vanished. He's gotten thinner and thinner, worn to the bone with Adelaide's work as well as his own to do. Apart from this minimal contact, Esedra's grandson doesn't really seem to live in the town where he first learned to walk. It's as if he's waiting for something, on the back burner. I wouldn't mind bumping into him in the street by chance, and with any old excuse invite him to play a game of chess just to kill the time. It would be the test of my life.

There's something about the lad. A commanding air. I see it, and at the same time I have to suppress a shudder of rage, because I also see Tempesti's face. The face he turned on me that day when I approached his table and dared move one of his chess pieces. "So that's what the old drunk wants," I muttered to myself when I happened to see Samuele through the chinks in the fence, his eyes glued to the flagstones. I think back to the way the chess master stared at my mouth before widening his gaze to include the rest of my face. A sign. That's what I was looking for. A distinguishing feature we all have, however old we are, or whatever we are wearing. I imagine it as a glimmer with a life of its own that also lives in other people's gazes. When the two meet, there is a spark of recognition, and you know you are kindred spirits. A call is answered. Instead, I had stood there like a rejected animal, unable to make that electric connection.

I would like to go and meet the two of them at Due Porte, like we used to do in the old days. I'd grab a chair, place it between them, and make a Sicilian opening on the chess board to show them who's who from the start. And see the difference between those who see their talent at chess as a gift of the gods and those who fill hundreds of notebooks with everything there is to know about the game, from A to Z. And then laugh with a hundred mouths at the sight of talent thrashing discipline. Because discipline can change shape as life goes on, and it can also leave you. As it did for Niccodemo Tempesti, who went on the wagon when he got older, and as it did for Esedra's Samuele, who lost his head for something as idiotic as jealousy and women. While I'm still here, the same Alvise as always. Quiet as a guillotine.

The truth is that ever since the lad walked back into the gates of the old town my blood has started to boil again. Nothing is the same as before. Every time I walk down Via di Mezzo, I feel my breath catching in my throat, as if a pack of wolves has been let loose in Le Case and they are lurking in every corner, on the hunt. I live on the edge of a ravine, and Iolanda hates it when I hand my plate back half-eaten. I have the appetite of a little bird. All I can see is the chess board prepared for battle. In the meantime, my wife's bustling fills my days. It's the backdrop to my obsession that is wearing me down, but it all started with her. One day I'd like to find the voice of a high tenor and shout it out to her face. "My dear woman, that day many years ago, I was about to beat Tempesti who was crowing over me. I was facing off the chess master and my game had risen to the challenge. But at one point, I took my eyes off the board to seek you out, and you weren't even watching. The spell was broken. I lost everything, including the game, as well as the prize money from the tournament. Instead of two days by the sea, that afternoon I fell sick. My nerves were shattered, and they still are today. This man here may have wasted your life, but your light-heartedness lost me my place in the pantheon. With everything that goes with having held the scepter for a second and then having it yanked out of my hands. Being clawed by the devil would be a tickle compared to that."

If there was one thing I wanted to be, it was the hero Iolanda had been looking for in that corner of Maremma. I have never felt as handsome and truly hers as I had done that day when I was on the brink of winning. I had been a giant. A ray of light. I had been worthy of her and my feelings for her had been unwavering. We would be equals in everything, strong and solid. And yet she had been the only person there who missed seeing me in that state of grace, when my sweat had been liquid gold and my most humble thoughts had had the brilliance of a diamond. "Iolanda, look at me!" I had screamed inside, at that moment of glory. "Iolanda, I'm setting fire to fire." She hadn't been there. Nobody had been there, even though there had been a crowd around the table. Just Tempesti's voice saying, "Your turn." I had felt the floor open up and swallow me whole. I fell here, to the floor below, like any old animal.

Many years have passed since that autumn festival in '69. Gilera has lived in Belgium half his life and he'll probably stay there to die. Gianni died a while back, but we were all expecting it as he had heart palpitations all his life. But the fact that he killed himself to avoid military service leaves a sour taste in my mouth, as if he had been murdered. Sometimes I take a flower to his grave and I stand there staring at the old photo. I look at it so intensely that I can hear his alarmed little laugh, which was never pure, in my head as if he were right next to me. A wave of tenderness washes over me so strongly that I start to cry. Not because I miss him but because I miss the way I was back then, when I was free of that obsession of sitting on the champion's throne. Maybe the throne never really existed but I needed it to show Iolanda I was worthy of her because the only time I ever got to slide my backside onto it, she had gone to the bar to get a San Bitter. By the time she got back, I was a different Alvise. My eyes were sunken and my soul flickered weakly like a wick about to be drowned in the melting wax.

I tried anyway to be her king. In this game of life there is always a threat lurking somewhere, and if you don't have a move prepared, you pay dearly. I've been holed up in this defensive position for forty years and she is my guardian angel. Since she is the queen, she's the strong one of the two. Just as strong as my heartbeat when I see her shuffling towards me with Calamaio's pot in her hand. "You're an idiot," she sighs, a smile lighting up her face and my world with it. "You'd hidden it in the larder, behind the cookies." A ray of sunlight falls over her face and the scar on her forehead flashes for a second, like a wisp of angel hair.

I'd like to tell her that of all the games I've ever played or would like to play, the one that I play with her every day has no equal and I would like to carry on playing it for the rest of my days. She would almost certainly answer with something like, 'Was that supposed to be a compliment?" But Calamaio is ringing the bell insistently. Iolanda gets up. Before going to answer the door, she straightens the collar of my shirt. And runs her hands through her hair. Then she says, "I'll go and see what that numbskull wants."

From the Secret Diary of
PIERA DEL CASINO,
Dwarf

In the summer, we used to drag our chairs up to the window and pull ourselves up onto them, our elbows resting on the windowsill. Kids would come up to our neighborhood in the old town and suddenly materialize as they rushed up the stone steps from the widening in via del Mezzo. They used to tie old sheets around their necks as capes and brandish wooden swords. As they approached, they would hug the walls and raise their cardboard shields. Until they would pull out their blowguns. Giuliano would tap my elbow, telling me to move back a little. But I wanted to see, see, see . . . curiosity got the better of me, and sometimes I would get a bullet in my forehead.

They would use dry olives. Or chewed-up paper projectiles that would stick to the windows with saliva. We would hunker down and watch the missiles rain down on us. Giuliano would collect them and bring them to me so we could share them out. Then we would lean out and retaliate with a shower of our own.

The battle would go on for up to half an hour. The kids down on the steps would lay siege as we responded with fire from above, as if we were in a tower. We would watch them raise their shields into a protective shell and wait until our spray of bullets was exhausted, yelling all the while. It was like a silent film. Including the piano accompaniment. Including the breathing. I saw mouths gaping with shock, jugulars bulging as they yelled. The pack of kids may even have had a battle cry, but we had a protective skin made of silence. A thick skin. Nothing could pierce it, neither a breath nor an echo.

When we talk about that time, we still refer to it as "our days of silence." Like we're nostalgic about it. Like it's a dream from another life. We lived inside a bell jar. Not locked in, just protected.

Because God wasn't concentrating that day as he modeled the clay to make our bodies. He was paying the kind of attention you would if your house were on fire and you had to fold your underpants into a drawer. The result was twin dwarves. Deaf mute from birth.

We used to love coloring in. We loved inventing new signs for things. To say "crayon" we would hold up our right index finger. To say "get that" we only had to look in the right direction and tighten our fist twice. We had an alphabet of our own that made us feel special. But most important of all, we held a secret.

Living in endless silence didn't mean we didn't listen. Le Case talked to us. With its earthquakes. Sometimes they were so mild they didn't even make the lampshades swing. But we could feel them. While everyone else went around their business in town as if nothing had happened.

To say "it's shaking" we would place the palm of our hands on our foreheads and shake our heads. I invented that one. Whenever it happened, we would stand still even if we were under a hailstorm of bullets. I would turn to Giuliano, my eyes unfocused, *listening* . . . To say "Can you hear that?" I shrugged my shoulders twice. He said "yes" by rolling his head backwards. Quakes were like itches. A tickling of the bones. They caught us by surprise even in our sleep. I would suddenly sit up in bed, turning around to where my twin slept. He would already be staring at me. We would peel ourselves out of our bedclothes and run down to the cellar.

We had learned what to do from Daniele, our eldest brother. One day, he came home with a little swallow in his hands that he had picked up in front of the house. It had a broken wing.

While he was showing it to us, he lost his grip and the bird flapped madly against the floor and then fled into a corner of the kitchen. It didn't want us to come close. If anyone took a step towards it, it would open its beak wide and start to flap again, beating its head against the wall until it nearly broke its neck. Eventually, Daniele bent down and picked it up again, showing us how to calm it.

His hands were cupped in a protective embrace. The head of the little bird poked out between his thumbs. Our brother bent his head down and heated it up with little puffs of breath. Maybe he was talking to it, too.

To begin with, the little swallow tried to get away, jabbing at my brother's hand with its beak. Daniele kept breathing onto it, his lips so close they could easily have been pecked. At one point, the little creature calmed down, as if it were sleeping with its eyes open. Our brother continued with his warm breaths while uncurling his fist slowly until it was completely open. Daniele handed me the bird and gestured that I should carry on with the breathing.

When there was an earthquake, we did the same thing. As far as we knew, we were the only ones who sensed the light tremors. If we were home, we stopped whatever we were doing and ran down the steep steps into the cellar carved into the rock. We would head straight to the far corner where the bare rock jutted into the room like a lava field that had solidified thousands of years before and we would hold it, breathing onto the rock surface. We would carry on like that for minutes at a time. Until the tremors stopped. Le Case had calmed down and we could go back to sleep.

* * *

I would draw a cat and show it to Giuliano, raising my hand, three fingers down and thumb and pinky out: our sign for "cat."

That was our way of saying it. Or he would draw a cloud on a sheet of squared paper. To say "cloud" we indicated a circle over our head. "Bad weather" was the circle rotating fast.

To say "Daniele" we tapped our chins, because our eldest brother had a pointed chin he was embarrassed about, which would stick out even further when he laughed. He never laughed, in fact. "Roberto" was a hooked finger at nose level because he had a pronounced hook in his nose. To say "Mamma" we put a thumb on our cheek, because that was where she always planted her kisses whenever she got us in her clutches. The sign for "Babbo" didn't exist. We didn't really want to talk about him.

He was always so serious. Everybody's mood took a nosedive when the door opened and he appeared on the threshold. His face was blighted by a stony, staring scowl. Our father looked as though he was in permanent mourning but we had no idea what for. He hardly ever spoke and when we saw his lips move, Mamma would usually nod or look down. He never deigned to look at us, not even by mistake. Giuliano and I were invisible to him. Like ghosts. Pockets of air to ignore or walk past. He never came into our room, not even when we had the flu and were shivering in bed soaked in sweat under the covers. If he caught Mamma in the act of looking at our drawings, he would walk past without bothering to glance at them. She would clap her hands and smile, as if to say, "Do some more."

We had lots of notebooks. Sometimes we would grab one at random and start testing one another on the scribbles there. It was the only grammar we knew. We turned everything that existed in the world into signs but only the ones we wanted to include in our silent universe. We didn't have way of saying "tears" or "pain." It was if these things didn't exist.

Then, one day, there was a storm.

* * *

The kids from the lower streets were quite nice to us. After the battles we would sometimes go down and join the pack. They often ran ahead, heedless. They were long-legged and lithe and they took the steps two at a time. But it was nice being accepted for what we are, without any special regard. Their indifference made us feel normal.

They were obsessed with a game we never understood, which was why we had such fun playing it. Once we got to Piazza dei Sospiri, Giuliano and I would clamber up the last steps holding onto the rope which had been put there for old people who would never have been able to go down to the store in the winter owing to the slabs of ice that formed there.

The other kids would surround us. The girls would smooth my hair down my back. They would pick some flowers and weave the petals into it. They would make string necklaces with a stone or flower pendant and hang them round my neck. And give Giuliano leather laces to tie around his wrists. It even happened that someone would untie their cape and give it to us. It was as if we were being knighted. We two monsters would suddenly become sovereigns, decked out for our investiture. Gods to venerate. Then, as always, the procession would begin.

More steps. Going up, towards the narrow alley that leads to the clock tower. But on these occasions, the other kids wouldn't run off home. They walked behind us and we headed the parade. I often thought about Mamma, wishing she could see us just once. Or else, I would look at Giuliano, who would stare straight ahead looking invincible. The viewpoint was the highest place in town. Apart from the flagstones and the clock tower there was nothing. Just wind.

* * *

It was the summer of '52. The weather was turning that day. The skyline was low, pewter gray. The air was still and stifling. The rumbling of thunder was inaudible but we could see the bolts of lightning like white gashes discharging their voltage down in the valley. We could *hear* it because it was as if the world were ripping apart and it echoed in our bellies. It was different to the earthquakes at Le Case, though. It was a loud rumble that didn't come from under our feet.

We climbed the steps in the middle of the electric storm, the purple clouds seemingly right in front of our noses. We reached the viewpoint. As usual, we let ourselves be led to the door. The kids positioned themselves behind us. Then one of them stepped forward and knocked. The others started retreating down a couple of steps. Some of the kids found it hard to stay put. They wanted to turn tail and run for it. They watched their companion flatten his ear against the iron rail across the door and listen. Then there was a scream and everyone started running.

We watched them charge down the steps. Some dropped their shields or their blowguns and didn't come back to get them. They only stopped once they reached the center of the square. They herded together, shoulder to shoulder, waiting with bated breath. They were watching us, the dwarves from the old town dressed as prince and princess. And we watched them from up there. They looked like a swarm of flies. Our terrified subjects. We stayed there for a long time doing nothing. The kids were restless, as if Le Case might open its maw and swallow them up whole. We were the only thing holding the town back. But as time passed, they started to get bored. The clutch of boys started to break up and their eyes started to wander. Some of them shook their heads. Those who had lost their weapons during their escape headed back up the steps with their tails between their legs. Then they went off in dribs and drabs, leaving the two of us up there dressed up as mad emperors.

That day in '52 they ran away. That day boredom got the better of their euphoria. We watched the first little brat leave the group, followed by another, and then another . . . I leaned over Giuliano, gyrating my hand as if I were tightening a giant invisible bolt. In our language it meant, "What does it mean?" He opened his palm, which meant "I don't know." A second later I felt a tingling in my tummy. It was as if someone had tugged at my hair from behind. Then, everything went white.

When I came to, I was sitting on the ground soaked to the skin by a storm that had torn the sky apart. The first thing I saw was some of the kids. They were yelling something, a fair distance away. I turned around and saw my brother. His hands were on his ears and he was staring into space. Maybe that was our way of saying "I'm scared," but we had never really expressed it before, which meant the feeling didn't exist. I understood immediately, though, that his head must have been splitting as much as mine was. The little punks were still yelling. Although I was feeling weak, I focused for a moment on their mouths. And that was when I realized I could hear them. I could hear the torrential rainfall that was pinning me down to the flagstones. I had lost my protective silence. Then I fainted again.

* * *

Mamma, with our brothers, came to get us. Daniele picked me up in his arms and Roberto carried Giuliano. The whole way down the hill, I never took my eyes off my twin. He, too, did not have the energy to lift a finger but from his expression I could see that we had changed. Up there, at the door, of the clock tower, something had happened.

Babbo was home. He didn't even turn around when we came in. He stayed in the kitchen when Dr. Salghini came to give us a checkup. He moved his finger back and forth in front of my eyes and gestured that I should take a deep breath. He then moved on to Giuliano, spending more time on him because he looked sicker than me. He couldn't even lift his arm. But in the end, he smiled and approached our mother with the air of someone who wanted to say, "There's nothing to worry about." Our sign for that was rubbing our lips with the back of two fingers as if we were shining them.

Our convalescence was long. Mamma came to feed us, first me then my brother. She was always smiling, and a smell of lavender filled the room like fresh air every time she came in. I gazed at her as if it were the first time that I'd set eyes on her because she was speaking and I could hear her voice. It made me feel faint. I would stare at her face the whole time and she would stop and stare back, the spoon midair. She would say a few words, which I didn't understand, with a worried look on her face. Then her expression would melt into a smile again. Finally, there was a new sound that left me completely bewildered. It was my own voice: a meaningless, primordial long vowel. A lament filled with questions.

* * *

Learning to speak at the age of nine was hard. We would practice at night, helping ourselves with signs. I would raise my hand, thumb and pinkie sticking out meaning "cat." Then, I would whisper the word "cat." I may have heard Roberto say it at dinner time. We would sit on my bed in the dim light. Giuliano would draw a circle over his head and try to pronounce the word "cloud." "Cloud," I would repeat with a shiver of fear.

We had to rebuild our whole world. Would we know how? Would we lose our way? My twin knew full well how anxious I was since my eyes were on sticks all the time. When I was overcome, he would grab my head and press his forehead against mine, which in our language meant, "only us." I would look at him. I tried to express it with a precise word: "secret."

We spent our days listening to what everyone in the house was saying on the sly. Meanwhile, we pretended nothing had changed. To begin with, we thought our mother was called "Ma," because that is what Daniele and Roberto called her. Giuliano was "frog" and I was "little frog" to them. Instead, Mamma called both of us with the same name, which was "my treasure." We didn't learn one word from Babbo.

And yet, despite our initial disarray, I suddenly realized that I was really enjoying our secret education. Learning the names of things was fun. Transforming an object into a sound felt like magic.

The two of us went on playing our old signing game. That was how we expressed ourselves in front of everyone. Mamma had even learned some of our words, like the sign for "combing," for example.

On Sundays, if it was nice weather, we would wait for the kids to come up from the streets below with a different kind of trepidation. We were now able to hear their battle cries. And we found out they called us different names from what our family called us. We would go up the steps to the clock tower and we would hear yet more words.

* * *

Legend has it that the clock tower had once been inhabited by a wicked sorcerer who could create a gale with his mouth and suck curious children up in the gusts. One day, he vanished. Weeks went by before the people in Le Case noticed that in the evening the windows in the clock tower did not light up. When they went to check, they found the walls dripping with blood, clumps of drenched hair sliding down them. The sorcerer's clothes were carefully folded on the back of a chair but there was no trace of his body.

The realization that the gang from the lower streets weren't dressing us up as sovereigns was atrocious. They weren't taking us up to the viewpoint to venerate us but to get their kicks by using us as bait. Lambs to the slaughter. Their fantasy was that the door of the clock tower would open and the sorcerer would pull us inside with his claws, slamming the door behind him.

We continued to play our role, however. We would watch whichever hapless kid had been selected for the counting game go and knock at the door. He would lean his ear on the iron bar and stand there listening for a few minutes, his heart thumping. Then he would yell, "He's coming!" and they would all run for it.

We used to let them observe us from the safety of the square below. Despite what had happened the previous year, the kids went on playing their perverse game. We would watch them down there, looking minuscule and useless. They would stand there until boredom set in and then they would leave. Only at that point would we ourselves go up to the door and flatten our ears against the metal. Knock-knock. We heard a low banging noise from deep inside. The Sorcerer's steps as he came down the stairs of the tower. Or maybe it was just the giant, grinding cogs of an ancient clock.

* * *

A lightning bolt. We found out years later that this was what had smashed the bell jar we'd been locked inside since birth. Sometimes we would sneak up into the tower on our own and inspect the burn mark that had been left on the flag stones of the viewpoint. That was the spot where we had been reborn.

I often told myself that our world of silence had been much

better. The one we lived in now was deafeningly loud. On the other hand, I knew that words had their own secret resonance, especially the few words Babbo ever uttered, usually in no more than a grunt. To sign "happiness" it was enough to rub our chests over our hearts but to say it was another matter. Something would hatch out of it. Spoken words had many layers.

Even the quality of silence changed. It was no longer a vacuum. It spoke. In Daniele's sighs, for example, when he watched Susanna from the window as she strolled by. Or in Roberto's surly expression the day Babbo came home with the news that he, too, would be getting a job at the Ribolla mine, that he would be starting out as a laborer down in the tunnels where there were often fires.

Giuliano and I would whisper to one another for hours at night. At first, it was to compose a new alphabet. Later, it was to practice. We soon learned to piece together halting conversations, stopping every now and again when we couldn't find the right word for something. We would then momentarily go back to signing.

We would even speak in our dreams like Mamma did while she was doing house work, convinced nobody could hear her. Sometimes, she even used to sing along to the radio. I would stop whatever I was doing, besotted by those sounds that I would never have been able to imagine back in my world of silence. Giuliano would often dig an elbow into my side as he walked past, bringing me back to my senses and reminding me to play the role of the little deaf-mute dwarf. It was hard. I would have liked to break out in song. One evening at dinner, Roberto knocked a glass off the table, which shattered into a thousand pieces on the floor. I was so shocked I turned around without thinking. Giuliano was right there beside me, pinching my thigh under the table. I turned back around again and met my father's gaze. He was staring at me. It may have been the first time in my life that he had kept his eyes on me for more than a distracted second. He glared at me so intensely that I held my breath, as if he were strangling me with his gaze. Then he started chewing again, slowly. So slowly I came out in goose bumps.

* * *

Giuliano was better than me at keeping up appearances. A bomb could have exploded right next to him and he wouldn't have batted an eyelid. Little by little, I learned to do the same, even though it meant living in a permanent state of alert. Since the episode of the broken glass, Babbo had changed. While before he had never bothered to look at us, now he would keep a close eye on us. We had become his home entertainment. He would set traps for us. Spoons were suddenly dropped on the floor and he would register the slightest movement in our pupils or check whether our breathing had changed. We could not allow ourselves to show any fear when thunder and lightning filled the sky in a storm. When a door slammed in a draught. When a dog barked. Nothing would betray our secret.

We sometimes talked about it at night. Had the time come to reveal what had happened to us? But Giuliano was convinced we should hold on to our advantage. We had neither height nor strength on our side. We were destined to a life that was different from that of the other townsfolk. The lightning bolt that had struck us in front of the clocktower had been a gift from God. People would pay gold to have our special power: knowing the truth about people. The kids from the lower streets went on escorting us on our processions, calling me "Queen of the Toads" and Giuliano "King of the Mongoloids." We just smiled, and pretended we were having fun as usual.

One evening we made a pact. In everyone's eyes we would be the same old freaks. It was our new shield. Our secret weapon. I looked Giuliano in the eye and I said, "Yes." He came up to me and planted a kiss on my lips. In our sign language it was a seal. In words it might mean something like, "I swear."

* * *

When there was the explosion in '54, we were eleven. It was a Tuesday. Daniele threw the front door open with a grim look on his face. He had to get his breath back before he could open his mouth. "The whole town is out in the streets," he said. "They say something has happened down at the coal mine." He swallowed. He was so pale his eyes looked as if they had popped out. "If you look down towards the sea there's a column of smoke."

Mamma dropped the milk jug she was holding. We sat there, staring at our breakfast. I managed to get a mouthful down, although my stomach was churning. Babbo and Roberto had both taken the 7-o'clock bus for the early morning shift.

Our mother ripped her apron off and dropped it on the ground. She came up to the table and said, "You two stay home," pushing us down into our seats to indicate we shouldn't move. Then she left with Daniele. She didn't even change her shoes.

We could see people flocking into the new town from our window, including the miners who had come off the night shift. They ran down the slope in the baggy work pants they had thrown back on in a hurry. A rumor was bouncing off the walls and under the porticoes. "The Camorra mine! They say there's been an explosion at the Camorra Mine!" At that very moment a woman was walking past. When she heard the voices, she looked up in the air and then fell onto the ground in a faint.

It was a long day. Le Case had emptied out completely, even the cats had vanished. It felt like we were the only ones left. We made the most of the situation and talked out loud. When

Giuliano opened his mouth, it felt like a slap. He was talking louder than I'd ever heard him speak in living daylight. I was sure we could be heard as far away as Siena. "Roberto has been buried underground," my twin said. I didn't say anything but the fact that he had said it in words changed things. You could pretend you hadn't heard things. I could pretend not to hear them, or decide not to repeat them, but they existed anyway, and they stuck to your skin like filthy mud.

The inhabitants of the old town didn't return to the neighborhood until the early afternoon. Especially the old folk. They looked like a chain gang, each one holding onto the shoulders of the person in front of them. The women were drenching their handkerchiefs with tears and wailing into their cupped hands.

"Damn the Grisou Dragon," they yelled. "He wakes up every ten years for the kill. He started with the firedamp back in '25 and he still wants more. That monster down in the Ribolla is always there but the Montecatini company doesn't give a shit. I wish the headquarters would get blown up, along with those bastard managers!"

Because there were so many people on the street, we opted for silence again. There was nothing to talk about anyway. Mamma didn't come home, and neither did our brother. "They've called the carabinieri," we heard someone call out down below. It was one of the two old geezers who always sit on the bench down at St. Bastian's. "They think there'll be a revolt. I wish! Think of those poor families. There are wives and children travelling down from nearly all the Maremma hill towns to stand at the mouth of the Camorra pit and wait for the remains of their loved ones to be hauled up . . . They say there were 47 bodies in the first cage that came up. It would be a miracle if anyone has survived." The other man noticed us at the window. He nudged his companion with his elbow as he knew full well whose kids we were. But there was no stopping his friend, who gave us a mean smile as if to say,

"My dear little monsters, the night is still young. Things will be even worse tomorrow." Then he turned and said to this mate, "What am I supposed to talk about in front of those poor kids? The problem isn't when they realize there won't be anything left of their father, not even a hair. The problems will start a month down the line. Here's what will happen: there's a family with no one to go to work and a string of kids, only one of which will be able to give a hand and bring the bread-and-butter home. In any case, the explosion could have gone off right here under their noses and those little savages wouldn't even have turned around."

* * *

They came back before dinner. They had been sent back home by the authorities together with everyone else so that the rescue operations could take place without the miners' families blocking the entrance to the shafts with their bellyaching. Daniele looked like a ghost. He grabbed the carafe of wine and slumped into a chair, knocking back one glass after another. Mamma tried to smile at us but she was shaking all over and could hardly stand. The first thing she did was rush to the stove and throw some dinner together. She needed to keep busy. Sitting doing nothing would have killed her. They didn't say a word and I wanted to shout out loud. I wanted to ask them about Roberto and about Babbo. I went and sat down next to my older brother. I put my hand on his forearm. He didn't move. He just stared into space. I was shocked to see a tear trickling down his cheek, his face smooth as marble. It dripped down his chin and then onto his sweater.

When they knocked at the door, I felt a sharp burn on my arm. It was Giuliano who had seen me jump up and wanted to knock some sense into me by twisting the skin of my elbow. There was a dark pall of death shrouding the house and no one took a blind bit of notice of us. Our mother ran to the door in such a hurry that she lost a slipper on the way.

Mr. Palazzesi walked in. We knew him well because he often came around to have a glass of grappa with Babbo, especially in the winter. Also, he was the father of one of the kids from the lower roads I really liked. I'd recently learned his name, which was Marco.

"Aldo, for the love of God." my mother sobbed, throwing her arms around his neck. "Let him in," Daniele said, pulling his mother back into the house both elegantly and determinedly.

We watched them sit at the table. Our older brother found a clean glass, filled it up, and stuck it under Palazzesi's nose. He didn't touch it for a while. He just stared at the wine as if he were listening to a speech. He was as black as charcoal and there was mud and tar encrusted on his clothes and face. "Aldo . . .," my mother found her voice. He shook his head. He looked around at us, the deaf-mute dwarves. Then he looked at Daniele and his smile made me want to tear my hair out. Then he looked at our mother and his gaze froze.

He started talking in a leaden voice, as slowly as if he were sleep-talking in a dream. Palazzesi vacillated from angry outbursts to forced chitchat. He was looking around as if he had been born yesterday.

"I was on the team that was working on a new branch of the Raffo pit," he said. "At one point there was an acid taste on my lips . . . " He stuck out his tongue to show us. "A second later, the earth was shaking and we were wrapped in a cloud. I couldn't even see the miner standing next to me. We got out as quick as we could. That was when they told us that there had been a gas explosion in the Camorra pit."

He picked up his glass and emptied it grimly. Daniele filled it up again and poured one for himself. He was shaking so much he had to hold the carafe with two hands.

"We went down straight away," Palazzesi went on, his eyes

wet. "We knocked on the pipes but they had all cracked and water had flooded the chambers. When we were forty meters down, there was a deep well. We counted seven bodies floating belly up. None of them was Bramante. Further on, a landslide blocked our way."

That evening I learned something else about words. They can be millstones. They can be blades. The father of that kid I really liked, Marco, was not mincing his words. He was talking about his day in the belly of the mine so crudely that Mamma, Daniele, and the two of us lost all hope.

"We managed to clear an opening and get the rope down past the landslide. I went down the tunnel head first but I lost consciousness as soon as I got in. Carbon Dioxide. I only came to once I was back up."

Mamma looked half dead. She stared at a spot on the table, her hands loose in her lap. Like us, she let the story wash over her, knowing full well how it was going to end. We heard about bodies being dug out from under the landslide, others who were carbonized, sitting with their backs to the walls of the tunnel as if they had been protecting themselves from something that terrified them. Others again had scratched at the rock face, their nails torn to the quick. The afternoon rescuers resurfaced, leaning on one another, their lungs poisoned. They had to wait for the firemen and breathing apparatus before they could go on with the search.

I suddenly found myself racked by loud sobs. Giuliano tapped me on my thigh a few times but he wasn't trying to stop me. I tried to hold back my tears but I couldn't. Worse, my bawling set Daniele off. He buried his face in his hands, his body heaving, the tears raining down. Palazzesi had stopped talking. He sat there, shuddering. It felt like he was saying, "Even the deaf-mutes have got the message. No use adding anything else." Mamma didn't move. Grief had pulled her face into a rictus which almost looked like a smile, as if she were thinking back to something nice that had happened a long time ago. It was terrifying. Then she looked up at her husband's work mate and said perfectly calmly, "When you go back down tomorrow, do me a favor. Dig carefully. Make sure you don't mess up any bodies with the machinery."

* * *

The following day, we went to a hangar belonging to the Montecatini company where the bodies had been laid out. That's when we saw that Mamma's fears were groundless: there was hardly a trace of the miners. Giuliano and I were waiting outside, under Palazzesi's watchful eye. He was convinced we had no ears, so he didn't take much notice of what was being said around us. Like a woman from Montemassi, for example, who was being held upright by force and yelling that she had recognized her husband from a darn on his sock.

The fire from the gas explosion had spread to the main tunnel in a flash, causing the walls to collapse. The miners who had been brought up from that point were lumps of coal. Dentists were called in to open mouths and inspect fillings, bridges, silver caps, or any other form of identification. Their clothes had fused with their skin and everything was in shreds. From what we could make out from the talk, the only recognizable men were the ones who had been in the side tunnels and had thus not been in the direct line of the fire. But they had suffocated agonizingly slowly.

Babbo and Roberto were still lying at the bottom of the Camorra mine when the state funeral was celebrated. There were thirty-seven coffins wrapped in the Italian flag, a helmet on each one. They were brought to the church on open trucks through a crowd big enough to fill a thousand towns like Le Case. The grief was more than plain grief. I could read it in people's eyes and I knew that somewhere there was a word to express it because words can express everything. In the end, I found the word. It was "injustice." Every single face betrayed rage and indignation. I also saw the embers of an unacceptable offence flickering behind it. The dead were still burning inside the living. In the meantime, the most colossal silence I had never heard hung over them, like the calm before a storm that would destroy the world. Instead of claps of thunder, there were a few voices raised against the evil mine owners. There were rows of policemen keeping the crowd in order as they followed the makeshift hearses. The long snake of heads moved forward and for us dwarves it looked like a high wall of bodies. Despite their number, they proceeded in an orderly fashion but every now and again, there was a bottleneck and we were kettled in by the advancing column. Then the procession would set off again and longer steps were required to catch up. For me, this meant breaking into a run. It was in one of these moments that I got lost.

There was an infinite forest of legs all around me. It was hot down there and the air was thick. The mass of bodies behind me was surging forward and it was impossible to resist it. There was no way I could scream. Another jam. I lashed out at the skirts and pants. I had already started to cry. Until I felt myself being yanked from behind.

He was a skinny young man, Maso was. I let him drag me away from the river of people. We soon found ourselves in a kind of corridor between the funeral procession and the crowd lining the streets that had come to watch. There was a cordon of policemen keeping the two apart. Maso was pulling me along by the wrist as if I were a dog on a leash. We moved along the slipway for a bit and then tried to cross the police cordon. They let us go through. We had to negotiate more crowds on the other side. There were moments when I felt my feet lift off the ground. We finally reached an opening where I saw familiar faces from Le Case. The Maso boy accelerated at the last minute and I almost tripped. When he saw his family, he dumped me at their feet like carrion in front of an animal. "I found this thing," he said. "A minute longer and the crowd would have trampled her."

I was picked up and dusted off. Their touch was cautious, not out of concern for me, but for themselves. It was as if they were scared of catching a disease, especially the women. I was a glass statue that only magic could keep in one piece. They didn't want any blame if it broke. They were too busy throwing the horns behind their backs, shielding themselves from the evil eye that a freak like me might cast over them.

They were kind to begin with. They gave me a handkerchief but I didn't know what to do with it. "We'll take her home this evening," one woman said. Then another ugly one chimed in, "What if we don't? It would lighten the load for Ines, poor thing. She's had a hard enough time with Bramante working down the mine. Now things will be worse than ever. This little thing may be a dwarf, but she still eats and shits like the rest of us."

That day I understood two things. The first was that holding a funeral without a body kills you. Your grief is a dark, bottomless pit because, in addition to the agony of your loss, there is also the feeling you have been robbed and defrauded without even the comfort of a body to preserve. However badly treated that body had been in life. The second, that Giuliano had been right all along. We had a gift. Right there among the riffraff of Le Case, I heard everything the old vixens were saying. Even in the presence of their coffins they'd badmouth the dead inside. One said, "Maybe God's wrath was brought down on them because they were first cousins and shouldn't have gotten married. Bramante was working in the guts of the Camorra pit where the explosion was. It was a punishment." Another added, "It's true. If I were Ines, I'd sell those two freaks to the circus. At least they'd be good for something. I'm not saying it to be mean."

I scratched a finger non-stop. In our old sign language, it meant something like, "If you go on like this any longer, I'll hurt you." In the world of words there was one that matched the sensation rising up my gorge: "vendetta."

* * *

Fifty years later, I'm still cultivating the same hatred. At the end of the day, I have had the satisfaction of seeing Le Case gradually but inexorably fall into disarray. Still today, we stroll around the old town and nod our greetings to the townsfolk. Together, we witness the grievances simmering in the blood of these derelicts. Their life drags on the same as ever, as if they were dying of thirst and unable to find their way through the mirage of a life that never really existed.

For example, we go into the grocery store and give Mario our shopping list. He smiles furiously at us because he likes our business and we listen to his latest adventures. "What can I say?" he keeps whining as he wraps our sandwich fillers painfully slowly. He always faces away from us so we can't read his lips. "It must be my arteries thickening. But I have fallen for her, hook line and sinker. Every morning I wake up and it feels like a knife sinking into my ribs when I realize I won't see my beautiful Eleonora at the door of the store anymore, with her pale little face and dark expression. She came from nowhere, and she reeled me in just like that. It got so bad I was thinking, 'Look what a bitch life is. It spits you out half a century early and then it laughs at you when you get the message that you're too old.' It's enough to ruin your liver for life. In a month I've turned into skin and bone. And that's without considering the extra work and double the trouble at home with Adelaide first a little better and then a little worse, ending up always in the same place: ready to leave this world, and then deciding to stay. Not that I hope she does go, for God's sake. She's still the person I married. Rather, I dwell on my fate and I can't stop. Was it really necessary for me to come across that beautiful young thing at my age? To experience all that anxiety? On a good day, I'm disgusted at myself down to my marrow. With my wife on her deathbed, the guilt has been killing me. And yet, I dream about my sweet Eleonora every night. In the dream, we're here at the store doing nothing special. I can smell the shampoo in her hair. I watch her profile while she stacks the shelves and then I call out to her. She turns around. Every time, I'm on the verge of saying it to her face, my heart thumping, "Let's run away together." That's what I'd like to say to her. That's what's always on the tip of my tongue. But someone inevitably walks into the store and I lose my nerve. Which is what these four walls have been doing to me since the days I was sent to collect the debts that the Ponenti family owed us: they've been killing me. In last night's dream, that old hag Isastia came in, and the words stuck in my throat yet again. That was when I woke up with a start and found Adelaide lying next to me, almost bald, practically a skeleton. The main thing is that she doesn't die in her sleep. I couldn't bear the idea of sleeping for a few hours with a dead wife next to me. Look what you're making me say . . . The truth is I envy the two of you, you know? At least you're sheltered from all this and, being disabled, your way is paid by the rest of us who pay our taxes down to the last cent until we're bled dry. I wonder what those hands of yours get up to after you turn off the lights? You must be at it so much you'll go blind. Of course, you're human like the rest of us, with the same desires. It's funny but if you think about it, there's no future for obscenity except more obscenity. Bramante hit the jackpot with his first two boys but his cum was less successful with you two, punishing you with those deformed bodies. The whole family was punished, in fact, because nobody lives on air and I bet you're happy to dip your bread in a bowl of soup every now and again. Then there's the tragedy of '54 to reckon with. Poor Roberto. Such a kind lad. Maybe too kind. Some people said he was a bit of a nancy boy, if you know what I mean . . . but we never got the chance to find out, did we? Watching poor Ines with her frayed nerves get sick and slowly die was terrible. In this whole story, the only one who got the right end of the stick was Daniele. It's a good idea to get away from Le Case early or you are stuck in its stranglehold and anything that happens later is a shit-show that ruins your life and poisons your blood. That's how Daniele dealt with his father and brother's deaths. He went to Belgium and set up a little restaurant. As far as I know he's still sloshing around there. You two are the only relatives he has but he won't even call you. Just to show you're a hindrance to him still today. I can't help wondering what purpose you serve. And yet you keep on going, dressed in those diminutive clothes of yours, while my Adelaide who hasn't set a foot wrong her whole life has been struck down by disease. And then the lovely Eleonora from down in the valley vanishes from one day to the next, after twisting the guts of an old man like me who, to add insult to injury, still has to slave away to pay your way with his taxes. So, am I supposed to feel guilty for rounding up your account every time you come shopping, or what? I only do it to get a crumb of justice in this deplorable world . . ."

* * *

At Le Case, people carry out their own vendettas. Hatred breeds hatred and their cries are stifled by the silence of wasted lives. An exasperated silence like a rumble that's been going for thousands of years. That rouses monsters. I'm always shocked by the extent to which people need to vent their rage in somebody's face. Every time I walk out of the grocery store, I feel like shimmering gold.

Don Lauro lives in the clock tower now. If a boy knocked on his door, he would hear the priest coming downstairs, exhausted by insomnia. Our dear officiant steals the collection money to buy bootleg liquor. Mario himself puts bottles aside for him and gets a tip for the trouble.

Dr. Salghini, on the other hand, plays with his tinctures and sends these people back to the Creator. That's how he gets his kicks, with the idea of taming the giant. But the giant lives on in the eyes of every single inhabitant of the town. Two days ago, yet another coffin was nailed shut. They called the agency from Roccastrada that had a gurney with crawler tracks to get it down to the road to the new town. The two-hundred-odd pounds that Giovanna Ginanneschi dragged around with her are now resting in peace. Our trusted doctor worked hard to achieve this great result, urging the fat spinster up in the old town to follow a diet that clogged her arteries day after day. They say she had been on her way to see the local fortune teller and have her cards read, up in the last house, after the big bend in the road. She must have felt the air go out of her lungs. There was no more room since they were stuffed to capacity with sausages and pig-trotters. It was still a masterstroke on the doctor's part, though. He started on her case when she was just twenty, giving her pills to calm her nerves after a love affair that never took off. He then bombarded her for the next three decades, one drop of poison at a time, until the grand finale. What would that sparrowhawk Salghini say if he knew that Vilma was still alive in someone's secrets, treated worse than an animal, a shadow of the wife that disappeared forty years ago. A wife who, after Giovanna's induced death, has been left in the clutches of her grieving, lonely mother. Just imagine. It was Alfredo dying in his sleep at twenty-three that triggered Giovanna's nervous breakdown to begin with: a beautiful girl whose fate was to die without ever kissing a man, if you could even call him that . . .

They do everything themselves here. That is the way it is in Le Case: you come into the world here and the place slowly kills you. And if death doesn't come knocking of its own accord, there's a pathetic doctor waiting in the wings ready to give you a shove of encouragement. As for us, if we haven't been sent off to the next world with a vial, we owe our salvation to a bolt of thunder. Ditto for all the fun we have with our silent subterfuge, where even the dead are not what they seem. Take Serraglini, for example, who buried his twin and took his place. Every now and then he comes and knocks on our door and pokes around the old furniture in our cellar. We make him a cup of tea. Like everyone who speaks to us, he turns to one side just in case we can lip read. Then, after a few minutes, he harks back to the same old story about Sonia, who gives him a shock very time he bumps into her in the street. "One of these days, my heart will give out and I'll die in her arms," he says. "A repeat performance of a show that was so popular a couple of years ago."

* * *

Going down to Staccioli's in the morning to buy the crosswords is always a huge pleasure. Sometimes, I take him a note with an order for the latest book. In all these years, nobody has ever bothered to ask themselves how come a deaf-mute like me, who has never even been to school, can read and write. They see I have two eyes in my head and opposable thumbs and that's enough for them. While I'm paying, I hear people say things like, "Books were invented for retards, housewives, and freaks of nature like Piera. Their lives are not worth living so they read a few dumb stories to give themselves a little flutter, even though it's all in the imagination." Then they go down to the Due Porte and drown themselves in wine at ten in the morning.

Antonio calls me often. He says the last novel is still at the top of the bestseller list, one year after publication. "In a month we'll be coming out with the new one and you are still riding the wave," he says. Then he tries once again. And I have to say it once again, "I don't want photographs or interviews. I'm not interested in going to the talk shows. I must remain anonymous." And then he gives up. "Okay, but after twenty years you could at least have a coffee with your agent," he grumbles. "I would pay a fortune to see you face-to-face just once." He wishes me a good day and puts the phone down.

It's a pity, because it would be nice to see the faces of those wretches. "Deaf-mute dwarf, Queen of the bestseller lists." I can picture myself sitting in the TV studio describing my efforts, the hard work and passion I put into my first blank pages. I could also add something about my rigorous studies, which began in secret with brothers' elementary school textbooks and continued by writing novels. Giving objects a sign and then a sound. Until I launched myself like a rocket out of Le Case and into the world. Won prizes. Traveled. Saw oceans and foreign lands beyond what I could glimpse from the rocky crag our town is built on. The same rock we used to embrace down in the cellar in secret when we had the magic power of calming tremors that nobody else even felt. Then the lightning bolt happened, a miracle of black magic. I once asked Giuliano straight out, "Can you feel the tremors now?" He looked down and shook his head.

Le Case is like a show put on for our benefit only.

* * *

We write long letters to Daniele. He writes back with the same enthusiasm, only now he has to dictate them because his sight is not as good as it used to be. Our older brother is the only person who is in on the secret of our books and he's the only one to benefit from the fruits of our labor. We have wonderful nephews who have been able to afford the best schools. The only condition is that our pact of silence is never broken. That sounds funny coming from us.

Once a year, Staccioli sees me coming into the store in a frenzy of anticipation, usually around Christmas. "Here comes the crazy dwarf," he says, as usual. He leans down and pulls a plastic bag out from under the counter. Last time, Dino Valenti happened to be there with a carton of Marlboro cigarettes tucked under his arm. "Don't tell me they've finally sent her a gun to finish herself off with?" he quipped, scowling like an impenitent Fascist. Staccioli stuck his oar in, "She's fixated with this big writer from who knows where. She never misses any of them. Listen to her panting, like a bitch in heat. Any minute now she'll be yelping."

It's nice when I get home, though, with my package. Giuliano is waiting for me with bated breath. As soon as I walk in, he rushes up to me and whispers excitedly, "Do you have it? Let me see!" I show him and he grabs it out of my hand. Then he runs into the sitting room to start reading.

Everything there is to know about Le Case is in my books. Names. Surnames. Tragedies. They describe the neglect, filth, and loathing that envelop this spur of rock in the Maremma hills. The betrayals, hypocrisy, and ignorance. At first, Antonio was convinced the setting was all in my imagination. Then, one day, he called me in a state of agitation. The second book had just come out. The rights had been bought across half the world. "You lied to me," he said. "I'm here, now, in Le Case . . . And what do you know? I couldn't swear on it but the woman I ran across five minutes ago on the street looks terrifyingly like the widow Isastia. There's also a Via di Mezzo. Oh, and there's a bar with a sign on it that says, "Due Porte." I went in for a coffee and, guess what? The guy behind the bar looked just like Maso. In the corner, there was a man playing chess on his own . . . " I didn't say a word. Antonio went on: "I don't know what you are aiming at. The only thing I care about is that you go on writing your stories. I just happened to be passing by, and I thought maybe . . . " As usual I had to say no. He implored,

"Just a handshake? Please?" I chuckled and put the phone down. Just to be on the safe side, however, I didn't go out for three days in a row.

There are millions of readers in the world every year who stick their noses into these wretched lives. In the summer, buses crowd the car park at the Bel Sole, disgorging French and German tourists. Families take selfies in front of the Due Porte bar. They go into the grocery store with the excuse of buying something so that they can meet Mario and hear him spitting out his infamous "Tankyu!" The cheekier day trippers stop passersby and ask if they can take a photo with them as a souvenir. I look at the lost faces of my neighbors and see them wondering whether they are being taken for a ride yet filled with a meaningless pride. Then, of course, there are the graveyard tours. The old ladies fall silent when they see the paths invaded by clutches of foreigners. They carry on snapping, but this time they are taking pictures of the tombstones under the astonished eyes of widows and widowers who chase the miscreants away with brooms and pails of water.

This is why I don't want to die. I would miss all these stories. I have created an army of readers who know everything there is to know about the intrigues of a certain Mariella Mantovani. They follow the decline of a former champion like Tempesti with passion. They would kill to know how Dr. Salghini's struggle with the giant will end, or how Don Lauro is coping with the grinding of the giant cogs of the clock. Anyone who is able-bodied comes up to Le Case and takes a stroll around this strange zoo, being careful not to leave any animal feed behind. They take the "author's advice" at the end of every book seriously: do not interact. Do not alter the ecosystem where these lost souls graze. Every April, I call Antonio and ask him to make detailed enquiries into how many copies have been sold or ordered up here in this hilltop town. The answer is always the same: one copy. Mine. I smile because at Le Case they would rather go under the guillotine than leaf through the pages of a book. And I can carry on making them a laughingstock all over the world for as long as I like.

* * *

I don't accept even a tube of cream from Dr. Salghini but he's right about my heart growing tired. I know. I can feel it. The novel I am about to write will be my last.

I have this new character I need to work on. I'm read the crime reports that got everyone excited years back. Samuele, Esedra's grandson. One of the many scraps the world has spat out our way. He came back to live here just before Eleonora disappeared, the same girl who has driven Mario to despair, to the point where today you can count his ribs. I go into the store in the morning and listen to people talking but it feels like I'm the only one who has made this link. It must be because I am well-trained in picking up the hidden stories that keep Le Case in its orbit. In a perennial stalemate.

But he is impossible to approach. Samuele never leaves the house except on a quick shopping expedition. I would so love to hear him open his mouth and confess to things that would make anyone's flesh crawl. I could even dig up the truth about that poor girl who fell off a cliff in Bonifacio. And while I'm at it, perhaps discover that he hasn't lost his touch and has made a twenty-year-old girl from the valley vanish from the face of this earth so that nobody is even looking for her.

The truth is that the show is going to be mind boggling and I'm going to miss it. A letter with my confession is ready. Giuliano is looking after it somewhere, only he knows where. Sometimes he comes up to me looking like a lost kid. He's about to tell me something but then he changes his mind. I try and encourage him. "The show will be fantastic, you'll see." My twin smiles weakly. "I'll sort it out on my own," he says. I give him a caress and then I stop with a jolt and remind him, "You have to say you never knew a thing, remember!"

He'll be the one to tell the world. He will reveal the letter where I state categorically that everything in the novels is absolute fact, down to the last details. Although I'll be checking out before seeing the shocked faces of everyone in town, on the positive side I'm comforted by the idea of Le Case being invaded by carabinieri. Anyone who has not already paid with their life, will end their days in a cold cell. Others will just be ashamed and close themselves behind their shutters, which will look just like their tombstones. TV cameras will invade the streets and the newspapers will have a field day trying to reconstruct the abominations of each and every character, splashing them onto the front pages. From the town's pall bearer to its gigolo, from the assassin to the beggar man to the thief. Le Case will be beamed through every television in the world and Antonio will see sales of my books hit the roof. Curious onlookers will come running from every continent, armed with cameras to capture all the filth they can. At that point, though, many of the apartments in the old town will be nothing more than a line of abandoned rooms. In many living rooms, rope will hang from the beams. Then the ghost stories will start, just like the ones that flourished in Via delle Scalette. People who fled to other shores back in the day will find themselves with worthless property, every last brick collapsed in a pile of rubble. Until finally Le Case will return to the rock it was built on. And to the woods.

"You'll have to travel a lot," I tell Giuliano when we talk about it. "They'll ask you to return the money from your invalidity pension but with what we have set aside you'll be able to pay ten judges and a hundred court cases. You'll go as far away as possible from here. You'll find somewhere you like and take my ashes with you. When you bury me, leave a space for yourself next to me."

My twin smiles when I say this and his face lights up the room with its sweetness. Then he raises a hand. He draws a circle in front of him and goes over it twice. In our old language, this sign meant something like, "Carry on." In the world of words, it means something more precise: "Forever."

Adele Centini -5
The Isastia Widow

There's a trick for getting into cold water that I've always used since I was a young girl. You have to jump in. There's a moment when your throat constricts and you can't breathe in or out. In old age, you feel the icy shock in your bones and it makes you want to faint. The only way is to abandon yourself to it, as if you were in the mouth of a wild animal. The acme of pain is when the freezing water reaches your soft nether regions, places Marcello or any man who ever set eyes on me used to long for. In any case, it's a fleeting moment. Mamma always used to say, "The more painful it is, the better it is for you." And then she would push my head under.

The thing slipped out before I was three months' gone. It was the size of a frog and I didn't even feel it coming out. They threw it in the garbage without showing it to me. They wrapped it in a rag. Worse than this, though, were the grim faces around me. Especially my mother's. She wouldn't look at me and her hands shook like never before.

The specialist came from Civitella. He sucked my insides out and had the sheets changed, saying I needed bed rest due to all the blood I'd lost. I felt a wave of fatigue wash over me but I had received orders not to sleep. "At least one night and one day," the doctor said as he put his tools away. "Wine and red meat, in large quantities." Stella, who had turned into an enemy in recent months was leaning over me and tucking my blankets in. All of a sudden, she smiled. I'd almost forgotten what it looked like. "They saved your plumbing, at least. You'll be able to produce the required offspring." Then they all left. Mamma was the only one in the room. She dragged herself over to the sofa next to my dressing table and curled herself up on it with her back turned. Five minutes later, she was already snoring. Which I wasn't allowed to do because after drenching my clothes with all those pints of blood, I could easily have drifted into unconsciousness and been stuck there for eternity.

Colonel Isastia did not have me or my clothes thrown out of his house onto the streets. He simply vanished the following morning. I spent what was supposed to be my wedding day in my room watching a thin ray of light filter through the window. My mother kept the curtains almost completely drawn. She sat in an armchair in the corner of the room all day. She only got up to go to the bathroom and returned a minute later. She held onto the arms as if she were on the edge of a precipice, her head bowed. She hadn't said a word since the day the scorpion came.

I slowly recovered my strength. I had occasional cramps in my belly but even these little inconveniences soon came to an end. But I never got out of my nightdress and I spent most of the day upstairs, like an imprisoned princess in a tower. They brought up our meals and treated us respectfully. The fact was that, despite the events that had sabotaged the wedding, the colonel had not left instructions as to what to do with me. This meant that the most recent dispositions were still in force and the whole household followed them to the letter, wary of a wrong step or a disrespectful look. Solino came straight out with it one day as he was collecting the trays. "The colonel has vanished into thin air and has sent no news. And here we are wringing our hands thinking the worst."

The more time went by, the more my hopes were raised. He was a man of the world: he knew the way things go when young people want to have a bit of fun. And he had never once expressed a desire to touch me in that way. I said this to my mother, who was beginning to get a little color back after the earthquake of the wedding cancelation, even though she still sat and stared at nothing for hours on end. I said, "I think he'll come back and say he forgives me." A jolt went through her, as if a horsefly had landed on that wild boar's mole on her forehead and stung her. She looked at me with an expression of disgust combined with unspeakable pity. Rather than instilling a little courage in me, she strode over and started ripping my trinkets off. The necklace with the oval zircon gemstone. The bracelet. The sapphire ring, the same color as the Holy Virgin's cape. She wrapped them all up in a handkerchief which she then tucked up her sleeve. The only jewelry she left me with were the diamanté earrings. "When the time comes, they'll have to find something left to strip you of," she muttered. As she walked away, she added, "And they'll have a ball as they do so."

I was fully recovered and being stuck inside all day was beginning to make my stomach churn. Mamma didn't want to take any risks, though. She was scared that if we left the mansion, we would find the locks changed when we got back and would be forced to scratch at the door like dogs. The colonel had still sent no news after two weeks. I was so exasperated, I was on the brink of giving up on the properties and sending them all to hell. Better a nice breath of fresh air somewhere aside from an upstairs windowsill. Then there was a knock at the door. It was one evening when spring was announcing its presence like a siren, bringing with it the sweet smell of mimosa blossom. I looked up from the book I had asked to be brought to me. It was Mamma. She said, "Your trunk is at the back of the wardrobe, and inside there are all of your best clothes. Grab the first dress you lay your hands on from the ones hanging there. Leave the other ones there. Don't be greedy. It's a miracle we still have a home to return to."

When they assembled us all up in the hall, Stella was already crying. Instead of a suitcase, she had a cloth bag with her few possessions thrown in. Solino was the one that made my heart bleed: he was holding a single photograph. He kept repeating that his son needed bread and salami since his bones were fragile. Marcello stared at his feet like a condemned man with the noose already around his neck. Santo was smoking but it looked more like he was biting the cigarette. Standing in front of us was a bailiff. He said he had come from Siena. An ugly, fat man with a pig's face, legs like sticks, and a pomaded handlebar mustache. He was flanked by two young carabinieri officers. The one on the right had the face of a fascist and kept his hand on his holster. " . . . And that is that," the bailiff concluded. His cold eyes inspected us. Then he pulled a face that feigned both boredom and amazement. "So? Shall we get a move on? Be good, people. Don't make us be mean." The officer with a blackshirt's scowl clapped his hands twice, as if he were herding turkeys into a pen. We were driven outside. From one moment to the next, we found ourselves in the market square like refugees.

In the whole time I had lived in the Isastia mansion, Santo had never spoken a word to me. He turned to me then as the whole household looked around not knowing which way to go, especially since night was falling and the buses were not running. Santo bent down and whispered in my ear, "I'll be kind to you because you're so young but I would love to know what devil put you up to this, throwing me to the pigs at the age of fifty." And off he went without even waiting for an answer, down Via Mozza, the street that still dips down into the fields and disappears into the woods down in the hollow.

Mamma started walking towards the old town. She held her head straight and her gaze steady. She didn't for one second think of offering any of the poor wretches, especially the older ones, a room for the night. I followed her, clutching my things, my head hanging, and I could feel my back burning with their enraged looks. A few curses may have been flying around but my heart was thumping so loud I couldn't hear a thing. "It's good they left you the diamanté earrings, I suppose," she muttered as we got ahead of the others.

When we got to Via delle Scalette, we pushed a dresser in front of the door. Then Mamma went into her room without saying goodnight or helping me make my bed, despite my recent convalescence. I flopped onto the little-used mattress which had not yet adapted to the shape of my body and stared up at the ceiling. As I turned over the bailiff's words, I transformed them into a movie in my head. I felt a twinge. It wasn't my body this time. It was in a place deep down, deeper even than my soul I reckon.

I could see him, Colonel Isastia. I played the whole thing out in my head. He was sitting at a card table up there in France with an expensive bottle and his face deformed by drink. Envisaging him that way gave me more pain than I knew what to do with. It touched a spot that I had never associated with him. And yet, it vibrated right there and a thought started clanging in my head like a bell. "Maybe," I thought, "I was actually fond of him and I'm only realizing it now as I imagine him lost out there on his own."

The bailiff has summarized the situation succinctly, "The owner of the Villa and all his other properties in Tuscany has lost everything with his gambling debts." This was where the movie plot took a twist. Because there were no heirs to carry on his name, he had thrown himself to the wolves. They had taken more than twenty days to tear him to pieces, but they had finally succeeded in picking his bones clean. Rather the wolves than leaving his family fortune to that wretch of a half-brother, born out of wedlock. The irony of the situation almost made me laugh but then I felt the cramps. Only then did I understand how much damage my superficial behavior had caused. I said to myself, "He was about to give you everything and you betrayed his trust. Did you need more proof of his love for you?" Maybe the colonel really did want to have a baby with me to continue the family line in an honorable fashion. Now I missed the way he didn't touch me. Through all those months I had received a single trinket that was worth more than all the gold and gemstones in the world: respect. The respect that a stupid creature from the wilds of Maremma like me had never encountered before. "That's what people brought up on bread and ignorance get," I said to myself. "You receive a treasure and you use it to wipe your ass and then you throw it away with the dirty water." Without taking account of the fact that, thanks to me, whole families had been thrown out into the streets without so much as a by your leave. I saw them projected onto the ceiling, too. I reviewed all the faces I had come across on our trips to inspect the properties. Until the bailiffs ugly mug came back into the picture. He had tried to provide an explanation in his fancy speech but it was hard for people to grasp the truth: all the colonel's possessions now belonged to a few stinking rich gentlemen wallowing in their wealth in France. They had had the good fortune to find themselves at the playing table with a man who was desperate. At one point, Stella had stepped forward, her face streaked with tears, and asked, "Where is the colonel? We'd like to speak with him." The bailiff had snorted like a wild boar. By way of an answer, he had turned to the carabiniere as if he were telling him a secret. "The casinos are full of people like him, you know. That's how it goes: once they've paid their dues, we know how it ends . . . " The officer had guffawed.

Mamma started going out with a blade hidden up her sleeve. All she had to do was shake her arm for it to slip down into her hand. "You've decapitated half the families in the region with your whoring," she would say when she was in the mood for compliments. "It's by no means impossible to imagine that someone is harboring evil intentions towards you," she would say. "First and foremost, the colonel's half-brother." In truth of fact, they didn't even look at us. Nor did they waste their breath to say so much as 'good evening'. Mario handed over the groceries and Mamma took them without a word. But one day I felt the earth shake under my feet and it wasn't one of those quakes that strike Le Case every now and again. The newspapers were filled with the news: Marcello had been discovered on the ground in front of his house with his throat split open.

The colonel's body was never found. "He must have ended his days tossed by the waves," Mamma said one day while peeling the potatoes, as if she had been talking about the weather. Since the wedding fiasco, she had stopped looking at me as she spoke. And she had stopped noticing how I looked. I could make up my face like a clown's and she was more interested in a fly buzzing by. She had also stopped eating, though she had started tippling, filling her wine glass by mid-afternoon. On the first of every month, she would send me to the bank to take out enough to live on. There was a little income from the old house still coming in and, considering how modestly we were living, it could go on forever. I had been brought up to watch out for things, however, and one day I said to her, "We should get ourselves a little earner or in two- or three-years' time we'll be going hungry." She shrugged. "In two- or three-years' time I'll be six feet under. You want a little earner? You're good at giving it away. If you put a sign up, there'll be a line outside the door all the way to the Buonconvento."

It was awful seeing Mamma drink herself to death. I had convinced myself that if I had used my beauty once to get what I wanted I could use it again. Added to the fact that I had been training for two years and knew how to keep a villa spic and span. That was when I discovered what the people in Maremma are like. They all agree to mind their own business but mostly to mete our punishment whenever anyone makes a false step. If you get into somebody's bad books in this place, you don't just die once. They make you pay day after day.

They slammed doors in my face. Actually, they never came to open them. Rather, they yelled from the window. One said,

"We need to take some bread to all those people you ruined first." Another shouted, "We don't need mosquitoes like you in this house, sucking the blood out of us." At the Friday market, walking among the stalls, I occasionally saw Esedra being helped with her bags. She used to smile at me but one day she yelled so loud that everyone could hear, "Did you ever find a place for that little glass pony I sent you with such affection?" The woman standing next to me answered, "This doll plays at being a little pony herself. She's not going to leave it on the dresser to gather dust . . ."

Mamma was right even about her death. One morning I found her in bed with a big smile on her face and her eyes wide open, looking up at the wall behind her head. I could see from the door that her blood had stopped but I didn't go and take her pulse. In fact, I started doing the housework as she grew as rigid as a stone statue with its mouth open. I didn't go and knock at Dr. Salghini's door until midday. I hadn't turned eighteen yet.

As the hearse went by, the men didn't even doff their caps. They carried on smoking or shoving their hands into their pockets as if nothing had happened. The storekeepers didn't lower their roller shutters. Don Lauro and I were the only people in the procession. There was not one condolence card. And I was still trying to process the loss. I looked at myself in the mirror and felt nothing. I wanted to slap myself. "No child should be indifferent to a parent's death," I said to myself. And yet I felt like whistling as I went around the house sweeping up. I kept the windows open to air the place out. In the evenings, I laid the table for one and happily knocked back a few glasses of wine. I was sometimes so tipsy that I went to bed with the dirty dishes still on the table, leaving them for the following day. It was like falling into a black hole. I would wake up in the morning on top of the covers still dressed. I found this so funny I started my day with a good laugh.

When I went out later in the day, my good mood soon took a turn for the worse. And not long after, the good moods disappeared altogether. I started to feel sorry for myself, drinking alone like an old woman. I didn't exchange one word with a living soul, not even by mistake. I spent my birthdays on my own in my room, but Christmas was even worse, though it wasn't exactly a great celebration when Mamma was still alive. But at least someone was there. Someone to tell those old chestnuts to. I started invoking the spirits from the old jail. Begging them to pull my hair, or grab my feet at night . . . But nothing ever happened. Not a sigh. I sometimes dreamed of leaving Le Case. I imagined myself walking barefoot on the beach, on the island of Elba on the horizon. When I woke up, I was so desperate to catch the first bus that I started pacing the room for miles at four in the morning. But when the time came, I was never brave enough. "Half of Tuscany knows what happened," I told myself. "Maybe I'll find the money to pay the rent and then find myself with the same grim faces as here, people who can't wait to see me humiliated." If I had wanted to start again for real, I would have had to leave the region altogether. I flopped into my chair, dangling my arms, because this place was the only family that I had left, even though it treated me like the least important piece of shit. I had been brought up with a peasant's mentality. Everything was possible but without anyone to teach me, I didn't know how to go about it. I was consumed by fear. Every day that went by was a day I wasted, immobilized by terror and exhausted by a solitude that was becoming second nature. In the meantime, the For Sale sign I had hung on the front door rotted month after month, as had always been the case in that building. I watched the seasons go by from the window. My savings had been slowly running dry but suddenly the money seemed to be running through my fingers faster than ever, even though I was consuming exactly the same amount. I had just turned twenty-five and my beauty was quickly losing its bloom.

One fine day, I realized by doing a few sums that my nest egg would only last me another six months. After that, I would have to cling to Don Lauro's robes if I wanted food on the table. Or I might even have to sell off the trinkets at basement prices.

Seven years had gone by since Mamma died and I had been turned into the wicked witch. What happened with the colonel had faded into distant memory and everyone who had been thrown out after he lost his fortune had found their way. I was the only one who hadn't. I was ready to break my back in the fields but if I knocked on any of those doors, I would be chased away with a stick. I felt a gaping chasm of terror deep in my heart because it was perfectly clear that the carabiniere could do nothing about it: people were killing me in broad daylight. They wanted to see me prostrate at the door of St. Bastian's, begging for a crust of dry bread to dip into water. The women were the worst. The fact that I was beautiful made them swell with envy like the toads they were. I could already picture myself having to roam the streets to steal scraps from stray cats. Or creep into orchards to fill my apron with fruit and risk a rifle shot. I went down to one meal a day, which I ate on the tip of my fork. I would wake up in the mornings with a tingling feeling in my head and bunged up ears. All it took was a few chores and I was shaking with fatigue. My ribs were beginning to show. At night, spasms of hunger woke me with a jolt. But I was ready to let myself die right there and then, like an animal seeking a ditch to creep into, rather than go and ask for help again. The townsfolk watched me walk by like a shadow of myself but not a soul said a word to me, not even when they saw me lean on the wall up in the old town with my eyes closed, feeling dizzy, with a buzzing in my ears and my knees gone to jelly. Eventually, I made up my mind: I went to the bank and I took out the last of my savings. Then I went down to the grocery store and cleared the shelves grimly. I said, " . . . and I'll have 8 oz. of head sausage. No, make that 12 oz. And that big bottle of wine. And bread, of course. And a nice portion of anchovies . . . " By the time I made my way home, the heavy bags were cutting my arms off. Once I was inside, I laid everything out on the table and started opening up the packages.

I ate and wept loudly. Snot wet the bread that I gobbled down. I knew this was the last decent meal I would have before throwing myself at the priest's mercy as I'd once seen the Calabrians do after an accident at the mine. I was a girl then and Mamma pointed them out to me. "If you ever end up in their position, you may as well kill yourself on the spot. I could have done it that day, to rid myself of the agony of slow starvation. The kind that gnaws at you by the hour. I was sorry to ruin the beautiful face that my father had given me before disappearing to Greece. A face that now looked like a skull. My hands were the scariest, though. They looked like a dead woman's. I could hardly bear to look at them as I cut generous slices of bread with the strength of a baby sparrow. In the meantime, I threw lumps of cheese down my gullet without even tasting them. With the opened packages in front of me, I thought to myself, "Maybe this is how I'll end my days. With my stomach cleaved open." And the tears started rolling.

I only stopped when there was an unpleasant reflux that brought up a piece of barely-chewed sausage. I gritted my teeth and sent it back down again. Dying is all very well but squandering the last of my money on food, only to chuck it up again, was not acceptable. My stomach was so distended it felt like I had ingurgitated everyone in the town. "I wish!" I said to myself. If it was possible, I felt worse than before because I had eaten too fast and now it was all sitting there like a brick on my stomach. When I sat down, I felt I was drowning. Pinned in my head was a postcard of me when in a couple of days, I would swallow the last mouthful. I decided this, too: I would go to bed and to hell with it. Beautifully made up and in one of the best dresses I had taken away from the Isastia Villa. It felt like a satisfying revenge on these hard-hearted people. They might even make up a story about my ghost, which yells all night. I had been thinking of myself as a spirit that terrifies passersby on the stairs so heartily that after a while, I began to feel a little better.

I still couldn't breathe properly so I decided to go outside. Breathing was even harder in the narrow alley. I ignored it and made my way up to the old town at a fast pace. I was soon up at the viewpoint under the clock tower. I could see the whole Maremma plain. I leaned out over the parapet and looked down at the rocky precipice and the scrubby bushes. I was on the verge of letting myself go but when the weight of my head made me tip over for real, I pulled back with my hands so forcefully that I ended up on my ass on the cobblestones. "If I die, it will be someone else's doing," I said, firmly. "Anything, but I will not do this to myself."

I started back home, my head hanging so low it was under my feet, and I suddenly felt a shiver of nostalgia for that simple gesture that is walking out in the world. There was a lump in my throat. Then I saw a ticket on the ground. It was there on the last part of Via di Mezzo. It hadn't been there on my way up. I could swear on my life. I bent down and picked it up.

They call me a "widow" behind my back, taking the piss. Or to remind me: "It's been forever but let's never forget the nature of certain events." Something like that. The fact is that they wanted me dead but I have survived, and done well for myself without ever having to stomach a day's work. The pleasure I get from showing off my good health and all my trinkets comes with a high price but it still fills my days.

Ten years ago, they even set the tax inspectors on me. They were two big men who spoke with an accent from down in the valley. I made them a cup of coffee. They minced their words, sheepish. I lived off almost nothing but that nothing wasn't bread and water. In Le Case they saw me go down to the store every morning and fill my fridge, while the widows on their husband's pensions had to count the pennies to get to the end of the month. The tax inspectors were wide-eyed when they checked my bank statements. They saw there was a tidy sum there but before they asked me about it, I said straight out, "I'm the one who won the lottery in '66," and showed them the papers, duly stamped and taxed at source. I'd had the nest egg all this time, and I was still doing well. "I own the house. Investing the original capital has given me more than enough interest to live on. In fact, I have almost earned more than I started with. Without asking for a cent from the State." After they left, I went and bought a necklace that I still wear and all the tittle-tattlers have a seizure when they see me stroll by under their balconies.

But sometimes I look at myself in the mirror in the morning for a long time. These are the days that start badly and are bad all day long. Because maybe getting the winning lottery ticket should have brought me back to my senses. So, I ask myself, "Adele, my dear, were you right to stay? All you needed to do was take the loot and shoot off to Liguria, say. Maybe you would have found a husband and had some kids there . . . " These moments are really terrible. I usually run to the kitchen and open a bottle. I ride the storm one glass at a time, the boat bobbing perilously on the waves in the unique darkness of my soul. I tell myself this was meant to be. That sometimes people are like trees: each one is different and they do not grow where they do by chance. They put down their roots in one spot and grow strong there, caressed by the wind. And this is where I was born, kissed with the fortune of a rare beauty. Leaving this place would have changed my blood and the rest of my life would have been missing something. I have lived and continue to live as a reject, it's true. But at the end of the day, this is the background setting I like. Including the bastards who live here. My presence here is a constant slap in the face for them. My flesh may be flabbier but my spirit is indomitable. Le Case requires this of its townsfolk: all or nothing. Every corner of Maremma is the same. It bellows inside you, for good or for bad. People from this region have thick skin, especially on their back sides which is as impenetrable and hoary as pig skin. I'm of the same ilk. Everyone wanted me to die of starvation but I stuck it out, and am still here, which makes them shit bile by the bucketful. It would have been too easy on them if I'd disappeared, ending up as the subject of a century-old fairy tale. "I'm here and I'm shoving the fact in their face," I tell myself when I'm on my fifth or sixth glass. Usually, it's already dark outside and my dark thoughts have already run their course. If not, I empty the bottle and collapse drunkenly on my bed, skipping dinner.

Esedra's death was a challenge to my convictions. She died unexpectedly and I was left gasping like a codfish. I was truly upset. I joined the procession of sad faces shuffling down to the graveyard. Everyone was saying she was a saint, but I knew how evil she could be behind people's backs. Over the years, I had been devising a plan to exact my revenge on her because, let's face it, if she had behaved like a normal person in the beginning, nobody would have tied a thread three times around the banisters. Nor would there have been a miscarriage caused by that scorpion wrapped up with the glass pony. It was her fault that everyone in the household had lost their positions. And she was at the root of the colonel's vanishing act. I used to spend whole nights planning my vendetta, especially in the winter at nightfall with the dishes still on the table. It was like a glittering treasure hidden at the bottom of a drawer: getting my own back would soon return things to the way they should be. Back to their natural order. But then Esedra suddenly went and died on me, depriving me of one of the trifles that kept me going.

One thing Mamma always said was this, "What goes around comes around." And she was right. Two years ago, I was jumping up and down like a madwoman when precious little Samuele was being pilloried on TV and in the national papers. And before that, I got so much amusement from that family's roller coaster fortunes, especially when her daughter ran off with a man from out of town and left Esedra to look after a toddler. At the same time, however, it really annoyed me because having to look after her grandson had given her a new lease on life. And when the results of her upbringing were making everyone in their right minds sick, I would dance down to Mario's like a ballerina to buy a flask of the new cask wine to keep me company and increase my pleasure listening to the news. I would lift my glass and toast, "To your health!" The entire nation was enthralled and disgusted by what he had done but my heart melted. There was always a stupid little voice harping at me, like a flea in my ear. "A life's effort for these fifteen minutes of lustful pleasure?" I kept it quiet with flask after flask. Sometimes I would get angry and answer back. "Okay, so it was a bloodbath but I'm going to enjoy every minute of it." With more wine down the hatch.

I was as nervous as a suitor as the court mulled over the first verdict. Condemning Samuele meant finding the person who had brought him up guilty. Imagining him under house arrest made me wake up as light as a butterfly. Then came the day when he escaped. They came to pick him up and found the apartment empty. It didn't last long. They caught him as he was taking the exit onto the provincial road. When I heard how the chase had ended up, I laughed my head off. The whole of Italy watched with bated breath and nobody held their breath longer than me.

Esedra's grandson had been sentenced to years and years. I had to pull up a chair when I heard they had captured him. He had been so desperately scared of jail that he had climbed onto his motorbike and tried to make his way up to these very mountain peaks where he had grown up. But it had all come to an end very suddenly on a hairpin bend. Precious little Samuele had seen a pickup coming his way and veered to avoid it. He had flown off the road and down the precipice.

In the TV report, they interviewed Sonio Nencioni from the old sawmill. He barked into the microphone and stared with bloodshot eyes at the camera. "Who's going to compensate us? It's a miracle my workers didn't go down the rock face behind him. They swerved the other way to avoid the speeding bike and this is the result!" The camera panned over to the pickup, with one side crushed from the headlights to the taillights. Nencioni was still baying in the background, "I pay my taxes!" as if that had anything to do with it.

I rubbed my hands so hard I could have lit a fire. Just as I had done that day when I heard that nobody knew who had won the lottery and I suddenly remembered the ticket that I had found by chance on Via di Mezzo when I was so deeply depressed. Actually, maybe I was even happier now: the blood was fizzing in my veins. But I didn't like what I heard on the shows. I saw all the onlookers and TV cameras crowding around the hospital entrance. All of a sudden, a doctor came out from behind a cordon set up by the carabinieri to keep the rubberneckers at a distance. The doctor said the young man had sustained life-threatening injuries. The crash had switched his brain off, exactly like a kid I knew who tripped over a football and hit his head on the sidewalk, a kid called Ernesto, but everyone called him Little Fly because he was so weak. That day in mid-May he was brain dead but his heart kept pumping blood around his body. He was in a coma for a week but then it ended as it should.

The idea that Samuele was in the same limbo between life and death made me sink back into the usual depression. "If you dare go and die on me, too, I'll come over and deal with you," I roared with my eyes glued to the TV news. My breath caught in my throat as soon as the theme tune came on. But the news was always the same: he was still in a coma. And I was drinking twice as much wine as before: Dutch courage to keep me going. Until they suspended the trial. "A legitimate impediment," they called it. "Like shit," I said out loud. Gradually, the story became old-hand and most people accepted that Samuele's condition was God's will: he metes out justice with one hand and gives candies to the devil with the other. I was so nervous I bit my nails to the quick. It felt as though Esedra was sticking it up my ass a second time around and I couldn't sleep.

Around that time there was a big earthquake, as if Le Case had suddenly decided to shake off all the aggravations living in its belly, especially mine. The tremors were strong but most people didn't feel them because they were fast asleep. Don Lauro was the only one who nearly died when his ceiling collapsed everywhere except where his bed had been. When people woke up, they found cracks in the kitchen walls and upturned furniture. Wedding pictures that had come off the wall, the frames warped and the glass shattered. But we all went out as normal, even though out houses looked like a particularly mean ghost had been rummaging in them, going through our things without asking. I watched the townsfolk talking softly to one another as they walked in the narrow streets. They exchanged greetings with smiles that smacked of an averted tragedy. Then they went back to their everyday lives, stifling with their daily habits the effects of the earthquake that had sent them out onto the street looking like the corpses they were.

I bought the papers but Samuele was still playing Sleeping Beauty on page five, holding me in a state of suspense that made me tear my hair out. Then there was the final nail in the coffin: the case had been archived. Insufficient evidence. He received a suspended sentence for his escape attempt, but that was nothing. Esedra's grandson had been let off even though he was still plugged into machines at the hospital. For the second time, I was being impeded from serving up my dish of revenge. I wasn't the only one who had it in for him. In those afternoon-talk-shows, they still talked about it. "So, was it the Holy Spirit?" Others in the street conjectured, "He was lucky to find a lawyer looking for publicity and get away with it. There was even a motive. Think of that poor girl's parents . . . " In the meantime, the graffiti on the walls of the house in Via Urania made you come out in goosebumps. Everyone said a monster had been living here. A monster who would have to watch what he did in this town if he ever woke up after the accident.

Esedra's boy came to at the end of June, after having his every breath pumped into him by the wheezing machine. His face was all over the 12 o'clock news. The same doctor I had seen in front of the hospital before was speaking. He said that the patient had opened his eyes. His vital organs were all functioning but he needed time to recover. In any case, he was already talking . . .

Two years ago, I said to Calamaio straight out, "Luigino, dear, look into my soul." He thought about it for a while and then nodded, with that typical expression of his that was both mortified and teasing. Eventually, he picked up a pastel crayon and started to draw.

"The outside reveals the inside," my mother would sometimes say, blathering as usual as she stuck her finger in the ash of the stove to make herself some dark eye shadow. She used to enjoy watching the workmen on Sunday morning, their day of rest, drooling on the church steps as I walked past. "Look straight ahead," she would warn me. "If you so much as look these dung beetles in the eye, poverty will cling to you, alongside those lustful gazes that would disgust the devil himself. It's best if they look at you as they would a loaf of bread in the bakery window. A nice crusty one that would split the stomach of someone so penniless they can't even afford a slice."

Well, I let Calamaio cut the loaf of my pale, flaccid flesh with his bare hands. "If there is any beauty in here," I said that morning, the first time we went into Room 112 of the Bel Sole, "find it and pin it down, hammer it down if you have to, in your drawing." I hadn't taken my clothes off in front of a man for years. The last time I had revealed so much as an inch of flesh was when I was with Marcello, when life and body both were reveling, before I was exiled within the four walls of my house. Every pore of my skin had started yelling that I was lonely. Draped over the chaise-longue, I looked at the tips of my toes as if they belonged to another person. I said to myself, "This body has been through everything and nothing but deep down it has fought a real war. That is what Luigino must find and draw."

He makes another attempt but, in the end, he leaves the room with a heavy heart. He never lets me see his sketches. He gathers up his pastels and runs away like a soldier surprised to find himself in an enemy trench. The last image I have of him is always his watery, dejected eyes. I let myself swim in the silence that follows, and is so different from the silence between us when I am posing for him. This silence is a lake with no shore in which I bathe at the end of every session. It takes cold water to combat and thereby exterminate the icy touch of naked skin. "The more painful it is, the better it is for you," was another of my mother's sayings. I stare up at the ceiling for a moment and then I go down to get my first dunking.

When I ran into him a month ago, I thought all the stories about ghosts had suddenly come true. It was a misty evening, the kind that creates a veil between you and your surroundings. I saw him walk past me, his head bowed and a bag of shopping on his arm. It was Esedra's grandson, Samuele. Yes, him.

I stood there at the bottom of the street, brushing against the wall like in the old days when I would walk through Le Case, my knees weak with hunger. "I must be dreaming," I said to myself, my heart galloping. "Maybe my obsession has turned into a mental disease and I'm seeing shadows." But that evening, rumors were already beginning to spread: certain shutters on Via dell'Incrociata had been opened.

Even though precious little Samuele had been cleared of all charges long ago, people thought the verdict was wrong. Many were ready to move on from words to deeds. That was why he was holed up in this Maremma hilltop town. He was opening up the rooms where his grandmother had once given him such tender loving care. And there he was, in my maws like a little bird.

It was as if Esedra had headbutted her tomb and cracked it open so that she could come back and live in her house. I walked up to her neighborhood using the back path. I came out on the corner of the water fountain and settled down to spy on the boy's movements, my back flattened against the wall of Mariella's house. I had seen so much about him in the news, and read so many articles in the papers, that I was almost beginning to think of him as a celebrity. He never did very much. I went up and laid siege to that quarter of town at all times of day and night. If I was lucky, I would see him go out, only to come back five minutes later with some shopping.

After a while I almost started to feel sorry for him. I rebelled against the impulse but I couldn't help myself. It was as if I were reliving my own troubles back in the day, when we were thrown out of the Isastia Villa and we lost the goodwill of the townsfolk. Samuele's life was like a carbon copy of mine. The days went by under the silent scorn of an exile that would have tested the patience of a saint. "Look how things have turned out," I would say to myself. "They are torturing him just like they did me." I knew the torment he was going through. I stared up at those dark windows with a compassion that I knew well because I had experienced it for decades looking at myself in the mirror. At the end of my stakeout, I went home with a bittersweet feeling that somehow calmed my anger and helped me sleep at night.

As the days went by, I started to notice there were other things going on. It's hard to imagine but the comings and goings in Via dell'Incrociata were unbelievable. It was like Piazza del Mercato on Fridays when the market was setting up. Take the son of that peasant from the Marches, for example. Some mornings I would see him scuttling out of the dark alleys like a spider. He would walk up to Samuele's motorbike and start stroking it, standing there looking around him, caressing the fairing as if it were the belly of his bride. Or again, I would catch sight of Divo if I leaned out a little into the street. He would stand there at his window, his jaw set like a small-town Duce, staring at Esedra's house as if he were peering into the depths of hell, without moving a muscle.

Whenever Angiolino walked by, I would pull back, hide behind the house and only resume my spying in snatches. I noticed a change come over him in the last few yards before he reached the door: he would suddenly alter his gait as if he were stepping out of someone else's shoes. If he had been humming, as soon as he turned the corner, he would stop and hang his head and scowl. Once, he dropped his key as he was trying to put it in the lock. He cursed out loud and, for a second, I thought he must have been drinking because he never usually says anything dirtier than "Maremma Marinade!"

The most interesting thing I noticed up there was the girl from the valley, the one they have finally stopped looking for. I would see her peer out of one of the porticoes like a kitten trying to have a nap. To start with, she would just stand there and look hesitantly up at the windows. Then the visits started. She would check Mariella's windows and then run across the road like a flash of lightning, race up the stairs, open Esedra's door, and disappear behind it. In that very spot, someone else's face appeared. At first, I didn't recognize the outline because it was right behind the window. One day I walked around the neighborhood and caught a glimpse of Sonia Serraglini from behind in the alley. I don't know whether she was following Eleonora or whether she was spying on Angiolino, who is identical in every way to her dead husband. To this day, it still makes me sad to think of it. "Look at that poor woman," I would say to myself, and still do. "She keeps an eye on poor Achille's twin and maybe she even thinks it's him, just so that she can feel he's alive for a moment."

I stopped my spying when I saw Eleonora's gaunt face in the newspaper. I had begun to convince myself that their fling was a slap in the face for me. Rather than being crushed by solitude and silence, Esedra's grandson had had his fifteen minutes of pleasure with a bimbo who caught a bus bright and early somewhere in the Ribolla area to see him. I had never had that luxury. Never again did a man look at me that way. They nailed the blame for what happened to the colonel on my forehead before I had turned eighteen, and the label is still there today. They didn't see me, they saw him. If any of the bolder men in town had been tempted, their temptation withered like dead leaves. In the meantime, I had to stand by and watch the waste when those same workers chose a hag to keep them company rather than marry me. When I still looked like a queen at forty. They left me there to rot.

I listened to the rumors distractedly. Everyone said the bimbo's disappearance reeked of violence but I was the only one who knew the truth. And yet I didn't say a word. My intuition told me this was fertile terrain for burying Esedra in another scandal, perhaps even worse than the one I had seen on TV. There was a chance I could use it beat her down once again. "Where do you think that young girl has come unstuck?" I would say to myself, watching the pickup from the sawmill crawl by Rodolfo's bar. The workers there made your blood freeze. They were fearless and hungry as wolves. The way they glare at you made you want to cross yourself. I laughed so hard it made me feel ill. "Samuele, my dear. This little elopement is going to cost you dearly," I chuckled as I dunked a slice of bread into my wine. "I've seen the face of that good-looking Albanian nursing his betrayal. Just breathing next to him is enough to create an electric storm."

I love it when things go this way. I hunker down with my dreams of revenge for whole afternoons. I'd love to have a magic wand to freeze this moment forever. The temptation to solve the mystery is overwhelming but if I talked, the smirk that comes of holding somebody else's life in the palm of my hand would have to be wiped clean. If I clenched my fists, all hell would break loose. But I don't and I'm happy with that. I pat myself on the back for keeping everyone's breath bated. Sometimes I look at the reflection in my wine glass and think, "Impersonating God is fun."

I always make my final dunk last longer. Sometimes I stay underwater so long that my body rebels and my legs start kicking of their own accord. I long for that moment of terror when the urgent need to breathe starts to give my soul cramps and I feel all the little veins tingling, plucking at my skin. I hold on without giving in to my craving for air, my throat screaming and my hands clinging to the edge of the bath. I hold on even longer. My heart is hammering so loud it sounds like barking and the surface of the water changes color as I glaze over. Locked inside me there is another Adele Centini wailing like a siren, yelling at me to open my mouth and take a deep breath. But I don't give in to her. She goes crazy, banging her forehead against the walls of her prison down there. All I need to do is let go, unlock my jaws, and inhale a mouthful of bubble bathwater. But I would be overcome by fear and my kicking would flood the bathroom, giving Susanna at the Bel Sole another low-season chore.

When I come back up for air, it is as if God has just created me out of the depths. The Adele that lives inside me fills her lungs with air in one gulp, like someone dying of thirst at the water fountain. Tremors shake my body to the quick. I chuckle and embrace my diabolic side. Stifling the words until I get my breath back, I finally say, "So this is it . . . you actually want to live . . . Even though you complain all the time . . . "

After my cold-water adventure, my body vibrates strangely, making a sound like the clang of metal on metal. I feel as though I am looking at myself from the outside as I place my feet on the bathmat. I reach for my robe, twist my hair up into a towel, and look at myself in the mirror. I like what I see. It's as if I were saying to myself, "Despite everything, you are still here." But there are other days when I feel so sorry for myself that I would like to jump out of the window. The same words go through my head, but the echo is different.

I go back to the little porcelain peasant girl. I take my trinkets out of her begging dish, one by one. Room 112 is the usual lake of silence and my movements hardly create a stir.

After my bath, I like ordering a cup of tea and drinking it by the window as I watch Le Case being swallowed up by the night. Even the telephone looks like porcelain. To call Susanna I need to dial zero, but my hand is shaking. Again, with that feeling of detachment, I watch myself dial emergency on 112, the same number as this room. The call is answered after one ring: "Carabinieri." A gust of warm wind billows inside me. Eventually, I give in to the temptation. "You know the girl you have been looking for?" I say. "I know where she is."

Renato Staccioli,
the Tobacconist

When Babbo told me we had to go down to the Tuscan Maremma I slammed the door in his face and went to the bar to drown my day's wages in drink. Baldo had heard the news and when he saw me come in, he said, "Here's another one tempted by bright lights and a comfortable life." I stuck my elbows on the counter and Moreno came to stand beside me. He gave me a shove and when I turned around, his face was an inch from mine. "There are hundreds of little fish swimming down into the valley in the Limentra river," he grunted. I looked at his black teeth. "The main thing is not to forget the ones who stay up here. Especially those who are still owed from six months back. Tell your father." Then he put twenty lire down. "Baldo, give him a drink. He'll need a little protein for the journey."

I was sixteen and the idea of leaving Maddalena Cancelli at Saverio Marchesini's mercy made my blood boil. But the debts we had on the farm couldn't care less about that little love affair and Babbo made that very clear. "There are charcoal kilns down in Maremma. Some people have done very well for themselves in five years. There's no point in gawping like that now. Do you think I'm happy to leave your mother in this shit hole? We're going down Monday, on the first bus to Pistoia."

And suddenly all my dreams were dashed. Maddalena hardly wanted to see me. Maybe going away was the best thing I could do for her. Marchesini lusted after her blond curls and Barbie doll's curves but unlike me he didn't have the kind of debts that tarnish your day and in the long run ruin your life.

The morning we left, I didn't even turn around and look out of the window where my mother was sniveling, holding a hankie in front of her mouth, even though Babbo had told her loud and clear the night before, "Don't even think of making a scene." He had given her a squeeze before opening the door and then he had pushed her away like he did with the animals because he didn't want us to see his scrunched-up eyes. "When life is a bitch . . . " he started as we walked down the ridge to the bus stop. "Look at me, Renato. Forty years old and I'm still having to travel to patch things up and stay afloat. Poverty has filled my shoes since I can remember and it's still with me."

We arrived in the pitch dark. As soon as I set foot in the place, I realized that there was nothing new. We had to make charcoal with the wood we collected in this new place just as we had done back home. The group leader was called The Comrade, or at least that's what everyone called him. He had come down ten years before from the same Pistoia mountains we came from. Babbo had banged on about it for the whole bus trip. "He started out as a lowly worker and he's built himself quite a reputation. He's even brought his family down from Pavana. You're young. Make sure you get into his good books."

We were lodged in the town. We were supposed to sleep in an eight-bed dormitory with a bunch of Sicilians, though many preferred to stay in the woods in stone hovels near the clearing so as not to have to walk the three-mile path before dawn. I was one of these. I didn't mind going down to the tavern where they called us Lombards even though we came from the same region in the Apennines as them. I enjoyed pushing the cart to and fro, taking the new charcoal to the warehouse. The Comrade took a shine to me right away because I managed to do up to three return trips a day. In the evenings, he would give me an extra-big portion of bread, onion, codfish, and fortified wine to give me strength for the following day. "You'll go a long way," he said once, with a pat. I said, "For now I'm happy with the distance I walk every day." He laughed out loud and scratched his belly.

In the early days, my blood used to boil but over time I began to see Maddalena's face as an effigy that gave me the courage to carry on and see the charcoal season to an end. Living in the woods all the time sometimes gave me the feeling I was in another world. I saw the same chestnut trees and the same centuries-old oaks. As the moon waned, I chopped down the turkey oaks and cork oaks. The Maremma hills were less rugged than the Pistoia crags where I had first learned the trade. Anyone with the experience of cutting wood in the scrublands around Le Case worked twice as hard and produced more.

If there was nothing to transport, I threw myself into preparing the wood. Mostly they gave me the task of separating the branches because I could read the knots better than anyone and set the saw or the ax where the green wood was as soft as butter. Or I would cut back the paths between the various charcoal kilns. The woods were like anthills, filled with charcoal-dusted workers, columns of smoke here and there, like chimneys. I would strengthen the dry-stone walls if the kiln had been built on a slope. Most of all, I liked controlling the draughts after the wood had burned for two weeks and the main shaft had been sealed. When the flames leaped up, I had to move everything down and pierce new air holes so the fire didn't go out. No mistakes were allowed. The Comrade would waste no time kicking you out if the whole load went up in flames.

The charcoal burning season started in the spring and ended in mid-autumn. We went back to our part of the Apennines in the middle of October and Mamma was so thin it scared me. She didn't look sick, though. She was happy to see us. She was so nervous she could hardly stand so I went and kissed her sitting in her chair. Her eyes shone when she saw the money that we had brought home. Working double shifts and never going anywhere meant we had set aside a small treasure. I didn't even have time to wash my face before Babbo looked over at me and said, "Go and call Moreno, will you? Let's get rid of this piece of shit who has been ruining our lives for over a year."

That very evening, I went back to propping up the counter at the bar. I didn't say a word but Baldo poured me a glass of our wine and said, "I can see it in your eyes. You left a boy and you've returned a man. Is that what the Tuscan Maremma does to you?" At that moment, the door flew open. A gang of young men came in.

The kids from Porretta do this from time to time, especially on Saturday evenings. They pile into a car and drive up to the top of the mountain, behaving like cowboys. When I clapped eyes on a certain person, I went straight back to my drinking, hiding my head between my shoulders. I knocked my glass back in one gulp, put some coins on the counter, and said, "Baldo, give me another." But before he had time to pick up the change, a hand swept down and scooped the coins up. "Get one for me, too. We're celebrating tonight and they'll be hearing the racket as far away as Sambuca."

It was Marchesini himself. I'd last seen him down in the car park at the square, where disco dancers from the valley drove up on Sunday mornings if they'd had an all-night dalliance with a local girl. "They come up from the hot springs and steal our girls" someone called out from the low wall on the other side where I used to sit and have a smoke every now and again. "And we sit here drooling after them." Most of them couldn't understand what it was about the out-of-towners that tickled the girls' fancy when there was such good meat on offer closer to home.

Someone touched my elbow. "I know you," Marchesini murmured. "You're the charcoal burner, the one from Picchio." I looked up and saw his fresh, young face as smooth as alabaster, without a single furrow. I nodded. He looked at my hard, calloused hands and charcoal-encrusted nails. It felt like he was peering into my underpants. Then he picked up the glass Baldo had poured for him and chinked it against mine. "A toast," he said as his eyes rolled up in his head. "I'm getting married to-morrow. Dutch courage, you know."

The rest of the gang was tanking up and getting the party going in the big room. I turned around and saw two old men grimly throwing back the last of their amaro and getting up to leave. One of them gestured over at Baldo to put it on the tab. And off they went home. Some local kids did the same, leaving their half-drunk glasses of fizzy drink behind. Marchesini's crowd were spoiling for a fight, even the walls could see it. The tall, lanky one they called Tamarindo accosted Barros, who was drinking on his own and usually only opened his mouth to ask for another whisky. People would steer clear of him because he had a reputation as a boxer. He was the right height and all neck. They say he killed a bull with a bare-fisted punch in the head when he was a boy. By contrast, Tamarindo was a beanpole and looked well brought-up. Except that he had been drinking that evening and was swaggering like a smart ass. To the point that he was taking the piss out of a man who could stare down a three-hundred-pound wild boar from a yard away.

"Which means that, starting tomorrow, you'll have to treat her with more respect," I heard Saverio Marchesini say as he stared at his wineglass. I looked at him without saying a word. He knew he would get nowhere by needling me and he chuckled to himself. Then he went on. "I used to see you, you know, down at the Valentino disco. Every Sunday afternoon you were there, sat in your usual corner, with those headlights of yours on full beam. I said to myself, 'The charcoal burner is spying on Maddalena as if she were the Virgin Mary.' Sometimes you even managed to catch her eye for a moment. Whenever it happened, you would run behind the column. Who knows what goes through women's heads but the fact is, being timid like that won you points. I could see it because Maddalena turned around looking for you with an enamored smile on her face. You hid. And then I came along."

I picked up my glass and knocked it back in one gulp, as I had done the previous one. I grazed the counter with my knuckles as if to get up. But Marchesini turned towards me. He leaned forward a little, too. "May the charcoal piles of Maremma be praised!" he said, his breath reeking of vomit. "I can't explain it, but it's true all the same: you were the only one I was worried about. Maddalena has never looked at me like that . . . Then the season came around and you vanished, leaving the coast clear. I owe you more than a sweet wine!"

We heard a crash behind us. Baldo almost leaped onto the counter yelling, "Hey!" But Tamarindo face had already been smashed in and he was lying on the floor, surrounded by broken glass, wailing. He was pissing blood from his nose like a fountain. Barros sat down again, as if knocking out that big lad had cost him no more effort than scratching his butt. Baldo was shouting, "Closing time! Thanks to you, my evening has come to an end!"

None of Tamarindo's drinking companions dreamed of teaching the boar hunter a lesson for punching their friend in the nose. Two of them somehow got the beanpole onto his feet and dragged him out. Marchesini came up to me before leaving as if he was about to say something. Then he winked. And added two pats on the back for good measure, as if we had been at elementary school together. Finally, he walked out, without paying for my drink or his own.

Finding out about the wedding made me toss and turn in bed for weeks. Poverty had robbed me of everything, including Maddalena who had felt like a match made in heaven. In the meantime, winter was on its way. Everyone said it would be the harshest in a long time. Babbo counted our savings every evening and Mamma would say, "What are you doing? Do you think the money is going to have babies?" He would close the wooden box with a scowl, looking like he wanted to jump out of the window. Then in December he came out with it: what he had set aside burning charcoal was not enough to keep us going until May. We started to ration the chestnut flour. We picked out the finest animals to take to the market.

Early every morning I went down to the tavern where casual laborers gathered. The farmers came to pick up extra hands for the day and I was always one of their top choices because I was young and didn't complain much. In the end, I liked the work, even though it meant getting up when it was still dark and resisting the potato dumplings I took with me to work and whose delicious smell made my nose fall off. They would load me onto the back of a truck and take me off to a different job every day. Many boys my age went down into the valley to warm the chairs at schools or colleges but I knew every inch of the forest and I did the work of four men on my own.

The first snow played its usual havoc, blocking the roads, and making the woods around the farm hard to get to. But I managed to fill the shed with logs. When the bad weather came, the spectacle was always the same: the sky looked as though it was going to crash into the peaks of the Apennines and smash into a thousand shards like a mirror. It often looked like a solid sheet of metal that hung there without stirring, while the clouds drenched the whole area. All of a sudden, it was like living in a deserted town. Passersby bent double, their heads wrapped up in thick woolen hats. Looking out from the farm, all you could see of the other houses was the thin streak of smoke coming out their chimneys. The silence split your eardrums and anyone who spoke did so quietly, as if they were praying. It was already dark at four in the afternoon and in that contrary world, it almost felt like a blessing because at least you didn't feel guilty doing nothing.

We killed a turkey for Christmas. Well, Babbo did. He

brought the creature into the house holding her by the neck and was pretending to be having a great time of it. But you could see his stomach was in knots at the waste. On the table, he put half a bottle of wine, which would usually last us for three nights. At the end of the meal, he rested his hands on his knees and said, "I went down to see Moreno yesterday. He's a good guy. He said if things got really bad, there would be some government subsidies and that we shouldn't worry about a thing."

Maybe I should have understood right away because the subsidies had always been there and Babbo wasn't saying anything new. But that evening I saw things for what they were, as if I had suddenly developed an extra eye: we would never claw our way out of poverty. It was like a disease that sometimes lets you take a few steps to make you feel better but soon came back to tighten the noose. We could pile up all the charcoal in the region and it still wouldn't make any difference. The realization made me want to throw up. But I would rather be choked to death than face my mother having to wipe up a rejected meal.

Babbo had not finished. I saw him eyeballing me and I understood that I should hold on to the chair tight. Mostly because he was smiling. "We talked about it," he said. "As you see, it doesn't matter how hard we work. We can kill ourselves but things go back to where they were . . . It may be painful but in certain cases it's better to step off the treadmill in time, otherwise we'll end up getting crushed by it." I stared at him and I could feel my forehead itching, as if there were ants crawling all over it. He looked down at the ground for a second and then looked me straight in the eyes. "I've written to The Comrade down in Maremma," he said, in a voice that sounded like iron clashing with iron. "He knows your worth and he's happy to have you in his team down there. You'll be given accommodation and good wages. Not like here where there is no hope for you."

I was already in tears. Seeing me in that state, Mamma

yanked a hanky from the sleeve of her cardigan and dove into it with her whole face. She started heaving with silent sobs. Babbo was also sad about the words that had come out of his mouth. His lower lip started trembling. To cover up his feelings he started talking again, in a firmer voice this time. "Don't worry about us. To be honest, it means one less mouth to feed. Maybe you'll be able to send us a little something from your wages and one day you'll see us behave like gentry. It will be better than asking for another loan from Moreno, who lives off the interest for the whole charcoal burning season." His voice suffered a sudden death in his throat. So, he knocked a glass of wine back. The silence of the entire Apennine chain seemed to shroud the farm. "You'll go down in the new year," he said eventually. "The Comrade can't wait."

I spent New Year's Eve at the Valentino disco with enough money in my pocket for three drinks. Everyone was singing and dancing and I was there behind the column thinking of the fantastic Christmas present poverty had handed me: exile from my habitual haunts. Maddalena had combed her hair into a high ponytail that brought her face out beautifully. She threw herself onto the dance floor with her new husband. She didn't lift her eyes to look into the usual corner once. He, on the other hand, kept looking over at me and at one point it looked as though he was smiling at me, as if he were rubbing my face in his good fortune. I felt myself fall apart inside. I drank my second glass of champagne and decided to go home. There was still one hour to go before midnight.

I heard the chimes in Piazza Santa Maria sitting on the low wall as I had done when I was a child. You could hear people celebrating in the houses and a few people threw some plates out of the window. The wind was biting so hard I felt numb. I saw myself there, as lonely as ever. And suddenly, there in front of the bell tower, it came to me: was the fact that I would soon be leaving really that bad? At the end of the day, what was there to keep me nailed to the rock face here? I didn't have any real friends. Poverty had deprived me of friendship for years. Since elementary school when I had been forced to go to work rather than playing bowls or soccer in the street, in fact. I would join them on Sundays but they treated me as if I had come from outer space. Not being part of the gang meant that they saw me as an outsider, one of those boys you hardly know that you had to make friends with from scratch every time. I spent the summers at the charcoal piles rather than in the fields catching lizards with slingshots, and I never had the chance to splash in the fountain or dive into the Limentra. It was the same for all the years that followed. If only it had made us rich, at least. I was in the bosses' good books here but the pay was always the same, enough to take one step forward and another back. And that's not counting the worst of it: the fact that Maddalena has linked her destiny to Marchesini, with all the sacraments to boot.

I would miss the farm for sure. But Babbo was right when he said I would be sending money home. I preferred the idea that my parents would be lulled with a little luxury than watching them tightening their belts day after day, dipping their bread in the same sauce for a week to eke out the last suggestion of flavor. Last but not least, there were good workers in Maremma but none of them had suffered the pangs of hunger I had. Over the last charcoal season, I hadn't seen a single worker who was even close to my age. Thinking about it, it would probably be a great relief at the end of the day to work half as hard and be paid double.

When I got home, my parents were sitting at the table peeling tangerines. My father had taken out the basil liqueur that was only brought out on special occasions. There was less than an inch at the bottom of the bottle with the wilted basil leaves and left-over sugary syrup. "Back already?" Babbo said, his head popping up like a fighter cock. He pushed a glass towards me. "Sit down and warm yourself up. See how this stuff sings inside you." But I stood there, shifting my weight from foot to foot. I looked at them both as I rubbed my hands like a demon. "Listen. Waiting around for my beard to grow like this is killing me with boredom," I said. "I'll leave on the second, on the first bus after the holiday. On the third, I'll be under The Comrade's thumb and that will be that."

Thinking back to those days now makes me feel it's someone else's story. Nobody who walks into the store here would ever imagine it, even though many of them knew me in the early Maremma period. Even though they may not know my story, they may remember the wild, lost look I carried around with me to begin with. But most of them are no longer around. People in their sixties who come to buy the newspaper here were in diapers when I rolled up in Le Case that second day of January.

Among the poor wretches who are still here to tell the tale, for example, there's Divo. I hardly have time to lift the roller shutter before I find him at my side talking about the weather and the news that he has just heard on the breakfast news. "I would know what to do . . . " He almost always starts with these words. He's so sick of life that you feel like giving him a hug and saying something like, "Chin up, old man. You've had a good run." I remember him as a boy, when he used to drive me crazy asking if he could try pushing the charcoal cart. He was like a locust, with quicksilver running through his veins. Then life hit him. Or rather, Mariella did, eating through his stomach with her constant cheating, hardly bothering to do it on the sly. He always looked the other way and to this day dons the expression of a hardline fascist. Nobody stops to talk to him for more than two minutes. You can smell his eau de cologne from thirty feet away and he never leaves the house without shaving. He comes in for cigarettes and dumps a pile of loose change on the counter. There's always a gold medal with Mussolini's face on it among the coins. He'll pick it up and murmur, "If only someone like him came along . . . " Over the years I have come to this conclusion: anyone who wants law and order so much is hiding something. Or is secretly screaming out to be saved.

Today is chaos. Divo shoves past all the other townsfolk crowding the shop and comes right up to me. He looks at me and says, "That idiot of a wife I'm stuck with burned the coffee this morning so my routine went to pot. I only caught the tail end of the morning news. What did I miss? They're all agog but there doesn't seem to be one person who can tell me anything with a semblance of logic, for Christ's sake."

I stick today's freshly printed newspaper under his nose. When he sees the photo on the front page spread, Divo blanches. He juts his jaw out in a pose that would have made him popular in the fascist days. "I knew it," he mutters almost to himself. He takes the paper away to read it in the corner with the slot machines. The next customer is Sonia Serraglini. "One for me, too," she says.

There hasn't been an uninterrupted flow of customers like this since '66 when we sold the winning lottery ticket. Le Case had been kissed by fortune and the following morning they were lining up all the way back to the road that leads up to the old town. Everyone was fighting to get into the photos or to be picked up by the TV crews that came in from Grosseto. Many of them came over to me and whispered in my ear, wanting to know who had won, "Renato, you can tell me . . . " I shook my head and my legs were trembling. I kept on saying to myself, "Laugh. Just laugh." But my instinct was to burst into tears thinking of the winning ticket I had in my pocket. I saw the crowd and my head span. In the meantime, I revisited all those images from my life, from absolute poverty back in the Apennines to when I came to Le Case. Those early years of hard labor, when I worked as if I had the devil at my door. The Comrade who made me team leader before I was even twenty, and me convincing myself, heart in hand, "Look how things have turned out, my dear. Ultimately, Maddalena did me a favor when she rejected me. I'm beginning to see the fruits of my labor."

Some people in the store took great pains to show us their tickets. "See here?" they shouted. "I'm not the one kissed by good luck! Was there ever any doubt?" Everyone laughed, a little bitterly. I thought of my father. My mother. I imagined them at the farm, living on whatever little they had always managed to eke out, enjoying not having to pay off Moreno any longer thanks to the sums I managed to send them every month. They had already won their jackpot and then they won it again when they came to see me get married in St. Bastian's.

My mother had never been outside the province and she felt faint all the time. "The air is hard here," she kept saying throughout the three days she stayed. I watched them walk around the apartment we had rented in via Mozza: it looked as though they were floating in a world of dreams, both of them. I think of my father again when he would lock horns with the fridge. He complained all the time, "So, it's the fashion to keep bombs in the house nowadays, is it? So long as you're happy." That was when I took him aside and told him I had set my sights on a store that might be on sale. It felt like perfect timing because the banks were generous and I had set aside a little savings to get myself started. He stared at me for a few seconds and then he pulled a disgusted face. "Newspapers," he grumbled. "With all the illiterates in the world since the war? I get the cigarettes, of course . . . In any case, getting into coal would be a hundred times better."

Now I had a billionaire ticket in my pocket and I could already see myself driving up the hairpin bends above Pistoia to bring the glad tidings that Caterina was expecting, as well as the big, fat news that a jackpot like this would mean we could throw in the towel for eternity. I would have to be careful how I told her, though, because Mamma was already taking aspirin for her heart and it would be throwing caution to the wind if I turned up on her doorstep without any warning.

Maso even brought round a case of champagne. "This is going to have to be enough for everyone," he proclaimed. "At least that son of a bitch who has won will have to drink to our health on the sly!" I didn't bother to check whether anyone was exploiting the bedlam to slip stuff from the display cases into their pockets. People kept on coming up and touching me. "Renato, put some color in your cheeks! We're hardly at a funeral!" But there were others who simply couldn't stand the idea that someone had become a millionaire overnight. "It's not necessarily lucky," they said. "More money, more worry. I'm happy with what I have and I'm proud of it." At one point, I saw Caterina just outside the door. Nardini must have given her one minute's leave to come and join the party. She tried to come inside but the crowd pushed her back. She hung behind with her hand on her belly enjoying the show. I had the impulse to strip off all my clothes and shout out loud, "It's me! For once, good fortune has set her sights, and more, on me!" I stopped myself. The store was still in hock to the bank and anyway everyone knows it's best not to shout certain things from the rooftops. Every now and again I would touch my pocket. Just lightly, with the tips of my fingers. It felt like touching red-hot iron.

They started leaving in dribs and drabs, following the TV cameras. It wasn't even midday and the store was suddenly empty, the hubbub from before still ringing in my ears. I swept the floor. There was a shaft of light coming in through the door. I was spellbound as I watched the golden dust mites dancing in the sun and saw in them a radiant future, free of burdens. Caterina came to mind, as she always does. That evening, after her shift at the sewing school, she would see me come into the kitchen looking grim. She would immediately make a scene and ask what was niggling me, whether per chance there had been any problems at the store. Only then would I take out the winning combination. I envisaged slapping it on the table with a huff like I do when the bills come in and griping, "This is what happened." Then I would sit back and enjoy the show.

If anyone were to ask me, I wouldn't be able to say why I played the lottery that day. I had never wasted my loose change after paying for a coffee like that before. I thought back to the moment, three days before, when I had suddenly been taken by a strange mania, starting in my gut. I had been preparing to close up and walk back home for lunch when I saw the block of tickets and muttered to myself, "Just this once . . . " As if my strings were being pulled by an angel, I had gone over to the shelf and under the neon light started filling the blanks with random crosses.

The ringing of the half-hour bell nearly made me put one in the wrong place. I turned the key in the lock twice and started walking up Via di Mezzo. The agitation gnawing at me meant I couldn't eat a thing. I was happier to add two glasses to the mix. I put the ticket on the table and stared at it. "Dear Caterina," I kept thinking. "Come Sunday, you can forget the sewing that tires you out by evening so much that your eyes are like pinheads. The days when we had to make tea with jimsonweed will be over." At one point, I thought I was having a fit, stuck halfway between laughter and tears like a madman and it felt like I would never recover. I shook it off and walked around the room until the bell rang two o'clock and brought my feet back down to earth. I picked up the ticket, stuck it in my pocket, and closed the door behind me.

I don't know what Mariella was possessed by. I had grown up between her legs and rather than getting sick of her, she continued to hold me under her sway. She had that way of always wanting more, everything was a game to entertain her enflamed body, without the annoyance of feelings. She would open herself wide like a deep throat and with ten turns of the lock, hold you there in the frenzy of her buttocks which were as firm and white as pillars. I especially liked her ardor when she grabbed me by my hair, as if being plugged up was more important to her than breathing. She would kick open the door of the charcoal hut on the edge of the woods just outside the old town, past the church up at the top, and sometimes she would say, "Bad girls get charcoal. Really bad ones get the charcoal burner."

It got to the point that it felt like you were doing her wrong if you didn't stop by to dip your stick into her juicy hole for half an hour. And there was no suffering or jealousy: Mariella needed a good hard fuck for her own reasons. It kept her properly alive compared to everyone else. Every Monday I would arrive at the glade, and our heels would fly in the air. If I happened to miss an appointment, she would make up for it a week later, attacking me almost angrily and kicking me in places the sun never reaches. It didn't feel like adultery. To begin with, it was what I needed to relieve the boredom of hard labor but then the habit stayed. Mariella was a free zone, without the feelings that grow into an annoying attachment. She would often lift her skirt saying, "Go gently today. That mule Giannone has been having his way with me. This morning, I could hardly get out of bed."

That day, too, I went for a shag in her furnace. As usual, I found solace there, her kisses like a mother's embrace and her lady cave still raging hot after a visit from a certain townsman with a well-turned truncheon in his underpants. Twenty minutes later, I was back in the street, flattening my hair and taking care to put one foot in front of the other because my legs were still tingling. I even had a little appetite. Before opening the store, I stopped by the house to down an crust of old, dry bread.

In the afternoon, the adrenaline started pumping again. There were a few more curious onlookers trying to catch me out by asking me if I suspected anyone at all. They counted everyone, excluding one another. "Out of the six of us, not one has had the stroke of luck they're talking about," they decided together. Then another came, and another . . . In the end, there was quite a substantial group. They had decided to hang out at my store rather than at the Due Porte. I counted the minutes. Partly because the more they conjectured, the more the circle of potential candidates shrank before my eyes. "The population of Le Case doesn't reach a thousand," old Nencioni said, "and you can count me out." "Me, too," Serraglini added. "You'll see the way the world goes," Barberini commented. "I bet it was Don Lauro who won the lottery, and the millions will go straight to Rome where bishops piss into gold cups." They began to gang up against me, asking whether the priest had thrown a few coins away on a ticket. I shook my head. One of them asked, "What about Manolo?"

At closing time, I had to practically throw them out. I started pushing them towards the door, especially after Divo barked, "What if it's our Renato who has won the lottery, eh?" Their eyes were all over me like headlights, but I managed to huff, "Yeah, sure! If I'd won, I certainly wouldn't be here listening to your conjectures. Any anyway, you know perfectly well I can't even finish a card game so imagine how much I know about the lottery . . . " Having reassured them, I shoved them out of the door and pulled down the roller shutter.

I walked up the road with Divo, of all people. Every time I entered his wife, I felt I should keep him at a distance afterwards in case he sniffed out my betrayal. "Well," he said at a certain point. "This evening someone's going to be looking at their boring old broth with new eyes. To be honest, I'm fine as I am with a secure job and fair pay. The only reason I like fantasizing about winning millions is Mariella. First, I'd take her on a nice trip somewhere. She doesn't complain but her days are all the same, reduced to taking care of the house. Think about it, Renato. It must get pretty boring, enough to kill a bull . . ." I carried on walking without saying a word, looking down at my shoes.

I went into the kitchen looking grim, as I had imagined I would all day. Dinner was on the table. Caterina smiled at me, but she didn't have time to greet me before I slumped like a deadweight into my chair. Then she made a scene asking, "What's that face for?" I was searching through my pockets, continuing my performance. I saw her put down the ladle she was holding. "Renato, your silence makes me think the worst . . . " My stomach was doing acrobatics, and I was tempted to pull my mask off and give her a hug with tears in my eyes. She came closer until she was a hairsbreadth away. "Why are you crying?" she murmured, her voice already trembling. "Renato, say something!"

It happened right then. I felt a shock make my hairs stand on end. My breath was as dry as cement and in a second my mouth was parched. I must have looked terrible because Caterina took a step back. "Renato, tell me what . . .?" She completely lost it.

I leaped back to my feet, tipping the chair over backwards. I had pulled my pockets inside out but there was no trace of the winning ticket. "It's not there," she heard me say, my words transforming doubt into certainty. "It's not there," I yelled. I couldn't stop searching through all my pockets. "It's not there!"

I shoved the table with a thrust of my back, knocking the flask over and spilling wine over the dishes. There was nothing on the floor. I looked under the soles of my shoes. Then I retraced my steps from the front door to the kitchen. "It's not there, It's not there, It's not there . . . " I started whining. When Caterina approached me, I nearly shoved her away. She looked at me with a terror I'd never seen before in her face. The same terror she could see in mine. "It's not there," I repeated. She tried to murmur something like, "Renato, please . . . " but I opened the door and ran out, my eyes glued to the flagstones on the street. "Renato!" I heard her yell behind me but I had already turned the corner.

Losing millions in exchange for a quick shake of a gigolo's dick is enough to make you gag for the rest of your life. There is no cure. It becomes the first thought that scratches at your brain when you wake up and, from that moment on, every minute has a target on it. It didn't stop even when I was asleep, when it turned into the feverish delirium. I suddenly found myself with that scrap of paper in my hand, and was about to tell my young wife when a minute later I heard Caterina say, "Renato, get up! The newspapers have come in!" I opened my eyes and saw her in her nightgown. The light was on in the corridor from where the smell of coffee wafted in.

In the early days, I would lock myself in the bathroom and try to throw up but all I could produce was an acid froth. I would splash my face with cold water and say to myself, "It's a long dream. Now I'm going to wake up and nothing will have happened." But everything stayed the same and even buying the store at a bargain price felt like nothing. I had this sensation that my existence was fading, on the point of vanishing, its outlines blurred. I groped my hands with my hands to give me an idea of who I was. "In your misery, you caught a fleeting glimpse of a golden cunt and then the skirts went down straight away," I said to myself. One evening Caterina came home all happy because she'd received her first salary. I looked at the coins in her hand and started bleating like a lamb. She came up to me and stroked my head. "Renato, I'm happy to do the work. I've even learnt to make frills." And then I really started bawling my eyes out.

When Divo was not working, he would come and strike up a conversation that lasted half a morning. He looked sprightly, with a twinkle in his eyes that a cuckold who is aware of his situation shouldn't have. The gossip about the winning ticket had already waned. It would go underground for a while and then come up every now and again. I kept my eye on Mariella's husband and waited for the whistle. In the meantime, though,

I was punishing her by not going to our rendezvous at the hut where, with all the stripping and dressing, I must have lost the blessed ticket. It was a clear message that read, "My dear friend, I know you found a little gift in the midst of all that rabbit piss. I'm waiting for you to take the first step." But nothing new ever happened. In fact, one day Divo came over to complain to me about his fridge. "I signed a hundred promissory notes to get that thing into our living room. Just as I'm about to pay them off, the motor has gone to pot. They say I have to start the whole process again, as if money grew in the folds of my scrotum."

They were good. They didn't risk ordering even an ounce of prosciutto more than usual. Meanwhile, Caterina would come up to me and say, "Look at this, will you? There's your first gray hair there behind your ears." But that was the least of it. I stopped talking altogether and I nibbled at my food at mealtimes and left most of it on the plate. Her belly kept on growing and I didn't care a jot. When I saw Michele come into this world my first thought was, "This spells more bills instead of that treasure chest from the thousand and one nights I had my hands on."

Sometimes I stood in front of the bathroom mirror in the mornings and said to myself quietly but clearly, "You're on the wrong track. Can't you see the great things you have built with your own hands? Forget winning the lottery. Nothing has changed." I got to the point where I actually convinced myself. I had spent the best years of my youth sleeping in charcoal stacks in the woods, hard at work burning charcoal for the holidaymakers who went out for pizza in Follonica. I had taken years to rid my body of the stench of the earth. And to relieve my father of his obsession with his debts to Moreno, allowing him to grow old in the peace and tranquility he had never known. We had a fridge in our living room, too. On Sundays in July, we used to climb up to San Martino and get a slushy from the kiosk there.

And Michele was a healthy and lively boy . . . In short, not being happy was ungrateful of me. Then Caterina would come to the door. "Have you fallen down the toilet?" she would yell through the door. "The store doesn't open on its own." I would count out twenty of Salghini's drops, the ones he gives me to calm my nerves and my heartburn.

I couldn't stand any kind of conversation. The only time I could bear the world was when I was on my own, in silence, when I turned the handle and started dwelling on things again. It was like licking my wounds in perpetuity. It was as if I had been destined for it. Maybe my doubts about Divo persisted, but the years went by, and I saw him in the same old pair of shoes, never a gust of wind shifting him from his normal routine. "Maybe Mariella kept the winning ticket," I thought to myself. "Maybe it's sitting there waiting for the poor wretch here to give up the ghost." But he kept going and was even impetuous. "What a great way to enjoy the jackpot," I said to myself sometimes while I was doing the store accounts and stopped to think about things.

The only relief I had was with the deaf-mute dwarf sister. She would come in to get the crosswords and if there were no other customers around, I would hang out with her for a few minutes to talk about myself. I would always stand at an angle so that she couldn't read my lips. She always looked at me with those bright little unhappy eyes that were just about level with the counter. "Piera, my dear. Let me tell you about the brick I have had to swallow," I started as I turned away from her and picked out the crossword magazine from the stand. I felt goosebumps coming up because talking about my misfortune with anything that was not an animal made me feel as if I were inside a crystal ball. As if my wretched origins had come back to haunt me, only this time in a more underhand way, cursed to consider even precious things mere crumbs. Which made me feel like a crumb. Every day it started with a slap and a voice railing against me. "What were you thinking of? Get back down, charcoal burner. Crawl like a worm!" And I crawled.

Caterina left me a little gift on the first of September, '73. She took the afternoon bus and went off to Sasso Pisanoto, where her sister had settled with a rag-and-bone man who had struck lucky and now sold antique furniture. I kept reading the note she left me, where in a few words she expressed the simple concept that she didn't like living with a mope and that it wasn't good for the boy, either. Never a smile. Even on saint's days it was like having a corpse in the house. There was one line that struck me in particular: *You have grown used to living in your own shadow and that shadow is eating us all.* In short, Caterina had become bored of throwing all her feelings into the pig swill. She had striven with all her soul to look after me like an angel and I hadn't even noticed her. It was the same with Michele. In fact, he was growing up as morose as me, full of silence and not at all sociable with his peers. Towards the end of her letter, she said, *You haven't so much as touched me for three years. Please excuse me if I'm not drawn to those Monday country jaunts of yours.* When I read this, I felt terrible. But I didn't rush to the phone to plead with her to come back. I didn't run down to catch the first bus out of town. No. I moved a chair and slumped into it. My first thought was, "Listen to that lovely silence."

Divo leaves his newspaper with the toy cars. He turns and says, "Unbelievable."

All this agitation turns me inside out like a glove because it makes me re-live certain moments from a different perspective. I watch as the mass of people move towards the door and at that moment, I see that the TV van has gotten stuck at the widening of the road on the curve. Somebody comments on it and my heart pops. "It feels like '66 all over again!" Except that now I have nothing in my pocket. Not even a family.

The TV cameras today are very different gadgets to the ones back then and the cameramen are dressed for a war. When the townsfolk find themselves in front of a microphone, they get off their high horses and reveal themselves for the animals they are, with inexistent grammar.

"You think I didn't guess there was a storm brewing?" Divo asked me, his chest puffed up and his arms folded over it. "But of course, I always see mirages where they don't exist . . ." I may be wrong but as he says this I feel as though there's a lump in his throat. "What do you think?" He goes on without looking at me. "Did he take Eleonora by force or was it just an elopement that went wrong?"

I notice Mario in the corner where all the stuff left over from the summer has piled up, where the postcards with "Greetings from Le Case" visibly fade year after year. He digs an elbow into Divo indicating a customer I rarely see in here. His clothes seem to hang off him he has lost so much weight. He is standing there staring at the hubbub going on outside through a gap between all the random supplies piled up against the store window. Then his sharp shoulders shudder and Divo comes and whispers in my ear, "What's he doing? Is he crying?" I shake my head. "I have no idea," I murmur. He gives a deep sigh. "He employed the girl at the store. It lasted as long as a dog's bark, but he must have grown fond of her. At least she was a breath of fresh, young air that distracted him for a couple of hours from the catastrophe that is Adelaide . . . Now look how he takes the news."

I'll never be able to say this, but the truth is that I always liked Samuele. His dark expression reminds me of my Michele. You can tell boys without fathers in your gut; you don't need to say a word to them. There's something feral about them. They have two ways of looking you in the eye: one is to challenge you. The other is not to look at all.

On some days, I go down to the city to get an earful of

noises that don't exist in Le Case. It's usually on Wednesdays, which is closing day. I love walking in Piazza del Sale. Or I go and get a Campari with an inch of white wine at the bar on the main drag and sit under the spell of people strolling. Finally, I take up my position on a bench at the Sienese Keep. From there I can see the high prison walls and the barred windows. I imagine what life is like behind those closed windows along Via Saffi. Sometimes, my imagination is so strong that my heart starts beating because I know I would die there in no time at all. The real blow comes when I hear the reinforced door open, though. It doesn't always happen. If it does, I have to hold tight and sit firmly because the earth suddenly bucks like a stallion: it's Michele coming off his shift. Just seeing him walking twenty yards down the road looking at the ground and vanishing into the parking lot at the Misericordia is enough for me.

A prison warder for a son. When I think about it, his situation is not far from mine: a recluse, I am, thrown into a corner of life ever since a ticket fell out of my pocket, as if I had been sucked into a ghost's mouth. All the days that would go on to become years were on that slip of paper. The same ones I have consumed since then, but wretchedly. And more and more I find myself thinking about that world, this one's twin, where instead of all those shenanigans that I went through in '66, I had yelled straight away with all the breath in my body, "I've hit the jackpot!" Then I go through all the facts again but from that point of view. Michele's birth, for example, when the movie transforms the brick in my stomach into delirious happiness.

This is what happens when someone narrowly misses out on their rightful life. Especially when that someone grew up a charcoal burner in the Apennines, when some mornings it hurt to breathe and at night you fell asleep sucking a dry chestnut to keep the pangs of hunger at bay.

I glance over at Divo and say to myself, "My friend, I wish

you had actually pocketed the prize . . . " He turns around suddenly and looks at me as if he had heard the rumbling of my thoughts. "In any case, this must be said," he says. "Sometimes newspapers are just looking for headlines, especially if they lean red . . . I mean, are we really sure those two are actually dead?"

Iolanda Barberini,
the Housewife

Dead as doornails! I swear, Rosanna my dear. There were even TV crews here this morning. Switch to Channel 4 and you'll see. You might even spot me there in the middle of all the hullabaloo. Luckily, I'd just had my roots done. Just so you know, I'm the one in the cream coat. You know, the one I wore on New Year's Eve . . . Yes, that one. I don't know why, I just woke up with a feeling that I wanted to look good. Who knew I would run into the TV cameras? Anyway. Look what happens when the law makes asses of us all. They're happy to let the dregs of society walk free but if anyone pays a bill late, they skin them alive and boil them with their clothes . . . Yep, that's how it is. Listen, how's Feo doing with his back? You tell him: he'd better watch the sea air down there in Arcille when it's muggy. One cold draught and his sweat will turn into ice and stick to him like a punishment.

. . . Oh look, seven-brains is over there, his eyes melting at the sight of the checkered board. You've certainly had your cross to bear with that husband bloated with drink. I have to deal with Alvise who knows nothing about you or me. If at least he'd lost a few marbles like some do at his age, when they get it into their heads to act young all of a sudden . . . But no. Luxuries like that have been left behind for a while now.

. . . Yes, here too, Rosanna, dear. It started clouding over an hour or so ago, at midday. It's dark enough to scare you. One of those storms that come in and shroud the peaks, when it goes from day to night from one moment to the next. The valley from my window looks like a dustbowl. And the squall! Gusts that feel like shoves and they're still blowing. You'll see as soon as it's over, it'll be paradise out there.

. . . I remember, yes. We had that nice room back then when very little felt like a lot. Not like now when we complain about everything. In those days, when there was a storm, I used to slip into your bed and every time you would say, "Can you hear? It's Jesus moving the furniture." I know I've always been sentimental but look at what happens as you get older: you start thinking about the trivial things and it breaks your heart. In any case, having set my sights on someone like Alvise, who has taken all the poetry out of living in this world like normal people, what can I do? If only I could turn the clock back . . .

. . . Look, I was as gobsmacked as you. You know that we're all pretty trusting folk here at Le Case and maybe that's why nobody noticed a thing. Even the carabinieri, who you would have thought would be on the alert. But who could have imagined that the girl from Ribolla spent all that time holed up in the house where that saint Esedra used to live? It's true, though: God is the only one who knows whether she was there of her own accord or not. Be that as it may, last night that oddball who is still learning the ABCs of life decided to get on his motorbike and take the poor girl with him. Did he knock her out first? Were they attempting an elopement? We are back to square one—nobody knows . . . But listen to how it happened: the motorbike glides silently by Rodolfo's bar down in the new town and guess who was out there smoking a cigarette in the cool of the night? That's right, him of all people. The Albanian lout. The one whose garden was dug up by the army after the girl vanished to see if they could at least find her bones. And there's more. The devil gets into the man, and he goes and calls the rest of his clan. People I wouldn't introduce to my worst enemy. No sooner does he break the news than they're already piled into their pickup and on the churl's tail.

. . . Yes, because in the papers they say they found brake marks on the hairpin bends. Imagine the scene: a chase. In the dark woods to boot, with the risk of an animal crossing their path at any moment. You already know how it ended. At the umpteenth bend, the motorbike loses its grip and flies off the road into the Toninelli's patch. It's always been a dangerous spot that. And on top of everything else, it seems there was some loose grit on the asphalt, the stuff that sometimes comes off the trucks. Anyone who knows this place drives at a snail's pace down that bit of road. But despite the signs, guardrail and reflectors, there's always some idiot who crashes into the olive trees of that man from the Marches. Only, the boy wasn't just risking his own skin: he was dragging a valley girl in her early twenties down with him, may she rest in peace.

. . . What can I say, Rosanna? What did our poor Ma always used to say? "It is idle to swallow the cow and choke on the tail." At least there's one less devil around. Pity about the girl, though. You should have seen her: she was small and taciturn, but she was so sweet it melted your heart. It's one of those terrible curses of life when a tender branch is suddenly cut off and it's like it was done to spite you. Don Lauro says there's always a design and I'd love to believe him. But it's sometimes hard, dear sister. Eleonora had every right to choose an unsuitable boyfriend if she wanted to. But if you had looked her in the eye, you would never have said she wanted to do anyone any harm.

. . . You're right. "These things are demeaning." And today feels like a death knell with this black sky that creeps into your bones. The squall feels like it's going to smash the windows. But don't worry: Alvise, dead man walking, won't notice a thing . . . Yes, I'm talking to you! Don't you feel as though they're pulling our house down?

. . . Do you see what I mean, Rosanna? The roof could fall

on his head and he wouldn't take his eyes off the pieces . . . Rosanna, can you hear me? Rosanna!

Hey? You there! The world's coming to an end and the phone line is down. But staring at those little figurines is more important for you. You're so useless. Go and check the window upstairs at least . . . I wish it was a hurricane, I say! One that lifts the roof off the house. Look, I would throw myself in like a flash. I beg you! Jesus, can you hear me? Send me a typhoon to lift me up and take me away from this godforsaken land of Maremma forever!

I was thinking. For dinner I'll make you some breaded cutlets, the ones you love as if you were a kid. Shall I?

Amico Fritz,
Niccodemo Tempesti

Don Lauro's body has been out cold for two days in the sacristy of St. Bastian's and not even a dog can come up to town and say a mass with all the frills to give him a decent burial. They say the problem is the driving rain that has brought the mountain down and flooded the streets with mud. Any little priest willing to give the last rites to a highly respected colleague, will have to wait until they open the road. And the forecast is not favorable, to say the least.

That's how they found Don Lauro. He was in the confession box, gripping the chair as if he were holding on to the edge of a precipice, his eyes wide open. It transpires that Divo's Mariella was the last person to kneel there. I'd give my left leg to hear just half of the stories she has to tell. It sounds like you need to have a sturdy heart to listen to them.

In any case, I'm fine like this, hidden away. It's not like life in Le Case on a normal day is a carnival. Out the window I can see the same empty road as usual, the only difference being that right now it is a river of sludgy water, flowing in an endless stream, which can't seem to find peace. All the lava in hell wouldn't be enough to wash the conscience of this place. Every stone contains the evil in the heart of the crag this town was built on, and its very essence is on show now more than ever: a dead priest left to rot without so much as a blessing. That just about sums up the spirit of this place. Every person that walks these streets represents it. Including the cats.

Meanwhile it feels like the end of the world. Come to think

of it, there could be no better stage for it. The growling in the sky sounds like the grumbling we have all harbored in our guts our whole lives that has finally been given expression. The thick clouds are a curtain hiding the sun, to the point that at midday it feels like it's time for bed. At Mario's they say they haven't seen a season like this for half a century or more. "We're going to be pushed off and it'll be sudden," they whisper, and in their faces, you can see the glassy gaze of people who expect the worse. They go deathly pale when the earth shakes for the umpteenth time, and the lampshades start to swing. That's when they start whining, "We haven't had any shuteye for over a week . . . " Going down past the old town is an adventure, facing the slapping rain and wind that doesn't know where else to go. You could easily crack a rib. But they attempt the journey anyway, running to Dr. Salghini like evacuees to ask him to prescribe sleeping pills. Or they go to the store with bits of ceiling plaster in their hair. They go straight to the shelves, anxious to fill their shopping bags with tin cans and liquor bottles. The only person who is actually enjoying himself is Mario. Even though today's bread has not been delivered, he's found a way to sell all his supplies. Like the boxes of tomato paste from last year that are flying from the shelves even though they are about to expire, and he's selling them at full price.

I should have said "*Auf Wiedersehen*, Signora, thanks for everything" right away to Mamma. "I'm going home, though I don't have a home and I'd joined the army hoping it was my chance to win at bingo." Maremma has this terrible way about it: first, it shows its best side in order to get you on board. Then it never lets go and reveals itself for the wild beast that it is. One day, you realize that the province has coiled its way into your veins and you try and take a step back and shake it off. But by that point, the strings have been tightened. In return, you get a scrape on the chin on the church steps and not much else.

There are some nights when I dream that I am in my uniform

looking smart with a gleaming rifle. "I'll get through this war, and I'll carve a path through all the chaos," I thought, my soul on fire like all eighteen-year-olds. "Maybe I'll steal a path from someone else who is less on the ball," I repeated to myself more insistently while I was undergoing training here to fight the partisans hiding in the woods. We spent our days drinking and teasing the young ladies. They couldn't get enough of it, and it was easy enough to get them to lift their skirts when they caught sight of an officer. Their husbands were either down the mine, at war, or fighting as partisans, and they were happy to get laid in their cellars. They thought that at the end of the war they might be able to say goodbye to their hovels carved out of the bare rock and wave their hankies from the turrets of the tanks like movie stars. All you had to do to get them to unhook their bras was mention a city somewhere. There were mothers who encouraged their young daughters, putting them out on the balcony like fresh meat at auction. You would get a tasty morsel if you went up the stairs.

Eventually, I found a pretty little mare of my own. We used to meet in secret near the abandoned hut on the edge of the hollow. Our bodies were so perfect that we looked like marble statues when we engaged in the act. The fact that everything was secret drove us so crazy with passion that we would tear each other's clothes off. We couldn't even pronounce each other's names. Our vocabulary consisted of desire and turmoil as we waited for the next appointment. That was when rumors about the Americans started.

We heard about the dark shadow advancing inch by inch and no major action impeded the progress of the marching armies. World events had brought the two of us together and now they threatened to separate us forever. Until one afternoon I had to tell her, "I'm leaving tomorrow." Her answer was to grab my waist, but I had to pull her off. I tried again. "I'm leaving." She looked at me for a moment, her face darkening with the rejection. I said it once again, adding a few slow gestures. "I have to go home. I'll be killed here." Finally, she understood. I saw her eyes fill with tears. At the same time, she shook her head. None of this was my fault. She threw herself on her knees and I was about to pull her off me again because I really wasn't in the mood. But instead of clinging to my legs, she started drawing on the damp earth. First, she outlined a clock face. Then the hands. Then she pointed at me. And at herself. The message was clear, "The two of us, at that time, here."

The terrible thing about war is that it leads to impossible love affairs, which are worse than bombs. That evening, I had someone cover for me and split off from the last section of the platoon. I ran through the village to the hut. There were others like me who had slipped away to say goodbye to their lovers before retreating and vanishing forever. When I open the crooked door of the hut, I found her on her knees in front of a candle stub. She had made up a bed of fresh hay. Next to the bed there were two bottles of wine she must have found somewhere. I threw my rifle onto the ground and took her there and then.

I opened my eyes, turned my head, and saw she was still there, her hair stuck to her forehead. Her lips were moving as if she were speaking to someone in her dreams.

Daylight was streaming in through the chinks in the walls. I struggled to my feet and realized that, despite the sleep, there was still wine in my bloodstream. First, I had to relieve myself in the corner, rocking back and forth to make sure I dumped it all more or less in one place. Then I attempted to straighten my uniform, which felt as if it had exploded on me. In the end, I managed. I lifted a slat and looked outside beyond the hollow. A second later I was hugging the wall of the hut. I had had such a fright that I felt like I needed another shit.

The little mare looked up when she heard the midday bells ringing. I started downing the dregs of wine left over from the night before. I needed it to settle my hangover. She gave me a little smile. And I said, "You can fucking laugh." But she didn't understand me and went on making coy faces from a distance. I felt like putting a bullet in her head right there and then. "My platoon left at dawn," I said through my clenched teeth. "Basically, you're looking at a dead man walking." She was half-naked and I kept on saying to myself, "My friend, you've just thrown your life away for a bit of young flesh, when there's no end of that in the world. The best possible outcome is that I'll be in handcuffs by tonight. But even the stones know that in situations like this, a non-commissioned officer can be 'disappeared' in a second. Just to make a point."

Not receiving the attention that she had been hoping for, she got up and sulkily glanced out of the high window beside her. She stood there for a whole minute. When she finally turned around to look at me, I saw the same fear on her face that was stamped on mine. She was a prisoner, just like me. Realizing she was on her own in the company of a Kraut made her world fell apart. She started gathering her clothes together so painstakingly it was agony to watch. I looked at her and shot these words at her. "Can you have only realized now that I'm a brother to those soldiers with death on their berets?" But after a while I came back to my senses and understood that it wasn't her fault. Maybe I, too, in her position, would be feeling a little sad. It wasn't a good moment to be found with a German soldier. She was sincerely sorry. That look spoke novels. Because she must have a mother there in the village or a baby brother in diapers. Our love affair would be considered blasphemous. She risked her reputation, if not worse. In the end I went to the door and threw it open. Light flooded the hut making the glass of the wine flasks glisten. I looked down and gestured for her to go out.

I was standing there completely exposed, no doubt in the cross hairs of a pair of binoculars. This scared her. She took a few little steps in no particular direction as if one hand were pulling her out and another holding her in the corner. So, I kicked the wall. The noise shocked her, and she came back to my side. I could feel her gaze on me, but I refused to budge. I didn't shift mine from the straw that we had spread around during the night. It looked as if she was about to say something, but I wouldn't have understood anyway. Instead, I could feel her breath on my face. There was a fleeting kiss on my cheek and she disappeared.

I waited in the hut until nightfall. I told myself that since it was in plain view, they wouldn't send anyone to check the place out. There must be other priorities. I didn't move until after dark. I covered the distance that separated me from the tree line in no time at all. Then I vanished into the undergrowth without looking back once.

There was one good thing: the arrival of the Americans had forced the partisans off the hills. They had had to get out of the scrub. Apart from wild boars, there was no one I was going to bump into. I scrambled up the mountain that looms over Le Case on the Siena side and didn't stop to catch my breath until the climb became truly impervious. I put my rifle down and chose a slab to lie down on.

I had nothing with me. My face stung from the whippings I had received from overhanging branches as I had cut blindly though the woods. It was my first day of desertion and I was already as hungry as a wolf. The idea that I wouldn't be able to satisfy my hunger made my throat constrict and I had to fight to catch my breath. They had sent me to Maremma to fight those partisan pigs and now I was the one in a trap. If I'd been in the mood, the situation might have seemed comic and even given me the chance to laugh a bit. But with an empty pit in my stomach, the cheer soon drained out of life.

I looked at the lights of Le Case. They looked like fireflies you could catch in your hand. I tried to guess how many there were, thinking what a far cry it was from Rosenheim which, compared to this spit of a town was as imperial as Vienna. At least a two-day train ride away. And there I was, clinging to a mountainside like a goat. Imprisoned in the wrong uniform, which I couldn't take off and throw into a bush. It was getting warmer, but the night air was still harsh. I counted my bullets, and it was like counting the days that I had left. In any case, I said to myself, "If you start whining, I'll finish you off." Because it didn't change anything all. I'd been alone in this world all my life and things had never gone too far wrong. At the end of the day, maybe wandering wild in the woods was better. In the orphanage where I'd been recruited, I'd had to watch every step. The only thing I missed was the chow that was served up as regular as clockwork at mealtimes. Anyway, I was having an adventure of my own for once, however miserable it was. I was the one seizing the day, not the Army or Miss Böhm, with her hideous frown that made me feel like I had come into this world wrong as soon as she clapped eyes on me. I was scared enough out on the mountainside to piss my pants but after a while I felt a certain euphoria. So I ate that instead of bread. Then I bundled up as warmly as I could and holed up there staring at the dwindling lights. My rifle butt against my chest was my salvation. At one point I started imagining I was cradling another me with all my might, one that needed to be looked after. It was a nice thought that gave me courage. And that eventually lulled me to sleep.

On the third day I fainted for the first time. When I opened my eyes, I was face down in a puddle. I pulled myself up onto all fours, expecting to see a forest of rifles pointing at me. Instead, it was just me. And the usual scrub full of nothing. I had a weapon but, in my condition, I didn't have the strength to kill an animal and skin it. I tore leaves off the bushes and chewed them for their sap, especially the ones that oozed milk.

I spent most of my time curled up in a ball at the foot of a tree with my stomach on fire. Or else, dropping my pants on the spot with bouts of diarrhea that produced nothing but yellow water. I got to the point where I was licking stones. I plucked up insects and ingurgitated them, fighting the urge to throw them back up. Berries and snails went straight down like gobs of snot without my even chewing. To begin with, I thought I could feel them moving in my belly, which had in the meantime been transformed into a hole under my ribs. I squatted down at streams intending to quench my thirst with handful after handful of water. Usually, I ended up feeling dizzy and coughing so hard that I risked vomiting everything and sending the acid drool up my nose.

I had tried getting to the road on the other side of Le Case where I thought there wouldn't be any of those American soldiers that infested town. But I was wrong. There were enemies everywhere. Even at night there was no way of getting to the provincial road and to the railway line in the valley. As if that were not enough, I found myself on the wrong side of the mountain, which was all forest. Not a single farmhouse, nothing. Just trees and more trees as far as the eye could see. Looking down from the peak, I was sorely tempted to lift the safety catch and end it all right there. It was a sea of green. On one side, my escape route which was under siege. On the other, miles and miles of woods. Now I could see why the partisans had chosen these mountains to hide out in. I felt sorry for them, too, because living for months on end in that nothingness must have made more than one of them weep. You needed to have strong convictions to survive in these conditions. So, I said to myself, "Nobody would dive into this hell, sometimes for years, with their loved ones at the mercy of invading forces, if they weren't truly convinced that they were on the right side."

I remembered the way my fellow soldiers had dealt with a woman they had discovered carrying medicine up to the partisans in a double-bottomed basket. First, they struck her face with the butts of their rifles until she spat her teeth out. Then they smashed her kneecaps, leaving her slithering on the streets. Anyone who tried to help her was sprayed with bullets. A young boy had been pulled back just in time by the crowd before he ran over to his mother. The woman lay there at the edge of the town for five days. We even set up a duty roster to make sure she never got any aid. She died. With a last burst of strength, she had tried to pull herself up, but she collapsed right away, crashing back down with her legs splayed unnaturally under her skirt. Now I felt her presence right there beside me. In the dark woods, I imagined looking down and seeing her hand gripping my boot.

I even discovered the walls of a parish church overgrown with trees. They were just ruins but I made sure not to stop there and take a look because centuries-old abandonment like that gives me the creeps. Rather, I inspected the perimeter of the mountain peak obsessively from one side to the other. If I tried approaching the road, there would be American soldiers, who seemed to be multiplying as if they had decided to occupy every inch of Maremma. I squeezed out every step. And despite my good intentions, I prayed for a good ten-minute cry to wash the salt from my tears. Then I discovered a chestnut grove near a glade a hundred paces under the crest. There was a stone hut there, identical to the one where, until a few days ago, I had been making sparks with a flesh-and-blood girl in full bloom.

On the side that overlooked the town, I saw a small plot. I sat behind the treeline and observed the place for a long time, waiting to see if I could make out any movement there. But there was nothing. I could hardly control myself. If I had obeyed my instinct, I would have hurled myself down those few yards and dug up the potato roots with my teeth. It was late afternoon by the time I convinced myself I could move. The sky was gray, and gusts of wind brought a few drops of rain. I took a few steps away from the tree cover. Without branches over my head, I felt stark naked in the middle of a town square. I was too weak to hold my rifle properly. The barrel swung with the tremors of my body. Then something happened. It was as if the soul that I had been dragging along beside me had reached its limit. I could see it clearly, amid all the bellyaching, saying something like, "I'm stopping here," and throwing itself on the ground like a spoilt little girl. I looked at the plot. I would have liked to run there. But my body wasn't responding. It was the end of the ride. There was nothing left, not even a cough. My legs were a house of cards. A blast of air was enough to knock them from under me. I lay with my face in the mud. In my ears, a long whistle, like a train leaving the station. That was when I thought, "I'm coming, Rosenheim. I'm coming."

Mamma would come every morning but, if there were no impediments and the weather was good enough, she would come in the evenings, too, with a candle for the night. I never asked her anything. She didn't even look at me. She came into the hut and put a half-filled bottle on the floor with a crust of bread and a lump of cheese wrapped in a tea cloth. One morning, she lifted her skirt and produced a light blanket she had wrapped around her legs and hidden there. Before she left, I would say thank you in my language. She would nod imperceptibly, her eyes downcast, and then scurry off.

At the time she was in her late forties, though poverty made her look twice as old. She would come from Le Case early in the morning carrying the first two pails of shit. It was usually the stench that woke me up and I would stand on the threshold of the hut and watch her toiling over her vegetables. She would carefully pour the slop around each plant and then go over to the grove and pour the remains under the chestnut trees. Then she would head back to town. An hour later, there she was with another load.

She emptied all the cesspits in her neighborhood and used the muck as fertilizer. A hell of a favor to all the backsides in the old town as this meant they didn't have to plunge their hands into their own stinking sludge. In exchange, she would receive a little money or leftover food from people's larders, even though times were hard for everyone. In addition, her garden grew luxuriantly. And so did the trees, which in the fall were laden like rich people's Christmas trees with sweet chestnuts in their spiny sheaths.

I don't know what went through her mind harboring a German deserter in her hut. One morning, she brought me some decent clothes that were more or less my size. Any rags were better than my military uniform, because they meant I couldn't take a step outside the hut. I had recovered my strength by then, even though I still looked like a skeleton. Opening my eyes one evening, there was a face looking down at me. "I'm innocent!" I yelled instinctively, raising my hands in surrender. But then I realized it was her, Mamma. The fact that she was there at that time of night was not reassuring at all. Maybe the Americans were scouring the woods, and she had come to warn me. I jumped up and loaded my rifle. I went to the door and leaned out to look. Everything looked normal. Everything was black, as usual. I saw she had come to my side and gently taken my wrist. She made as if to coax me back into the hut. I dug my heels in and said, "I'm not going anywhere. If they find me, I'm dead meat." But she kept on tugging. For the first time, there was a hint of a smile on her face. "If you sell me to the enemy, I'll kill you," I muttered. She was looking at me and her eyes were sincere. She dropped my arm and gestured for me to follow her. She blew out the candle out and walked out into the night. The pitter-patter of her footsteps grew weaker second by second. Eventually, I slung my rifle over my shoulder and followed her.

Thinking back to those months, I sometimes have to quash a wave of nostalgia. And yet being holed up in those three rooms drove me crazy at the time. The days were all the same. The most I could do was stand at the window for a few minutes and look down into the alley where the sun never shone through the shutter slats. She went out, came back in. She didn't even lock the door. "If you don't attract attention, the ill-intentioned will walk straight past," she later explained. But for the time being I was inhabiting the house like a ghost, even though nobody ever came by. A phantom doesn't really exist without anyone to scare. We would sit at the table in the evenings, and I would listen to her. She pointed to things and told me what they were. I would repeat the word. There were no notebooks because Mamma couldn't read or write. Then she would show me Niccodemo's portrait, in uniform. She would put a little water in a tin bowl and wet a comb. Then she tried to comb my bristly hair into the same style as the young man's in the photograph. As she did this, she would hum a tune.

I realized right away that Mamma was a little off her head. But in all the years I spent in an orphanage there had never been anyone who had offered to take me away with them to a real home. In the meantime, I had become a man. Now I was being welcomed in an area of the world that had been torn apart by war and penury. And by a woman who had taken me into her humble abode thinking it would bring back the son who had never returned from the battlefield. I went along with it, partly because I didn't have a choice in the matter. In the meantime, if I made an effort, I was able to have a basic conversation. She would swoop in like a hawk and say, "You can still hear the accent. If you want to see the light of day again, you need to speak just like a Maremma toad, dragging your words out as if it was too tiring to say them. So, I kept on practicing, day after day.

It was almost July. Out of nowhere, there was a general commotion and the roads in the old town were filling with life.

News flew from window to window, and I heard it as it came through and grasped what I could. A clutch of soldiers in shambles had arrived in town having wandered in the woods on the western front for a few weeks after the end of the war. A band of men who had been holed up on their own in at the middle of nowhere, holding a position for no reason without receiving any news of what had happened.

There were lots of sudden apparitions of that kind in the first few weeks and, every time, my blood ran cold at the idea that I would be thrown out and lynched from one day to the next if a certain Niccodemo were to show up. Because normal people were the real enemy now, not the Americans. Le Case was a hotbed of partisans who still had stashes of rifles to hand. If they so much as sniffed a Kraut in their midst, they would get over-excited and I would vanish into someone's cellar forever. But by the beginning of June, I had already calmed down. The good-looking lad in the portrait on the dresser had left me his room. It was not me that had wanted to steal his life. It was his mother who had dressed me in it to assuage her grief, replacing her son with a young soldier who had chanced upon her hut.

Through the slats I could see a line of people making their way up into town. "Some of our own flesh and blood is back!" they yelled as they relayed the news. A small woman fainted, and they lay her out on the flagstones. She thought her husband was a ghost. He was speaking to her with perfect calm, but she went on looking straight through him as he were playing a trick on her. Then they hugged but the woman still couldn't believe it. Worse, she looked almost offended. That was when I heard the door.

Mamma was well-known, mostly because she went door to door emptying latrines. The rest of her business didn't exactly make anyone in Le Case tear their hair out. Niccodemo's return, mixed in with all the other soldiers coming home, was hardly noticed. There were no festive gatherings or rowdy crowds celebrating, unlike with the other returnees. Mamma would slip out quietly as if on tiptoe and sometimes people would approach her and ask, "How's Niccodemo? Who knows what he has been through . . .?" Or "There's been a saint watching over him, like all the other disbanded soldier trickling back to Le Case from the frontline." I only heard about these comments much later. Mamma would say little or nothing in return. She made it clear that her son was still struggling with the effects of the war and the terrible deprivations he had been through. Niccodemo needed rest and didn't want to play the hero and risk a nasty breakdown.

The townsfolk were all too ready to believe it and this was a good stopgap for us. There were plenty of people traumatized by the war. I soon came to hear stories of men who spent days on end at the window sharpening a knife. Or sitting on the front doorstep, their gaze so empty of life that it made your hairs stand on end. Others were driving their family crazy, waking up at night screaming so loud they woke the whole neighborhood. For many, the real war was only just beginning with the resumption of normality. Just when it was time to roll up their sleeves and put back together what was left of the province and the entire nation.

My only concern was whether I would be able to spit out a few words properly so that I could pass as a local. One evening, Mamma got the usual tin basin ready. Instead of the comb this time, she took out a razor with a black blade, which she started sharpening with a smooth stone. She wet my hair with drips from a cloth. Then she said, "Stay still," and started shaving me.

She did a good job. I could see why she was doing it, and I didn't know whether to laugh or cry. "We'll get both of us killed," I muttered, though she couldn't understand a thing. Meanwhile, I looked at myself in the rusty mirror. "We don't all look the same just because our heads are shaved," I said.

She tapped me on my shoulder. I turned around and saw her holding a dish filled with a pile of ash she had taken from the wood stove.

She rubbed it in dark rings all over my head and, with that dusting, covered the blond roots of my hair, highlighting the contrasts. She dipped her little finger in the ash again and ran it over my eyebrows, tickling me as she did so. She even dabbed it between my eyes. "Imagine if it rains," I attempted to joke. But she had disappeared again. She came back a second later with more of her son's clothes.

I picked out the less smelly ones. After I had done up the last button of the unbelievably worn shirt, I turned to look in the mirror and stood there for a moment, catching my breath. Because in the end, seen from a certain distance, I had actually stolen a resemblance to Niccodemo. I was gaunt in the same way, for example. And the shaven head, now that I was dressed as him, was also striking. Without considering the black powder Mamma had used as makeup. It was hard to see through the deception. In any case, my face was much thinner than his and I discovered my ears stuck out, which I had never noticed with long hair. And then there was the problem of my eyes. His were decidedly black while mine were hazel going on green.

I saw Mamma come out of her room. I had to get to her as quick as cannon fire because when she saw me, her heart missed a beat. But she was a tough woman and quickly shook off her emotions. She had a hammer in one hand. In the other, a nail as big as the ones that hold down train rails.

I thought she must have lost it entirely and was about to nail me to the wall like Jesus on the cross. Instead, she put everything on the table and went to get the usual portrait. She turned it towards me and pointed at her son's smiling face.

I looked at the picture and then at her, without understanding. "This," she kept saying. Eventually, I looked more closely and realized what she had been getting at: Niccodemo had a broken tooth. Right in the front. A diagonal crack. That was what made his face unique, but you had to know it to realize. I looked up at her. Then I cast my eyes over to the hammer and the nail, which was as thick as a thumb. "Are you joking?" I said in a feeble voice. She didn't understand but she smiled anyway. She pointed to the chair that she had taken out from under the table for me, as if I were at the barber's.

I started going nuts and running around the room. "No do!" I said in her language. "No do!" But Mamma had made her mind up. After a while I over-heated and a trickle of sweat ran down my cheek like a teardrop as thick and dark as crude oil. I calmed down and attempted to convince myself that, compared to everything I had been through, a chipped tooth wasn't such a big deal after all. What is more, we needed to do it to convince people. Without a gap in my mouth there was no way I could go down and mix with the former partisans in town whose only dream was to worm out a fascist and bring him to justice. I didn't think they would take the bait, but I couldn't go out and shout that I was a doppelgänger gone wrong. My only plan was to mingle as little as possible and play along with my mad mother's game while she taught me what she knew about her language. And then vanish into thin air back to Rosenheim.

I screamed into a tea cloth for a whole hour because, as she rammed the hammer home, it slipped and split my top lip and gouged out a bit of gum alongside the tooth. I spat out blood like piss and when my tongue found the chipped tooth, it struck a nerve and I saw stars. I filled the tin bowl with red spit while she bustled about bringing me fresh rags to stem the bleeding.

When the torture was over, I went to the mirror and saw myself there, the ash dripping everywhere and my mouth as swollen as a mule's. But at least the tooth had been properly broken. With my smashed-up face, it even looked like I had two fat cheeks to show off. In short: I was a rough copy of Niccodemo.

If I had walked to the Due Porte bar right there and then, at first glance they would have taken me for him.

I went out with Mamma the following day. I was so nervous I had to fight my instinct to throw up. I walked with my head down, my eyes nailed to my feet. We went down to the store for a spot of shopping. It was less than a hundred yards from home, there and back, but the procession nearly killed me. I was waiting to receive a tap on my shoulder at any moment and turn around to find a motley crew ready to drink my blood. But nothing happened. Mamma walked in front at quite a fast pace, and I traipsed along behind her, hiding behind her skirt like a retard. The old men stepped aside as we went past and whispered into one another's ears. I could feel their eyes on my back like a spray of machine gun fire. Every now and again, we stopped. Especially if one of them came forward, I stared down at the flagstones and left her to do the honors. "The war has finally gotten to him now." I was to get a better picture later on but at the time I missed most of what they were saying and was on the point of fainting. Another town gossip with her eyes flitting all over the place said, "They've sent him back practically deformed and with every tragedy in the world on his shoulders, none of which should be weighing on young men at that age. Imagine, yesterday he collapsed on the floor as stiff as a board. And cut his mouth open while he was at it." The townsfolk studied me in detail, with a great deal of pity and a great deal of horror. They saw how diminished I was and said to Mamma, "My dear, you know you are not alone. It's impossible to imagine the slaughter our boys have had to witness. The main thing is that they are back in the fold. There are so many of us who are left with nothing but their grief."

Then there was the story of the thirty-year-old builder, one of the first to come home. One morning, he shot himself in the mouth. A shockwave rocked the town and everyone said that weapons should be hidden away, even in the houses of solders who hadn't seemed too distressed at coming home but had then left free reign to the nightmares that had festered inside them.

Meanwhile, I fed bits and pieces of myself to Le Case so that the town could digest Niccodemo's new face slowly. They saw me as I was and were horrified by the change. And that was how they remembered me. More than anything else, they were shocked by my empty gaze and my silence. Mamma trained me with two words that I could repeat until I was blue in the face if anyone ever struck up a conversation, "Bad times." That's what I said, quietly. Somebody or other would stop me in the street and encourage me to talk with an opening like, "Niccodemo, you're looking good!" I would look away and say, "Bad times." The poor wretches were eating their hearts out. Some of them would come up and give me a patronizing pat. "Buck up, young man," they would mutter. "It'll soon pass. You'll find a nice wife and then you can set all the horrors of this rotten world aside."

After a while, I started taking my little jaunts a little more calmly. I still rubbed black ash into my hair, but my face was no longer swollen, and nobody took much notice. I focused on looking like I had a screw loose, tied to my mother's apron strings as usual. When we were walking around town, she never looked at me, not even once, as if she were both disgusted and ashamed of me but had to put up with her lot. It was all grist to the mill of our deception. In the meantime, other rumors reached Le Case that did nothing to dispel my fears and persuaded me not to lower my guard. News from the north, and from Emilia-Romagna in particular, was that the partisans had not disbanded at all. Fearing that fascists wouldn't get the punishment they deserved, they were making house calls and committing terrible atrocities. The news rekindled all the hotheads who had been holed up for months on end in the woods and had come home in some cases to find their wives carrying other people's babies. And there was I, a German soldier, hiding in full sight, right there under their noses. I went out nearly every day but never for long: ten minutes at most. Just enough time to remind the townsfolk of Niccodemo's gaunt face. Then I scurried back inside. Most of the people I ran into on my morning outings were either old men or housewives doing errands. Lowlifes whose advanced age and sacrifices had cast a pall over their minds. Duping them was tantamount to duping the entire province. But Mamma was the one who had the masterstroke when one day she dragged me down Via di Mezzo and past St. Bastian's. We emerged right in front of the town hall. She went to the counter and applied for a new identity card saying I had lost mine who knows where. As she spoke to the clerk, I was standing a few feet away and she cocked her head in my direction. "With all the trauma he's been through, and is still going through now, he simply can't remember where the papers went." Five days later, we returned to pick up my identity card with my photo clipped on it. The date of birth was four years before mine.

The weather turned cold in mid-November, after an October that was so mild it felt like Spring had returned. For Mamma it was a bad sign. "From one day to the next, the wind will be pushing us around," and she wasn't far wrong. I helped her carry shit in the mornings. It was a job that kept everyone at least ten yards away even to say good day and, as I toiled alongside her, I continued to familiarize the townsfolk with my face while hiding any precise features. We wrapped up warmly from head to toe and went down to the chestnuts where it had all started. We were able to have a decent conversation at that point but outside the house it was better not risk too much. In the evenings, we went back to our exercises in front of a crackling fire, and she continued to rap me over the knuckles for my pronunciation. "You sound like a broken trombone when you speak," she hissed. "Do you want to get rid of that Austrian accent or not?"

Rosenheim was still a mirage even though I could easily have gotten out of Mamma's hair by then. I even had an identity document to produce at the border. And yet, I stayed at Le Case, and I probably wouldn't have known what to say if a spirit had suddenly appeared out of nowhere and asked me out of the blue, "Why don't you leave?" Ultimately, Niccodemo's life was quite nice. Every minute that went by at Le Casa was a surprisingly appetizing and amusing vendetta. Orphans grow up with a feeling that for ordinary people they're just a disturbance, and I had been plagued by this sensation all my life. For once, I was imposing myself right in the lion's den. I was living an adventure that I had sought out since the day they first put a rifle in my hand. By that point, I wanted to see how things would end.

"Keep yourself to yourself," Mamma said when one February afternoon we decided I was ready to go out on my own. I pulled the collar of my jacket over my ears and touched up the black which was left on my eyebrows. I felt like a kid on his first day of school. "If anyone asks you anything, think about the words before you open your mouth. But in general, keep up the dazed look. Pick the shopping up and come straight back home.

Apart from a moment's surprise at seeing me come in alone, nobody took much notice of me at the store. I grabbed the bag full of our usual provisions and was about to head back home like an obedient dog. Except that it was a nice day. Yes, it was cold, but the sky was so wide open and blue that it reconciled me with the world and all my best intentions. On the spur of the moment, I turned on my heels and started going down the hill.

It was such a pleasure to be walking around town like a normal person. I answered an old man's greeting and didn't keep my eyes on the ground the whole time. I finally found myself in front of the Due Porte bar where the road narrows. The very idea of it warmed my blood. A second later, I turned around and headed straight for the door, throwing all my chips in at once.

The men's gazes were like a slap in the face. Those who were looking the other way received an elbow-dig, bringing their attention to me. "This is going to end up with a beating," I said to myself. "Stupid me, I'm asking for it." In any case, I found the strength to drag myself a little further inside and close the door on the town behind me. There were a few grumbles here and there. Then, as if by magic, everyone went back to what they were doing. I saw a free table on my left, right in the corner. I sat myself down in the chair and cast a look around, acting as dazed as I could.

To tell the truth, it felt as if something unusual had just happened to catch the onlookers' attention. I soon realized, however, that I had simply been a momentary distraction. A fly passing through. They were mostly old men, and they crowded around the tables in an almost funereal silence, at most whispering to one another. Every now and again there was some cursing and one or other of them heaved themselves up, sending half the town into disarray. They went straight for the counter and ordered a glass of wine to throw back in one gulp like medicine. Until I heard a yell, "The queen can't make that move! Only the knights can! Your brain must be full of worms if you haven't learned that yet."

That afternoon, I didn't see so much as an inch of the tablecloth. The drunkards in the Due Porte had their backs to me the entire time, totally absorbed in a pastime that alienated them from their surroundings. After a while, I got up and went out without a single person noticing. In exchange, when I got home, I found Mamma on the doorstep. She was hugging herself and her teeth were chattering with nerves. As soon as I got close enough, she started slapping me and pulling me into the house by the lapels. "I tell you to come straight back and you go off for a stroll!" she yelled. "Who cares, right? I'm the one who's eating my heart out. I imagined all sorts of things happening to you. Cretin!"

It was at times like these that she convinced me. She was

smacking me about a little, but she was breaking my heart with the affection of a real parent. If to begin with it made me shudder, over time I grew used to it and I told myself, "She's protecting me." There was no point in wondering whether she actually thought I was Niccodemo or whether her attachment was that for an acquired son. The main thing was that her blood ran cold if I didn't answer immediately.

I started going down to the Due Porte bar more often. When I walked in, they gave me a half-hearted look, but there was always some nasty comment to go with it. "Here's the guy who would have been better off if he'd been blown up. We already have enough village idiots in Le Case." I didn't mind them thinking that because, by making me out to be an idiot, they gave me a refuge without knowing it. Anyway, they let me go near the tables where furious battles were always being enacted. I found my corner and stayed there. Cigarette smoke burned my eyes and, since I never uttered a word, after a while they forgot that I was there. In the meantime, I watched the chess matches. There and then, I knew that the catastrophe of the orphanage and of war, the fighting in a foreign county and then hiding out in the woods for months, my whole life, in fact, had one aim only: to learn that game.

I was so obsessed I even made my own board. I used lumps of coal for the black pieces and pebbles for the white. I had found one shaped like a horse's head that I started carrying in my pocket as a talisman. All the while, I studied the moves at the tables in the Due Porte bar. I soon started to chafe at the bit: the games were all the same, there was no flair. Those old men had a many-faceted gemstone in their hands, and they were only looking at two or three of the thousands of possible facets. One man shifted a knight distractedly and I already knew that in four moves that would be the end of it. On the other side, however, there was a similar lack of talent, with the result that the game could go on for hours with nothing ever happening, pieces left unprotected and a chaotic spectacle of pawns sent blindly forward.

They used the chessboard to take their pieces for a stroll rather than to fight real battles. I would die of boredom watching them. It was as if I had an invisible book in my pocket, written in one sitting, which had never been surpassed anywhere in the world, but all around me there were herds of goats interested, at best, in eating the pages. The game gave me power, but I had to let it contaminate me from the inside. I memorized most of the games and played them when I got back home my own way, finally giving vent to my instincts. The matches lasted at most two minutes. Then, one day, there was a brawl.

By then I had understood the great thing about chess: it's all or nothing. Checkmate was like the recoil of a gunshot. It stayed with you for days. In the bar, defeat was never taken lightly, partly because they were betting with shots. If someone happened to come on a bad day, they would end up leaving, slamming the door behind them, their wallets a lot lighter, yelling that they would only come back to the pig sty of a bar when and if it started raining upwards. This happened with a man I had seen there often whom everyone called Moresco. He had started his day on the wrong foot and continued to lose badly. With a final curse, he lifted the chess table and tipped all the pieces onto the floor. His adversary had been a handsome man named Pallino, who had a special gift for stirring things up even when he was just saying good evening. He burst out laughing, deep in his gullet, relishing yet another victory, while most of the guys in the bar were pulling the chairs out and scrabbling for the pieces. Moresco was livid because losing control like that in front of the others was like stripping down to his underpants in public. Pallino's belly laugh had sucked the last drop of respect out of him, until he went into a blind rage and lunged towards him to slap his face. It was a pretty lame slap, like that of a jealous girl's. The room went quiet. Pallino laughed louder than before and the men in the bar followed suit. A red mist descended over Moresco, and he took his rage out on one man in particular who had been chuckling in his ear. He shoved him with his shoulder and almost succeeded in sending him flying. A free-for-all broke out but nobody was taking it too seriously. The brawl lasted no more than a minute. Moresco picked up his jacket and stalked out, sending the bar and everyone in it to hell. After a moment of silence, thick chortles filled the room. "Great way to get away without paying your debts," one of them said. "He's not fooling me. I take photocopies with my brain, and he owes me three." Throughout the whole fracas, Pallino's face never lost its smirk because he had enjoyed crushing the man's pride. "Next?" he joked. The men said that, given the melee, it might be a good idea to put the chess pieces away for the night, together with everyone's nervousness. Just then, the whole bar went quiet. I had appeared out of nowhere, and I had sat down in Moresco's place, placing the pieces into their starting positions. Pallino looked at me, the same smirk on his lips. The only thing he said was, "Today I've been kissed by a saint. More shots are on the way." Then he lost nine games in a row.

The streets look like muddy snakes. Looking at the swinging lampshades makes me feel I'm floating on the flood tide. From my window, I can see into all the other windows in the street, at least the ones that are lit up: dark silhouettes standing there like restless ghosts contemplating the destruction. Maybe they're spying on me in the same spirit. The crashing storm rattles at the windows, as does the driving rain which chucks buckets of water against the panes, whipping against them. My thoughts return to the room where Don Lauro is rotting away by the minute, and I tell myself that this is what a town with no soul looks like.

It's impossible to go down to Mario's because there's a real risk of not living to tell the story and ending up at the bottom of Via di Mezzo swallowed up by the mud. The phones are dead. But we're the lucky ones up in the old town. Down in the new town the landslide must be burying them.

It's as if all the shit that Mamma had taken up to the chestnut grove over a lifetime wanted to make its way back down again, all at once. That's the bad thing about Le Case: one way or another, things come back to haunt you, with accrued interest. That is what happened after the early days, when my face was well and truly imprinted in everyone's gaze and nobody thought for a minute that the wrong person was in that body. Mamma had also stopped blackening my face and hair and I thanked my lucky stars that Niccodemo had been an introvert who had steered clear of company all his life and spent most of it holed up at home.

I already had a certain reputation with the old men who had no jobs to go to. I could beat anyone from anywhere. Then Sundays at the Due Porte happened. They were the best: the bar filled up with customers not only from Le Case but from neighboring towns as well. Once the entry fees were collected, the tournament began.

The first time I was nervous. I asked Mamma to give me the money to sign up for the competition and she answered, "You must have gone weak in the head." I had to beg her on my knees and swear that if I didn't bring home the prize money, I would do the shit rounds on my own for a whole month. Eventually, I saw her vanish into her room and when she came back, she handed me the money I needed. "Here you are," she said. "Go and throw the proceeds of my sweat away. But don't come to me whining that your plate's empty at dinner time."

I shot to first place in the tournament in the first hour, and nobody could believe it. I kept my head down. I hardly said a word, and when I did it was in a whisper. They saw this half-wit war veteran flaying saints alive on the chessboard. Someone muttered behind me, "He's turned into one of those circus acts where one minute he can't tie his own shoelaces and the next he gets obsessed with something and suddenly becomes famous. There was a retard from Tatti like that: he painted pictures and people came all the way from America to buy them. But if you left him alone even for ten minutes, he was capable of drowning in a glass of water. He had his art, and Niccodemo gets his kicks from chess. Who knows? Maybe his mother, poor wretch, has won the lottery and doesn't even know it."

I laughed with a chickadee in my belly. I watched as these petty men with hard fascist faces sat in the front row and blew smoke in my face at my opening moves as if to put me off my game. Three minutes later, they had already lifted their backsides from the chairs, their pupils shriveled to nothing. "It's not all pawns and rooks," the most disappointed among them commented. "Once the game's over, some of us go back to having a life. Others have nothing else."

The players in the vicinity were all a waste of space, even the wealthier ones. There was no fun in setting my traps for them on the board. I moved a knight forward and none of them bothered to ask themselves why I had left it there to be taken. They captured it, looking all the while, as if they'd done something crafty, and that was that. This exemplified everything about them and exposed their souls for what they were. I took it all into my stride. I would put some bait out there and then after three long moves checkmate them. It was great sending them home deathly pale and mortified. Playing against me was like stripping off in the main square and revealing their flaccid flesh but they couldn't help themselves.

On normal days, they never let me play. The old men confiscated the box of chess paraphernalia like nasty kids who horde a ball to themselves. I was perfectly happy to sit and watch because by that time, the idea of spending the whole day walled up in my room did me in. I stayed close to the chess board, though, because I felt at home in that magic world. Until chess became my undoing.

To begin with, I thought I was being hexed: I ended up in the newspapers. Me, of all people, who had spent the last year or more taken up with the idea of hiding and had even gotten to the point of changing my skin and becoming someone else. But I quickly climbed up the tournament ladder, making anyone who had bet against me regret it. I even started earning decent money, which I always gave to Mamma. I made her throw the shit pail away. Let someone else come and collect her shit now.

And yet, even though I got to see the cut glass and bright lights of many different cities, I felt as if I was being spied on in the one place that was just my own, which had nothing to do with the name I had adopted, and which was not evident from the newspaper headlines. I won an umpteenth trophy, but my smile was never unforced. Part of it was the gap in my mouth, the tooth that had been chipped with a hammer. Another part was the impression that crawled on my skin like the itch of a flea. I shook hands and watched the countryside go by from my train seat. Wherever I was in the world, there was always this feeling of doom that robbed me of feeling complete satisfaction. It was like being stared at by a stray cat squatting in the grass. I didn't know it at the time, but the cat had a name and that was Le Case.

Twenty-six years before, I had been scouted by a talent-spotter who had landed at the Due Porte bar with the idea of introducing me to the world. Twenty-six years later, the same character sent me back there after one more defeat. "You've lost your touch," Tancredi said one day. "It's not something you think about but kids with a talent for the game are springing up like mushrooms. You only notice when you see them playing. And anyway, I'm too old to be your impresario now. The world has changed. Everything has changed."

I didn't even get through the round of sixteen. The flame had been extinguished, not from one day to the next but gradually, very gradually, in that bastardly way that suddenly leaves you standing in your underwear. I lost the important matches, and that crow of a wife I had married to make me look good and make people envious also disappeared. Debtors were scratching at my door at all times of day and night. Having signed away all my property, I found myself from one day to the next back in Mamma's old rooms. From where Le Case had never ceased to call me, tickling me on my back.

There is no insult given that you pay more dearly for than success. Especially in towns filled with peasants whose backs have been broken by routine and hard work. When they bumped into me on the street, they would come up and give me big hugs, devour me with their eyes to see if per chance they noticed a worn shirt cuff. They broke into big smiles that seemed to say, "Now eat your queen." The worst were the idle fascists, whose wives had been drilled by various townsmen more deeply than in the mines, and who, after many years, had gained a black lung and a pension for their efforts. "It's a nice world, isn't it?" I heard them mutter behind me one afternoon, the Due Porte almost empty. "I hope he doesn't think he can come and shit it all out again here."

Maso was my only friend. He came and sat at my table and brought a glass for himself, too. We were both in our fifties, but we looked like two old men. Our conversation always drifted to the past. He talked more than me because he felt ground down by serving at the counter. So, he opened up with the only person who had actually looked around this Earth, while he had had to hang up his spirit of adventure in that morgue of a bar where every day was an echo of itself.

I first noticed Samuele when he noticed me. He appeared out of the blue one ordinary morning, walking into Due Porte with that grim look on his face. His school bag was hanging off one shoulder. He slung it under a table and slumped into a chair. He was thirteen years old.

We grew fond of the boy, especially because he had no desire to make friends with anyone of his own age. He was a stray mutt, full of rage, a symptom of all the things he wouldn't have even known how to express. He was upset by the way the bullies treated him, beating the life out of him in the school corridors and on the bus. "I'll smash their heads in," he used to say but he never did it because, every time he tried, he was fenced in by the others and his hatred melted into fear in no time at all. It was safer to wriggle his way out of the scrum, the ugly words shouted by the kids from his neighborhood raining down on him like stones.

I remember the defeat a few years before. It was at the Due Porte. There he'd been, sitting in front of me. It was a game, letting novices play with someone who knew how to move the pieces. I had thought about him occasionally since then, especially after the knocks I had taken from the new generation. Samuele had been the first to slap me with a checkmate. That was when I started to lose my talent. It wasn't the boy's fault. He somehow represented the beginning of my downfall. That might be why I didn't have much sympathy for him after what happened.

In the dead hours of the early afternoon, we were like a little family: me, Maso, and him. As time went by, he started to open up, telling us about his old grandmother and the father he had never met. He never spoke about his mother, and we soon understood where the wave of anger that washed over him day and night came from. It was his abandonment. Samuele felt as if he had been picked up and thrown away like an old cigarette butt. I recognized my younger self in him: all those years in the orphanage when I would stare at the shadows of the big windows at night in the silence of the dormitory and try to drive away the idea that I was destined to live a life floating on nothing because I had no roots. Or again, I would feel as if I was disappearing, with a lump in my throat at the thought of a mother who had left a crying bundled-up baby on the sidewalk, right on the edge of the sewage ditch. To my mind, no state of poverty can justify something like that. Samuele had the same cross to bear, which made him walk with clenched fists without even noticing. At least there had been chess to help bring me back to life and I still went around with that pebble shaped like the head of a horse in my pocket. I had found a haven in the game because it opened up infinite routes for me. One day, I placed the chessboard in front of him with a little trepidation. I felt my heart burst when I recognized in his gaze the same spark that decades before had been in mine. I soon realized that Samuele harbored the same destiny as me and would be able to build vast new worlds with it. He moved rooks and bishops and galloped with knights. As if he were redesigning the board.

In the end, I found myself in the same role as Tancredi. I taught Samuele the best way to take out all the other player's pieces. Once he'd learned to appreciate the sweet pleasure of the blood sport, he became ruthless. In provincial tournaments, he would annihilate the other young players, brought in by parents convinced they had given birth to a phenomenon. He never boasted about it. He just wanted more. He would study his next adversary from afar and then lean over towards me. "Nine moves," he would say after observing the way the player walked or looked around him, without even touching any of the pieces. Nine moves later and the other kid would be sobbing into his mother's skirt. Samuele was cold-blooded. His method revealed a great deal about him: he created chaos and disoriented anyone who challenged him, including me. Then, he divided the board up into strips and attacked one piece after another. By the fifth or sixth move he'd usually checkmated his surprised opponent. Victory was point-blank, like a rifle shot.

Those were good years, despite how bitter they were for me. Little by little, Samuele created a new character for himself outside chess, applying to the outside world the same clear-sightedness he applied to the game. He also brought me back to life; the nurturing of a genius allowed me to discover the bright side of chess. My life had been full of hardship, but my days had been filled with light because under the mucky waters of my daily routine there was a new alphabet which was only ours. We spent whole afternoons at the table without saying a word. We would then trudge back home together like mercenaries after a bloody battle.

When he started to move away from me, I started drowning myself in drink again. Samuele was besotted by the city, and he felt duty-bound to keep up his studies, given how much his dear grandmother had sacrificed for him. I would sometimes see him walk by and we would make a date for a match which never materialized except against myself in my corner of the Due Porte bar. Until one day he simply vanished, taking everything away with him.

The most terrifying thing is the ring around the sun which is desperately trying to show its face but can't because the clouds are too thick. Every now and again, like now, some of them come so low that they crash right into the town, covering the walls and filling the streets. From the window I can see what looks like a platoon of ghosts floating in mid-air down Via di Mezzo. Emerging from the foggy folds, I catch fleeting glimpses, shapes of people, but just for a second like in a feverish dream. I know I may be obsessing about this but I'm sure I saw Don Lauro's face in the storm.

Today is the fourth day. The light bulbs seem to be holding up but it's a small miracle: it feels like I'm going through an eternal night, with the electricity going on and off all the time, like an animal gasping for life. And here we all are, holed up in our rooms, counting the breaths.

I saw Samuele again in the papers at Maso's but this time it wasn't because he'd won any trophies. Then, a while ago, I almost dropped my whisky glass at the Due Porte when the news came in. He was back in town. I opened my eyes wide and saw a film reel in my head: he had been sent back to Le Case just as I had many years before. I imagined him coming through the door of the bar with the weary air of a practiced traveler looking for some peace and quiet. He would see me sitting at my usual table, as always, laying world events out on the chess board to dry. Because Samuele knew how to lose himself there exactly like me, finding solace in the bottomless pits of the board. I had been flying solo for too long.

But he never came. Maso said we should just wait. The burdens our boy had brought back to Le Case were not insignificant and this town will skin you and stop greeting you just for a sideways look. After the first few weeks, I gave up hope. I got out of bed in a black mood. I went to the Due Porte and started drinking early as a rebuke. "You want to do yourself in with the drink, do you?" I heard Maso say but I didn't deign to look at him. I hung my head and went back to the bottle.

I didn't dare go and knock at his door. Samuele had his own special way showing me his indifference. Or maybe he thought that someone like me couldn't understand the difficulties that had forced him to return to this hellhole to lick his wounds. In all that silence, I heard an even louder silence calling out: his final detachment, which wounded me to the core. Then, a week ago, I bumped into him coming out of the store.

He almost knocked me over. He was closing the door behind him and turning around to walk back home. We were face to face and about to bump chests. We stared. His face was as expressionless as ice. I wanted to say something but not a word came out of my mouth. I was dying right there under his pallid, soulless gaze. Then he looked down and stepped to one side as if he were avoiding a stranger. I watched him as he disappeared, stooped over, protecting his face from the first gusts that were already making the alleys howl. "Samuele . . . " I managed to call out but it was just air, and the cross-draughts swallowed it up on the spot. I stood there for a few minutes icing over. I had gone numb. He had just robbed me of all the heat I had managed to preserve.

I'd be willing to bet on it: he didn't even recognize me. Maybe he really has gone off his head as the gutter press has been insinuating for the past few months. Or he's ashamed. But the Samuele Radi I know has nothing in common with those eyes, which were black holes totally lacking in emotion. My Samuele was a dark creature, for sure, but he had a whole range of emotions at his disposal, which he would pour out onto those few inches of the chess board. All the silent matches I have been playing through the years have been against him. And I am still playing against him now while outside the turbines are turning Le Case inside out, stone by stone. So, I go over to the table where my pieces are lit by the last whimpers of electricity, as the supply dwindles and fizzles out. I sit on the black side. I look straight ahead of me into the void. And I say, "Your turn," and turn the board around.

Marco Palazzesi,
the Chief Physician

When I close my eyes, I return to that evening in early June when Babbo put his spoon down abruptly making a commotion. A deathly silence fell over the table. Mamma turned into a salt statue and was about to get up because she was probably expecting him to have another fit of nerves. She said, "Aldo . . . " and it sounded like a hundred questions wrapped up in one. But he held up. He didn't cup his face with his hands and start sobbing as he'd been doing for days on end. On the contrary, he shifted his gaze towards me and said, his eyes flickering like a flame, "In September, you'll have to start studying. Enjoy the summer while you can. When the time comes, I don't want any fuss." I nodded. Then we went back to our meal.

We didn't talk about it at home but the explosion at the Ribolla mine had changed him. Babbo had such a baleful expression in his eyes that it gave me goosebumps. He had new furrows on his face, deep chasms on the edge of which he only just managed to keep his balance. I no longer saw him as normal. If I tried, a sense of shame rose up inside me and made me turn my head the other way. Since the explosion, Babbo walked around as if he were naked. I would flee into my room whenever he collapsed onto his knees for no reason, even as Mamma ran over to hold his head up. He would be taken over by fits of crying that would make him shake all over like there was an earthquake inside him. I had to stuff my head under my pillow not to hear his moans. When I emerged from my room, I would find him sitting at table, his face looking like old parchment. "Hey, little soldier," he would say, with a ghost of a smile. Then his gaze would wander off, and he would be trapped in that mask. Mamma laid the table around him as he sat there like a sleepwalker. She spoke to him in the kind of voice you would use for retards, "Aldo, move your elbow, please . . . " Babbo would sit there completely still, glassy eyed in his depression. Sometimes I had to touch him to bring him back to life. He would come back to his senses batting his eyelids repeatedly. Then I could smooth out the tablecloth properly.

"We need to be patient," my mother said to me one afternoon. "There are some events you can't digest in a week." But the months went by, and I watched a man crumpling up somewhere inside him in a place I didn't even know existed. "Look how low Babbo is," I said to myself. "The worst thing is that he noticed it day after day, too, as he sank into the chasm without being able to do a thing about it." It got to the point where he was only sleeping half an hour a night. Meanwhile, it's not like the bills stopped while his brain settled down and Mamma's face began to furrow with apprehension. The larder was crying out to be filled. It was most obvious when I came in from playing with my band of friends. Until a few weeks before, I would come home to a snack of bread and sugar but now there was nothing left. One day, I dug out an almost-empty jar of jam but, when I opened it, I found a thin layer of white mold. Mamma took it out of my hands and stirred it with a spoon. "What's the problem," she said, her face pulled into a laugh though even an ass could see that she was torn up about it. "It's just penicillin!"

Babbo was not the only one. Some families had accepted the terrible events and were licking their wounds and putting away the little compensation they received, which was anyway better than nothing. But there were other kids whose parents were suspended like dazed ghosts, understandable after a beating like that. The older folk were fed up and plotted ways to get their revenge on the Montecatini company. One day I heard someone say, "These lands were controlled by brigands until yesterday. Maybe the bosses don't know this little detail. Things are not going that well for them as it is . . . " More than a month had passed since the tragedy, but the aftermath of the shock was still in the air in the whole region because they announced they were closing some of the shafts. "They're going to pick up and leave," people said in the streets. "The ones who'll get their last salary for dismantling the machinery before being packed off to retirement are the lucky ones but most of us will be taken off the payroll from one day to the next. Thinking about it takes my appetite away."

We were already there. Babbo was broken inside and there was no way he could go out to earn a day's wages. Talking about the mine was out of the question. If he so much as heard the word Ribolla, you had to rush to his side and reassure him that everything was over. When tragedy had struck, he had thrown himself into helping his companions with the determination I had always known he possessed but he was now paying the price. There was no way of erasing what he had seen from his mind. He had been buried by the Camorra explosion as much as the others, even though he was still walking around the house. Back when he was fit and well, he used to say as a joke, "I survived a war and then they stuck me down a mine to give me a rest." The mine had been like a boil gathering pus for years. All the debris that had been piled up exploded at once producing a stench that was enough to catch in the throats of half the province. At the same time, it turned a model worker into a nervous wreck who could hardly find his own mouth at dinnertime.

He started to recover in September when Mamma gave me the news, wide-eyed with happiness. "Babbo has been given a job with Cutini, the lawyer. Taking care of the villa, that's it. Just outside the new town, on the road up to San Martino."

I should have been happy for him, but I considered it a

woman's job and the first thing that came into my head was how I was going to tell my friends. I knew perfectly well where that big house full of windows was. We used to go there a lot, especially on summer Sundays when the rich family would call in a band and parked cars would line the road all the way up the hill. There was a gap in the ivy-clad fence that was big enough for one of us in turn to look through. We used to spy on the parties of those people whose wallets were always stuffed. They were so rich they had ice cream delivered straight to the door even in November.

But Babbo was beginning to feel the earth under his feet again. That was the main thing. He had walked barefoot through the flames of hell, but he hadn't forgotten what he had said to me at the beginning of the summer vacation. In the evening after dinner, he nailed me down to my notebooks and checked my homework. To begin with, reading came hard to him but as time went by, he became more fluent and started checking up on me regularly, to the point that I would sometimes run to Mamma, bury myself in her skirts, and start begging to be sent to bed right there and then. I didn't even care about eating the last tangerine. He would start reciting the usual rosary of how studying would free me from a life of deprivation. To encourage me to fall in love with the pages I had to study, he would tell me all about the wealth he had seen at the villa, which had at least thirty rooms. And lots of bathrooms. But the thing that made me gawp the most was the idea of having a fountain in the living room. As soon as he told me about that, I sat down like a good boy. Babbo broke out in a smile and went on describing the high ceilings and vast terraces that were so big I could play football with my friends on them. Eventually, he would always end up with the war. "The Germans used to live there," he would say. And then he would start telling the story that made me laugh the most.

He told me about this character he called Amico Fritz. I

could picture him in minute detail. I imagined his adventures, which started one heady, drunken evening. "The Americans were heading up north fast," Babbo said. "They did away with every Nazi they came across, liberating Italy from that plague. Marco, just imagine the scene. All the platoons posted in the area are ready. At dawn, columns of soldiers will be hastily retreating after living scot-free off us Maremma folks. Amico Fritz dives deep into a haystack. It is his way of saying farewell to the girlfriend he's been having a fling with since he first arrived. To drown their sorrow at separating, first they kiss a little and then he kisses the bottle a little. Until he is dead drunk, his girlfriend flicks on the forehead and, seeing there is no reaction, hurries home in the middle of the night. When Amico Fritz opens his eyes, it's broad daylight. He drags himself up to a standing position and makes his way outside as steadily as he can. The first thing he does is look down the street and he gets the shakes straight away. Instead of German jeeps on the tracks, he sees vehicles belonging to a different army, including tanks and trucks cram-packed with American soldiers. And there he was in a Nazi uniform. Without any luggage, in the belly of the enemy. They catch him in the crosshairs of their binoculars almost immediately. The first yells can be heard from the procession. Amico Fritz doesn't waste any time: he runs into the woods with the whole of America on his tail."

I had to take this story to bed with me because Babbo would always stop just as things were getting interesting. I used to enjoy making up a different ending every time. At one point, I had a dedicated notebook which I labeled, "The Adventures of Amico Fritz." In one version, he even became a father. But what made my hair stand on end was when suddenly, he would say, "What if he were still here living among us? Have you ever thought about that? Sometimes the best way to hide is in plain sight." Babbo had come out of his bad place by then, as if he had spent a long time screaming in an underground chamber.

There was a new light in his eyes. It looked as if he had fallen in love with Mamma all over again and he would often come up to her from behind and hug her suddenly, nestling his face in her hair. In the evening, he came back from the lawyer's villa the picture of contentment and tucked heartily into his dinner. His debt to suffering had been paid and he was flourishing. He spent all day in those gilded rooms, keeping the garden tidy and polishing the mirrors. The Cutini family only remembered they owned the place in the summer, or on certain days when the lawyer would come from Siena on a clandestine assignation with a signorina. For the rest of the time, it was Babbo who got to inhabit those rooms. There was often nothing to do and he spent whole afternoons on the veranda with books from the library and a glass of lemonade at his side. His main task was to be on the other end of a phone call, which could come at any time. "Everything okay?" Cutini would ask. If there was an important repair job to be done, a team of handymen would arrive from Grosseto. "During the day, I'm the guardian of a royal palace," we would hear him comment at dinner when he was in the mood for joking, "and in the evening I come back to this shithole." Mamma and I would look sideways at him. Then he would add with a wink, "Nobody is better off than me." Until one day, he came back with the news, "Cutini says he doesn't want the villa to stay empty on Sundays. If we want, we can go ourselves. Let me be clear, they would add this service to my pay packet."

It was like being on vacation. Suddenly, that day of rest became our obsession. We couldn't wait for it to come. We used to get up just past dawn and head up the road towards San Martino with a small bag. The first couple of times, Mamma just stood there because she was terrified of touching a glass. Babbo looked perfectly at home, laying the table for lunch with the gold-leaved plates. I would get lost in the corridors and in hidden corners of the garden. I didn't mind leaving my band of friends behind for a whole afternoon. In the evenings, we would head back home feeling slightly sad. Babbo would close the big gate behind us, and we would walk towards the old town back to our house. One day, Mamma said, "Are we sure that these tastes of another life are a good idea? On Mondays, I wake up with a brick in my stomach." Our whole house could fit into one room in the villa. I would throw myself on my bed at home and feel as if I was in a stair cupboard.

You soon get used to earning money and living it up. When summer came around, the parties started again and Babbo had a long face when he told us. "This Sunday, they're coming down from Siena with the whole troop," he said, making my guts twist. "They're even bringing their own butlers." We had to spend that Sunday inside the four walls of our house, which felt like they were suffocating us. Mamma sat at the window sewing. I spent the whole day on my notebook. It didn't even cross my mind to go and look for my friends. To do what? To spy on all that wealth through the gap in the ivy? The Adventures of Amico Fritz were much more fun, thank you.

Cutini had given tender meat to the wolves to taste and now they were howling at the full moon and asking for more. Mamma's taste for the good life was such that one day she looked at us with a smile and said, "I'm not coming tomorrow. I don't feel up to it. I fall in love with something that's not mine and then I grow less fond of what we have, which is not very much but until the other day it was enough. It's not good for me. And it won't lead anywhere good, either." And she stuck to her decision. There was nothing we could do to change her mind. That Sunday I walked up towards San Martino with Babbo and spent the day inside a rich person's picture frame. But without Mamma it was only half the fun. Her absence brought me back to my senses, and I heard her voice in my head, "Keep your feet on the ground. Nothing you see belongs to you and it never will." We went back in the evening, before dinner. We preferred to go home and eat at our own table, where we sat elbow to elbow. But at least we could look one another in the eye.

When the lawyer proposed to Babbo that the whole family move into the villa, there were days when you couldn't hear a pin drop. It sounded like a good idea to me, but Mamma dug her heels in. She was sorry to leave the home she had inherited from her grandparents. "It will change us," she said one evening. "We'll be living a novelized version of our own life." Babbo swallowed these words in silence and tried explaining the matter to her calmly. The Cutinis were growing older and more apprehensive, and they couldn't sleep knowing that the San Martino villa was uninhabited at night. Despite the guard dogs on the loose and the locks on all the doors and windows. We had the chance to take over the whole of the top floor and live for most of the year without ever being disturbed by the shadow of another person. We would be able to stay for the vacations, too. Mamma was not being asked to join the servants, who usually followed their masters when they left the city. And there would be no expenses. On the contrary, we would be able to rent the house we had always lived in and make more income from that. In short, it was a great retirement plan. "I'm thinking of the boy," Babbo said in front of me. "Once he finishes secondary school, we 'll have the money to send him away to study, without running up debts like all those people who live off canned food for half a century so their kids can go to Florence."

It only took a few weeks for Mamma's doubts to fade and eventually she grew accustomed to the endless corridors. But she never stopped repeating to me, "If you touch anything, remember it's not yours." She felt ill if an ornament was knocked over. Her stomach clenched the whole day long and she would stare out of the window, obsessed by the idea that the boss's big car would pull up in the drive. She would rather have bumped into the devil.

The first party we were invited to, she spent the day in her room. But she dressed me in my Sunday best and spent half an hour getting the knots out of my hair with a comb. When the time came to go downstairs and greet the owners of the villa, Babbo tried to convince her, but she started dry heaving at the thought. She grabbed her nightie and hid under the covers.

And yet, Cutini was so ordinary that if anybody saw him on the street, they wouldn't have been able to tell he was a lawyer and wealthy landowner. What struck me about him was that he didn't have a single hair on his body, not even on his eyebrows. He went around with that polished bald head and long, wrinkly neck. He reminded me of a dried-up turtle that had lost its shell. He looked at you with those light-gray eyes that made your blood run cold. The slit of his mouth was indistinguishable from the skin of his face, which was filled with liver spots and little green veins that stuck out and looked like cracks in his cheeks. His clothes hung loosely. He wore his shirts with the cuffs unbuttoned and only the tips of his fingers on view. "He finds clothes itchy," Babbo once confided. "His skin is like tissue paper . . . he looks like he's about to be carried away by the first gust of wind. Who would ever have said this man commands half the region?" Apart from this, his manner was that of a loving grandfather, even towards me who was nobody to him. "Let's get this little frog settled, too," he would say, stroking my hair with those hands that were so like a child's, with dainty, transparent nails. Then he would sit with all his relatives and listen to the complaints that they took turns bringing to his attention. He would look into space and sit there with a blank smile on his face, nodding every now and again. Eventually, he would pat whichever nephew or son-in-law it was on the shoulder as if to say, "I'll deal with it." Babbo always used to say, "There are important people in Rome who are afraid of him and will sit a whole day in the waiting room to speak to him." One day, I turned suddenly and said, "What if he is Amico Fritz?" My whole body caught fire at the idea. "Look at that disguise!" The next minute, I dashed off another adventure.

Mamma, too, started coming down to the garden for the parties. The first time, the lawyer's wife rushed up to her. "My dear," she said, handing her a glass of champagne and dragging her towards a clutch of upper-class women. "Finally!" I saw her come back in after the party looking sprightly and walking on air, buoyed up by bubbly and good spirits. I stayed outside in my fancy clothes with a nice cup of pistachio ice cream in my hand. In full view of the gap in the ivy fence.

When I arrived in Siena, the table was already laid. I was fourteen and my blood had been poisoned with something I hadn't been born with. I had become accustomed to being called "little lord" by the wait staff at parties and I knew every member of the family I had come to the city to meet. They treated me as an equal and with an affection that my real uncles and aunts had never shown me, even less so now that we had acquired connections.

I was especially close to the lawyer's grandson, Raniero. He was going on seventeen and behaved as if he were already an adult. He encouraged me to explore the local dives and drink a lot. In the evenings, he would come and throw stones at the window of the seminary where Cutini had found lodgings for me, for which he had only charged Babbo a pittance in the form of a donation. I would open the window and lower myself onto the street. Getting down was easy, though I had to be careful not to twist my ankle. Getting back up required an accomplice to give me a leg-up because even if I jumped, I barely reached the windowsill. As soon as the bells of the San Domenico Cathedral rang ten o'clock, there was Ranieri's gravel, regular as clockwork. And out we went into the night.

He was always complaining about his father, who had spent so much time in the capital that he had found a new, young wife and left his mother in Siena with the Ghibellines in a vale of tears. Tears that the son of the lawyer's son had to deal with. I kept a close eye on him. Especially when he was on his fourth glass of wine, when he would suddenly turn to me looking upset. "They're ruining my best years," he would say. "And they already wasted my childhood by making me study fucking *bon ton* instead of playing. Sometimes I would extend my arm and pat him, as if to say, "I'm here, I'm with you on this." It seemed to be enough for him because his face would melt into a smile and he would stare into space for a few seconds. Then he would come back to his senses and say, "Come on, let's go to Nenni's."

The place looked perfectly normal, nothing ostentatious about it. Donna Nenni would come to the door and spy us there on the third-floor landing of Via Stufasecca, 17. "Here are the little lords," she would hiss from the other side of the door. And then open the door.

This is what happened when you hung out with any of the Cutinis. Doors were opened before you could say half a word. And that was how we would get into that apartment, which was cozy, lit by candles, which were everywhere, even on the floor, lining the corridor as you came in. Nenni was more or less my mother's age, but she was uglier and her makeup was caked on, lipstick staining her teeth. She wore loose tunics and walked barefoot in the house so as not to make a noise with her heels. We had to do the same. We left our shoes in the entrance, where there were usually several pairs in the corner already. That was how we were able to tell what kind of people had come for the soiree.

The hostess made me feel dizzy, which was why I never wanted to look her in the eye. It amused her. She enjoyed laying a hand on my shoulder, for example, and using her thumb to stroke the back of my neck. I struggled with all my might but by the time we got to the living room, my dick was standing to attention, and my only concern was that nobody in the room would notice. It was unlikely, given that there was so much cigarette smoke in the apartment that we had to grope our way around in the thick fog. There was no music, and everyone was talking like they do at the seminary, their voices under their heels. If anyone happened to sneeze, Donna Nenni was instantly at their side, like a devil. "Quiet!" she whispered, her eyes flashing a threat. "You can thank that prioress, Senator Merlin, for outlawing us. If she'd had more fun in life getting laid, we wouldn't be holed up here in secret." There was a picture of this lawmaker in every room instead of a crucifix and Nenni often used to stick her tongue out at her.

Raniero would head straight for the drinks cupboard and pour a glass of something strong for me, too. He always looked like he was going to the gallows even though he was in a house of pleasure. Every now and again, we would hear a dull thud coming from one of the rooms. A second later, Nenni's hisses made my hair stand on end. "Hey, you in there! For St. Brigit's sake, take it easy. Do you want to see this place closed down?"

We would sit there waiting on the low sofas in the semi-darkness as if in a dream, the murmur of voices sounding like they came from the great beyond. The only entertainment was Nenni herself, who was thrilled to receive the scion of the Cutini family and would always stand outside one particular door knocking madly. We would usually see a man coming out and scuttling down the corridor a few minutes later, huffing and puffing, with his pants still open. Donna Nenni would come along smiling from ear to ear. "Come, Raniero," she would say. "The girl is ready." He wouldn't get up right away. To begin with, he would stare at nothing as if he had just received a terrible diagnosis. Then he would throw what was left of the liquor in his glass down the hatch. "I'm off to drown in my Gorgon," he murmured, looking askance at me. And he would make his way to the room in a hurry. Leaving me staring at the flickering candles.

I could have done the same. Between Babbo's salary and the rent from our old house we were starting to save a significant amount of money, and it was piling up. Every week, I received notice of a deposit, but I hardly touched my bank account, because if you're going around with the heir to a fortune, it's offensive to offer to pay. But the very idea of going into one of those rooms made me burn with shame. Nenni no longer bothered to ask me. "It's blasphemous to take pleasure unwillingly," she had said the last time, and that was enough to get me excited. I was more likely to think about a girl when I was safely tucked up in bed at the seminary, where I suddenly had the courage to do everything.

Then Agnese, the albino girl, came into the picture. I followed with my eyes the shape of yet another run-of-the-mill family man walking down the corridor and, a few minutes later, there she was. She appeared like a ghost in her sky-blue gown. She looked as though she was made of snow. She flopped into the low divan in the corner and lit a cigarette. Bare feet. Hair tied in a high bun, as white as marble. The flickering candles turned her hair silver every now and again. Agnese's face was that of a twenty-year-old, but her coloring was an old woman's. And she didn't say a word. She lay there making cats' eyes. She didn't throw a single glance at me and I really thought, "I'm in the company of a ghost," and sat stock still, holding my hands in my lap the whole time she was there.

The silence felt different when we were in the same room. It was heavy and felt like it would crush me. One minute felt like fifteen. And I stole glances at her to see what a girl's face looked like when she'd just had sex. But she looked as shiny as freshly fired porcelain. If Nenni asked me outright which room I would choose, I would say number two like a shot as I never hear a peep out of it. But Agnese was not the kind of girl you fantasize about under the bedcovers. Whenever I thought about her, I imagined her on the other side of the city looking back at the seminary with an offended expression on her face. And my dick would instantly shrivel in my hand.

Ranieri would always come back looking grim, as if he had been given a belting. The hostess would rush up to him with chocolates and proffer her greetings to his family. I often found myself thinking that if that place continued attracting so many clients, it must have been down to a certain person whose fingers were in every pie. A person who decides people's fates. After his quickie, Raniero never said much. Once we were outside, he was desperate to get back to drinking and strode off. Nor did he provide any details, unlike my classmates who loved boasting even though they didn't even know where to look for their dicks. We would usually go and hole ourselves up in some tavern and, even when the chairs had already been pulled up onto the tables, the innkeepers would start getting bottles and glasses out like nobody's business. They would launch into long conversations as if they'd never in their lives opened their mouths. And I kept on thinking, "He has the whole city at his disposal and yet he's a lone wolf. Some bell tower or other would ring midnight. We would walk back up to the seminary lurching drunkenly. We would jump over the fence and often tumble over like cooked pears. We would shove one another to remind ourselves that we risked waking up the student priests with our laughter. Eventually, we reached my window and Raniero would offer me his shoulder to climb up on, however unsteady he was on his feet. One evening, as I was pulling myself up onto him, he kissed me.

I revisited the scene for days afterwards. San Domenico rang ten o'clock and there were no stones at the window. I conjured up my last moments with Raniero—he stared at me for an interminably long time after pulling away. I had no idea what he had been trying to say but the last few glasses of wine had still been in his blood. I burst out laughing. I laughed so hard it made me feel ill. I collapsed onto the ground and stayed there for a bit because I'd been about to pee in my pants. By the time I lifted my head, he had gone. I ran to the road, but it was no use. He had vanished.

With the icy air, the inebriation soon passed, and this helped me look at things from a different perspective. There was nothing I could use to lever myself up to the windowsill. The only thing I could do was spend the night there mulling things over. Some of the time, I grew angry with the crazy Raniero Cutini. The rest of the time, I shuddered at the thought of what I'd done. Had I lost him? Had I just slammed the door on a powerful family? At dawn's first light, I ran to his front door and saw the servant they called Albertino leave the house. It was his turn that morning to get up at an ungodly hour and pick up the basket of bread for breakfast. I had come hugging the walls. I was so cold that I was sure I'd lost my nose because I couldn't feel it even if I touched it.

Days went by. One morning, I obtained an hour's leave and rushed over to the Classical Lyceum to watch the students as they filed out. I saw Raniero lighting a cigarette, surrounded by other young men. I walked towards him. When he caught sight of me, I stopped in the middle of the road and waved at him. He looked at me for a second and then went back to talking to his friends. Then he left, crossing the road without once looking back.

I earned my high-school diploma in '67. After the end of the semester, I went back home and instead of the garden on the mountain side of the villa, I found a tennis court. "It's the Cutinis' new pastime," Babbo said, convinced I would want to try out the game immediately. Instead, it hurt me that I hadn't been consulted about the new development because the message was loud and clear: this is not my place. The owners could completely transform the property I lived in from one day to the next with a tap of their magic wand.

Sometimes, Raniero came on Friday evenings and left on Sundays. We hadn't exchanged more than a distant greeting for years and had certainly not spoken. He was a good-looking young man with the world at his fingertips. He brought packs of well-off youths down from Siena, most of whom were nonchalant about the grandeur of the villa. The table we most often used for dinner was piled high with delicacies all day long. The waiters changed the food according to the time of day. Breakfast went on until two in the afternoon and then guests picked at dishes as they passed by until dinner time, when the table was cleared and freshly laid from scratch. At bedtime, there were bottles of milk, orangeade, and champagne alongside trays laden with cakes and dried fruit. Just in case anyone woke up with a rumbling tummy.

At weekends, we would eat in the kitchen at the small table as the servants who had come in from the city bustled to and fro with the food. We would go up to our rooms without passing through the living room, the one with the fountain in it. We often heard music being played and lots of laughing. Babbo would be sorry when I looked upset. Sometimes he would rest a hand on my shoulder and say, "Come on, we need to talk about what faculty you're enrolling in." Mamma said nothing, in that way only she had, as if she were yelling, "This is what happens when we lose what does not belong to us in the first place. In the end, we get used to a life that is nothing but a carousel."

Even on the top floor there was a living room with a fireplace. This was the room I had used since I was a child to do my homework in, and you could see the whole of Maremma out of the window. This was where we spent our weekend evenings when the house was taken over by the young masters. Babbo would relax on the sofa and light a pipe which he had started smoking after meals. "Cutini sees you as an engineer," he would start, legs crossed, puffing out clouds of smoke like a steamer. "Do you really not like the idea? It would pave the way for a government job. Or do you still want to study medicine? Are you sure you are up to it? You need a firm hand above all else."

He wanted to hear me say it over and over again and I did. I didn't know how to put it any other way. "As soon as you are born, from the first day onwards, little by little you start to die," was what I usually answered. "It's a subject that never goes out of fashion. Basically, it is unlikely there will ever be a shortage of demand . . . "

He would sit there thinking, his eyes stuck to the ceiling. He didn't look at me, but I could feel him scratching my insides as he gazed into my future so blatantly it made me nervous. "Dr. Marco Palazzesi . . . " he would mutter, his words mingling with the thick smoke. He would turn to Mamma. "It sounds marvelous, doesn't it?" She would smile, her face pulled as tight as a slingshot.

I didn't talk willingly about where my inspiration had come from. If I really looked at myself in the mirror and confessed the truth of what I saw there, it wasn't Cutini's wealth or power I envied but rather the reflexive and subservient way those who had dealings with him revered him. It was the same even with his close relations. The hold the old man had over them was branded on their faces: he pulled their lives along behind him and they enjoyed the benefits without being worth even a toenail of the head of the family. Even worse, the only thing they brought to the table was trouble. Cutini was surrounded by people with only one talent and that was to complain. And he would nod and give them a pat on the shoulder. Off they would go, their tails wagging, content with the kind of petty laments rich people indulge in. But the lawyer's icy gaze was already set from the first good morning of the day, even if it was his son greeting him. He was already weakening your will. He was already sucking your blood. Because all it took was a gesture from him and the sky over your head would change color from one minute to the next.

I wanted that power. I didn't tell Babbo, but my ambitions for the future amounted to that. Sovereigns and beggars alike, all lining up to see me. Soon they would be knocking at my door saying, "I beg you, save me!" And I would save them because it was my vocation, and I was dedicated to it. The souls that I pulled from the abyss of death would somehow belong to me. Nobody would dare touch a corner of my garden, they wouldn't even be tempted, because I would be there guarding the sanctuary. Nobody would banish me to the kitchen table for dinner, like I was a refugee.

The lawyer, Cesare Taddeo Cutini, died on April 12, '77, at the age of eighty-nine and the event shook the earth under everyone's feet. Nobody could have imagined the secrets he had taken with him to the grave, or the business ventures he had left unfinished, leaving all the useless dogs to fight over the bones. I was already practicing medicine. I enjoyed hearing of the tragedies that occurred throughout Italy. That summer, in the province of Siena alone, two very important people committed suicide. Nobody would have guessed they harbored such intentions. Old-school businessmen and politicians were falling like flies in the capital. I doubt I was alone in thinking that these deaths could not all have been the result of divine intervention.

In the new year, the lawyer's secrets exploded in the family's face and the ripples spread far and wide. Cutini's real occupation came to light: he had acted as a watertight dealmaker for powerful people from different walks of life. After the war he had cleverly wormed his way into every facet of the country's reconstruction and was soon masterminding vast armies of grabbers and snatchers at every level. "He built his reputation on other people's ruination and rubble," Babbo commented as his eyes ran over the newspaper. "Worse than Amico Fritz . . . " Without Cutini to oversee the spider's web of favors and counter-favors, the family business was on the brink, and one crack was enough to bring it tumbling down. All the embezzlement and sleaze came out in a sludge. Paraded out of their homes in handcuffs, the small fry began to sing. The list of names was beginning to look interminable, and the revelations were becoming awkward. One fine day, the carabinieri arrived at the villa and put seals on it. All the Cutini properties were seized. The bank accounts frozen. Close relatives were put under surveillance. Including Raniero.

Ironically, we seemed to be the only ones ultimately to gain something from the situation. Babbo already had a generous pension and his wages from the last two decades had accumulated interest in an account in the Monte dei Paschi bank that Cutini himself had advised him to open. In addition to these savings, there was the rent money from our old house. I had already managed to secure myself a permanent position at the hospital so even the small expenses I had run up as a student had been eliminated. The tax inspectors sifted through our papers for a week but eventually they had to admit it: there was no trace of a backhander in our pockets and any tax due had been paid regularly, down to the last penny. The half a million that continued to accrue interest in Siena was as squeaky clean as a kid's face.

We didn't participate in the foreclosure auction and Babbo ate his heart out when he heard how much the family from Massa had paid for the villa. But Mamma didn't want to hear any complaints. As soon as the subject came up, she would fly into a rage as if it were the first time she had said it. "I don't give a damn if the Cocchi family enjoy the place after paying two cents for it! There are so many people in Cutini's wake, and they are all looking for payback for some slight that has ruined their day. Am I supposed to spend the rest of my life worrying that someone might come and throw a bomb at us just for the satisfaction of it? We had our time there and, considering how things ended up, we have managed to get out with our bags full. In any case, the villa was built on a foundation of certain predilections that I'd rather shake off right now."

And yet, Babbo couldn't stomach it. Maybe he had secretly harbored the idea that he might finally establish himself like that lawyer who had clawed his way up from nothing, take us out of our misery, and make us wealthy. "If the rumors I hear are true, I'll throw myself under a train," he grumbled. "They say those people from Massa are thinking of emptying the property and turning it into a hotel. Up there, on the road up to San Martino! Can you imagine anything more foolish?"

Everyone in the area came to the inauguration of the Bel Sole. I even recognized a few faces from my old band of friends, but I did everything in my power to avoid them. I wasn't interested in hearing about how their lives had been ruined by being forced into marriage at twenty. I was happier to wander around the place with a glass of Prosecco in my hand, gazing up at the living-room ceilings, the new windows, and strangely shaped lamps. The Cocchi family had built a giant arch at the entrance. The fountain was no longer there. People crowded around the buffet and nodded their heads in time to the music being played by a small orchestra. I walked around feeling every change as an interminable slap that bit into my flesh. Most of the garden had been cemented over to make a car park. The only thing they had saved was the tennis court.

I made my way to the drinks table to grab another glass. "I knew I would find you hear," I heard someone in the crowd say, but I thought they were talking to somebody else. "At least, I hoped I would." I turned around distractedly and saw Raniero.

I didn't say anything. He leaned over the bottles as cool as a cucumber and poured himself a drink. He brought his glass to his lips and drank a drop as he looked around. Then he turned back to me with a big smile on his face. "So?" he said. "What do you think?"

I hadn't heard from him for ten years or so. The dramas revolving around the Cutini family had gradually disappeared from the newspapers. The most recent rumors I had heard were that half the family was behind bars; the lawyer's son got the hardest sentence. Raniero knocked the whole glass back. He took another. "It's way better than the wrack and ruin we let it fall into," he muttered, turning to look at me again. "Marco, I'm happy to see you looking so well . . . " At this point, I finished my glass in one gulp, too. Just like in the old days in the Siena drinking holes.

Half of Maremma had made its way up to San Martino for the party, everyone more interested in the refreshments than the villa's refurbishment. We ended up in a corner, hidden from most people, leaning against a wall freshly painted in off-white. My words fell like drops. Embarrassment was cutting me to pieces, but Raniero looked unruffled, as if we'd seen each other the day before. He stared at the old living room that was now a hotel reception.

"You may find it strange," he said at one point, "but I wouldn't go back to those days for anything in the world. Anyone who spoke to me was only doing it to get into my good books. It got so that the good days disgusted me. It wears you out in the end because when you leave the house, you have to don a mask that others have imposed on you. I couldn't do it. I was Cutini's grandson and heir and that was how I had to behave. I swear, it drove me crazy. Otherwise, you end up a cynical bastard. One of those men who repress their feelings to keep a stiff upper lip. The day you realize it is happening, you die of fear. You stand there with waves of rage washing over you. And you convince yourself that without the rage, you wouldn't be able to stand on your own feet. You tell yourself, "If the anger goes, I'll die." He turned his face to mine. "You were different. Of course, you benefited from your friendship with our family, but you didn't throw yourself at anyone's feet.

When I think about the way people fawned when they met me in the street, it still makes me want to throw up. Then things went as they went."

I was a little slow to notice. He was dressed simply but it didn't look wrong on him. The years had passed for Raniero, but he had kept his spark. For a moment I saw us from the outside, and I got that giddy feeling that life, with its sudden somersaults, keeps in store for us. A cursory glance would suggest that I was the rich man and he the less fortunate friend. He still had more charisma than me, though. In fact, Raniero Cutini now inhabited his name properly. It echoed around him, even if he didn't open his mouth. "It may well be," I muttered with my eyes firmly on the party. "But you dumped me from one day to the next without a second thought. I would see you come to the villa in the summer, and you could barely force yourself to say hello."

Raniero looked back at me with a combination of surprise and amusement. There was also some bitterness. "Are you really digging up that old story?" Then he shifted his gaze over to the Cocchi family, who were greeting guest after guest. "Twenty years have gone by . . . I can still see it. We would go into Nenni's boudoir, and my spirits were so low they'd get trampled underfoot. I had to take all her smooching as I waited for her to throw some desperate man out of room four. I never told you. Her name was Cristina. She was beautiful. She was kind. That fiery red hair . . . As soon as she saw me come in, she would run over and throw her arms around my neck. She covered my face in kisses. We had become friends. Then, after talking a little, we would try. I would lie down on the bed and let her do her job. Any boy in my place would have been wild with joy. Cristina's body was perfect, and she was good at what she did. But my body didn't respond. After a few minutes, it was pitiful to behold. She was giving her all and I just lay there frozen, staring at the ceiling. I must have looked like an animal on its way to slaughter. I would push her off, but Cristina never lost her smile. "Maybe it's me," she would say. And she would lie down next to me and hug me like a sister. "It's fine," she would repeat, kissing my temples in a different way. Then I told her. I told her my disease was nothing to do with her looks. It had nothing to do with my dick, either, which was perfectly capable of doing its job but would always come to life at the wrong moment. Cristina asked me about a new love interest I had told her about, if there had been any developments. I shook my head. "Nothing to report," I answered. I had so much rage inside me that I felt like bursting into tears right there in her arms. And in the silence of that room, I would accept her caresses and her sweet words. Then I would leave. I always left her a generous tip without Nenni seeing, or she would have pocketed half. Before going out, I would say to her, "If I ever change my mind, I'd like to fall in love with you." She smiled and said, "You can't decide these things." Well, she was right. Early on, I was experimenting with prostitutes to see if I really did have a strange disease. My father knew all about my visits because the following day he would look at me with a glint of pride that gave me the shivers. Imbecile fathers are obsessed: they feel validated if their boys go and spread their seed around with a few easy women. But at least I kept him happy, given that I was nearly eighteen and had never brought a girl home even by mistake. He was far more likely to see me hanging out with you, the janitor's son. He didn't ask any questions. But in my head, the questions were multiplying because just looking at you took my breath away. I thought at first it was a passing crush. I had been in love lots of times, suffering in silence. But it didn't pass. You didn't pass. I took you to Nenni's place hoping to glimpse a shadow of jealousy flit across your face at the idea I was having it off with that tart. I used to say to Cristina, "He's right outside but I really don't know what to do." That last evening, after so many others, I found her on top of me. She closed her eyes and kissed me on the lips. She'd never done it before. It lasted a whole minute. I watched her. I could feel her heart beating against mine. Eventually, she stopped. She sat there staring at me in silence. Then she smiled, even though she suddenly looked like she wanted to cry. 'A kiss doesn't lie,' she said. And she pulled away so I wouldn't see her in that state. She went to the dressing table in the corner where she kept her makeup. Without a word, I left her there. Well, even a child would have figured it out: after so many meetings, I had roused feelings in her, feelings that were not reciprocated. 'A kiss doesn't lie.' Her words continued to ring in my head as we walked up to the seminary. Maybe it was the drink because, under normal conditions, I would have preferred a bullet in the mouth. And yet I tried. We were standing there under the window of your room, and you were suddenly right there on top of me . . . I did it: I kissed you. Then your bewildered eyes were on me like a shot. 'Now he's going to punch me,' I thought. Instead, you started laughing. I saw you drop to your knees, concerned only not to make too much noise."

Raniero had been talking non-stop over the orchestra, his voice mingling with the chatter of the guests. He hadn't paused once: it had been impossible to but in, to explain or at least try. Maybe he was waiting for a reaction, any reaction, but I was paralyzed. So, he went on.

"You were the only one who knew my secret," he said. "It was juicy information, considering I was heir to an important family name. No second thoughts are allowed, especially when the line of succession is the issue. A pervert as an heir would not only have caused a scandal. It would have cast doubt on the passage of power. At home, all they talked about was Francesca, Consul Mattei's granddaughter. One Sunday a month she was invited to lunch with the rest of the family. She was nice and would certainly have been considered an appetizing morsel by all the boys in the province.

But it was torture for me because I was dreaming about you. I would sometimes brush my lips with my fingers imagining I was back there under your window when everything turned to nothing. And your laughter exploded in my face like bombs. But I was proud of myself that I had tried at least. With that kiss I had given you the keys to me and revealed myself. It was sad seeing you there that day in front of my school. You couldn't even cross the road. You didn't follow me or ask to talk to me. That spoke louder than words for me: you didn't feel an ounce of the passion that was burning in my veins. There was no point going on. I had to try and forget you. But I couldn't seek comfort with Cristina because I was causing her the same pain you were causing me. It was agony coming to the villa in the summer. I risked crossing paths with at every corner I turned. That was why I ignored you: you were keeping me hostage. I owned property as far as the eye could see but you were everything I could not possess. I would have thrown my name to the dogs if you had asked me to. "Francesca Mattei is a train that only passes once," my mother would say. "And anyway, it's not nice to keep a girl from such a good family on tenterhooks. At a certain point it becomes a matter of respect for the Consul . . . " When the corruption scandal broke, Andrea Maria Mattei was the first to be arrested. Alongside my grandfather, he was the puppet master of the criminal network that had emerged after the war. He died in his cell five years ago."

We stood there in silence for a few intensely painful minutes. Lifting my eyes to look at him was beyond me. Saying something, anything, even though I felt the ball was now in my court, impossible. Eventually, I lifted my glass, which had been empty for a while. "I'll get two more," I said, stalling, and hurried over to the drinks table.

I threw one down the hatch and filled it up again straight away. I had started to sweat. I woke up every morning knowing

I was going to be cutting people open but now my hands were betraying my nervousness. My wrists were shaking as I poured the champagne. The idea of going back to that corner made me want to jump out of the window and drive down the hairpin bends as fast as possible. Instead, I turned on my heels, trying to pull myself together and gather the courage to go and find my old friend. I nearly knocked old Mr. Cocchi over. He had been smiling so hard his face was stuck in a rictus. "Dr. Palazzesi, what a pleasure to see you here!" he said.

I had to listen to a cascade of words. I answered with a false smile and a series of nods. He claimed he had brought half of Tuscany back to life when in fact he had ruined a centuries-old villa by repurposing it as a provincial hotel. Nor did he spare me the poisoned arrows, with allusions to my origins and the years I had lived there. "The whole place was completely abandoned," he said at one point. "But you could see that it had been kept up well. I've been saying it all my life: property is wasted on the rich. It's left in the hands of loyal servants who polish the mirrors with the sweat of their brow." Then he noticed that I had two glasses in my hands. "Ah, I see you have company . . ." he whispered, casting his eyes rapidly around the room. "A friend," I said, careful not to nod in Ranieri's direction. He had once been the owner of the place, after all. The old man studied my face, his eyes slitted like a snake's. "Well, have a good time," he concluded. I threw him a final pleasantry. Then I stood there waiting for the party to absorb him. Only then did I move, intending to go back to the corner. But Raniero had gone.

If I close my eyes now, I see myself there at the inauguration of the Bel Sole, lost in the mirage of the giant living room where I used to spend my winter evenings running around and fantasizing about the Adventures of Amico Fritz. Still today, I wonder whether that encounter ever took place. It is fixed in my memory like the vivid images of a dream five years before.

A bat of my eyelids and I'm back here in my office on the ward in icy, neon-lit solitude.

On the door outside there's the plaque I dreamed of with all my heart when I was a boy. Doctor M. Palazzesi - Chief Physician. So many people come knocking on the door. With their hats in their hands and their eyes cloudy. They don't even sit down. They prostrate themselves on my desk. The words are always the same, "I beg you. You are my last chance . . . "

Years ago, I thought being someone's last chance would give me power. I had the arrogance of youth and if an operation ended badly, I would pull the sheet up over the patient roughly and go down to the cafeteria for a coffee. Then something happened. Not from one day to the next. A color that started filtering in gradually. Just a streak at first. I had no idea that darkness had invaded me like that. Until it was inside and I finally understood. I wasn't taking their souls. I was taking the pain, the darkness, the confusion. I was at a tipping point. Every now and again something arrived on this side and found me on the front line. It was as if I were in front of a giant mouth. I stood there as useless as a fly in a storm as the world gradually extinguished itself into oblivion after the gigantic effort of life.

One day, Samanta came to my office. Her marrow was already infected but the eyes of the young girl struck me deep inside where, perhaps, there was still a little light. After the operation I ended up in all the newspapers, praised as a saint. Phone calls from all over the world started to rain in. People were willing to sell their mothers for one consultation with me. Even so, I knew that her cardiac muscle would degenerate and inevitably lead the little girl to a sad fate. It was just a matter of time. That was when I saw the meaning of everything printed in giant letters. It was so banal it broke my heart. My work was not to save lives. I was delaying the inevitable, if anything. I gave people a few days, maybe hours. That was all. I had been given the privilege of being in a position to try, but the most I could do was work hard to keep a few people on the edge of the precipice. The rest was simply the decaying of flesh. Birth and death. Why make all that effort? The answer to the question killed me and it was little Samanta who had provided it: despite the disease, she had spent six beautiful weeks with her family. Loved and coddled as never before. When the last emergency operation was over, when I pulled the sheet up over her face, her mother threw her arms around my neck. "Thanks for everything," she said, kissing me as one does a temple-stone. Then I went back to my empty house. I laid the table for one, as usual. There was so much silence. It was like a giant concert being played to empty stalls. Every breath I took fell to the ground and rattled like a spinning coin. Because I had nobody to share it with.

The emergency bell rings on my floor. The urgent steps of the nurses can be heard in the corridor. I wait, looking at the red light. After a minute, the alarm is still ringing. More steps. The door is thrown open. It's Nurse Marchi. She looks shaken. She stands there at the door, staring into space. She can't even catch her breath.

"Pull yourself together, Nurse," I say firmly.

She comes back to her senses. She swallows. "It's unbelievable," she says finally, her voice strangled with emotion. "The patient in Room 308 has just woken up."

Eleonora Borghi, *the Missing Girl*

I open my eyes and find myself sitting up in bed, my heart in my throat. In my head the screeching of brakes. Blinding headlights in the night. Then the long, long fall into an abyss. It's a horrible feeling, like going over a cliff, and it stays with me for a while longer. Eventually it goes. My eyes get used to the shadows little by little. And I see I am here twisted up in my covers. The shutters are rattling in the storm. It's the same sound of catastrophe I heard in my dream, especially the final moments. I pat the other side of the bed. He's not there.

No light, no movement from the other rooms. Samuele repeats it every day, "When I'm out, nothing must attract people's attention." These are the times I hate the most because they turn me into a ghost. I have to sit here in silence and count my breaths. I'm not even allowed to clear my throat. And the minutes never end.

In *Pride and Prejudice*, there's that moment when Jane hears that Mr. Bingley is leaving. She keeps the news locked inside her and carries on as usual, smiling away for weeks with death in her heart. She puts on a brave face even as the debris piles up inside her. Ten years ago, I used to die reading those pages. I bolted myself in my room and tried to gather up courage like her. Miss Bennet risked losing the love of her life. In comparison, my dramas were a healthy walk in the park. I had to deal with my problems but, ultimately, I wasn't losing a whole world full of emotions. I was just me, an ordinary girl with no future, living in a godforsaken corner of Maremma. It comforted me to know that once there were women tougher than soldiers' women who had to swallow nails. They sat on a chair by the window for weeks with their embroidery, locked in their deadly routine. And they didn't die. "Well, if they can do it, so can I," I'd to say to myself.

The minutes I spend alone doing nothing in this house are a test for me. Samuele says we have to wait for the right moment and then we'll leave everything behind. He really believes it. I can see it in his eyes. I drowned in those eyes from the first moment. One day, I had only heard about him. The next, I saw him and I was transformed. In *Pride and Prejudice*, there's that lovely moment when Elizabeth falls in love with Mr. Darcy. After all the fantasizing, he is right there, without a mask, introducing her to his sister Georgiana. Darcy explodes in her face. The day Samuele opened the store door there was a similar explosion. Suddenly, my blood was running in the wrong direction.

Mario read the expression on my face, but he never dared say a thing about it. Whenever he saw him coming in, he would pack me off on an errand and take over serving at the counter. In a way, I was grateful because when he was in the room my heart thumped so hard, I looked like an idiot and could hardly say a word. But in another way, I hated him because, even though it felt like I was on fire, the only place I wanted to be was right there under his hangdog gaze. I identified with it. Rather, everything about Samuele spoke to me about myself. Just being in the same place created a storm, worse than the one raging outside. The air changed and was charged with electricity. Though we hadn't even said hello.

It was worse in the evening when Borian made his way up Via di Mezzo. I hung my head when I met him, hoping he wouldn't see the change in me. I smiled at him calmly, recalling Jane Bennet's battles. He threw me one of those sideways looks that were hurtful because he didn't say a word and kept walking, looking down at the road and throwing his cigarette away.

It was all my father's fault. Maremma shits out people like him, who bring you into the world only to own you. "He's jealous," I heard my mother say for as long as I can remember. "But it's Babbo's way of saying he really cares." When she said this, she looked like someone who was hanging on, waiting for the last train with all her might. A minute later, the color would run out of her as her husband walked into the room.

He always looked grim and even when he laughed, it felt like something was bothering him. When I was younger, he used to pick me up from school, the excuse being that my anemia made me feel weak. His eyes ranged everywhere like a spray of machine gun fire: there would suddenly be a vacuum around me. If a boy spoke to me, we had to deal with his long face at dinner and that silence particular to him that made your ears go numb, as if someone in the household had just died.

Over the years it got worse. I wasn't allowed to watch the programs my schoolfriends talked about. Permission slips for trips were never filled in. I once asked for a secret diary, one of those ones with a little padlock. At table the air was as heavy as lead. "You'll have secrets once you've left home," he muttered, twisting his mouth into a snarl, crushing his napkin into a ball and throwing it on the floor. Then he got up. The chair scraped the floor, screeching like a flayed mule.

He made it impossible to like him. Mamma and I were walking on eggshells. She suffered the same torture as me: if anything, worse. She went out on her errands looking firmly down at the sidewalk, saying good day here and there in a strangled voice as if her husband were right there in her shadows, ready to pounce on her. "People tell me things," the idiot would grumble sometimes. "Ribolla is a puddle. I could hold every single person who lives here in the palm of one hand," he added, closing his hand into a fist. But nothing big ever happened. There was never a curse uttered in the house, never the whoosh of a slap. Babbo kept us under his thumb with anxiety. The kind of anxiety that churned in our stomachs and became rage, enough to topple mountains. I hid in my room and vented my anger on my pillow.

The holidays were terrible because my aunt and uncle came over from la Spezia. Mamma would be happy as pie that her brother was coming to stay for a week. Babbo became a wax statue and chain-smoked the whole time. He would go and open the hardware store even on Boxing Day, saying he had to do the inventory. Any excuse was good to get away from the house and not have to exchange a few pleasantries. Uncle Giovanni had gotten rich with his construction company, and for Babbo this was a fate worse than the plague. I could see from the way he eyed the car, which my uncle changed every two years, when he pulled up in the drive. He forced a steely smile as they brought in baskets laden with delicacies to repay our hospitality. For Christmas, I would get an envelope with a C-note inside. Babbo would come into my room and take it the same evening. "This goes into your savings book," he would say. "College is expensive."

The Bennet sisters' adventures were beginning to tire on me, but they were still my refuge. They took me away from that provincial backwater where the streets are filled with nothingness. High school was a daily calvary, especially in my second year when the girls started putting on makeup for real. I would overhear them talking in the toilets about how they had experimented acting like women on their dates and who had touched them where. A world apart from my old-lady cardigans and bated-breath greetings that would make even rats run a mile. It was as if the whole earth had decided to move on and leave me behind. As soon as I set foot outdoors, I felt as though I had Mr. Collins's pompous voice in my head when he snidely advised Elizabeth to dress adequately for her luncheon appointment with Lady Catherine de Bourgh.

And yet I was beautiful. Sometimes I would look at my body in the long mirror after my shower and touch myself a little.

I would always put a towel on the door handle to block the keyhole. I liked doing it standing up and looking into my eyes, holding the edge of the basin. I saw blue behind my eyes and my mouth would open spontaneously. Meanwhile, I was digging inside myself with two fingers. My heart thumped, partly out of pleasure, partly out of fear I might break something. Then there would be a knock at the door, and the sudden jolt would send my fingers off course, as if they were a pair of scissors. "What's going on?" he would bark from the other side. "Do we need to put ourselves get on a waiting list to take a piss?"

At school, I was friends with Valeria who was as unfortunate as I was. Only uglier, with rolls of fat that did her no favors. But she had an amazing surname—Amore. If my secret refuge was a book that I had found in Nonna Levia's boxes when I was still a little girl, hers was horses. She had grown up with them, and she always wore riding boots whose heels betrayed that she had trodden in fresh muck that morning. She talked all the time about one mad horse called Sheriff. But her favorite was Chamomile, who was exactly her age. She was a good-natured horse who allowed any kid who came to the riding school to mount her. I thought about the name, and it made me smile: the Amore Riding School. I would sometimes say to her, "You must be a little magic: you ride love!" Her eyes would light up. They were incredible, one was blue and the other green. As if that were not enough, her right eye was a little off-center giving her the air of a wise fairy. We are all unique, but Valeria was more unique than the rest of us.

In every other respect, we were spectators. We would meet in front of the school gates where the boys would put on a grotesque show with their mopeds and motorbikes. In the senior year there were a few kids who already drove a car. They would go into Via Meda, a narrow alley, and turn up their car stereos. We would watch love affairs bloom. At recess, we didn't race down to the toilets to smoke cigarettes. We sat on the steps outside the gym where hardly anyone passed. And we talked. Life in Ribolla and life in Albinia sounded much the same. But unlike me, in her family they breathed fresh air whereas in mine, when the five o'clock bell rang, my stomach clenched.

We took the very last day of school for ourselves. Another summer of letter-writing and phone calls awaited us but, once our exams were done, come September, we would no longer sit together in chairs vacated by the previous generation. We gazed at the store windows in the old center, where we had never dared go at that time of day. We gave each other this sad gift, experimenting for the first time the giddiness of seizing the day outside our normal routines. With the result that we saw ourselves as the provincial deadbeats we were. Except that we laughed about it.

I came back home red-eyed. Mamma was immediately worried and put a hand on my forehead to see whether I had a fever. But Babbo knocked twice on the table. "Is the free ride over for you young things now?" he growled. I stared at him without saying a word. For a moment he stared back but it only took three seconds for him to notice that something had changed. The rage of a lifetime had funneled itself into my look. He even pulled his head back a bit because he realized, for the first time, that I was actually offended. He grumbled something. Then he put his head down and went back to eating his pasta.

* * *

In the shadow of the storm, I watch the lampshade dangling above me like a hangman. Le Case feels like it's sinking inch by inch and Samuele is still not back. Usually, he's only out a few minutes and then I hear him come back with the shopping from the store, the very same store where until a few weeks ago I was the one handing over the groceries. I tell myself that maybe he has stopped in an alleyway or under a portico to wait for it to stop raining. But the lightning bolts are relentless, lighting up the room intermittently through the slats. Every flash reconfigures the shadows. At the umpteenth crash, I reach over to the lamp on the bedside table and feel for the switch. I stop at the last minute, forcing myself not to do it.

The storm outside is similar to what I felt inside me before I started university. I had to forget the idea of renting accommodation in Siena straight away but after a whole summer of torture at home, just getting on a bus that would take me away all day was a relief. Mamma almost made a show of force, insisting on buying me a cell phone, and I was happy to have the new toy because it made me feel like all the other girls around me. But I soon realized that I had fallen into yet another trap. Babbo called every two hours asking me if I needed anything. He put on a calm voice while interrogating me like a policeman. "I can hear someone talking," he would say. "Do people talk like that in class?" Or "Is it raining or sunny outside?" And I was racked with nerves because I knew his tricks by heart and I could just see him with the weather forecast in his hand. He counted the money I brought back, shocked that a sandwich could cost as much as three thousand lire. Something flashed in his eyes, and he couldn't keep it to himself. When he had totted everything up, he would say as a joke, "Should I ask you to bring back the receipts next time?" I didn't bother answering because by the time I got home, I was dog tired. I found him in a bad mood if the bus was half an hour late, which it always was.

It was a rotten life. My alarm went off before first light. I came back home in the pitch dark, especially in the winter. I threw down a hasty dinner. Then bed. It sometimes felt like I had closed my eyes for a moment and then, a minute later, there was Mamma getting me up to start the whole routine again. My life in Siena was wound tight as a top and I didn't have a second to enjoy the kind of pastimes other students talked about. I used the two-hour journey to copy out my notes though the roads were so full of bends it made me want to throw up. But at least the head of the family was happy because I came back every night to sleep in my own bed. Though it cost me my sanity.

It would have taken so little to change him. Seen from the outside, his problem was jaw-droppingly clear: Babbo feared the outside world, and he expressed all his fear with the people he loved. He would watch the regional news on TV and when he saw there had been a robbery, he had to take drops to avoid a panic attack. He didn't sleep a wink at night unless he drank a half carafe of strong red wine. Mamma worried about him. Over time, her husband's eyes were beginning to betray an imminent break-down. Being so alert all the time for no reason was wearing him down and there were certain moments when his heart would start beating fast for no reason, only to return to normal soon after. The attacks terrified him and left him drained. But deep inside, the torture would begin again: not only did he need to control everything, but he was scared another panic attack was just around the corner. If he was out doing a little grocery shopping, for example, an ambulance could drive down the main road of the town, and he would leap into the car to follow it. He had to find out whether something had happened to me.

"Don't answer back," Mamma said to me. "Babbo's not a young man anymore and if he has his thing, his heart will suffer." "His thing." That was what we had to call his attacks, which now forced him to be extremely vigilant I looked my mother in the eye and enjoyed the feeling of telling her the truth without any pity, "If he wants to be a normal person, he has to get through it." She smiled as if I'd just given her an explanation for why water flows downwards. Then she shook her head.

The fact he had panic attacks made me hate him even more because it kept us pinned down in the corner. If I found myself reassuring him during a phone call, it disgusted me to the bone. I was forced to create a version of myself that didn't exist and it was like giving into his pathetic, colossal need for attention. I used a particular tone of voice. At twenty, I still had to adapt to his view of the world even in the way I dressed. After being a silent torturer, he now played the poor victim. It made you want to knock your head against every wall of the house. We were supposed to defend him for precisely what made him deserve to be cracked open like an animal. And in the meantime, I was cracking myself.

The drama unfolded on a Friday. It was a study day, and I usually managed to have a quiet afternoon with no phone calls that made my hair stand on end and no wasted hours on the bus. Mamma would spend the day lolling on the sofa watching TV programs that her husband didn't approve of because they featured articulate women. He thought he was a better model for her, after a lifetime selling varnish and bolts to all the farming men in the area . . . At one point I lay on my bed. I reached up, instinctively and a little distractedly, to the shelf above, feeling for something. After a few seconds of groping, I wasn't finding what my hand was seeking. I let out a deep sigh and pulled myself back up.

It was something I did often, especially in the half hour before dinner. I would pick up *Pride and Prejudice* and open it at a random page. All I needed as a hook was to start reading the first line of the paragraph I would pick by chance, and I was inside the story. Then I would rest the book on my chest and continue it in my head. There were some passages I could recite by heart even if I covered the page. When the game went well, it was a kind of twilight sleep where on one side I heard the inner voice of my thoughts and on the other the settings, characters, lights, and even the smells. When I got stuck, all I needed to do was pick up the book and take another peek. For years it had been a great way to get to sleep at night, projecting myself out of Maremma with all my strength and landing in the Bennets' Hertfordshire.

The book was not there. I looked everywhere, even in my wardrobe. I had grown up reading those pages. It was as if my lungs had suddenly been pulled out. I ran headlong into the living room where Mamma was on the sofa. She was so surprised that she jumped and lost a slipper. "Who is it?" she yelled without thinking and saw me with an expression on my face that was certainly not my most attractive.

I felt a strange shadow over my head but for now I had to try and get rid of it with all my might. She looked bewildered, her gaze absent for a moment as she was consumed by a terrible doubt. Then she started searching for the book with me, opening cupboards and drawers.

Babbo came home at the usual time. He found us sitting on the sofa. I was staring into space. I had a pile of bunched-up, wet paper hankies on my lap. He closed the door behind him but didn't come into the room. He put his work bag on the cabinet in the hall and stood there contemplating us. "Has someone died?" he asked eventually. I watched him in the reflection of the dormant TV screen.

Mamma didn't say a word. Her hands were trembling, but she went on stroking my head. I swallowed a gob of snot. Then I asked him straight out, "Where is my book?" My voice sounded ugly, halfway between an empty breath and the cawing of a crow.

He puffed. He even ventured a smile. "What do you mean?"

"My book." Only then did he shift his gaze and look at me.

Babbo looked as if he was about to take a step back but, in order not to lose face, he took a step forward, covering the next tile along.

"Listen, it's not a good day. I don't feel like . . . "

I leaped to my feet. And I screamed all the hellish torment that had forever been burning inside me right into his face. Every word gave me throat ache, the kind that makes you spit thick mucus for days. "WHERE. IS. MY. BOOK?"

Mamma burst into tears. My screams had made the crystal glasses in the cabinet tinkle. He stood there a few feet away, gawping. Nobody had ever seen me in a state like that and I couldn't do anything about it because I had been knocking the dam down for years. My anger was overflowing.

Babbo tried to regain his composure. He even tried hardening his expression. "Ah, that book," he muttered crudely. "I picked it up a couple of days ago. I took a look, out of curiosity. All that stuff about little women looking for husbands . . . we've been watching you make yourself blind with that book for years." He cleared his throat. "In any case, don't you dare use that tone with me again."

I clenched my fists so tight I couldn't feel them anymore. "Where is it?" I mumbled, staring at him hatefully.

He seemed to shrivel up more with every second that passed. He threw a glance at his wife as if he were begging for help. Then he swallowed and tried to smile. "Listen—"

"Where is it?" I repeated. I even managed to take a deep breath and keep myself under control. "Please."

When I saw his eyes wander into space it was as if a gust of wind had suddenly erased me. It was worse than an admission. My hand flew to my mouth. "You've thrown it away," I said softly, very softly. The words hissed through my fingers.

I didn't wait for an answer. Something had completely and irremediably broken. My arms fell to my sides. "I'm sorry," he whined. "I'm sick. The doctors have confirmed it. But it's because I love you . . . " He went on in this vein for a few minutes with me standing there, miles away. I heard his words as if they were from another planet even though he was right beside me. "I have these moments," I heard him say. "It's bad. Something grabs my attention and . . . "

"I'm a whore," I retorted like a shot. Suddenly I was completely calm.

He looked up. We were so close that our faces almost

touched. I stared at him. Then I said, "Yes, a giant, wet, horny bitch."

Babbo looked at me, his eyes full of confusion. "Darling, what are you saying?" He muttered and he was already changing. I could see the early signs of panic.

I started listing names, like Alfio, the boy who works at the fruit and vegetable stand. I told him that we'd been boning in the storeroom for years. Or Alessandro Luti, who had had a thing for me since we were in elementary school: we had a regular ride behind the garbage cans at the barracks. And Salvatore, the guy who lives on the road to Montemassi. We'd been fooling around since he first got his driver's license, and he was nearly twenty-five now. Then I swept rapidly through the five years of high school as he slowly crumpled before my eyes. I hadn't missed many, that's for sure. I had been pounded by half the males in Maremma. Dario from Orbetello. Sandro from Grosseto. Palmi, Pieraligi . . . Cucca, who hailed from the heel of Sardinia and was shorter than me but whose dick was so big it put other men to shame. I even included that blimp, Ceri: just looking at him put you to sleep.

Babbo had already collapsed, rasping. "Maddalena, my drops," he hissed, reaching an arm out towards my mother. But she just sat there, staring out of the window. "Maddalena, help me. I feel terrible . . . " I walked straight past him and went to my room.

He was yelling in the living room as I packed my bags quickly. I ignored him completely. I bolted through the living room, out the door, and left.

I felt it in my legs: I could have walked for days. I had so much adrenaline in my body that I could have roamed the entire region without a drop of water. Every step I took further from home gave me a new lease of life. Rage and euphoria ran through my veins and that was all the fuel I needed. I strode forward with the sensation that I was coming out of a thick fog for the first time ever and that I was heading for a new place inside me. And there was that book of mine at the heart of the cobweb. In the middle of a blank page, I had written two words clearly, "Chapter One."

I enjoyed making myself out to be a tart like that. Locked up in the sarcophagus of a poor-spirited father's obsessions as I had been, at twenty I hadn't even had a first kiss. In fact, to avoid trouble at home, I had stifled those adolescent rumblings and treated crushes as a plague to be left to wither, never writing a word in my diary. The Sandro I mentioned in my outburst had actually existed, but I had never said his name out loud, not even to Valeria. She, on the other hand, would fall in love with a new boy every week and she would doodle millions of red hearts with her felt pens. Sometimes she would ask me straight out, "Don't you fancy anyone at all?" I hung my head. "It's all the same," I answered.

Breaking Babbo had been great. I had heard obscene words come out of my mouth associated with a merry-go-round of faces I had mulled over in silence. Every one of them had been a repudiated boyfriend, sitting in the pit of my stomach, like a flame that burns bright and is then gradually extinguished with repeated spits. I was full of dead bodies. First kisses and courtship stifled at birth so as not to upset a father's mood, even though nothing ever changed. Somewhere inside me there was a house of spirits infested with the ghosts of love affairs I had never experienced. Except for Ceri. He ended up in my rant by mistake. I wouldn't have touched him with someone else's cunt, never mind my own.

I was walking in the rain in the streets near the mine shaft. I didn't have a penny to my name and I was hugging myself as the ice started to penetrate my bones. Ribolla was already behind me. This felt like a good starting point. The few cars that drove by on the provincial road splashed me until I was soaked to the skin. When I heard one pull up beside me, at first I ignored it.

Then there was a honk of the horn and only then did I turn around, the way an animal would look if they'd been cornered, with a grimace.

It wasn't Babbo. It was a white mud splattered pick-up. Inside the cabin was a boy I had never seen before. He was leaning across the seats in my direction, intent on rolling down the window pane. Eventually, he leaned even further and said, "Rain bad. Take home?"

The mist had come down and partially veiled the tops of the mountains. Night was falling fast. I looked up and down the street. I realized that my adventure was about to begin. I drew closer to the window and said, "Okay but let's go to your place. Just until tomorrow."

He stared at me with an inscrutable expression. "You whore?"

I smiled. "I wish," I muttered but he couldn't have understood a word. I shook my head and opened the door.

* * *

If it weren't for the light from the crooked lamppost on the street outside, it would have been dark in here for a while already. It's cold and there are sounds coming from the other rooms as if flakes of ceiling plaster are falling on the floor. In the shadows, things are amplified. The shadows inside spread themselves out and make it darker. Samuele owes me an explanation. Leaving me here alone like this, worse than a dog, with my guilty conscience looming like a giant ready to knock the door down and crush me.

Borian was good to me. We lived in a kind of farmhouse partly surrounded by the woods and invisible from the road. You could hear cars passing in the distance. I was like Lydia Bennet when she eloped to Brighton with Mr. Wickham and caused a scandal. At the same time, I was a bit like a provincial

Snow White, with a farmhouse to keep tidy and a pack of boys who came back from the sawmill in the evening, famished.

I loved it when I heard the tires of the pick-up on the gravel. I rushed to the door even in bad weather. The lads who traveled in the back were the first to jump off before they had come to a stop, usually fooling around pretending to be acrobats at the circus. Their faces were almost always splattered with dirt. Borian was the last to get out.

It was a commune. The owner of the sawmill owned that abandoned property and since he wasn't completely inexperienced, he combined business with business by letting the gang of Albanians live there and take care of it so that it wouldn't be completely run over with grass. "Boss keep pay," Haris said one evening pointing at the walls around us. I smiled, feeling I was being implicated and not enjoying it. "In Maremma there's no such thing as a free lunch," I said, a bitter taste rising in my throat.

On Sunday mornings, we would form teams and clean the perimeter of the farmhouse. It was a way to keep the forest at bay, which seemed to want to take everything in its path. The boys picked me wildflowers. Especially Kristi, with his helmet of bristly red, almost orange, hair. He was the youngest and shyest of them all and could hardly bring himself to look me in the eye. He had special techniques for weaving stalks together and would leave bracelets and head garlands for me on my bedside table.

Vidan, on the other hand, was rough and continued to give me nasty looks, especially when he was drunk. Borian would come to my side. He would land like a shadow without my even noticing. He didn't do anything but his friend would stop staring at me. Or get up and go into another room taking the bottle with him.

I thought about it all the time: under different conditions I would have had less to laugh about playing the little mother. The boys loved me but the drink sometimes split them in two and their young faces were riddled with a yearning that made my blood run cold. It happened mostly to Pishtar, who most days would look at me hungrily. He would grab one of his mates' shoulders and start whispering in his ear. At times his words ended in a chuckle. Other times, they turned into a soft muttering and a proliferation of strange looks. Borian would intervene right away. "Go sleep," he would mumble. And I would disappear.

It was an unspoken rule we lived by: I didn't belong to anybody, but I answered to the head of the community. The others didn't dare challenge him. Not even Plator, who was the biggest and strongest of them all. In any case, if they stayed away from the wine, it was like living with a band of friends, they were the friends I'd never had. I thought, "If Babbo knew I was living with six hunks, he would have a fit and die on the spot." In the evening, I had first dibs on the room. Borian would only open the door a few minutes later. We didn't say a word. I watched him lift the blankets and place his knife under the pillow. He did it naturally, as if he were putting his keys on the chest of drawers. That was when I realized it was something he had always done. It wasn't because of me. Maybe he'd been taught to do it when he was five. Then he lay down and turned the main light off. Leaving on the kid's bedside light, in the shape of a globe. Because Borian was handsome and taciturn. Everyone feared him. But he was afraid of the dark.

Sometimes he talked in his sleep. They were long conversations in a head voice that at first gave me the shivers to begin with. After a week, I realized that wherever he was in his dreams he saw himself there, where he had first known the world. It always ended up with him whimpering which went on forever. Then he'd jerk awake, open his eyes for a second, his hand at the ready under the pillow, and look around, finally resting his gaze on me for a while. It would usually end with a sigh. And he would turn the other way and go back to sleep.

I called Mamma every other afternoon. They were the only moments I turned my phone on. "I'm fine," I told her. "I'll take the time I need." Because I had to cleanse myself. The first times, just hearing her voice made me sink back into the brackish water and I felt as though I could smell the stench of that house. Of that life. As the days went by, I started to realize I could deal with it. The main thing was that she stopped asking me where I was. I was twenty and I didn't need anything. I wasn't running away. I was not burning bridges. I wanted a life of my own and for now I had found it in a beautiful place, sheltered from everything. I would usually leave a long pause and I expected to hear her say something like, "Lucky you." Instead, she ended the call with a mother's words, "Take care of yourself. You know that anything you need, I'm here." One day, she was unusually merry. When I asked her why, she burst out laughing and said, "They've arrested Babbo. I bet we'll see him in the papers tomorrow." Splitting her sides with laughter.

The following morning, Borian went down into town early. Before going back up the hill for his work shift, he brought me a copy of the paper. I went straight to the local news and spotted the article. I sat there for a quarter of an hour, staring at it in silence like an idiot. Until I started heaving, working myself up gradually into a full-blown yell, beating my fists on the table with tears in my eyes.

Babbo had smashed Alfio Calzolari's face in: the boy who worked at the fruit and vegetable store in front of the church. He had walked in without any fuss and had started thrashing him. Then he had continued, kicking him in the ass as he dragged him into the little square. It had taken four men to stop him. Two of them were hurt so badly they had to see a doctor. I read about broken jaws, shattered cheekbones. And I laughed until I had no breath left. Kristi came down at that moment to have breakfast. He had stayed home because he had a touch of the flu. He looked at me from the doorway, sniffing. Then he pointed at his temple and said, "You crazy."

My phone calls with Mamma were especially enjoyable when I asked her for delicious recipes. "The recipe should be for seven people including me," I would tell her. She would mutter the first line of The Lord's Prayer. But then she would happily instruct me and sometimes I had to ask Borian to put some more money on my pay-as-you-go phone because I'd used all my credit chatting for half an hour about cooking. He would always say yes. And he would put on a sad face as a joke when I promised I'd pay him back. "Here is like family," he would mumble. And give me a hint of a smile, his style.

That was the most annoying thing about the situation. Borian had a thing for me, which was visible even to a blind person. Apart from anything, I was the only woman he had any dealings with. His infatuation was something soft in his life that provided respite from the grime, the hard labor and the nasty looks that he received from the locals. He behaved as a kind of protector. Maybe it was because he had been the one who had picked me up. Maybe in some areas of Eastern Europe that meant he somehow owned me. Thinking about it gave me the shivers. I had only just begun to belong to myself.

If he tried to look me in the eye, I blanched. When I talked to him, his breath would grow shallow and his face would flush. It would darken if I was more playful than I should be with some of the other boys. In the evening, before we all retired to our beds, he would make me write a shopping list for the following day. It was his way of letting me know I was important there. That he trusted me.

But the days were long. At first, I threw myself into cleaning the farmhouse with the zeal of a novitiate. But after only a couple of weeks, hanging out their clothes made me feel like a scullery maid. The idea that I had turned into a Maremma version of Snow White started to bother me. "I'll go from the frying pan into the fire without even noticing," I told myself. There wasn't even a TV set. Until not very long ago it felt like a blessing but now even that weighed on me. I would flop into the worn-out, crusty old armchair in the living room. It was already getting dark early at the end of September, and it felt even earlier because of the woods around us. I sat there looking at the paper with the article about Babbo in it. I spotted the advert on one of the last pages. It was out of date but I decided to try anyway, just for the hell of it. I turned my cell phone on and tapped in the number.

"I'm coming out with you tomorrow," I told the gang that evening. A tomblike silence fell over the table. All their eyes were on me except Borian's, who sat there frozen with his face in his plate.

I told them I needed to pay my way in the house. And that I couldn't be a housewife for the rest of my life. Pishtar was wide-eyed, falling from the clouds. "Why?" he blurted, looking at the others as if to say, "Have I missed something?" It made me laugh. I reassured them: first off, I need to see whether I can do the job. Even though a man with a nice warm voice had answered the phone. "God bless you," he had said once I'd introduced myself. Then he had unleashed a torrent of words trying with all his might to sell me on the job. He was so desperate that it made me wonder whether it was a scam.

* * *

Now I can see it clearly, even in the darkened room: destiny has led me to this point, here and now. The incident with the book, my outburst. Borian picking me up on the provincial road. But more in general, I have always felt my life was a millstone grinding me down. All those love affairs thrown into the trash before they had even begun, my feeling of being on the edge of a precipice. *Pride and Prejudice* picked out of a box by chance. For years it has been in my hands, burning with all the emotions that I might have felt if I only I had had a normal life. Meanwhile, I'd had to live with Babbo's insane jealousy. Like all miserable people, he was so buried by fear that he kept our lives within the perimeter of his own shadow. The experience of high school was like a festering wound I had to disinfect every minute. University was nothing but to-ing and fro-ing. All these things had to happen so that I would find myself there that day behind a shop counter in the middle of tiny out-of-the-way town in the crags of Maremma. The bell on the door trilling to announce the arrival of a new customer. Me looking up, tucking back a lock of hair that was hanging over my eyes. Watching him come in. And for the first time saying to myself, loud and clear, as if it were magic, "Everything has been perfect."

Borian changed on day one. I would catch a ride in the pick-up as far as the Meleta junction. They would turn left on the road into the woods that went all the way to Perolla. If they'd taken me all the way to Le Case they'd have gotten to work late and the bosses at the sawmill would have yelled at them. I didn't mind at all being on the side of the road, even when it was raining. I would stand at the bus stop and look down towards the valley. If I reached out with one hand, I could hold the whole plain in the palm of my hand. It was like I was holding myself.

Mario made me love the job from the start. I was more like a granddaughter he never had than an employee. He would come in smelling of hair gel and after-shave, and he'd tell me endless stories about the town. He would take these stories seriously and would usually come up with a moral, as if to say that people's lives are never wasted even when they live in a godforsaken place like this. "A stone in the desert," he would always say. He was always going on about this stone. "Right now, there's certainly one there somewhere. Sitting there being a stone, without anyone even noticing it. And yet, it is there. And if it's there, it means someone put it there for a reason." At this point, he would always pause theatrically. Then he would give a big smile revealing all his dentures and say, "We're all the same here in le Case."

Spending the whole day watching the crazies come in was fun in some ways and worrying in others. The women were mostly snakes, incensed that I had only just turned twenty. By contrast, the men looked as though they were floating in a faded world of their own, and my presence got their blood going a little. In the evenings, Borian would come up Via di Mezzo after work while the boys stayed in Piazza del Mercato in the pick-up. He never came close to me and would hardly greet me. What he thought of my occupation was clear enough. He looked daggers at anyone who walked by in the alleyways, showing that I was his. I felt like a little dog being led home after it has done its business.

I let the days go by, accepting the boys' long faces. When we got to the farmhouse in the evening, nobody had laid the table for them nor kept the house warm. The dirty clothes were piled up like when I first arrived. And now there were mine, too, which made it worse. The alarm was set twenty minutes early because there was an outsider who needed the bathroom. Moreover, nobody could touch me because the head of the household would go crazy.

Borian saw my getting a job as an insult. He didn't like the fact that I wanted to put some distance between us and it didn't get better with time. He would explode over nothing, especially if he caught the others whispering or casting looks at me. All he needed to do was grunt and they all hung their heads. But there was anger inside them, too.

Vidan was the one who usually harbored the most hatred. Sometimes, he would aim his dark eyes straight at me and they would strike me like balls of fire. But the worst feeling was the thought that I was trapped there without an exit strategy. Lying in bed petrified, I would say to myself, "Look what you've done." The idea of telling Borian I wanted to leave opened up terrifying vistas in my mind, and I had to control my imagination which would otherwise start galloping ahead. And, anyway, where would I go? I certainly couldn't risk the resentment of this band of thugs by going back to my family. With a father who was always on the edge of panic, who had just been given a suspended sentence. So, I simply carried on, walking a tightrope. The days chased one another fast but at the same time, my anxiety was taking my breath away. I started eating less and that was another thing Borian couldn't digest. "Finish plate," he would say if he found me looking rebellious and fiddling with a lettuce leaf. "No free food." I would regale him with a nice smile saying I was exhausted. And get up from table feigning a yawn.

With Mamma I kept up the tone of a young girl on vacation. Before saying goodbye, she always said, "Eat meat. You need the iron." Anemia was still my punishment. When my stomach clenched with nerves, the troubles started again. In the morning, I had to sit on the side of the bed for a few minutes before getting up. I was so weak, I saw white spots and it took a while before the whooshing sound, like two shells stuck in my ears, faded. I would pinch the sachets of sugar Mario kept in the back of the store in one of the many boxes. I would hide them in my pockets but in the meantime, I went around as pale as death. Then, one evening, I fainted for real and tumbled down the farmhouse stairs on my back side.

One minute I was climbing up to my room calmly. The next, I was on the floor with all the boys around me and Haris giving me little slaps. As soon as they moved me, I felt a burning sensation in front. I had banged my chest on the steps. Some of them were chuckling as if I were completely drunk. Then they picked me up like a sack of cement and carried me on their backs. I still had the rushing sensation in my head as if grains of something were traveling from one side to another. I kept saying, "I'm fine," meaning they should get their hands off me. A couple of them were exploiting the situation and were already beginning to manhandle me. They were like kids at a long-awaited party.

They only pulled back when Borian made his way through the huddle. He devoured them all with one dirty look and, as if by magic, I was left by the wall. They stood there looking at their shoes. Then they went back to their places one by one. I only noticed then that Vidan had not gotten up from table. He was wiping up the bottom of the pan with a piece of bread.

Mario never asked but it was visible a mile off: I was going through hell. When he first met me, I had been cheerful and now I was spending hours in silence, often staring into space. He was always on my back and there were times when I would have thrown him out of the window, the one that gives out onto a drop to the road below, on the side of the store with a panoramic view. Other times, I felt as though my reserve was melting and I had it on the tip of my tongue to say, "They're keeping me in chains. I've lived my whole life in a trap and every breath I take I'm still there, nothing changes. Even if I went to the desert, to that stone you like so much." But then I would bite the inside of my cheeks and say nothing.

I would vent with the deaf-mute dwarf sister but only when the store was empty after Mario had flown to his wife's bedside after a phone call. I sat there at the meat slicer and took my time, telling her all about my high-walled prison. She stared at me with those turtle eyes of hers, which looked as though they were contemplating something else all the time rather than looking at me. Or else I would start arguing with the Isastia widow who would drive me mad asking for discounts and demanding that we set aside the pig skin for her soups. She would open her puny little purse looking ill . . . Or again, with Don Lauro. Unlike the dwarf sister, if he found me alone, he would wait for the storekeeper to come back, taking up his position at the back of the store and discussing his shopping list from there. They would put things in their bags on the sly, like two brigands. Then my boss would come back to the counter and put the money in the cash register as the priest left with a big smile and a shopping bag full to bursting with liquor bottles disguised in the yellow paper we use for sliced meats.

Eventually, I fell on my face on the cheese counter. I didn't really faint. I simply collapsed and then caught myself at the last minute. Mario caught me just in time and walked me step by step to the storeroom, where he made me lie down on the wooden counter. Then he called the town doctor.

It had been a long time since I was last in that state, like a ghost, suspended in a delirium between sleep and wakefulness, struggling against a weird sense of weariness. When I was a little girl, I used to like it, except for that nausea that was always there, with a rumbling in my ears as a backdrop. I used to listen to the conversions around me, Mamma mad with worry and Babbo searching the cupboards for some vial or other. When I finally came to, the stench of vinegar was always in my nose.

But that time, Mario was looking at me. I lay there completely relaxed but I could feel him there beside me, his breathing heavy. Then there was a hand on my forehead. A few moments later, it was on my cheek. Those grandfatherly gestures were good for me. They warmed me up better than medicine. But it was a bit strange when all of a sudden, I felt his fingers on my lips. They were insistent, as if they were drawing the shape of my mouth. He smelled like freshly turned-out cheese. The wave of weakness was already coming to an end and if I had wanted to, I could have opened my eyelids right then and there, but something else kept me frozen, immobile. Mario was mumbling to himself, "Look at this beautiful flower . . . " I had to clear my throat to stop him. At that very moment, the bell on the door rang.

Dr. Salghini gave me a once-over as if he were a pediatrician. He was good-humored all the while, except when he saw the bruises that I had gotten from my fall, which I covered quickly to avoid having to give any explanations.

But the idea that Mario was on the point of doing who knows what, making the most of my fainting fit, disgusted me so much that I found it hard to hide. I started avoiding him, especially when he called me over to explain something important. Until then, I had always accepted his attentions gladly but now all I saw were devious tricks to get physically close to me and take a sniff or two. I would stiffen whenever he lay a hand on my shoulder and take a step away. I kept the smile on my face, but he noticed the change anyway. He was in agony. I could see it in his eyes, and he didn't understand what was happening to him. He would sometimes get grumpy and I paid the price: he would send me to search for some document or other in the files piled up in the store room. But usually, he kept himself to himself and that was that. With a glance in my direction to check whether the wall of silence we had erected between us was having the same effect on me.

After Samuele came into the picture, things got even worse. He appeared one morning, a morning like any other. He picked up a bit of shopping and when he walked out, my skin started itching as if ants were eating me from inside. Nothing like that had ever happened to me before and for a moment I gave in to my inner turmoil. Mario made me jump when he yelled from the counter, "Does Mrs. Barberini have to slice her own ham?" The woman was standing there waiting and looked gratified at my dressing down, which made her feel important.

I would listen to people's conversations. Anyone who came into the store eventually came around to the subject of the boy who had reopened the shutters at number 1, Via dell'Incrociata. They talked about him as if he were an animal with no hope of redemption. I remembered certain things about him, too, especially from when Babbo used to watch the news as if he were hunting game. "He's the filth of Maremma . . ." he used to grumble. "How is it possible that only madmen and imbeciles get to go on television?"

His presence alone, just a few feet from me, elevated me to a better place. Every time Samuele walked in, I was torn between the desire to steal a glance and the terror that he might notice one of my furtive looks. The worst was when Mario was not around. The ringing of the bell was enough to cut off my blood flow. If the dwarf sister popped through the door, I had to hold back a "fuck you," which she couldn't have heard, of course. But if he walked in, I wished it were her, and I was overcome by vertigo. My throat seized up as hard as bricks. My hands froze. I was walking on a cloudbank. "Can I help you," I would say in a faraway voice that came from somewhere deep within me. The good thing was that he never looked up, otherwise I would have detonated right there and then. The silence would grow like the rumble of an airplane coming closer and whatever I did felt wrong. Then he would come to the cash register. I would ring up his things with one finger but my heart was rattling so hard I would find myself hitting two or three keys at the same time. Then I would have to annul the transaction and start again. Samuele was completely unruffled. When we were done, he would take the bag from me and only then would he lift his eyes for a second. And that made my cup run over.

As soon as he walked out, disappeared, I'd almost manage to forget him. In general, his presence was like a ring of light that I couldn't bring into focus. This made me so angry and so desperate for him that I wanted to scream. I couldn't keep a picture of him in my head. All that was left was an idea, like when you stare at the sun for too long and it leaves an imprint on your retina. Until it fades and disappears. But the heat on your skin stays.

When Mario was around, I would keep my distance. Or else I would serve another customer, who would weigh every slice of salami I cut by sight. I would usually watch Samuele in the reflection of the store window. I would see a shadow coming from nowhere and flitting away two minutes later. But it stuck to me and I was different after it had gone. Mario couldn't forgive me. I would go pale and stare into space until closing time. It was like living with Babbo all over again. I had to deal with that possessiveness again. Except that now I didn't have a pillow to vent my emotions on because it would have made the handsome Albanian, who, every evening, put a collar on me in Via di Mezzo suspicious.

I started taking a lunch break and leaving the store. Sometimes even when the weather was bad. The first day, I walked blindly through the deserted streets as the cooking smells and TV voices wafted from the few inhabited houses. Then I found Via dell'Incrociata. The house opened onto an uphill road.

I would look up at that window without doing anything else in particular except hide behind the corner. If I saw a shape behind the window, I would immediately pull back. Or I would curse the ginger cat that was always there in the middle of the piazza near the water fountain staring at me.

My obsession with Samuele didn't pass. It was a completely different story from the infatuations I had beaten down into silence in the past. The more I heard people bad-mouthing him, the more fascinating he became to me. I was still picking at my food in the evening but what made Borian nervous at that point was seeing me staring into space in a way that completely excluded him. My body was sitting with the other boys at table but my mind was traveling far away. I went to bed with a light heart, for now I could see at the end of all those things that had happened, a door filled with light. This renewed my resolve and made me stronger. It even made up for the lack of iron in my diet.

I fell into his trap like an idiot. I was going on my usual stakeout. I had reached the end of the street and saw the light off in the window and the motorbike parked under the low roof of the storeroom. I stared at it and hid around the corner; I had goose bumps seeing his shape in the window and from the combination of proximity and trepidation. It was a tremor of pleasure that I enjoyed reigniting continuously. I assimilated the first shiver as it ran through me. I was about to lean out a second time when I heard someone say, "What are you looking for?"

I froze and looked around me. For a moment I thought I had dreamed it. Then Samuele appeared from the other corner and there he was in front of me.

I realized he'd been there from the start. Part of me was ready to make a run for it but I was struggling against a total paralysis. I was like one of those little animals that pretend to be dead. He looked at me. "Every day you come here at the same time. Do you have something to tell me?"

If I'd had a flick knife like Borian's I'd have slashed my own throat without thinking twice and died at his feet in a suitable fashion. Instead, all I could do was gawp. But I couldn't let him think I was nothing but a nosey parker, obsessed with spying on the movements of a notorious celebrity just to pass the time of day. "Sorry," I mumbled. That was the best I could muster. The stab I had felt when I first saw him hadn't passed so I turned slowly, hanging my head like a naughty little girl who was being thrown out of class. And I started to walk away, dripping with rivulets of shame.

"I didn't say I didn't like you coming," he said.

I walked faster. "He's going to kill me now," I repeated to myself. I could feel his eyes drilling into my back and all I could do was stare at the end of the alley as if it were a safe haven. I got there almost in a run.

* * *

When I think of those early days it makes me feel safe and dry, even locked up in this shadowy room in the middle of a storm. I see the way I crept back there the following day like a feral animal that doesn't trust anyone and was scared to stick its head out into the road. Samuele was already there on the step under the last porticoes.

We weren't doing anything in particular. I would get there and sit down to talk a little. Usually, he was the one to start the conversation, telling me how Le Case was stuck in its ways with no direction forward. "The tragedy will get to you, too," he often used to say. But there was no need for him say it because it was written all over his face: he was stuck in a place that was crushing him. One day, he looked at me. "Don't I scare you?" he asked me straight out. I shook my head. I would have gladly sat there on that step for the rest of my life. My only fear was that I wouldn't be able to see him the following day. I wanted him for myself but I also thanked all the unlucky stars that had brought him back to the town.

He never talked about it and I never asked. Being with Samuele was like settling comfortably into the middle of a perfect place: I didn't care at all how the world had shifted to bring him here. And I cared even less after we'd had our first kiss, which blew away all the fog of the past . I even got to the point where I thanked Babbo. His jealousy had kept me intact for the boy I was now holding so tight that our bodies were almost fused together. We reaped the best from one another, erasing all the ugliness that had befallen us and transforming it a light that shone in our eyes. We would sit and stare at each other for hours with a blend of awkwardness, happiness, and shock. I caressed him and every now and again sought out his lips. I felt like I was drowning if I went without. When it was time to open the store again, I would walk half-way down the road clenching my fists. But then I would suddenly stop and hurry back to kiss him some more, which never sufficed to keep me going until the following day. "I was in love with you ten years ago," I murmured sometimes. "But I didn't know it."

I let him undress me here in this room. It was Saturday and, as usual, the agony of knowing we wouldn't be able to see each other on my day off made us even hungrier. There was a dim, bluish light and our bodies took on the sheen of metal. Even the tearing of my flesh was beautiful because it was him doing it to me. But most of all, I could feel life resounding loudly in every fiber of our beings. Now that our two shadows were no longer floating aimlessly in the slipstream, life was much fairer. Even Le Case was thanking us. Making love there in the heart of that chamber of death, filled with people devastated by boredom, was as if music had penetrated its walls and added a touch of color to that waste of space.

My doleful look on weekends did not escape Borian's notice. He controlled everything I did, and I was going crazy under his oppressive cowl. "Eat dish," he insisted again that evening, digging his elbow into my sides to wake me from my reverie. I wasn't in the mood. I saw red and did something impulsive: I picked up my plate and shoved it towards him. "You eat it," I said sharply. Silence fell instantly over the table. Everyone put their knives and forks down. And stopped chewing. They looked as serious as if they had been about to go into battle and lob a hand grenade into the mix. I was tired of being under a yoke. I threw my napkin down on the table and left.

Borian came up to the bedroom after an hour. I pretended to sleep but I could feel his gaze on me. Then I heard the usual sounds: his knife under the pillow, bed springs. Followed by the click of the main light, waiting for the glow of the globe. But it didn't come. For the first time, he decided to sleep in total darkness. I didn't know it yet but my punishment had only just started.

When I opened my eyes, it was morning. It was the engine of the pickup on the gravel drive that woke me. I lifted my head and saw that his bed was empty and the covers in a pile. It was so quiet in the house you could hear a pin drop. I got up and counted the hours: thirty more before I could go to Via dell'Incrociata. I would be spending my Sunday doing the washing and counting every minute. I got dressed and went over to the door. It was locked from the outside.

I banged on it. "Hey!" I yelled, my voice still gravely from sleep. There was no answer. I crossed the room and opened the window. The icy air slapped my face. I looked around the yard: not a trace of the boys. I looked straight down and considered jumping. But it was an old building with high ceilings. I would have shattered my knees, or worse. "Hey!" I shouted again, hoping someone had stayed home. The only answer was the distant rumbling of cars on the provincial road.

My heart was thumping and my head was filled with images I couldn't banish from my mind. "They've locked me up," I kept saying to myself. I opened my backpack and rummaged around the bottom. Overtaken with nerves, I emptied the whole thing out on the bed. My cell phone was not there.

I started circling that tiny room, tearing at my hair. I could already see myself stripped naked and chained up like an animal. I wept and threw myself at the door. Panic came in waves making me feel dizzy, as if I'd been slapped hard. Eventually, I forced myself to take some deep breaths. I closed my eyes. Borian was not a genius but he wasn't stupid enough to believe he could do something like this without any consequences. Mario wouldn't take my unjustified absence lightly. The whole of Le Case knew who the guy who picked me up every evening on Via di Mezzo was. And then there was Samuele. He used often to say, partly to test my reactions and partly as a joke: "One day they'll tell you who I am and you'll run a mile." But the truth was that nothing, not even a natural catastrophe, would make me miss appointment with him.

Thinking about him helped me. From the first day I laid eyes on him, he had been a reason to keep going. And now, too, I needed to be patient. And hope that the gang didn't have plans to make me vanish for real.

I heard the crunch of the pickup tires on the gravel that evening. I went to the window and saw the boys getting out calmly, good-humoredly pushing one another around. Their commotion filled the house. They yelled, moved chairs around . . . Then I heard footsteps coming up the stairs. Once they reached the upstairs corridor they moved on to the other rooms. When the key started to turn in the lock of my room, I waited with bated breath. Eventually, the door opened and Borian was standing there on the threshold. He found me sitting on the bed.

He gave me a rapid, silent once-over. His eyes swept the room as if to check that everything was where it should be. Then he threw his jacket on the bed and left, leaving a slice of door open.

I saw the normality of his action as a perverse farce. I'd spent the day locked up without drinking or eating. First and foremost, I needed the bathroom. But I waited to hear his footfall on the stairs. Only then did I stand up.

As I went downstairs, I almost convinced myself that my torture would be limited to that: holding me in a cell for a day of fasting. In conditions that would transform me into a pathetic bitch, pissing in the corner. They had laid the table and there was a place for me. The wine was already flowing steadily. Kristi came up to me and handed me a glass filled to the brim. I took it without a second thought and threw it back in one gulp, which left me breathless.

The evening before, I had made a scene with the food that I had hardly touched, and I'd been punished for it. After a whole day without anything to eat, I threw myself on the meat that landed on my plate. I cracked hard crusts of bread with my teeth, scraping the roof of my mouth. Borian sat next to me with a satisfied smile on his face, taking delicate sips from his glass, his lips barely touching the rim. His look sent a clear message to the boys, "You see how to treat bitches like this?" Apart from that, it felt like a normal dinner. Except for the fact that I went on eating. The leader of the gang saw this as confirmation of his power: the punishment had done its job. I made myself look obedient, almost hamming it up. The idea that I could be hatching a plan didn't occur to him.

I played the role of the scullery maid to the bitter end. I cleared the table and stood at the sink for an hour washing all the dishes. I ended the show with a good sweep of the room, making the boys get up so I could clear away the last crumbs. Borian watched me from the head of the table like a contented lord of the manor.

The globe lamp was switched on again that night at the usual time. It wasn't hard to get to sleep because the day's ordeal had drained all my energy. For now, it was enough to keep up appearances as usual so that nobody would suspect anything.

The alarm went off early. Outside the only bathroom, there was the usual fuss between those who couldn't hold it in another second and those who took a century to splash their faces. Then the race to the pickup with the stench of Sambuca in the cabin from the previous day's drinking. They dropped me off at the junction and I felt like I was flying. "You're almost there," I said to myself. I said it again as I clambered onto the bus that took the workers from the Lucchini mine back home after their night shift.

The morning in the store went by so slowly my hair was going gray as I worked. Mario was sulking about all his problems and all the pathetic women in the town who came in to fill their fridges on Monday mornings. We even closed a little late. Then I was on my own. I waited for the streets to empty and then scurried out of the store and headed straight for the hill. I hugged the walls all the way up until I reached Via dell'Incrociata, my breathing so labored it burned my lungs. I went for the door like a missile and vanished inside. Then, there I was in the silent hall.

Samuele came out of his room almost immediately, looking a little disheveled and alarmed. He was about to open his mouth but I didn't give him the chance to utter a syllable. I ran towards him on the point of tears. The impact made him lose his balance. "Let me stay here!" I said, holding him as tight as I could.

* * *

And now he's not coming back. Even though he knows what I went through that terrible Sunday, locked in a room in a farmhouse in the middle of nowhere. Now I'm stuck here, pinned to this bed where Samuele has initiated me into womanhood. It's pitch black now and the storm is still raging. There are moments when I think that if it got any worse it would be the end of the world. But it goes on endlessly.

I went missing and that was that. To begin with, it felt like a liberation. Samuele would go down to the store to pick up a few groceries. He brought back news of people's moods. "At least they have something to talk about," he groaned, his expression darkening. I knew what he was saying: keeping me here was putting him at risk. The billboards of Maremma had my photo on them with the word "MISSING" in giant letters. The carabinieri had already turned the farmhouse inside out and put the workers at the sawmill on notice, interrogating them one by one. There was no other news, though all he needed to do was pick up a newspaper. "I have to keep to my routine," Samuele muttered staring into space. Then he looked at me and his face opened up into a beautiful smile. "If they find you here, I'm done for," he said. A second later, he was on top of me.

I think about Mamma, about Babbo. I can see her, in particular, gripping the receiver and madly dialing my number again and again, only to receive the same message: "unavailable." And that is the pure truth. Remaining hidden is the only way to keep everyone safe. If I were found, the news would make the rounds of all the papers, and the spotlight would be on Samuele again. He would be taken away from me. The sawmill workers are as mystified as everyone else. In my heart, I know Borian will never forgive me for the affront of eloping for love. And here I am, stuck in a vacuum as usual.

Samuele says things will be different later, that slowly we'll get our act together. For now, all I need to do is make a phone call. "Mamma, I'm fine." That's all. Without tossing and turning in bed thinking she's wearing herself down imagining me six feet under.

It's been five weeks and for most people I'm already a ghost. Maybe they're right: I live in the shadows and speak in whispers. If Samuele isn't home, I can't even flush the toilet. Then there are moments like these, when reality is blurred. I ask myself, "Is it all a dream?" Maybe when I open my eyes, I'll find myself back in the farmhouse in the early days. Or maybe I'll wake up with a start and I'll be reading about Jane's dance with Mr. Darcy in my old bedroom and Mamma will come in all out of breath and tell me dinner is on the table. "What's that face for?" she would cry, catching me half-asleep. "If you sleep now, you'll mess up the whole night and we'll need cannons to get you up tomorrow."

* * *

The slamming of a door makes me think there's been another gust of wind seemingly strong enough to sweep the house away. But the cold puff of air reaches the room. Then there's a click in the lock. Samuele has come back.

I prop myself up on one elbow. It goes quiet again. But then my anguish melts away when I see a dim ray of light coming from the corridor. I have to bite my lip to stop myself from calling out his name. I hear his steps and can see his shadow on the floor.

The light goes on. I have to shut my eyes tight and shield them with my hands. "It took you a while," I mumble. Samuele doesn't answer. He comes closer, sits on the edge of the bed. "Look at you. You're soaking wet. It's pouring like the end of the world out there."

He sits staring at the wall. He's pale and there are sticking plasters across his forehead.

"Has something happened?" I ask feebly.

Maybe he doesn't even hear me. Then his eyes start moving up the wall to the ceiling . . . he rolls his head back, staring at the lampshade that is swaying slowly. His face is lined with rain but I couldn't swear there were no tears there.

"Samuele, speak to me," I insist. "You're scaring me."

A shiver runs through his body. He shifts his gaze towards me so slowly it makes my hairs stand on end. Eventually, our eyes meet. His looks gaunt. A little candle of mucus is dripping from his nose. My stomach leaps when I realize his lips are starting to tremble. Then, his whole face falls apart. A sob catches in his throat and this time I can see it clearly: a big fat tear trickles down his cheek. "I'm back," he manages to say in a broken voice. "I'm back . . ."

He lifts a hand. He brings it closer and I am frozen to the spot, watching the scene from the outside. I feel his touch on my cheek. An icy touch that makes me catch my breath. And more tears fall. I am unable to formulate even one word.

He leans forward. When our lips meet, I can taste salt. Samuele is racked by sobs but keeps kissing me as if he were taking in gulps of fresh air. I let him do it and gradually melt. He moves down to my neck and I am suddenly on my back looking at the lampshade. He doesn't stop. I see a crust of paint peeling off the brass lamp and fluttering down onto us like a snowflake. He shrugs off his jacket and drops it on the ground. Then he throws himself back onto me.

* * *

There's a moment when the storm outside feels like it is at one with us. The thunderclaps make the windowpanes shake. He's on top of me, going at it as if he were pushing into the storm. I accommodate him inside me, clenching my teeth so as not to make a noise. It's painful and it's beautiful and I want more of it, forever, to the last day and beyond. Flakes from the ceiling continue to fall and everything still feels like it is being pressed into the frame of a dream. I'd like to ask, "What's happening?" but I'm being devoured by kisses. Samuele's tears are wetting me, but he doesn't stop. Until it becomes impossible to keep it to myself.

I open my mouth and I start screaming.

Samuele Radi,
the Monster

After making love, Eleonora collapses in an exhausted heap. And she usually falls asleep for a few minutes, like now. Eleonora's profile is as sharp as a knife blade. But in these shadows, she looks like a flaming sword that burns me first because I can't control her. "Let's leave tonight," she says every time she sees me come in. Holding my hands, she says, "I've found you and I'm not letting you go ever again." For a moment, I'm tempted to tickle her face to make her open those dark chasms of her eyes which I have continued to fall into, heedless of how hard the crash landing would be. Oh, to find the courage. The courage to tell her that . . .

. . . Clara had a beauty spot under her cheekbone, like a movie star. And she used to practice her fancy signature for hours, filling whole sheets of paper with the squiggles, her gaze drilling a hole through the paper and landing who knows where. "It relaxes me," she would say whenever I asked her why she enjoyed writing her name over and over again. Most of all, she liked drawing a kind of vortex where the letters got smaller as they were pulled into the center until they became a dot. Then she would lift her head and look satisfied. It was as if she had taken herself into the eye of her own storm, where the air was still and everything was becalmed. Clara seemed to want only one thing: to live in that spot.

To begin with, she didn't even look at me. She was in love with her black hair, which behaved very like the doodle she would draw on the paper napkins at the restaurant, curling wildly. Shiny vortices that she tried to tame by tying them up in a makeshift bun high on her head. They reminded me of a Gorgon's snakes. I would weave between the tables as clients lined up in front of her at the cash register to pay their checks. I would pick up people's garbage, greasy napkins and forks left lying around with lumps of leftover desert stuck in the prongs. I would throw everything onto the Coca-Cola tray, including the miserly tips I sometimes found under the ashtray. And as I worked, I would cast a sideways glance over at that mixed-race Maremma wonder with her shiny white teeth and incredible hands. Her father was right to put her front-of-house. If there were any complaints, they faded instantly in the eyes of whatever watery-eyed customers from up north who tragically found themselves on holidays in Follonica—an admission to the whole world that their lives were a complete failure—as soon as they set eyes on her.

At the end of our shift, we used to sit on the low wall looking out onto the camp site and smoke a cigarette. I loved it. It set us apart from all those fraudsters who would hang out on the terrace on the other side and stare vacantly at the sea. We didn't talk that much. We sat there staring into space as if we were taking stock of the world after the barbarians had passed by. Sometimes she would lift her head and say, "Whatever you earn, you should know that we don't pay you enough." She meant I was heroic to put up with the riffraff gazing at the bay, their eyes deadened by the city routine and the screaming kids in strollers. I would have liked to say that my real pay was the time I spent with her under the crooked roof with the stench of leftovers wafting from the kitchen.

The Baia dei Butteri was a soulless place that attracted soulless people. You could smell the neglect from miles away, especially if you took the provincial road from Solmine with its plume of thick white smoke day and night. The Scarlino valley stretched out in the sun, which scorched the rushes and bushes to nothing. Reaching as far as the sea, which was also an eyesore given that a pontoon had ripped in two the picture postcard view that tourists rushed out to the beach to snap, which they couldn't wait to show off once they got back to their slums. Instead, they bumped into the sulfur wharf, the water hot and oily from the treatment-plant waste pipes. Every now and again, everything would die. The fish would leap out of the ditch, wildly gasping for oxygen, and end up twitching on the banks. Or they would be beached by freak waves. The carcasses piled up on the shore and in no time at all, the air started to stink and it was hard to stop from retching. That was when I would look over at the giant Welcome sign hanging from an arch at the entrance to the campground, then to the beach where the kids would be scraping tar off their heels with plastic spades. Their parents would be a few feet away, dead to the world, done in by the heat. As soon as a camera was taken out, they would all plaster a smile on their faces that made you want to scream.

Amid all this decay, Clara was the only clean corner. I kept my distance, especially when we were alone on the restaurant veranda laying tables. I would start wandering around with a hangdog look, inventing chairs that needed straightening or glasses that needed a quick wipe to get rid of the dishwasher stains. But sometimes it was impossible to avoid her and we ended up back-to-back, maybe in front of the salad bar or by the dresser where we stacked the plates. We would make the usual comments about all the ugly, lame people forced to spend their August torturing themselves with a vacation there. Clara used to enjoy describing the people who were so crazy they decided to spend their free time in that handkerchief of plucked provincial scrubland. And yet I admired her father who had had the foresight back in the seventies to stick a kiosk up on the edge of the old pine forest. As time went by, he built the first balcony. Then a wall came up, and then another, and another

. . . The Baia dei Butteri was the result of his penchant for building without permits. And twenty years later, the whole project was amnestied, making a family of spoonbills and lathe-turners wealthy.

Clara's movements had that unauthorized spirit, too. Her very presence changed the tone of the place, making it suddenly take on the colors of the Caribbean. As long as she was in one slice of the picture.

By the end of the season, we were going around hand in hand but only when her father was nowhere to be seen. The veranda would be ransacked by all the surly retards who were still moping there on Assumption Day, crankier than ever because that place had put a sign on their foreheads reading, "This is what you deserve." This was what the fruit of all their blood, sweat, and tears was being wasted on. A place where the waiter didn't even wear a shirt.

Clara cast looks at me that were like electric shocks, sharp prods that sent me off course. I ended up getting the orders wrong, which drove Beppe crazy as he strove to keep the kitchen on track, and he would let loose with a spray of profanities. Or I would get the flashy clients' backs up by forgetting what the Special was that day. She would laugh at everything I did, in a kind way, as if she were screaming with her eyes, "You're handsome and you're mine." I didn't know what to think about the former. As far as the latter was concerned, I was prepared to swear to it on the stars that govern the universe.

We made love at the end-of-season party, while all the cowboys twerked their giant elephant asses outside, warmed up by the Sangria that Beppe had mixed up in a vat that afternoon and left on the floor. At one point he had taken his sandals off and soaked his feet in the liquid. "It's to give it a certain *je ne sais quoi*," he had grunted. Then he had gone back to chopping peaches and watermelons, throwing the pieces into the warm soup of cheap wine together with a dash of rum. The holidaymakers were throwing back the swill with abandon, swaying loosely to the music provided by an entertainer from Puglia hired for the occasion. He was chubby with a thin mustache, singing with a backing track and pretending to play the keyboard in an attempt to imitate Eros Ramazzotti.

Clara and I were behind the bamboo fence, which separated the veranda from the hedge that led to the back of the restaurant. I came inside her as my legs nearly gave way. As she climaxed, she grabbed the top of the fence and rolled her head back. A six or seven-year-old kid was spellbound to see a set of fingers suddenly appear over the bamboo. I watched him through the slits as I continued pumping. Eventually, our gazes met for real although he couldn't actually see anything. And that's when I went limp. Staring at the big, blue eyes of a kid with a buzz cut in a Barcelona soccer shirt.

We moved to Viale Uranio at the end of October. I was already living on an alien plane of reality: I was starting to think the kind of nice things that would have made my former self die of boredom. For example, now suddenly I was grateful for all the effort I'd had to make in life because it had led me to this precise moment: opening the front door confidently with Clara beside me. The musty smell almost took my breath away, but I was still thinking a new chapter was beginning for both of us. Then we spent the whole afternoon going up and down the stairs carrying the boxes with our old bits and pieces in them. Because you can have the best of intentions, but the past never stops pursuing you.

Another thing about her was this: with just four month's work, more money rained down on her than a good builder earns in a year. Her father had put one third of the company in her name and when the accounts were done at the end of the season, Clara cashed in a check with several zeros. While I had to squeeze every cent out of my welfare payments, eating at the restaurant over the weekends when I worked off the books. "One day I'd like to go back to college," I said every now and again, and there were times I actually believed it. She used to tease me because she didn't think I had it in me to be an archeologist. "On Sundays, we have to set off a bomb to drag you out of the house," she would say. "I can't imagine you in a jungle hacking at the undergrowth with a machete to uncover an ancient temple."

She was right because she would spend her Saturdays with her friends, while I had to run to and fro for miles at the San Lorenzo or at the Bavarian's place where I worked myself to the bone to avoid getting slapped around by the slave-driver proprietors who turned up their noses as soon as they saw me walk in.

Other than that, our life was an eruption of love. We would be at each other at the drop of a hat. Any little provocation would set our flesh on fire. We didn't do much but to us it felt like the essence of the world. Aimless strolls through Grosseto, a town which would give panic attacks to anyone. We could come up with whacky plans sitting on the cathedral steps. Waking up the next morning and seeing her doing things in the house made me feel like the luckiest man in the world, someone kissed by God. Every time, I had to give myself a pep talk. It was terrible when I watched her without her knowing it: I didn't feel I measured up. Clara kept me on edge. She was the glass doll I had always dreamed of having but she was always on the point of shattering in the first gust of wind. Smashing me to pieces, more importantly. Like never before.

The jealousy started the evening I shot out of the Bavarian's place like a missile, making the most of a rescheduled Serie A match that had kept all the retards glued to their TVs at home. In the old days, I would have stayed on to get paid to the last. But I went and asked, "Given the scarcity of human livestock, could I leave a couple of hours early?" Giancarlo looked at me, the bulbs of his eyes floating in the fleshy folds of his permanent eyebags. When nobody came to the restaurant it hurt his feelings, and he wanted everyone to stay there in silence sharing in the tragedy. "Your stomach for work impresses me," he said with a gurgle. I took it as a Yes.

I arrived at the Tredici Gobbi. I only took my helmet off when I was at the bottom of the stairs that led down to the ancient cellar revisited as an English Pub. Anyone who had seen me would have thought I was there to rob the place. Or a killer on an evening job for a mafia boss. The noise suddenly flooded my ears, and I was already sweeping the room with my eyes, so anxious was I to surprise Clara. I was anticipating her surprise, followed by a jolt of recognition, a shout of my name. Then, I imagined her all over me, showering me with kisses.

Instead, she was sitting next to a fancy guy. There under the arch, in a corner bench seat. There were empty glasses on the table, and I watched him bend down warily to take an occasional puff of a cigarette he was keeping hidden. He produced little clouds, but nobody seemed to be bothered. The worst thing was that they kept laughing. They were having such fun that at one point I saw her rest her forehead on that guy's friendly shoulder. A second later their eyes were awash again.

Maybe it was a minute. Maybe it was a hundred years. I was leaning on the counter in my waiter's outfit, a crash helmet hanging off my arm. All the while, I was experiencing pure terror. A deep well of anxiety made breathing feel like history: I existed but I was completely outside myself. I was no longer a person. I was an exception. I was looking at my beautiful Gorgon being handled by someone else. I was looking at the way he stared at her lips. And just like that, seeing Clara so carefree robbed me of all the complicity which, until a minute before, I had believed was ours only. I didn't even register her last movements before she turned towards me. I watched her as if I were looking through a porthole into another world. I didn't even make a face when I saw her frown. She looked as though she was struggling to bring my face back into focus from light years away. Until she finally opened her eyes wide. "Samuele!" she blurted out, making her way over to me.

It didn't make any difference that the others in the group were at the bar right beside me during the whole scene. It didn't make any difference what the guy's sexual orientation was, or finding out that Filippo had been desperately in love with a Maremma stallion who had gone to England to follow the fashion, leaving him to drown his sorrows in beer at the Tredici Gobbi. It didn't make any difference finding out that the laughs were the result of a whole toke Filippo had smoked sitting on that bench, blowing substantial puffs into Clara's face. Since she wasn't used to it, she had gone off her head on the spot like a twelve-year-old with a first glass of grappa.

All that mattered was me. That long blade that had suddenly stripped me down to the bone and further. All that was needed was the *idea* that I might lose everything and the next minute I had fallen into an abyss. Swallowed up into a darkness I had never experienced before. I was laughing and joking with Clara latched onto me, happy I was there. Inside, I was still licking my wounds, as if I had narrowly escaped total annihilation. Which was, in fact, just around the corner. The question that continued to float in the air was ruthless: was I sure I wanted to live like this? Completely prone. Constrained. Subjugated to that sentiment.

Yes, I wanted it. In fact, there was no question. I had no alternative. Now that Clara had come into my life, there were two possibilities: her or her. I could kick against the chains as much as I liked but it was in her eyes that I found confirmation of myself. Before I had been Samuele Radi like any other guy, mown down like everyone else by normality. Now I blinded everyone I met in the street with reflected light.

Everything about her was amazing. And therefore threatening. I started to feel lava bubbling in my blood whenever I saw her bewitched by some thought. "What are you thinking about?" I pounced like a bird of prey. Clara came back to her senses with her usual smile. "About you," she would always say. Cutting me to pieces.

Weekends had become a torture. There were so many sharks ready to eat her up out there. Sometimes, we would be in the bathroom together in front of the mirror. I was getting ready for my shift. She, for her evenings out and about, which she used to call her "tours." "Tonight, I have a tour," she would announce and I felt as though I was tumbling down imaginary stairs.

The tours almost always started with a dinner at Camilla's house. She was a 260 pound blimp, fixated with gloomy music and black lipstick. Clothes, shoes: all black. I hated her manipulative gaze. If I fell into its orbit, she would wink oddly at every word Clara said as if there were a hidden story that I couldn't possibly take part in. I was convinced that she spent their evenings out urging Clara to throw herself into the pool of boys. Camilla didn't like the fact that Clara was beautiful. Nor that she had settled happily with a hillbilly like me. Since she couldn't undermine her best friend, she undermined me. All she had to do was pull a face and I was on tenterhooks. She noticed. She enjoyed it. She continued.

Sometimes I would come home and Clara was still out. It was hard for me to deal with, and I started processing it by opening a bottle of wine at one in the morning. Until I heard her fiddling with the lock and her voice that I knew so well calling, "My love . . . " There were seven clacks of her heel before she reached the living room with the corner kitchenette. She switched on the lamp and saw I was lying there with the TV on low. The light blinded me but she was even more blinding, the way she always complained she was done in and recounted every detail of her evening without my even asking. Too many details. The kind of list someone who wants to hide something comes up with.

I had the illusion I was safe only when we were holed up between the four walls of our apartment under the bedcovers. This was how we spent most of our winter Sundays, in fact, with the rain whipping against the windows. I would be as happy as pie and she would gradually start fading. She needed to be out and about; it was her nature. For me it spelled mortal danger. It got to the point that I started lying to the restaurants, calling in sick on the sly. Giancarlo would roar at me, and I would hang up on him. Then I would come back into the living room with the news. "There's still not much work," I would mutter ruefully, whining something about how the pay would have come in useful. In the early days, Clara would leap with joy, happy to have me to herself and it cracked open my heart. She would start making lists of where we could spend the evening and with whom. That was when I would pin her down. "What about renting a film?" She would stare at me. Then nod, without making a scene. And I ate her up whole until the following week.

In quiet moments, she would sometimes try and lead me into conversations about things that made me see blue. Such as, for example, past boyfriends or girlfriends, the dreams we had when we were kids . . . I spat out my words one by one, as if they were on a drip-feed, partly because I didn't have any interesting stories to tell, and partly because I didn't want to encourage her to go on any longer. I didn't want to know who she had given her panties to when she was still a virgin, nor who the brainbox she had a crush on at high school was. My face darkened if she ever said she liked an actor, and he would be immediately struck off our list of films to watch. I got anxious when she told me about her senior year school trip to Lisbon because sooner or later a kiss, a caress, or a letter full of stupid promises would be mentioned . . . And as soon as it was, I would clam up and batten the emergency hatches over my ears. I would hear names like Marco, Sandro, and Raffaele but I didn't take them in. They were meaningless puffs of propelled air. Over time, Clara got the message. I usually didn't open my mouth until the following day. I would turn into a totem pole if she spent an hour in our room on the phone to Camilla the blimp or anyone else in her gang.

One evening she spoke out, "You can't go on like this. If you mistreat my past, you're mistreating what I am today. Don't you get it?" There followed out first real argument, when she let it all out. The bulging veins on her neck and forehead as she spoke were a shock. "I know nothing about you. Do you think that's normal?" she said to me at one point. "It's like you dropped into this world without a past. Everyone has a story to tell, even if it's a depraved one."

I opened up. Just like that. It happened unexpectedly, bringing her rant to a halt. She was so surprised that she pulled her head back as if I was about to slap her.

I talked to her about me, where I came from. About the silence a son grows up in when his mother has spent her life hugging trees and clouds. You end up feeling like a cloud yourself, the contours of your body blurring into nothing. Or you live with other people and try and do what they do: keep going. The journey continues, it has to, even when you've been curled up in a corner looking at your feet for a hundred years. You let yourself be carried along like a bored traveler looking out of a train window at the scenery. Because ultimately you like being detached. It's your secret.

Yes, I too had had my happy little moments when I was younger: panting with a throbbing heart while trying to unhook a bra. I had had my share of kicks in the face. Attempted things that went askew, taken long rides with the sea in view. Somehow, I had managed to find a safe harbor somewhere inside me, despite feeling one step removed from reality. If reality was a picture, I was always outside the frame. "Then you came along," I said, staring at my hands.

Her gaze on my skin felt like a firebrand. But by that point I was galloping along, words gushing out of me. She wanted to know who I was and I was telling her.

I laid out unthinkable vistas, which brought me back to my old life in this town on the crags of Maremma. It was pleasurable and painful at the same time because the dazzling figure of Nonna Esedra suddenly came to mind. I remembered how blindsided I had been by her death, which had surprised me in my twenties and sent my life totally off course. Bringing my studies to an end. Making me realize I was completely alone in the world without her regular phone call every other day at six P.M. But I hadn't let Le Case devour me. On the contrary, with what little inheritance had come my way, I had found a tiny apartment in Via Roma that looked more like a garage. My dance of death with off-the-book restaurant jobs had already started then and continued.

All Clara had to do was look at me. Her presence had torn me away from ten years of treading water and thrown me in front of other people. She had made me clearly visible. I was trying to express my feelings as well as I could, squeezing my brain so hard it hurt, but all that came out were a few random drops that had no relation to the great machinations I felt working inside me. Until I came to the conclusion that I could say everything in five words. I said them just like that, maybe without even realizing. "I love you too much."

If it weren't for the panic pinning me down, I would have leapt out of my chair. Clara had tears in her eyes. When she threw herself on me, I held my breath. I was confused. Finding meaning in that vague cloud had opened my eyes and shown me new configurations. The outlines were clearly drawn, and they looked like the grates of a cage. It felt like every square in her vortex had her name carved onto it and that doodle ended in a dot. The dot was me.

* * *

Eleonora has a mole, too, but it's so small you can hardly see it. Just under her right eye, like a tiny tear drop that is there for no reason. I see it now in flashes when the lightning illuminates the room. It's at moments like these that my thoughts get caught up and lead me back here, on top of her, having surrendered everything. I lean over a little, brushing her ear with my lips. "We'll never have enough of one another," I whisper inaudibly. She goes stiff. A shiver seems to go through her, or maybe the floor is shaking again. Because Le Case is breathing. It's panting. It's a giant wounded animal. The room is lit up in repeated flashes as the storm rages. The detonations in the sky are booming across the land and echoing in everyone's blood. But Eleonora is asleep. Perhaps she is dreaming.

The wake-up slap of spring re-opened the gates of the Baia dei Butteri. Bushes to cut back, licks of paint to apply all over, fences to mend. Clara's father employed a gang of foreign builders. They took their orders and threw themselves into their work, heads down, without saying a word all day.

Pulling up at the campsite in her canary yellow Renault, with Clara at the wheel, was a bit embarrassing. I felt like an invalid that needed to be carried around. Or like a poor bastard who had no choice but to shout to all and sundry, "I don't own a car." It was a sorry sight, especially for Alarico who, unlike me, acted tough and appreciated an ostentation of virility. Like spitting on the ground, which he did continuously. In the little room where he did the accounts, there was a bronze bust of Mussolini in plain sight. Whenever he walked past, he would rub the bald head as the faithful do in church with a saint's foot.

At the beginning of the previous season, Alarico had called me as a substitute. He had told me on the phone: their long-time waiter had broken his leg in mid-May, just as things were revving up. At my job interview, he had asked me pointedly, "Can you manage a twelve-hour shift?" I was still in a daze because a mysterious thing had just happened to me. After a decade, the job center had offered me a proper job with a contract and benefits. With these shifts in addition to my previous work distributing flyers, I would be eligible for unemployment benefit in September like any other normal person.

I sometimes thought about it afterwards and I told myself that nothing happens by chance. My phone number had been there all those years, buried in a drawer gathering dust. And then suddenly one afternoon a miracle had happened and my phone rang. The second I answered, my life shifted towards Clara.

She was radiant. After a whole winter in Viale Uranio living under my pall, she was finally out in the open air and she was filled with enthusiasm. Except that she dragged me along with her and this turned the tables for her father, too, who wouldn't deign to look at me. As soon as I came into his view, he would walk away with some excuse. Instead of saying hi he would yell, "Hey . . . " looking at his feet. The fact was that he would have to suck it up and tolerate my presence for the whole season. Because even the unauthorized walls could tell: it had been his daughter who had forced him to take me back.

During the restructuring, I showed I could work hard, even though I had no building experience. Most of the time I was moving boxes. Cleaning windows and floors. Raking millions of pine needles into giant piles. Clara would flutter here and there with quicksilver spraying form every pore. Returning to the Baia of the Butteri was like getting her reins back, after months of being on my leash. By the same token, seeing how eager she was hurt me, as if I had not been enough for her and she couldn't wait to get out from under my thumb. But I tried not to pull long faces or sulk. We would hardly say a word on our way home in the evening and by the time we got there, we were dead on our feet. The silence gave me the opportunity to dwell on the image of one of the builders who, unlike his companions, was quite brazen and had taken up the habit of stripping off his T-shirt at midday to show off his sculpted-iron physique. The show mesmerized men, too, even though we didn't have the same tendencies as that Filippo we'd run into at the Tredici Gobbi. He looked like Rambo, only slimmer. And he wore a Marine's metal dog tag that glittered.

My eyes would dart over to Clara and sometimes I would catch her in the act. She would be standing there somewhere on the veranda we were still setting up, momentarily but blatantly overwhelmed by his good looks. The agony of having to smile started all over again. One day, though, I did something crazy. I was watching the Albanian idol piling up his tools and picking them up in a bundle to take to the storeroom at the back of the restaurant near the freezer. I was the only one to see the shiny tag come off and fall on the ground. I made my move right away, as if I had been guided by another me. I went to the middle of the clearing and pretended to tie my shoelace. As I pulled myself up, I slid the glittering trinket into my pocket. And walked off.

I thought about it the whole way home. I didn't know what had taken hold of me and I didn't care. All I could see was Clara in the flagrant act of letting her eyes wander towards that young man with a low forehead and the body of an Achilles. Since I was jealous as hell, the image was followed by other more horrifying scenes: him and her, fucking on the sly, making the most of the fact that we were all engaged in our chores. One in particular made my blood boil but excited me at the same time: the two of them holed up somewhere looking at me as they fucked. Exactly as I had done all those months ago with her and a little blond boy.

I hid the dog tag at the bottom of a drawer. The idea was to sniff out whether my beautiful Gorgon ever found it. Would she have the stomach to tell me, or would she keep it to herself having no idea how that gewgaw ended up in the middle of all our clothes? I was testing her. There were moments when the idea of finding out she was having an affair felt perversely pleasurable. If, on the other hand, there was no evidence of her infidelity, I would simply mumble something about having found the medal on the dirt track leading to the campsite and who knows how it had gotten there . . . People who are sick with love have been known to set worse traps.

And yet, from the outside, I looked like an altar boy. The Samuele that Clara was dealing with was calm and relaxed and not at all bogged down by the meaningless manias he'd suffered from in the early days. But inside there were a thousand battles raging. All it took was an involuntary gesture of detachment on her part for me to interpret it immediately as a desire to get away from me. It was enough to see her rapt in the pages of a book for an alien me, who still lived in the dark, to sharpen his weapons. "Do you see?" the creature would whisper in my ear. "She's looking for something somewhere else." And my insides would start churning.

But my facade held up and, in appearance at least, we were going through a good spell as the Baia dei Butteri started taking in the first bookings. When the builders left, for a moment I thought I'd been an idiot. Only for it to start again a second later when the campsite filled up with losers from inland rolling down to the seaside for weekends. Every male of the species who flocked to the coast would be locking eyes with Clara. I often had to put up with crass comments that I downed like glasses of quicklime as I carried on my job as a handyman with friends in high places. Until, at the end of the shift, we would meet behind the restaurant and smoke in silence to get people's ugliness out of my head. The difference was that, unlike last year, when we lit up, Clara would start talking. "Tell me about Le Case," she would say.

It had become a kind of game. Of my whole long confession

the previous winter, what had stuck in her mind was the strange end concerning a strange place that seemed to hold endless fascination for her. So, I would dive back into my memory and look for characters and old stories that in another lifetime I had heard from Nonna Esedra, or appropriated as I had wandered the streets in the old town. After a pause of a few seconds, I would begin, "I was just a kid but there were still rumors going around about the Isastia widow . . . " Her jaw would drop as she listened. In some cases, I scraped the bottom of my barrel of experience so hard that I came up with unexpected details. Meanwhile, I carried on painting an extraordinary fresco that Clara loved losing herself in. "Are you making it up?" she would ask me incredulously every now and again, her eyes as bright as headlights. I shook my head. Lying a little, of course. But apart from a few improvised additions, the pedigree of Le Case was there in all its abomination. And she was enthralled.

We entered those rooms on the wave of my memories which were almost entirely untouched. We joined the dots of all the different characters' lives as if we were deciphering a rebus puzzle. The result was a description of a locale where everything stayed in its place, suspended in the fog of millennia. I came from there.

There were dwarves and murderers, brigands and madmen. Lovers torn apart at the peak of their affairs, monsters of solitude . . . Clara wallowed in the stories and eventually learned to call everyone by name. The great thing was that, by telling the story through the eyes of the kid I was, at a time when I observed everything and registered every detail, I was able to blend into the kinks of that circus of death .There were even some funny moments when I felt a kind of pride at having survived the mess, which was starting to take on the semblance of a legend. After all, the place was in my blood and, although I hated to admit it, everything about me spoke of that town, from the absolute good to the god-awful that rips at your flesh.

Sometimes we would have little fights when she would beg me to take her up to the old town in the afternoon and I would shake my head reluctantly, pretending to be less pissed off than I felt. Mario had become her hero. And she would have paid anything to meet Mariella or Don Lauro face to face, even for a second. She longed to test the deaf-mute dwarf sister or sit across from my old chess master and move a random piece.

I enjoyed seeing her so in love with the vocation that is life because it was as if it confirmed the sentiment for me. But the fact was that I couldn't contemplate the idea of going beyond the Due Porte and tackling the alleyways of the old town. The idea of going there and not seeing Nonna Esedra out of breath on the steps that led up to Via dell'Incrociata was enough to cleave me in two.

Clara would come out of the blue with phrases that took my breath away. "I was thinking," she said one day. "Le Case is female: she never forgets." Or, suddenly appearing at our bedroom door, she would say, "I've worked it out. I know who found the winning lottery ticket . . . " And she would knock me sideways with her wild eyes as she joined up all the dots, making absurd connections she cared passionately about. Her hypotheses usually got mixed up with the truth, adding to the shroud of mystery and clandestine double lives. "I swear," she would say, looking bemused by the number of irons in the fire, "I'd go and live in a place that like that in a flash." Then one evening she had a moment of inspiration. She whispered the words almost like a sleepwalker. "We should write it all down."

It was the subject of the season. I kept at bay all the hungry looks she received from the pot-bellied, delicate-heeled wrecks from up north who rolled in here every Monday. She started taking notes instead of practicing her signature endlessly, while the usual bloodbath took place on the veranda over dinner. "Leave your thoughts at home," I would say to her, making her start. Our gazes would meet between a dish of fried seafood and another of octopus and potatoes for a table of seven. And we smiled in unison.

I watched her feverish progress without imagining that a mad project of the kind could enrapture her to the point that she couldn't sleep even after walking miles during a double shift at the restaurant. And yet, it happened and the sheets of paper piled up. They were mostly odd phrases jotted here and there, jottings without a beginning or an end, with asterisks and crossings-out everywhere. Sometimes Clara would stop in the middle of lunch, which the staff ate early while some of the bumpkins were still in the bar ordering their cappuccino. She would take out her notebook and write a couple of words down, circling them with conviction. "This is really important," she would say. Then she would start eating again slowly, with the air of someone who can see things in the far distance.

We hardly spoke about anything else and by that point, the whole project was starting to come out of my ears. She had taken so many notes that she had filled three books and new underground passages continued to come to the fore. She was looking for symbols. Or she was creating them. A hundred days like this, with the summer pressing down on us. Idiotic long afternoons that went by in slow motion without ever extinguishing the flame of Le Case. If anything, it burned brighter. Until it was time for the end-of-season party and we were both dazed and confused, the effect of a whole tourist season spent with the scum of the earth.

Two musicians had been hired for the occasion. She was Cuban and roused the rabble by inciting them to dance. He was so fat he looked like half his head had been eaten up by his neck. Like the guy from Puglia the previous year, he was pretending to play the keyboard. Meanwhile, everyone was filling the plastic glasses that a smiling Beppe handed out with sangria from the usual vat.

Instead of secretly having sex behind the bamboo fence, we

spent that fifteenth of September at a table of our own that we had carried over to the sand. The jetty was lit up with construction work underway, as sulfur was unloaded from the umpteenth Spanish tanker moored there since that afternoon. The towers were so bright it was still daytime in half the region, ruining the sad fizzles of fireworks that Alarico had bought for the party. Clara went through her notebooks obsessively, turning the pages back and forth. "There's a gap here," she would say, pointing at a place on the page. Or: "This character can stay in the background. I'll make them appear here and there as the others talk about them. What do you think?"

I yawned. I had the weight of a whole summer at the restaurant on my shoulders, the last month without a single day off. All I could think about was that I would be able to sleep in the following morning, and I still couldn't believe it. Clara gave me a little dig with her elbow. "I like the idea of Le Case being a kind of monster," she muttered wistfully. Then she snapped out of it and said excitedly, "Is it devouring its inhabitants or are the inhabitants slowly tearing it to pieces?"

* * *

A monstrous gust of wind loosens the old shutters, which suddenly slam open. The crash is tremendous: the right shutter is lifted off its hinges and carried away by the maelstrom. The other one keeps on flapping, the hinges hardly holding. It makes me think of a wounded animal writhing so much it tightens the trap. Eleonora doesn't even notice. She carries on sleeping face down on the pillow. No amount of destruction could rouse her. I breathe as softly as I can so as not to break the spell. Her sleep is magic but as fragile as glass: if she opens her eyes everything will shatter, taking us along with it. So, I lie there frozen, keeping vigil over this suspended moment while all around us every atom seems to be gradually disintegrating.

The lampshade is swinging wildly. The creaking noise is ghostly and, as it sways, it scatters flakes of paint over our bodies which tickle our skin. The lightning bolts actually light up the room, giant camera flashes that flush out our desperate intimacy, snapshots that strip us down to the bone. And at the same time sculpt our presence here in eternity.

We decided on Corsica because the forecast said there would be bad weather for ten days straight. "The geniuses can't be right so far in advance," I said to begin with. I didn't want there to be any risk of the sun coming out halfway through our trip. Clara shrugged. "It says one hundred percent rain until Thursday. That's encouraging."

The sea was flat as a table in Livorno, despite the low, purple clouds on the horizon. It was great being on the deck as we sailed out, the wind whipping against us. All the other passengers were holed inside like moles as we felt an anticipation of the autumn on our faces. After the sweat baths of the summer, it felt like a dream having to pull our jacket collars up over our ears. We went and hid on the highest deck in a protected corner where we could at least talk over the wind without eating our words. For no particular reason, I said, "This is the first time I've been on vacation." I regretted it right away because Clara planted a pair of eyes on me that expressed a combination of confusion and pity. And maybe even fear. Then she took my arm and pulled me down to sit with my back against the vibrating iron of the ferry. "I brought something," she said with an expression on her face I'd never seen before. "Don't tease me, though."

Hearing her read the first pages made me feel bad. Then good. Then bad again . . . Maybe it was the long wave which kept rolling back unexpectedly that was making me feel giddy. In the meantime, there she was ransacking me. Worse, crushing me out there on the uppermost deck. Because reading about Le Case was equivalent to reading about me.

I listened to the story of Divo and the little retard and I felt as though they were molecules that had been injected into my blood at birth. Voices I had buried were being brought back to life by my girlfriend's pen. There were some scenes that tipped over a cliff edge of the imagination but mostly, its natural bent was all there. I recognized the place.

She went on for an hour or so. Then she stopped and we let a few moments go by without saying anything as the ferry continued to slice the sea in two. "Do you like it?" she asked softly. I wanted to answer with another question, "When did you write this stuff?" Because we'd been shoulder to shoulder for months and I'd never seen her with a pen in her hand, except for sudden occasional outbursts of writing in her notebook. But there she was with four whole chapters in her hand. This meant that if she wanted, she could do anything without my knowledge. I looked at her. She frowned. I stopped and held her there, her face in my hands, in silence. We stayed in that position for a long time, letting ourselves be rocked to the sound of clanging iron.

Corsica welcomed us with weather that would be considered lovely in November. We drove off in the canary-yellow Renault, desperate for a road trip and solitude. We enjoyed stopping off at stormy beaches or observation points to gaze out at the rocky giants pulling themselves up out of the sea. We had dinner in small-town restaurants. We slept in godforsaken inns. The following morning, we would go into the streets and mingle with the locals of some town who were busy with their little routines and it really felt as though we were in another world. Our aim was to drive all the way around the island, discovering peaks and crags that suddenly hair-pinned back to the sea. I was in love with the west coast because it gave me the impression that I was safely out of sight of Maremma, which I had never really left before. On the third day, when I saw a road sign for Grosseto-Prugna, I felt my blood run cold. "I can never get away from the place," I thought to myself, filled with fear. Before she got it into her head to go and take a look, I said loudly, "Please go on."

Le Case traveled with us. Eventually, those first pages set me alight, too: something was really happening. Clara begged me for more details, and I filled a whole leg of our trip with my talk. It was good for me because it was a little like looking myself in the eye. I was finally dealing with that giant baggage of grief I had been dragging around forever.

Whenever we weren't busy trying to find our way through some little village or other, it immediately became the subject of our conversation. We would sit in a tavern and order a glass of wine first thing. Then she would take out her travel notebook. She would take the top off her biro with her teeth. "Tell me about Calamaio," she would start. "What was he like?" Or, looking over at the squat tavern keeper behind the counter, "Do you think our Maso looks a little like him?" *Our* Maso, she would always say.

I began to think she was doing it for me. Maybe she thought I had been building a high wall for years and seeing the barrier on paper in the form of a story would do me good. This was why I didn't try and wriggle my way out. This was also why I showed my gratitude to her by taking part in the experiment.

There was a day when the heavens decided never to stop raining again, and that day we discovered the Bonifacio cliffs. The viewpoint was deserted and so was the old citadel. It felt like a divinity had prepared the place especially for us. I looked at the houses perched on the edge of the steep drop. And the seagulls, like lost souls mewling loudly as gusts of wind blew them off the cliff face. We were soaked. Freezing cold. But we didn't want to get up and leave behind that landscape, which was being shaped by wind and sea before our eyes. For a moment I was completely engrossed in looking at the rock stacks, almost in a trance. They looked as though they were setting off on a procession, the folds of their age-old tunics flapping in the storm. Until I was thrown back by a particularly strong gust. I came to my senses and looked around me. Clara had gone.

* * *

The tremor was so strong that the bed moved about six inches to one side. The rock that Le Case is perched on is gurgling, as if a snake of lava were slithering under our feet. Then in a flash, the wind rips the second shutter off its hinges. It flies away without a sound, sucked up by the whirling air currents. Leaving between us and the cataclysm nothing but a thin pane of glass.

They found her two days later wedged between the rocks.

There were people speaking to me, but it felt as if they were all behind thick glass, where the faces looked like washed-out shapes with no eyes or mouths. The only thing inside me was the memory of her last words in the ancient alleys. She had stopped near an old doorway, staring into the distance. "How could I have missed this? It's unforgiveable," she had said, grabbing her notebook. And she had started writing. "The girl with Amico Fritz. At the end of the war. The one in the hut. What happened to her? How is it possible that she never recognized the man she had once loved who reappeared disguised as someone else? Tempesti is famous later on. There are articles in the papers about him and all the rest." This was what we were talking about when we suddenly came out onto the viewpoint that left us both breathless. Clara had taken out her camera rushing towards to the parapet.

Face after indistinguishable face fired questions at me. They mixed with sleep and delirium. There were times when I felt everything had gone so dark that I had finally died. Or I had to combat an unhealthy reaction as I said to myself, like the devil, "Clara has gone. I'm free."

Over and over, they asked me, sometimes harshly, on an endless loop, whether I had been the one to push her over the edge. Every time it was like a rifle shot in the head. "I was looking at the giants," I managed to mumble, my voice sounding like it was coming from another room.

In the meantime, they turned Via dell'Uranio inside out as I lay there numbly on the sofa. They were looking for proof. A motive. Something that would justify something so terrible. Clara had been hale and hearty, mentally and physically. The idea that she might have thrown herself off the cliffs was rejected right away. Until the dog tag turned up at the bottom of a drawer. The first thing they did was stick it under my nose. "Do you know this guy?" they asked.

There was a first and last name that were impossible to pronounce embossed on it. They must have seen from my expression that it wasn't any old trinket. I almost burst out laughing. Eventually, I confessed. "I put it there." It was the truth.

Phone calls were made. There was no point insisting that I had taken it on a whim out of jealousy and that they were reading too much into it. But the engines of conjecture were already revving up. Everybody wanted the case solved yesterday and it felt as though I was slipping into a trap, and I didn't care one bit.

The builder admitted it right away. Yes, he had had an affair with the girl who had fallen off the cliff at the beginning of the season. They hadn't had feelings for one another. It had just been sex. No more than three times. Four, at the most. Well, maybe five but he wasn't sure. He said he had given the girl the dog tag.

"He's lying," I said, always followed by a strange silence. Even the fresh-faced lawyer they had fobbed off on me gave me weird looks. Because in everyone's eyes, the case was closed. Months ago, I had discovered the affair, waited until late September to make my move, holding out until the right moment, far from home and with nobody looking, before giving vent to my urge for revenge by shoving the two-faced bitch off the viewpoint. There were lots of witness statements from friends of hers: I was a gloomy and obsessive type, and I had never wanted to be a part of their gang. The one with the sharpest teeth was Camilla, who had been out to drink my blood from the start.

These things happened and that was that. I returned to my old perspective as a bystander, light years away, detached from the world. By the end, I could hardly say a word. Unlike the newspapers, which trumpeted their versions in banner headlines. They had found a little tasty morsel to tear to pieces, a distraction from the cosmic boredom of the provinces, where they only ever sold the odd copy here and there. They were baying for blood: before my trial I should be in locked up in Via Saffi with four turns of the key to give me a foretaste of the jail where I would be spending the next thirty years. Clutches of people gathered under my window and yelled curses up at me. Then one day I saw the builder on the television. He was sitting in one of those afternoon-TV pseudo-living rooms stuffed with pathetic women pickled in poison who happily produce tears on demand. I heard such terrible lies that my blood started pumping. Incited by the anchor woman, the monster described Clara his way, inventing an affair that gave the women in the studio hot flushes. He wasn't even a good actor. At a certain point he said that if he had known what was going to happen, he would never have touched the beautiful girl. He said it looking straight at the camera and holding my eyes. Somehow, he managed to make me feel guilty. He even pulled a sulky face. With a round of applause for his efforts. A few days later, I saw him bare-chested on a billboard advertising a designer jeans label. The slogan was, "Pick the fruit of your passion." That was when I lost it. I took what little savings I had and fled the apartment in Viale Uranio, even though I was under house arrest.

To begin with, I didn't think of going to Le Case. My main concern was to escape the trap. The motorbike glided over the asphalt, almost blindly negotiating turns and junctions. Until I found myself on the ring road without knowing how I had gotten there. Only then did I see the peaks in the distance beyond the plain that used to be full of sulfur. I changed gears. Then I accelerated so hard I almost dislocated my wrist.

* * *

The wind stops so suddenly that for a moment I sit there, orphaned by my senses. The silence it triggers is deadly. The rain falls vertically, gradually taking possession of the scene. Other noises start to make themselves heard: moans and clicks that echo as if we were in the belly of a galleon shipwrecked after the storm of the century. Then from a distance, the rumbling of a landslide that makes the windowpanes shake. Eleonora is breathing deeply, immersed in her limbo. Miles away, a piece of the world seems to be breaking off the crust of the earth and falling suddenly who knows where.

Le Case was deserted. I stood there under the last porticoes at the top of the road for hours. I could feel my blood pumping through me in waves. My escape had been so precipitate that I had nearly knocked a kid down who was walking in the middle of the road on one of the last bends before the town, right past the church. Now I was giddy from the journey. My feet didn't even feel like they touched the ground.

As well as my motorbike key, on the carabiner I was fiddling with in my hands there were still the keys to Via Roma. For some reason, I had never made up my mind to get rid of them. There were the newer, flat ones as well as the much older one for Via dell'Incrociata, which had become a kind of lucky charm for me. All the most important moves in my life were represented in that measly set.

Eventually, I decided. I set off, putting one foot in front of the other like an automaton. I walked across the little patio and stuck the key in the rusty lock. It felt like stabbing a giant in the chest with a dagger. Then I turned it. I had to fiddle a little until I heard the first click. The sound rang inside my ears rather than outside.

When I opened the door, the house responded with a waft of musty air in my face, like the puff of a sleeping dragon. I was almost tempted to turn around, make my way back down from the mountains in a hurry, and hole myself up in Viale Uranio again. Instead, I gathered my courage and crossed the threshold.

Everything was there under a veil of dust. It looked like a cloak of protection to keep me away: I was the unwanted molecule. The smells. The forgotten details that conjured up clear images like flares, taking my breath away. One of the chairs at the table was pulled out a little, as if someone had just gotten up and left the place.

I knew perfectly well that they would soon be coming to get me. I wouldn't resist, as I'd been doing all my life. For the moment, all I needed to do in that old nest of mine, which had sunk deep into the silence of the old town, was to get my breath back. The silence. I realized maybe that was what I had been looking for when I had come here like a shot. I touched the switch and the old lamp came to life, though it seemed to think about it first, gasping for life, as if it flickered with the last remnants of electricity that had accumulated over a decade in the wires. But the light went on. I had gone on paying the bills for Via dell'Incrociata, a commitment I kept over the years even though I had to eat out of tin cans to afford it. Because maybe I knew deep in my heart that I was destined to return.

I saw the master bedroom in the shadows. That was where I had kept vigil over Nonna Esedra for a whole night. There were the same flowery bedcovers. The mirror was still covered by a white sheet that had turned into an old rag. I went and sat on the edge of the mattress facing the wall and felt as though I might hear her voice at my moment, "Samuele, come down. It's supper time!" Then I let myself fall back, releasing a cloud of dust. And I stayed in that position, staring at the dark ceiling and waiting for the carabinieri to show up.

But they didn't come. I spent the whole afternoon sitting at the table, wrapped up in my jacket watching the shadows change as I waited. I didn't move until darkness fell over Le Case. Then I went down to the store.

Eleonora. Seeing her there at the counter of the old grocery store was like God's idea of a joke. There she was, a rare bloom growing in a crack of the highest crag of a barren outcrop . . . We barely exchanged a glance.

On the third day, I reached the conclusion that the carabinieri must be scouring the streets, taking for granted that I wouldn't be so stupid as to come and hide here of all places. It was anyway a matter of time: as soon as I went out, people would see me. I was in a place where everyone had TVs chained around their necks, bleating in distress to be distracted from the torture of a life where nothing ever happened. People who would be willing to murder one of their parents just so they could pick up the phone and feel like the protagonists of an event for a change. Especially if there is a glint of metal handcuffs.

There was another possible explanation: maybe the person in charge already knew where I was and had decided not to make a song and dance about it. After all, skulking in the belly of that old town dug into the rock was no different to being under house arrest.

I would step out of the house like a ghost, always at the same time. I walked fast, hugging the walls, and hugging the walls I would return three minutes later with a few groceries. I had no idea how long this getaway would last. In the meantime, I took care of the house as best I could. I lifted tons of dust polishing the old frames. I scraped the crud off the windows and mirrors. I washed the floors and whacked the blankets. It helped keep me sane. Because scrubbing away the dirt of the house was like scrubbing away a different kind of dirt that I had been carrying for years under my skin. There were some terrible moments when I would suddenly look at everything from another perspective. Maybe, without realizing it, I was preparing myself to be devoured by the mountain town just like everyone else. In her last months, Clara and I had been playing a dangerous game in which we had amused ourselves by moving the kind of catastrophic lives that abound in the boondocks like pieces on a board. "We were asking for it," I kept on thinking, and my blood turned to ice on the spot. Because in the end, Le Case had answered.

What little I was able to reap from this existence came from the clean-faced, skittish young girl who, like me, had ended up in this purgatory without a way out. She was my only light. The only gleam to shine through the fog in this place that never lifts until midday, and then floats back at four in the afternoon to shroud the alleyways. She would come into my mind at random moments during the day, interrupting my empty thoughts. It made it possible to distance myself from my despair. Then I would immediately regret it and could hardly forgive myself. In the end, I told myself it was normal: we were the only young people in town. Maybe it would help to talk to someone from a similar world to mine, at least in terms of age. Someone who hadn't had the millstone of the old town tied around their neck all their lives. Whatever the case, it was aberrant of me to want to make contact because the girl certainly knew who the guy who had been making the bell on the door to the grocery store ring at five every afternoon was. Where he came from. And why. In fact, she would always find a reason not to look up if per chance she was caught having to serve me. She grew twitchy, she dropped everything.

Then, one day, I saw a silhouette appear at the bottom of the street.

* * *

The umpteenth aftershock shakes a picture off the wall. The frame is old and the four-foot fall is enough to smash it to pieces. But I'm not sorry. In fact, for a moment, it almost makes me smile . . . When I was a kid, I would always stop and look at that print of a peasant boy with a straw hat and a sheaf of wheat on his shoulder, which was already faded back then. "He looks just like you," Nonna Esedra used to say when she saw me staring at the picture. Maybe she was saying it just to tease me a little. "No way," I answered firmly. I would stare at the boy with all my might but there was nothing about him that resembled what I saw in the mirror. There was one thing that drove me especially crazy: the boy was smiling. He was bright-eyed and happy-go-lucky. The idea of putting on a dumb face like that made me burn with shame. I couldn't explain it: did I really go around looking like that? If so, the urchins up in the old town, who were always ready to hurl their stupid insults at me, had been right. Usually, they would take it out on my mother, having heard about her from their parents or who knows who. They thought it would hurt me more if they brought her into the picture. But I didn't care a fig. Sometimes, I would catch Nonna Esedra holding a photo. If she saw me anywhere near, she would pull a simpering, sad face. "When she comes back, I have a few bones to pick with her," she would say solemnly, even though she looked like she was about to crack a joke. "As far as I'm concerned, she's fine where she is," I would always answer. Then I would go and get a glass of milk without feeling any emotion at all.

Eleonora is a watershed, dividing my life into two parts: before her and after her. Despite the disasters we had both attracted to ourselves, suddenly together we were made new. And forgiven. And important. Two distant points that had always sought one another out and that despite everything had finally collided in Via dell'Incrociata. Against all odds.

Sometimes I would tell her, "We had to go through tragedies to get to where we are now." She would change the subject immediately or silence me with a kiss. She was so bountiful that she accepted me as I was, stripping away everything I had been in the past.

As days went by, my fear of losing her became my primary illness, replacing everything else. I managed to handle it, but I couldn't control it: whether I struggled against it or not, it was a wave that dragged me out in its wake. And I had no idea what was going on in the real world outside. How wide the mouth of the trap was. At Le Case, cell phones were useless objects, and the firing line of staring eyes on the way out of the gates to the newsstand didn't bother me; so I went to get a newspaper to see if they were still eviscerating me.

We lived there floating on a cloud of love. Eleonora crept out of the store, raced up the road, and dived into my door. There were days when the sheer fact that she was in front of me made me think my life was perfect. That this was the only place I was supposed to be. With her beside me.

The agonies of Saturdays were the worst. The idea that we wouldn't be able to see one another for two whole days stopped us in our tracks. We were so distressed that we couldn't squeeze out a single word. Not to mention the threat of the carabinieri coming at any moment to put me in the dock, which would be followed by a cold cell. I resisted. I sucked up every moment trying with all my might to imprint it on my mind: It would be my gold standard. Gold that was so dazzling that it would help me get through the dark days.

The day Eleonora came to the house announcing she would never leave, I thought I was done for. An image sprang to my mind: me, a runaway, holed up in my old house with another fugitive. I couldn't even contemplate what the papers would say about the news. Imagining Camilla, that tenebrous pachyderm, commenting "He got over Clara quickly enough," was enough. I could practically hear her voice. Meanwhile, Eleonora begged me not to send her back to the farmhouse, where she, too, had been caught in a trap. She couldn't stay there one minute longer. That was when I realized.

There was a bigger picture that was taking shape in our minds. In most people's eyes, our love would look blasphemous, betraying the memory of the dead, aside from anything else. Two repugnant creatures who had found one another by chance in the meanders of a small town and sniffed each other out like ogres. We had become fused into one and the world was trying to abort us rather than thank us. Our kisses were good for the plants and the birds. We shed so much light into the world that even the Divo Valenti with his betrayed-Fascist jaw benefited from it without realizing it. But we had to fight.

We went onto the battlefield armed to the teeth. Silence. Patience. When I was out, Eleonora lived in darkness. Immobility. "Let's leave tonight," she said every day. I grabbed her hands. "We need to let the tsunami die down," I muttered. "They're looking for you everywhere." Then Viale Uranio came to mind. I couldn't believe that nobody had rushed up to Le Case to interrogate me yet again about Clara. By that point, curtains twitched at every window as I walked by. Rumors were rife. All someone needed to do was call the nephew of a friend and a gaggle of journalists would be outside my door. But it didn't happen. It was as if I had been forgotten. "Let's wait two more days," I said.

In the meantime, I didn't change my routine. Few, quick outings. Head down. Words whittled down to the bone. One evening, as I was leaving the store, I nearly bumped into an old man looking completely lost. I overtook him quickly and made my escape under the porticoes. When I got back home, I told her right away, even though Eleonora wouldn't know who I was talking about. "I saw Tempesti."

I had only realized it was him afterwards, on my way home. Substituting his face for the image I had preserved of him back from the days of the Due Porte had been a difficult exercise. The years had pulverized him and his expression had been reduced to pure bafflement. "The drunkard, you mean?" she said jokingly. But she soon realized it was not a laughing matter for me: I was devastated. That man had been the only father I had ever known and there he was, a ruin of his former self. There was nothing left. Le Case had sucked the life out of him and turned him into a zombie. There had been another chance meeting, too, right at the end of the porticoes, at the last corner before going up Via dell'Incrociata: the deaf-mute dwarf sister had suddenly materialized. As usual, I looked down and kept on walking to avoid meeting her eyes. But she stood in my path. It was impossible not to raise my eyes to that deformed little individual. Our gazes locked for a moment. "They've called the carabinieri." In her outlandish voice, like a decrepit little girl's, the words echoed in the penumbra. For a second, the idea that it had been the walls of Le Case to speak flashed through my mind. Then the dwarf scuttled away, ignoring me completely. I started back on my way thinking I must have dreamt everything.

Eleonora gazed at me, suddenly serious. She was sorry she had trivialized something that was as important to me as meeting my old chess master and seeing him ruined like that. I didn't tell her about the dwarf. But I was suddenly lifted by the crest of a wave of inspiration. "Le Case exists for one reason only: for us to leave as soon as possible." I grabbed her hands and said, "Let's go right now."

* * *

The rain stops, too. In fact, suddenly, everything stops. There are still drops and water spilling from the gutters. The last shudders of something that is settling down. Even the distant gurgling has come to an end. The sky is the only thing that is still alive: an infinite sea of silent lightning bolts. There is a peculiar red glow that tinges the low-lying clouds. The light filtering into the room looks like sunset and sunrise at the same time. Holding the longest night in the world prisoner.

The first few times, Dr. Palazzesi tried to explain what had happened in plain words. "There was a chase and you flew off a hairpin bend. They had to come in with a helicopter to get you."

I was in a hospital room. After weeks of immobility, my body felt like a piece of granite. And there was a continuous rumble that sounded like it came from a great distance, like an engine running at top speed but never getting any closer.

After the first day I managed to croak, "Where is Eleonora?"

"You need to rest," the doctor answered. Then he nodded at the nurse, who was wielding a ready-prepared syringe.

I fell asleep often but when I opened my eyes, I was still there. "They were following us," I mumbled with difficulty, hoping someone responsible would go and get the bastards. But nothing happened. They just stuck a glass with an inch of water in it under my nose and said, "Drink this."

Strange days, in total suspension. Everything felt like it was only half-said and my thoughts were the same: they derailed. Or worse, they evaporated and got lost. Leaving me there numb from the trauma of waking up and groggy with drugs.

I gradually got my strength back, however, and with my strength came a modicum of clarity, even though I still felt as though I was a little inside and a little outside my body. After the routine checks, Dr. Palazzesi would make everyone leave the room. He would grab a chair and put it next to my bed to talk to me for a bit. All the while, he'd be scribbling in a notebook he kept on his knee. I found this habit odd, as if he were a shrink rather than the chief physician looking after a random patient in his hospital. It felt like I was being paid special attention. Someone in his position was taking the trouble to spend time with me and only leaving me with others when strictly necessary. "Why are there two carabinieri outside?" I asked him every now and again. "I'm not the one they should be looking for." The doctor ignored my questions and urged me to speak. He took advantage my befuddled state of mind, which often led me to open my mouth without my commanding it. The thoughts piled up and I would follow the flow of the first one I managed to grasp hold of. But again, I would go nose over. My sentences sometimes hit a wall of oblivion, as if they had driven into a dead end. "Why was I saying this?" I would ask, disoriented and immediately enveloped in a giant mass of fatigue. At the same time, I had to fight a creeping sense of terror: I realized I was unable to keep a logical argument going without sinking into quicksand. Dr. Palazzesi continued to encourage me. "After a long sleep like yours, your brain needs to be stretched a little, too."

The image I was able to hold on to the longest was that of Eleonora. I missed her terribly, and I suspected that she had not survived the crash, and these two feelings triggered unimaginable peaks of agony. But they went on ignoring my crucial questions. Or maybe they had answered them, and I had simply forgotten after dozing off. If I talked about her, I didn't lose my thread. Except that I was immediately crushed by anxiety. Where was she? Were they hiding something from me? I would fly into fits of rage, which would leave me completely drained. Then I would give in and let myself sink into a strange twilight sleep where incomprehensible images were superimposed with lightning flashes, like the delirium of a high fever. One day, Dr. Palazzesi set the chair by my bed as usual. But instead of the usual pleasantries to break the ice, he stared at me for a second with unusual intensity. Then he said, "I don't know if you're ready. At this point, the only way of knowing is to try."

I was told a strange story about being intercepted by a police car in the Ribolla valley. The chase continued all the way up the winding, mountainous road. Until at the umpteenth hairpin bend, I ended up in the ravine after my motorbike skidded on a scattering of grit and flew off the road like a rocket.

"This is how the accident unfolded," the doctor said at the end of his story. "You were lucky."

I looked at him for a moment. I burst out laughing. "You're getting me mixed up with someone else," I said. And it was perfectly possible given that those roads were more dangerous than the devil.

Dr. Palazzesi had to look down at his notes. When he looked back up at me his expression had grown dark. "I know, you're convinced you've had a certain experience. It happens sometimes. It's the mind's way of protecting itself."

I, too, had suddenly grown serious. I was no longer amused. He sighed deeply and went on. "About two months ago, you left your apartment in Viale Uranio, breaking the house arrest that had been imposed on you. The police caught up with you a little later. There was a chase. You may not even realize you had a crash . . . That was the moment of interruption. The reality is that you were thrown into a ravine. In your imagination, you reached Le Case and that was that."

I was really scared at that point. "You're wrong. I have no idea where Viale Uranio is . . . "

Dr. Palazzesi smiled mildly. "It's called retrograde amnesia.

From what you have been saying, it would appear you have erased ten years of your past. But with a bit of patience, you'll see that."

I had had enough of the baloney. "Where is Eleonora?"

Silence fell over the room. He looked at me with ice-cold eyes. Then I heard him say, "Samuele, the girl you are talking about doesn't exist. She's just a false memory."

That was when I went apeshit. To the extent that the doctor had to call the nurses and have me restrained.

* * *

I try moving. As soon as I shift my weight onto my elbow, the bedsprings sound an alarm in the form of a thousand creaks. In the unnatural silence of Le Case, they sound like the screeching of an out-of-tune violin. Eleonora doesn't react. She's lying there naked and completely relaxed. The dim red light penetrating the room creates a perfect shape. Her curves are highlighted, light touches of a paint brush drawing her outline in the shadows. I finally manage to sit up. I put my heels on the floor and the ice filters through to the bone. With a thrust from the hips, I manage to get out of bed and then I'm standing there in the nude illuminated by the apocalyptic red glow. I take a first step. The cold tiles feel like they are rejecting my presence, as if I were walking on air. That must be how restless spirits move around.

At the time, I couldn't know it, but it was all true. The trauma of coming out of the coma had erased Viale Uranio, the Baia dei Butteri, Corsica. It had canceled Clara, with her Gorgon's hair. The only thing I remembered about that night on the hairpin bends of the hill-top road was the sawmill workers' pickup on my tail . . . until the crash. I couldn't swear on it but in my compulsive revisiting of those last moments I thought

I remembered a wolf peering out of the woods on the side of the road.

People came into the room and saw me lying there, a bundle of nerves. "You're bastards, all of you," I yelled. "You need to wake me up."

There were always two carabinieri outside and they changed shifts every eight hours. There was a young officer with a northern accent who would always poke his head in and look at me with a disgusted look on his face. If there was no one else around, he would say things like, "Your little bitch came to see me in my dreams. I fucked her to my heart's content," And he would give a pelvic thrust.

I missed Eleonora completely. I felt as though I'd been torn to pieces, the prisoner of a dream that didn't make any sense. I waited for sleep to come, hoping I would open my eyes and find I was back in my real life with a beautiful girl I had to save. "You're in denial," Dr. Palazzesi kept saying. "It's understandable. I can see why. On this side, there's not much going for you . . . but sooner or later, you're going to have to deal with it. Accept it. It's just a matter of time." Then he added, "Do you remember how you got to Le Case?"

He kept on asking me as if this were the key to everything. "I was born there," I grunted. At which point I was handed piles of documents attesting to my passage through life. Rental contracts. Short-term jobs from two, three, or more years before. While for me it was crystal clear: Nonna Esedra had only just died. That was why I had gone back to the mountains. I had spent those days in silence tidying up her few possessions. And then I had gone down to the grocery store as usual and I had met her, Eleonora. Their response was more paper. Some articles even said I was suspected of killing a girl out of jealousy. When I saw these, I would usually look around the room. "If you can build up all this evidence, and even have fake news published, it must be a walk in the park," I challenged them.

Dr. Palazzesi was patient. It wasn't just special attention. He really seemed to have taken my situation to heart, and he kept on plucking weird theories out of his notebook as if he were putting together a puzzle that I was clueless to help him with. But it was impossible for me to avoid his interrogations. "I've compared notes with people who know," he would say. "There's no question about it: it's all in your subconscious."

He meant Le Case. My craggy cradle that he knew well, too. "I know what it means to come into this world in the Maremma mountains," he would mumble occasionally. And that was where he grabbed me. That was where he scared me because he seemed genuine. When he talked about his father, who had lost his mind after the explosion at the Camorra mine, his eyes welled up, leaving me breathless as the monitors beeped along to my accelerated heart rate. One day he even mentioned the deaf-mute dwarves he had teased as a kid when he had been part of a gang of bored urchins up in the old town.

The hypothesis that fascinated him the most was always the same and it drove me crazy because he talked about it as if it were evidence. "The crash sent you flying right there, into the alleyways of the old town. You went back to Le Case. It's just that you have created your own version of events. For two months you've been the unconscious god of a place where you imposed your symbols, your memories, the standing or shortcomings you were subjected to or aspired to in the real world. You even created a girl you loved who needed saving."

It was a terrible time, but I slowly learned to manage it without needing to be sedated or restrained. I limited myself to staring at the ceiling and digesting the hogwash being fed to me by a country doctor in search of fame. I didn't bat an eyelid when he got excited by some solution or other and came up with things like, "The crash you remember, the chase with the sawmill gang on your tail, is clearly the product of trauma after regaining consciousness. In your version of Le Case, you died. A moment later, you opened your eyes in this room."

He was so insistent and sure of himself that I sometimes found myself remodulating some of the impressions I had of people I had mixed with in the past. Tempesti, for example, who had been like a father to me. But other men and women, too, whom I only vaguely remembered as secondary characters in a legend that had endured thousands of years.

And yet I still missed Eleonora acutely. Dr. Palazzesi was working with a scalpel, as if he were trying to cut and stitch a new conscience inside me day after day. My love for a girl whose profile was as sharp as a blade wouldn't fade, however many words I was bombarded with and however many mornings I woke up to find myself stuck in the same bed. One day I said it for the umpteenth time, from the heart, "If this is truly my reality, I don't want to be here any longer."

The mornings were the worst. After the shock of waking up, there was the rehabilitation. The carabinieri were there, posted at the door. They even followed me into the bathroom, to which I shuffled slowly. They stayed on the threshold and went on prodding me. The fresh-faced northerner was the one to give me the idea one day. "I'd know how to rehabilitate him," he whispered to his partner. "With a nice jump out of the window."

Ultimately, it wouldn't be to kill myself. It would be to go home. I was stuck in an evil world where I risked spending an eternity locked up in a cell, paying my debt for a crime I didn't think I had committed. A world without Eleonora, which was worse than everything else. I didn't care to live on a planet of that kind. "She's waiting for me," I would whisper from time to time and I didn't care if anyone heard. But sleep was no longer enough to get back there into her arms. I needed an immense leap. Or maybe everything had been a test for me. Was I willing to erase a universe in order to find another one?

I answered this question with an action while I was being

transferred to a room on the top floor reserved for prisoners who had almost fully recovered. Taking them by surprise, I loosened the guards' grip, ran down the corridor, and hurled myself headfirst against the sixth-floor window.

* * *

After two steps, I have to stop and get my breath back, shocked by how weak I am. The feebleness smothers me like smoke and for a moment I feel as if I have gone back to being that undefined thing, a body outlined in clouds. Then there is the dizziness. A sudden instability that I control in no time at all. Maybe because I'm used to the quakes. I've been here in the darkness of my old room for several minutes, with the floor that every now and again seems to turn into a sheet of water. The window is a rectangle of dim light filled with silent flashes. It looks like the gates of Hell. A few more tiles and I'll be able to look down there. To see the whole truth.

Dying is like the blink of an eye. After jumping from the sixth floor, I found myself in Via di Mezzo in the middle of a raging storm. An overcast sky. The street swollen with water higher than my shoes. The first thing I thought was, "I'm back." Words that you should be very careful not to put together into one sentence in Le Case.

I touched my face and looked at my hands over and over again. Maybe I had slipped on that treacherous shiny stone, hitting my head and losing consciousness for half an hour. In the winter it was my favorite warning to Nonna Esedra. "Watch out for those paving stones. They turn into a skating rink with this ice. The poor bastards up here have left enough broken bones along these alleyways, going from street to bed and from bed to grave in twenty minutes."

I had had an obscene dream that felt as though it lasted for days. But I had finally left it behind after a test of my courage. I was there, appreciating the wave of happiness that was washing over me at the idea that I had freed myself of that curse. All I needed to do was run to Via dell'Incrociata and throw myself into Eleonora's arms, saving her from the darkness. I would tell her everything, covering her in kisses, starting with the escape I dreamed of during what must have been a fainting spell. And then, I would say, "Let's do it tonight." I was ready to set out for real, despite the storm. Then something happened.

A bolt of lightning. The crash was so loud the whole street shook. When the darkness returned, I felt my enthusiasm wane. I had started to remember.

It was as if a divinity had funneled a new consciousness into my body. An eye opened wide at the center of my soul and in a flash, I saw the whole story, a bridge of ten years. Worse, a whole lifetime. The very life that Dr. Palazzesi had tried to show me day after day at my bedside in hospital.

Reliving the act of throwing myself into a vacuum almost made me drop to my knees. It had not been a leap of faith. It had begun to look more like a punishment, as if I had been forced to relive Clara's last seconds myself the day that I watched her drop off a cliff. A moment before, she had been standing beside me in the storm looking at a landscape. She had been pointing her camera down, her feet almost lifting off the ground, aiming at the waves crashing against the rocks. All I had done was take a step forward and bend over. All I had managed to do was grab hold of her leg but I had let her go. I hadn't even had time to yell. Or maybe I had yelled but a gust of wind had swallowed it up on the spot. Then I had looked at the giants, caving in to the storm. Until I had come to with a start, blown back by an immense gust of wind. And I had found myself alone.

When I was a boy, Nonna Esedra didn't like seeing me hunched over a chess game. It upset her to see me staring at the board for a whole hour, my hands in my lap, without ever touching a piece. Even when I came home from tournaments laden with cups and medals, she was unimpressed. "God knows what you see in those little squares," she would mutter without expecting any response. As a result, she couldn't stand Tempesti who, in her eyes, filled my head with garbage. "Listening to the gibberish of a desperate man like him is not going to solve your issue with not having a father," she once blurted out. It had hurt her to say it. I could see by the way she was holding back her tears. Then she changed tactic. She would bring me a silver tray with a white napkin folded into four laid out on it. On the white napkin was a small blue pill shaped like a sunflower seed. Handing me a glass half filled with water, would say, "Dr. Salghini has come up with a diagnosis for why you're not sleeping. This will help you go down under until tomorrow morning."

She was convinced it was my insomnia that caused my attacks. They came out of nowhere: I did things and said things and then I would come back to my senses without remembering anything. It happened more often when I was being bullied. Life at school was a case in point because kids of a certain age are animals and I often came home with a note from the teacher or with a suspension letter. It was a double torture: I was accused of doing things I had no memory of or saying things I had no idea about . . . or, maybe, I would punch someone's nose after yet another nasty comment. Or again, I would shout out obscenities at a schoolmate or teacher who happened to be on my street at the wrong time. Nonna Esedra would go and talk to the headmaster with the countenance of an army general. "It's not Samuele's fault," she would say, with me standing next to her. "Those bad boys and sneaky girls are the ones provoking him."

The pills had the desired effect but I lost my talent. They took the scales from my eyes. I grew more solid; I could feel it in the roots of my hair. And I slept like a log. But if someone stuck a chessboard in front of me, my moves were average. There was no magic. My face was drained of color until the evening, when it came back like a warm shiver. The world shifted minutely and I was my old self. I would lock myself in my room and start moving the pieces around but, half an hour or so later, Nonna Esedra would scream up the stairs like a bird of prey: "Supper time. Down you come!" And with desert, came the silver tray.

Taking my medicine didn't change the behavior of those wild packs of kids who bullied me, especially the older ones who lay in wait for me at the back of the bus. But at least I wasn't surrounded and beaten up for something I couldn't even remember. There were even some periods of calm when everybody seemed to forget about me. They kept me at a distance in any case. I had become the weird guy who might pounce at any moment. Even the teachers called me up to the blackboard with a different tone of voice after handing back my homework.

When I played chess, I built new worlds. Both sides were equal to begin with. Then something happened, even by the fourth or fifth move, if not before. Just like life. I loved the matches that surprised me, the ones where I had to use all my skills for both the whites and the blacks. I would lose myself in a labyrinth of opportunities and sacrifices, ruthless strategies and breathless recoveries. I had no use for technique. It was like walking: you don't have to think about it. What I loved about the game was the spectacular battle I raged against a Samuele Radi who was inside me and opposite me at the same time. It was great because I would always win, but I also lost hopelessly every time. All I wanted was to outperform myself, at least there on the old wooden board, where getting stuck was worse than being knocked out by a novice with a checkmate. Just like life.

Nonna Esedra's pills took my shine away. I could easily have tricked her and gone into the bathroom to spit the medication out. But I couldn't keep making trouble for her with my uncontrolled rage. Keeping myself calm put the woman who had brought me up on her own, never wanting for anything, in a good mood. It was important to keep Nonna Esedra happy because she was beginning to feel her age. Good humor was better medicine than the injections she took for her osteoporosis, which was giving her trouble, especially in her hip. Anyway, Dr. Salghini always said my problem would soon go away. He said it was normal at my age, that it was just a way to deal with the trauma of being abandoned.

But it didn't go away, and I was almost twenty. I could feel it in my college room where I took refuge after lectures. I could hear the TV blaring in the sitting room because Mrs. Volpileoni was hard of hearing and didn't know it. I would knock at the door and find her sitting in front of a wooden tray. She would point at the piping hot cup of tea and the box of cookies. "You need fuel for your brain," she would say. Every other day, Nonna Esedra would call at 6 o'clock on the dot. "Have you taken your pill?" she would ask, without even saying hello. "Yes," I would always answer, without ever having to lie. If I ever noticed I had missed a dose, I would immediately take a little sunflower seed out of the packet and wash it down, perhaps with some of that tea I had left on my desk growing mold. I never drank it. As soon as it got dark, I would open the window on the first floor and pour it out onto the quiet road below.

When I was very involved in my studies, or fell asleep without realizing it, I might forget my daily ration. Once, in a lecture, the whole class was looking while the professor called me out. "Do you think you're funny or something?" I gathered up all my things and ran out of the lecture hall without having any idea what I'd done. And I never found out.

One evening, Mrs. Volpileoni came and knocked on my door after her usual ringing. When I opened it, she was standing there looking pained. She looked at me for a second and then, searching for the right words, he said, "Samuele, sit down a minute."

Nonna Esedra had been found on the lower steps of St. Bastian's, which are as high as benches. She looked as though she had been sitting there, like many of the old ladies do at Friday market, resting before setting out on the last leg of the climb up to the old town.

"She looked lost in her thoughts," Divo said when he told me about it, his face tight. "Her eyes were open and everything. 'Nice day, my dear Esedra,' I said to her. There was no answer. So, I tried again, 'Esedra, I'm talking to you. What's so interesting on the ground?' It was a discovery I wish I hadn't had to make . . . She looked lost in her thoughts, that's what she looked like . . . poor Esedra. And then, look what happened."

I felt as if I'd been sent to the slaughterhouse. That was the day I decided to stop taking my medication. I put an end to everything that day. I threw myself into my work and left my rented room at Mrs. Volpileoni's noisy house, where the TV split my eardrums as soon as I walked into the hall. I went to restaurants where I ate and drank too much and I could have been arrested for disturbing the public peace now that I was old enough for handcuffs. And yet, nothing happened. I went back to my den in Via Roma feeling crushed but at least without my medication my light was beginning to shine again. I took the chess pieces out and started rebuilding my universe, in the eternal battle between me and myself. Since I was a little crazy, I had convinced myself that if I managed to beat myself, I would learn the secret that commands things. One of those secrets that can bring back the dead.

* * *

After all the darkness, in front of the window, I have to shut my eyes tight for the flashes reflected on the glass and the blades of white light almost blind me. Silence continues to torture my eardrums. At the same time, there is this floating feeling that is beginning to make me seasick. Then I hear a bell ringing in the clock tower. Just one ring. It reverberates inside me like a hundred earthquakes.

Maybe Nonna Esedra's death was the drug that finally got rid of the trouble I'd lived with all my life. I went through the days keeping my head down, staring at the ceiling in my spare time. Or forcing myself to go for a walk. Grosseto was great because it felt as though it was yelling at me every time that I went out looking depressed, my hands dug down deep into my pockets. It was keeping me in its sights. In the meantime, I looked at the people. From my distant spaceship, I looked at the store windows. Sometimes I even went inside the shopping malls, especially at Christmas when loneliness became an obsession. For the others, not for me. When everyone lives in a pack, a lone wolf is an eyesore. So, I blended in and sometimes I really felt like that drop of poison I had always imagined someone had dropped into the dough of my being. I would stand close to a nice little family staring at the wonders on a shelf. Sometimes I would even brush against the shoulder of a young mother or father who went pale at every bleat of the little dwarf they were carrying. And I would pretend I was one of them. For a few seconds, I would breathe in the air, grasping their names and unique smells. The way the wife smiled, like a cry for help that did my head in. The husband's shaky hands as he looked straight past the trolleys at the emergency doors with their crash bars. In that moment, people saw me as normal. I would say to myself, "This is what it's like to be normal." And it didn't feel like anything special. In fact, getting away from that cozy group was like letting go of a bag of bricks.

One day, during one of these experiments, I felt someone pull my sleeve. I looked down and saw a little boy. He was standing there like me, in an aisle of any one of those giant new, inimitable shopping malls. I looked around. Then I asked, "Are you lost?" He nodded. He was so scared he couldn't even speak. I stared at him for a while. "What's your name?" I asked calmly. "Michele," he somehow managed to answer. "Hi, Michele." I held out my hand. He took it.

Walking along holding little Michele's hand was strange. His heart was thumping like mad; I could almost feel it through his gloves. But I had a drum instead of a chest too, for no reason at all. We walked among all those people and every now and again, people looked kindly at us, especially the older women. I must have looked like a young father. Or a dutiful older brother. We walked past a display of lasers and another of clothes and I saw our reflections. That was when I heard a terrible shriek perforating my eardrums. "Michele!" When I turned around, I saw a woman in her thirties with makeup running down her face. She threw herself on her little boy and pulled him into a tight hug. Then she hugged me. She was sure I was taking the boy to the cash register to make an announcement over the tannoy. She couldn't have known that I was about to walk out and take him away with me.

I had inexplicable fixations like this that took me completely by surprise. Usually, they were things to mull over and not much more. They rarely turned into brazen actions. Like when I got obsessed with Minù, a kitten as white as snow belonging to Mrs. Straccali. She lived on her own, two doors away from me, in a house on the corner of Via Bolzano. She had this cheeky little kitten who would often escape onto the street. One day I found her in a little hut in front of the garage where I had made a den. I took her in. I kept her for two weeks, taking great care of her. In the morning, I would go to the bar to get a milky coffee and see the fat lady, her face drawn with anguish. She asked everybody in the neighborhood whether they had spotted her kitten in the alleyways. Minù would throw herself on the plastic plate, purring loudly. She liked being with me. And I liked controlling the destiny of an old lady, who sat at her window all day checking out the street. Sometimes I even passed under her window on my way to throw the bag with the dirty litter in it in the garbage container near her house. Until one day I put the kitten to the test. I opened the door. But she stayed there all curled up on the sofa. So, I picked her up by the scruff of her neck and took her back to her home. When Mrs. Straccali saw me with her kitten, she almost had a heart attack. She invited me in. I had to struggle for a quarter of an hour because she insisted that she wanted to give me a reward, a hundred lire bill! "If I had millions, I'd hand them over to you!" she squawked, she was so over the moon. In the end, I took the money and that was that.

I used to take people's pleasure away. Aside from the most sensational cases, it was like that with nearly everything. For example, I would create havoc at work at the Bavarian's place. Without anyone seeing, I would swap the forks and the knives if a table had just been carefully laid by Cristina, say, who maybe I liked. She always did what the head waiter told her to do. I knew it was normal but it gave me special pleasure to see her being told off when she swore that she had laid the table as usual. Or I would make my grumpier colleagues fight. In the supermarket, I would slip boxes of some product into old people's bags causing confusion at the cash registers.

I spoiled love affairs by dropping hand-written notes into people's pockets or handbags. I made anonymous calls from the phone box, taking a random number out of the book. I called at all hours of day and night from any area of the city. When someone answered, I would hold the line in silence. After a month I could detect a hint of madness just in the way they said "hello," their voice dying in their throats already at the first syllable. Everybody in the world has ghosts that from one moment to the next might start calling them at unthinkable hours. There were some people who were so exasperated that eventually they would try and make contact, "Mamma, is it you?" Or, "Carlotta, please. Talk to me . . ."

I would make bunches of keys disappear from the counter at the bar when the customer had put them down for a second next to their cup of coffee. Back home I had a collection of miscellaneous objects I lined up on a shelf of my old dresser. I would dust them often. Then I started finding things in my hands without even realizing it.

It would happen just like that. One second, I would be walking along a road. The next, I would open my hand and find an earring in it. Or a bag. Once I realized I was holding the lead of a gray poodle that was trotting happily along beside me. I let go immediately, running across the road at the first corner.

The attacks had started again. They usually only lasted a few moments but without the same consequences as in the past. I would steal things. That was all. And I was never caught. This meant that despite my condition, I was still clear-headed. And detached. One day, walking in the center of town, I suddenly felt something pushing on my leg. I pulled a silver frame out of my pocket. There was an old photo of a good-looking young lad in uniform. When I got back to my den, I looked at it carefully. At the bottom, on the white of the scalloped edge there was a faded inscription that read, "Carlo, 1943." It must have been an important memento and for someone in the family it must have meant a great deal. But more importantly, it didn't feel like something I could have swiped in the street or in a store on the sly. Maybe I had stolen into someone's house.

There was an endless shitstorm brewing inside me. I did everything I could not to let my thoughts go there because if they did, I would be trapped inside questions that were bigger than me. And I felt sorry for myself. I watched all that maneuvering and tried to bring other people down to the same level where I had been stuck for years. Or maybe I hoped to be caught and moved away from the stalemate. I carried on sitting in front of my old chessboard, armed to the teeth, in a battle against an equally motivated other self, to the point that

I was willing to die for that checkmate. Losing seemed to be my only destiny.

And so, I stole things. I dug chinks into other people's lives. It was my only way to force my way out of the cage of my days because otherwise the doors were closing in on me leaving me with no hope. I couldn't stand that prison. It was the supreme sign that had been sizzling like a hot iron brand on the thin skin of my forehead since the day I came into this world. From the day I was abandoned: plucked out of the vacuum of the galaxies and forcefully locked into the box of a difficult life. There was not a single person I could lash out at in revenge. There was everybody. Until one day, there was the unexpected explosion: Clara. With her immense light. The tsunami of her fulfilled life that took me from nowhere to somewhere. And locked me up worse than before.

All I had to do was free myself. As one would do with a Gorgon who may be beautiful but was still a wild animal that could turn you to stone with one look. And then decapitate you.

* * *

The echo of the bell fades slowly. Then the silence returns and as usual, I am orphaned in this void. I decide to open my eyes. And from this window in Via dell'Incrociata, I see the whole truth. It's a terrible view but at the end of the day it brings relief. In my ears I can hear a distant rumbling, even though the Maremma valley stays mute, as if waiting. The glass of the sixth-floor window. The fall. Only to land here again, in this middle earth, in the crawlspace between life and death. Where at least I met love.

From behind me I can hear a rustling. And her voice. "Are you awake?" The earth starts shaking as she speaks. From the red glow in the sky, a distant crash sets the storm off again on this night without end. Almost in its death throes.

Le Case
Via di Mezzo

Divo Valenti waited for the end of the world sitting at the kitchen table with his wife. He was on the point of telling her about a certain note he had found years before with a list of all the men she had entertained. "I felt so sorry for you, Mariella," he would have liked to say. "Living with an obsessive need to be filled up, you spent your whole life like an empty sack . . . " Then then there was a strong tremor and the woman's face crumpled. "Hold my hand," she murmured. He held back, as if tempted to take his revenge right at the end. But then he rested his hand on the table and wove his fingers through hers. Despite everything, there was a big smile on Divo's face, and tears welled in his eyes. Mariella was overwhelmed by a feeling of boundless love. She never managed to express it, though: at that very moment, there was a crash. And the ceiling came down.

* * *

Just outside town, in the last house past the big bend, Graziella Serri spent the last moments of her life with her Tarot cards. Every round, she picked out the same card, as if it had been calling her from the center of the star. The wind was battering the shutters. The thick mud slide that had been snaking down the road for days and had buried the last buttress of the church, made a squelching sound. She was reminded of her Nonna Velia's words when she had taught her how to read the cards. "This is the punishment of arrogance," she would say, pointing at *The Tower.* "We will face harsh punishment due to our lack of humility." Graziella had been no more than a child and she used to run around the house holding the card. "It represents the Tower of Babel," her grandmother would comment as she carefully took it out of her hands. "A symbol of the arrogance and pride of man who desired to rise to compete with the divine. And God himself sent them tumbling down."

On days when the little girl frowned more than usual, Nonna Velia would add, "To put a halt to the blasphemous construction, all God had to do was snap his fingers. And unleash a storm."

* * *

Mario Silvestri took care of his wife to the last, though his heart was not in it. He had been reeled in by a girl's smile. "Come on, one more drop of soup," he said, bringing the spoon closer to Adelaide's face, which already looked like a skull. She lifted her hand and lay her icy palm on her husband's cheek. And smiled, her eyes filled with compassion.

* * *

In Via delle Scalette, the thick mud was stagnating with nowhere to drain. As it eddied and swirled, it pushed its way back up the alley, picking up debris and carcasses of stray animals in its path. Adele Centini was so famished she was scratching the walls. When she looked in the mirror, she no longer saw herself. She saw the head of an ass. All that money invested and yet she had never thought of spending a little on stocking up the larder. And now she was trapped in her apartment and desperate. She opened the cupboard doors wide and sucked up the crumbs with a wet finger. She licked the empty jam jar. She thought she could hear all the prisoners who had died in that place laughing at her. Or worse, her mother's voice cawing like a crow from her room, "Eat that bank note!"

On the table there were Calamaio's notebooks that had resurfaced after the first landslide, the one that had walled her up alive in her own home. "Luigino, my dear, the mud must have surprised you in the cellar," Adele had thought, her heart cleaving at the image of the kind man ripped to shreds and carried down to the valley alongside the town garbage and debris without anyone ever finding his body. Her sadness was aggravated by another source of distress: she had finally got her hands on the sketchbooks. Peeking inside was like desecrating a tomb. Calamaio had never shown her any of his portraits and perhaps Adele should have respected his wishes . . . but then she opened them anyway.

Le Case. Every page contained a sketch not of the Isastia widow but of a view of the old town seen from Room 112. He had painted what he saw through the open window behind the chaise longue where she had lain in the nude for him so many times. When she saw the landscapes, she felt fear but then she burst out laughing. "I did ask Calamaio to draw my soul as a painter would see it," she told herself every time she thought about it. "And what did he do? He painted the mountainside and didn't even put me in the picture."

There were moments when the hunger pangs were so acute, she almost vomited spit. She was no longer herself. She ripped out the pages and stuffed them in her mouth seeking relief. She chewed and chewed until the paper had become a pulp that she was able to swallow. Leaving the sketchbooks in shreds, torn to pieces on the table.

* * *

The bottleneck at the Due Porte was another point where the silt was unable to drain and had created a plug. Until it smashed through the glass store front. Maso poured himself an inch of vermouth that he knocked back in one gulp. Then he looked down and started doing what he always did: he started rinsing the glasses. "Today the weather looks bad," he muttered to himself through his teeth as the sludge reached the foot of the counter. "It's for the best. At least I can close early . . ."

* * *

The first spur cracked and split off, bringing a piece of mountain into the hollow, shattering slowly and making as much noise as a city. From his kitchen window, Domenico Fiorani saw a chunk of the ridge break off, dragging enough trees and earth with it to bury the entire region. His father was sitting at the table staring into space. When the rumble of the mudslide came closer, he looked up. "Now who's going to pay us back for our trees?" The son smiled. Then he shuffled slowly to the table and stood behind his father. He took the hunting knife he always carried with him out of his pocket and slit his father's throat, taking him by surprise. He didn't let the man's body drop. He lifted his head and clasped him to his chest. "At least I did it," he muttered, as his father thrashed his arms as hard as he could. "At least I finally did it . . . " Until the mud smashed through the windowpanes and swallowed up the house.

* * *

The beginning of the gale had surprised Angiolino at his sister-in-law's house. He had intended to stop by for one of his usual visits, when she aged a hundred years every time she found him on her doorstep looking so like her dead husband. Pepita had been keeping her eye on him for a week, having convinced herself he was her previous owner. And Sonia Antichi was going visibly crazy at the idea of being stuck in the house with this replica of her Achille. And yet, she liked it in the evening when, exhausted by all her worrying, he crawled under the covers with that faggot of a brother-in-law. They didn't do anything in particular. They lay there in the dark room as the cracks and rumbles carried on outside, with the cat purring contentedly at their feet.

* * *

As Le Case started to sink, Dr. Salghini went to his window with a glass of cordial in his hand. He saw the clock tower lean towards the cliff edge and then crack in half and vanish behind the mountain. He smiled. With the same expression as when a patient takes their last gasp.

* * *

Susanna Cocchi was applying her make up in the mirror. She had already seen the hollow filled with ooze, boulders as big as ships rolling down and then being sucked up by the swirling mud. The eastern peak had taken the form of a horn cut in two and all that was left of San Martino was a buttress, the trees holding on for dear life by what was left of their roots. She penciled around her eyes with her eyeliner again. After putting on her lipstick, she pursed her lips to make sure it was evenly applied. Then she went over to her wardrobe and took the wedding dress out of the nylon case where it had always lived. She slipped it on leaving the zipper open at the back because there was no one to help her do it up. Then she sat on the bed. As the Bel Sole tipped over the cliff edge. Like everything else.

* * *

At the umpteenth tremor, the chess pieces fell onto the table, breaking their ranks. Alvise Barberini let out a curse. He looked up and saw Iolanda on a chair that she had randomly placed in the middle of the room. The lamp shades were swinging over her head like a pendulum that had gone crazy. "Aren't you going to leave your toy soldiers now that it's the end of the world?" she asked with an ugly look, her soul stuck in her throat. Her husband looked at her for a few seconds. Then took a deep sigh and bent down to pick up the chess pieces.

* * *

Piera Del Casino decided to write a letter to her brother who had been dressed in his best clothes and laid out in the other room for the past two days. *Dear Giuliano, In the end you were the one to check out first. Le Case, too, is bringing the heavens down to confirm everything you've been saying: there's no getting away from here . . .* Books were flying off the shelves, including the ones she had written, attracting all those curious bystanders to this corner of Maremma. *This is how the town is getting its revenge, by going down a sinkhole. It's good news ultimately. It will make the newspapers go mad tomorrow. All this evil locked up in itself like a monster that can't stand how abhorrent it is. Which is vanishing like everything else that is hopeless . . .* She looked up. And started singing a song out loud. The same song she had heard her mother sing to her when she was a little girl. The end caught her right there and then. She didn't hear a thing. Night fell all of a sudden, and that was that.

* * *

The peak facing Siena cracked off in one piece, holding itself together for a few seconds before crumbling into the valley below. Renato Staccioli felt the earth lurching under his feet but managed to get to the window and grab onto the sill with all his strength. Sinking, he saw the other neighborhood that was still resisting on the other side of the hollow as the lightning bolts drew cobwebs in the black and red sky. The image he took away with him was that of Maddalena Cancelli at the Saturday-night dances in the Valentino club. He saw her so clearly that he fell in love with her right there and then, as if it had been yesterday. And he held onto her to the last. Of all the stupid things he had down in life, he didn't want to waste the good fortune he had been blessed with. A good death, with his heart on fire.

* * *

Caspar Huber was staring at the chess board in the dim light of the bare light bulb. The pieces were arranged in an English Opening with the white advancing its c-pawn into C4. The knights were having a face-off. Dust from the ceiling, which was cracked with deep crevices, had fallen on the board and onto the player's head. The man was playing on the black side but didn't make a move. He had been stuck there for at least two days.

A final tremor opened a gaping hole in the facade. There was a rumbling as the house collapsed, and the room was left to the mercy of the maelstrom. Caspar Huber didn't lift his eyes from the board even though all the pieces had flown away. Around him, papers and old newspaper cuttings. Pictures were torn off walls. Furniture tumbled as the floor bucked wildly. He stared at the checkered board holding onto it tightly with both hands. Because it had happened just like that during the darkest hours of the cataclysm: he had suddenly forgotten how to play chess. A light had gone off somewhere, leaving him there like a kid trying to work out a gigantic mathematical formula. Even though he had spent an entire lifetime on that board. The apartment was proof: it was overflowing with medals and trophies. Everything was falling into oblivion in the eddying mud flow. And then came the landslide. Caspar Huber was carried away with all the debris. Without ever really knowing who he had been.

* * *

The farmhouse on the edge of the woods was swept away by the first rock fall from Mt. Alto. The boys saw the landslide from the window, trees folding in its path like blades of straw. The only one who wept was Kristi, without making any noise. Borian sat at the table and peeled an apple. He liked taking the skin off in one long snake. He laid it in a concentric circle on his plate, which was shaking. But he didn't manage to finish because the roar and the darkness had become one and the same.

* * *

The storm was slashing against the hospital windows. Marco Palazzesi walked into the room. Having closed the door behind him, he stood there for a few seconds, the jabbering of the journalists still in his ears. News of Samuele Radi's suicide had traveled far and wide but they were still pushing him for more details. Dr. Palazzesi reached his desk. He slumped into his chair and thought how complicated that netherworld is, where someone might lose or find random piece of themselves. Or turn into a god lording it over everything. Maybe even disguised as an outcast, mingling with people in a place like any other in a corner of a godforsaken province. Or of a dream.

* * *

Eleonora opened her eyes. She had to wait a few seconds to realize where she was. Recently, it had happened often when she woke up from the deep slumber she would fall into after making love.

In the penumbra, she could see the shape of Samuele. He was standing there at the window. A purple light made his silhouette glow. There was an unnatural silence. "Are you up already?" she said eventually. Pulling the white sheet up and wrapping it around her.

She reached Samuele, being careful not to be seen from the outside. The creaking of the lampshade echoed around the room. Eleonora leaned against the wall. "You're trembling," she murmured, looking at him.

He was naked. And he was standing there, his eyes lost in the deep throat of Maremma. Eleonora saw the lightning reflect in his glittering irises. Then Samuele turned around and froze, as if he were suspended there, his smile hardly stretching his lips.

Their fingers wove together. First gently, almost playfully. Then clasped tightly. "It's just a storm," she said, without looking outside.

Samuele pulled her gently towards him, bringing her out into the open. Then he held her tight. Eleonora pressed her face into his chest as if she were hiding. But finally, she made up her mind and looked out into the hollow.

She saw the destruction. And the darkness that kept advancing. There was nothing left of Le Case except the buttress of rock they were clinging onto. The rest was a sinkhole of debris and flames that flickered on the blurred line of the horizon. The Maremma valley had been transformed into a morass of fog and thick sludge that was being siphoned into the chasms. The last bit of the mountain crumbled at that very moment, sending more silt into the crevasses. That was when she, too, remembered.

In a flash, she relived the argument with her father. All the rage she had stoked for years had exploded on an ordinary afternoon because of an old book that had vanished from a shelf in her old room. She had run away with the idea that she could walk for days without any regrets towards a life she had been forced to give up before it had even been lived, just to indulge the obsessions of her pathetic father. Who that one time had committed a far more serious mistake: canceling even the games of her imagination. Eleonora had grown up in the vacuum of the valley and, at the same time, in the wide-open spaces of Hertfordshire in another era. There, she had grown into a girl and then become a woman, imagining herself as a Bennet. There, she had found comfort when she attempted to kill off the mysteries and tumults of her age by throwing herself headlong into certain passages where Darcy at least suddenly walked into the room. Taking that alternative world from her had been like killing her. She had made the only choice possible: seeking out a new life by striding down the old mine road without a penny to her name. The town already behind her. Every step motivated by rancor, to the extent that she hadn't felt the fine rain that had blinded her as every passing car splashed her with an icy spray. Until there had been a honking of a horn. Seconds later, Eleonora was already lying face down in that terrible ditch that lines the provincial road.

Now she was weeping as she held her boyfriend tight. Her nails sank into his flesh when a final tremor made the floor lurch. She was racked by sobs, taking her breath away. Then from another room there was a crash.

"It's just a storm," she repeated through her tears.

* * *

During the chase, the man driving the white pickup had been surprised by a missile coming at him full speed from the opposite direction. He saw it bursting out from the driving rain, followed by the blue flashes and the screeching tires of the police car on its tail. He had instinctively veered to the right to make room. Mowing down a girl who had been walking with her head in the clouds on the side of the road. Samuele never knew this.

Just as he never knew that Eleonora had not died on the spot. In fact, she was still hanging on in a hospital room without any sign of improvement. Her father hadn't left her bedside for a second. He had kept vigil over her sleeping figure reading out loud from that same book. At the same time, he had kept a vigilant eye on the monitor that kept track of his daughter's every heartbeat. Every now and again, he would rush into the corridor and ask the chief physician to step into the room because maybe he had seen a twitch.

Over the previous weeks, the man struggled to deal with the clamor when the boy next door came out of his coma. The very guy who had contributed to the accident that had befallen his only daughter. It had been impossibly hard. The thin wall was not sound proof enough to smother the bastard's yells and of all the names in the world he had continuously screamed one in particular: Eleonora. Dr. Palazzesi had stopped by often to explain the strange phenomenon. The patient must have heard it from the nurses or it must have reached his ears from the ward . . . "Subjects in a vegetative state can preserve the ability to grasp information and elaborate it in the depths of their consciousness." That was what the chief physician had said. He never mentioned the dramas the boy had been through. Thank God it was all over now. A flying leap out of the window. If the man was surprised to find himself thinking about it, he said to himself, "Divine justice."

For many days their two bodies had lain close to one another, separated only by a wall. Now they were hugging in front of a window that looked out onto a scene of infinite destruction, both imprisoned in a final break. She couldn't find peace, shocked by the things she had remembered about herself, by the events that had brought her to this place.

Samuele held on to her. He knew nothing about the world, but he could say one thing with certainty: Eleonora was the most real thing that ever happened to him. He looked at her and, smiling, said, "Thank you for having dreamt me."

In the hospital room, the man was reading out loud the scene where Mr. Darcy comes to the ball, arousing first admiration and then aversion in all the bystanders for his haughty ways.

Without any warning, the light on the screen stopped flashing.

About the Author

Sacha Naspini was born in 1976 in Grosseto, a town in Southern Tuscany. He has worked as an editor, art director, and screenwriter, and is the author of numerous novels and short stories which have been translated into several languages. *Nives*, his first novel to appear in English, was reviewed on *NPR's Fresh Air* by Maureen Corrigan, who called it "delightful and affecting."